ALBERT QUIMBY

some things change

by George Opacic

Albert Quimby

Author: George Opacic

Publisher: Rutherford Press

For information, contact:

> Rutherford Press,
> PO Box 648
> Qualicum Beach, BC, Canada V9K 1A0
> info@rutherfordpress.ca

> https://rutherfordpress.ca

ISBN # 978-1-988739-45-8

Working at the World Headquarters

*Give me a friend who will weep with me; the
laughers may be found anywhere*

Early morning sun glints off flimsy, faded and cracked vinyl- or metal-clad buildings that support enough moss growing on the roofs to feed a herd of goats. Passing through this "dead zone" – abandoned light industrial districts – Albert moves as quickly as he can. You never know who might try to stop you.

In and out of harsh morning shadows, his "beater" of a compact car drives aggressively around the obstacle-course of potholes.

The car hits crumbly-edged pavement despite the driver's deft driving. This leftover district in Burnaby used to have businesses that employed at least thirty people each. In these latter days of TV (*The Virus*), most of the businesses are much leaner, or, as here, closed.

The soil under the crumbling pavement is concrete-hard and can no longer raise enough dust to be swept onto a pan. Rainfall no longer comes as steadily.

Albert shakes his head at the landscape. "Talk about dead. And the changes are happening faster." He continues with his thought: *The virus slammed into these places and swept them over the edge. Where did it take the detritus? If this looks crappy here, what do the rubbish heaps downwind look like? And back home? My god.*

Coming to a slightly better block, he bounces over the curb toward a weed-filled, rough laneway that sits between two metal-clad building walls. As he enters the lane the driver looks up and does his standard snort at the painted sign on the front of the left-hand building. It says, across a grand but faded and peeling red arch:

`Pietri Enterprises, Inc.`

`World Headquarters`

In the small chain-link fenced parking area behind the building, Albert Quimby zips backwards into a tight spot – "his" spot. The one thing he most values while working there – he has his own parking spot. He slips out of his car; clicks the car lock, twice; unlocks the building door then lets himself into the World Headquarters.

Albert walks like a harried chipmunk – more so these days than ever before. If he sported a tail, it would be twitching high over his back as he hurries down the dark hallway. Even the many years he's been in Canada haven't eased his nervousness.

At the edge of the fluorescent-lit front offices, Albert turns into his tiny office and plops onto his hand-me-down chair. Without a pause, as if he had been forever glued to the chair, Albert wakes up his computer with a mouse shake, enters the six-digit PIN, and screws up his mouth in concentration as he carries on working through a software problem. *Boss wants an elegant e-commerce solution on the back of this cheap collection of freeware. Here's me pasting html5 into scripts and hoping this almost-redacted version of php can hang together long enough to get an elementary e-commerce package done. At least in Montreal I was able to do some real work on my AI, with real software…*

Absently, Albert takes from his shirt pocket the new memory-stick he purchased yesterday. With a quick glance at its orientation, he installs the stick into a slot on the front of his computer. His salt-and-pepper hair flops in loose curls over his ears and neck. A week's growth of beard pokes up unevenly over his face. This is his private chuckle, knowing it makes him look like Lenin. He wears a polyester computer-geek outfit, including pens and pencils in his shirt pocket (no plastic holder). His pants used to be wrinkle-free.

Albert's thin frame is restlessly on the move, even sitting. While typing alphanumerics with one hand he twirls a pen in the other hand. If it goes flying, as it does every once in a while, he finishes a section of code with both hands then, pausing for thought, pulls out another pen from his pocket. The only picture in his dark little space shows a beach with bright sun glinting off rolling surf hitting white sand that arcs away for kilometres. No people are to be seen. The picture has been cut from a magazine. It has now a caption, and the page shows wrinkled glue marks where it is attached to a piece of cardboard. It is enclosed in a recycled chrome frame and covered with glass. In the bottom right corner a business card has been inserted against the glass, under the frame. It prominently announces "Pietri Enterprises, World Headquarters". In small type is "Albert Quimby, Vice President".

A call on his cellphone elicits a suspicious stare. *Who the… OH! What the hell's **he** want? Andrew walked away years ago and told me fuck off forever, after… the incident.* "Well! Is this really Andrew?"

"Hey, man. Hi. Yeah. Like, how you doing?" Albert notes the very slight quaver in the voice.

Staying polite but thinking, *Doesn't quite sound steady like he used to.*

"Andrew! I'm doing great. How the hell are you? Haven't heard from you for… years."

"Yeah, listen, man. I miss talking with you, too. Even if you *are* a commy dickhead… Listen, Al. I don't want to fight. Can we talk? What are you doing tonight? Ah… I got something serious to…"

"Serious?..." *He never did finish his sentences.*

"Can't talk over the phone. You know. Coffee tonight? How about the place in Po-Co we used to…"

"Coffee. Sure, Andrew. See you there around eight?"

"Eight. Thanks, Al. See you then."

Albert stares at the beach picture for a few minutes, remembering life before The Virus. *Sounds peculiar. I know it's him, but…. Andrew calling me a dickhead is rich. Last hockey game we played I was clobbered from behind not once but twice and he didn't raise a finger to help. When I asked him where my winger was, he swore at me and stormed off the ice. He got dressed and left without another word. Wouldn't answer my calls. Never heard from him again. So what's he want, now?*

Albert shakes his head then refocuses on his computer screen. Saving the file, he gets up with athletic dexterity, intuitively avoiding a bare dangling bulb overhead (this time) and his spare suit-coat hanging permanently at the side of his cramped cubby-hole. He heads for the laser printer that his boss won at some business thing, to retrieve a printout. *We'd still have a noisy dot-matrix monster if the laser hadn't been free. To Piero, it's all about* **money**. *There is nothing else in the world. Absolutely nothing. And yet he has no clue how to actually make it. Andrew! What the hell's so serious? Christ! He better not be thinking of spilling the beans!*

Albert thinks guiltily at the beach picture. *Have to get rid of it.* He drops his newly printed papers into a worn yellow folder.

Distracted, Albert ambles down the haphazardly painted hallway with his folder in hand. *Andrew. And I haven't seen or heard from Tasha for… half my life.*

At the boss' office he gives a short, one knuckle knock on the expensive oak door then walks right in.

Behind his desk, the stout boss, Piero Pietri, is hastily doing up his zipper as his secretary, Cloe, gets up from her knees. Pietri buttons his expensive suit coat and looks quickly and with bossly purpose around his room, chin elevated. *Looks for all the world like a little Mussolini.*

Pietri scans walls that are covered in oak-fronted shelves bent in the middle with heavy manuals and magazine boxes. None of which were ever read for more than ten seconds. *So impressive.*

"Albert! Hi! Come right in. I want to speak with you. About… about… Cloe! The light! It's, it's not working, no?"

Pietri points up to one of the fluorescent fixtures that's been flickering for a week. Cloe brushes down her pleated skirt as she hustles past Albert, head down, ignoring the question.

A glance at her averted red face pulls out thoughts that Albert actively suppresses. *Why does she wear those old-fashioned clothes? Trying to put Piero off? Or does he want her to dress that way? STOP. Boss' Moll… Could never let my guard down with any woman. Honey pot…*

Shaking Cloe from his thoughts, Albert turns to Pietri. The boss puts on his business voice. "Albert. What you got?" He takes a step back out of habit then leans forward to take the folder from Albert, mumbling, "Good; we don't need social position no more, eh?"

He nods at the folder. Sitting down into his huge "Boss's Chair", Pietri is engulfed in the leather cushions.

Albert doesn't smile at the scene. *Normal shit.* He forges ahead with his job.

"Social distancing. Last year." He points to the folder, "That's the Indonesian proposal. Mustafa Seraben. Remember the guy who wanted…"

"Yeah yeah. You put together good proposal? I finish it. He's one of the *Big* Boys. I have to add some special things. Get lotsa work from him."

Albert sits down in the chromed guest chair across from his boss.

"First of all, Piero, did you hear that Seraben's government just got dumped after their virus riots? And, can I take a minute to talk about my salary?"

"Dumped? What you mean dumped?"

Saved by his ringing phone, Pietri picks it up quickly. He speaks into it as if he has to yell across the Atlantic.

"Pronto?… Ma, Maria… I'm very busy, in an important business meeting… Ah, Albert and some Big Boys… Indonesia, you know… But Maria, I don't have time to talk now… No, they're not going to be coming for sup… Maria, listen… Maria! Listen, where's the lights, you know?… The lights, the lights, for the ceiling… The long ones… Yeah, the tubes… But but we can't be out! We just bought a box this year, no?… Maria, you use them up too much in the store!… Ok, TWO years… Ok ok, so where we got them?… Lighting Supplies? Is someplace cheaper?… Used already?… Why we buy used lights?… How much!?… Ok, we buy used lights… I'll send Albert. Where's the place? Never mind, I'll get Cloe to find the invoice."

Pietri yells louder, "CLOE!"

She can be seen through the doorway, where she had resumed typing accounting data from a pile of invoices. Before his yell, she switches windows on her screen and is calling up the AP invoice information. Albert notices the curls in her light brown hair gently bouncing as her fingers flow across the keyboard. She mumbles and sends a print instruction as Pietri yells at her. Albert shakes his head of forbidden thoughts and walks to the printer. His boss is lost in the conversation with his wife. Albert retrieves the invoice copy and sits down again as Pietri continues, oblivious, yelling at the ceiling and walls, free arm waving.

"CLOE! Find the invoice for the lights things –- the the tubes for the ceiling. Show Albert where the place is… Maria… Mari… Maria, please!… Yes I remember her… When?… But Maria,

Saturday I go out with the Big Boys… You know, Gino and Vladi and Louie and and… We have a very important business meeting… Ahh… Maria!…" He remembers something important.

"My lunch… Maria, my my lunch! Did you pack my lunch?… Don't need to dis-fect everything, Maria! You go over the board again… Ok ok. What did you make?… Ma Marie, I'm a growing boy! How can I eat only some sandwich until tonight?… Ok… Ok bye… Bye, Maria… Bye, Maria… No, I can't buy him another computer! He's already got that good one from here… What do you mean games! He's supposed to use it for school so he can become a bigshot lawyer like, like… Marie, bye, I'm busy now… Maria, I keep the Big Boys waiting too long! **Bye!**"

Pietri puts down the phone and is surprised to see Albert still in the chair.

Albert finds himself wondering whatever happened to the universe he used to live in. *This guy actually believes his ramblings mean something important in the history of humanity. They are nothing more than trumpabolic magnifitudes. Words stolen from English, stripped of any significance whatsoever. Strung together in some appearance of grammatical order. Puffs of light smoke in magnificent solitude. And yet here I am, working for this idiot. What's that make me? Less than significant? And how did a guy like Vladi insinuate himself into Gino's operation? Tasha said we're not supposed to be in the same county…*

"Albert. You have to go get some more, some more lights, tubes. Ask Cloe where we got them. Get a box. Ok?"

He brushes off any further discussion by quickly grabbing a file folder, opening it and putting his nose into the first page available.

Albert gets up, invoice in hand, and heads to his little cave.

It used to be a broom closet. Literally. There is no door, because then there wouldn't be room for his four-by-two foot (*whatever the hell that is in kilopascals – can't remember any more*) loose plywood desktop. The bare light dangles loosely on a wire from the ceiling, catching the occasional draft from an overhead air vent, so that it casts angular moving shadows off the computer that he put together from leftovers. The computer's main box, sitting on a concrete block, holds up one end of the desktop. It has a gaping hole with wires hanging out where a cd-rom drive used to be. The other end of the table is supported by two wall brackets he had found in storage. An old monitor fights for space on the desktop with a keyboard and a mouse.

The screensaver scrolls by slowly on his monitor:

`Vice President Albert`

`World Headquarters`

`W H A T E V E R`

Albert stares at it, blankly. *So what the hell's got into Andrew that he wants to see me now, after ignoring me for all this time. Shit, I hope he didn't get something like complications from The Virus. He did sound really tired. When we were back in… god! it's been over fifteen years!*

A sound like a boom box set on high, shakes the walls.

"ALBERT! YOU GONE YET?... CLOE! Did Albert left already?"

Both Albert and Cloe answer at the same time.

"No." "Not yet."

"Albert, come here for a minute!"

Folding up the Lighting Supply invoice copy, Albert pirouettes out of his room and puts the paper into his back pocket. As he enters the boss's room, Pietri winks and motions for him to close the door.

"I talk too loud. Don't want to bother Cloe… Albert, I want to tell you just a few things about my family, so you understand me better, eh?" He pauses to collect his thoughts as Albert closes the door and resumes his seat.

"My great grandfather, back in the old country, he was, he had a different last name. Because a lot of people got mad at him and some other Big Boys, then. He was just a barber, but he, ah, made lotsa money and people was, what's the word… jealous. They was jealous of him."

Albert nods and smiles a little. Pietri notices the smile and resets his speech.

"Did I tell you this already?"

Albert shakes his head but keeps his face in friendly-attentive mode.

"No? Ok. Anyway, just because they give away their land when they sit in his chair, and he holds the the razor a little longer to their neck –– only enough so they could sign over the papers –– well, the people got jealous and the government made a law soes the Dons had to give back some land. And for this, even though my grandfather change his family name for chrissake! there's some people –– you won't believe this –– even today! some people are still *jealous* of my family. There's one of them here, in Burnaby, even, who keeps saying things about me. He lies and he lies… So, I want to give you warning that if he talks to you, don't say anything."

"Who is he?"

Pietri leans back in his chair, taking his mysterious pose.

"If he talks, you'll know him. Just remember what I tell you. Ok?…" Pietri tents his fingers.

Relaxing after his thoughtful exercise, Pietri smiles engagingly . "Now, you know how I said you would get a big raise after a while?"

"After the first six months – a year and a half ago."

"So now I give a hundred dollar more! Eh? How about that?" He smiles like he just donated half his fortune to the needy of the world.

"So now I'm up to four-fifty per week?"

"Yeah. Maria gonna be pissed off. She'll say, why give it to Albert? Give it more to our son! But I want you to be happy here, Albert."

Right. Money equals happy. "Thanks Piero. When is Junior going to start working here? Is he out of the college, yet?" *The kid and his wife and probably their dog all get a big salary…*

"Oh he wanted to stay another year to to, work on the, what do you call it? the graduation degree…"

"I thought he was at the college upriver?"

"Yeah yeah. Close to go. He still sleep at home cause he don't know to, to social – what-you-call-it…" Suddenly changing to an ominous tone, "When he get home…"

Albert cuts in, "So now the college is giving graduate degrees?"

"Oh yeah, sure. But only if you know the Big Boys, the the President, you know. Not everybody can do this." He nods in agreement with himself.

Albert rolls his eyes as he gets up. "Ok. Anyway, I'll go out and get the fluorescent tubes and I'll grab lunch on the way."

Not long later, Albert is carrying the box of fluorescent tubes through the back door when he hears Pietri calling for him.

"Cloe, what do you mean it take a hour to get there and back, he's been almost a hour already! Oh, there you are. Albert…"

Pietri's voice lowers several levels as Albert comes in carrying a long box. He puts the box of tubes in a corner of Pietri's office. Pietri stands up to think and pace.

"Albert, I want you to go to Seattle to see a friend of mine. He's one of the Big Boys. You're my Vice President, so I want you to meet Fabio. Is really Big Boss. Personal friend with government boss in Ottawa *and* Washington! He's really Russian Jew but we, ah, all call him Fabio 'cause his name… never mind. He is a smart man. I hate to say it but maybe even more smart than me. He plays violin. Wanted Junior to play but he said he was busy. Baseball." Pietri snorts.

Not impressed, Albert shoos a reluctant Pietri away from beside his chair. He pulls the guest chrome chair under the flickering light fixture, brings over two tubes from the box and carefully leans them against the desk, within reach. Pietri backs out of the way reluctantly, glancing under his desk several times.

"Albert. Don't touch…"

"Don't worry –– I won't touch your shotgun… What does Fabio want from you, Piero?"

Relaxing, Pietri backs to the window that overlooks a side street. As he talks, he appreciatively watches the occasional women as they walk by.

"Listen, I just wanna use his address so I can get things mailed there…" A younger figure hurries by the window, late from lunch. Pietri gazes at her lecherously up and down while he can. Then something down the road gets Pietri skittish. He backs away from the window slowly, scanning along the street.

Albert continues replacing the tubes. "What's the matter, Piero? See her husband?"

"Funny. Ha ha. Husband." He walks along the wall, brushing nervously against the bookshelves, toward his desk, still glancing at the window with concern. He comes up with a distraction. "What I said about that jealous guy…" Then pivots away from the thought. "Never know what crook try to break into my office. Valuable stuff in here."

Albert smirks on the other side of his mouth. *Always with the distraction technique.*

Pietri forces a tone of slyness, "And listen, I was just thinking. Why don't we set up a company in Seattle and use Fabio's address. Like he do, is good to have shoe in two country, no? Could be useful for getting… ah, computer parts for you."

Albert rolls his eyes. *Parts from* this *century would be good. Current software even better.*

"Okay, Piero, what do you want me to do?"

Pietri walks back to his desk to reach across it for a red folder. He opens it and waves one of the papers, nearly brushing against a precariously leaning tube. Albert reaches down quickly to protect the tube.

"This is what the lawyer give me. He said all we need to do is get these to Seattle and we got a company in the U.S."

Albert nods, finishes by closing up the fixture cover, then he steps off the chair.

While stepping down he replies. "Gino called me yesterday about it. He didn't really know what you wanted. Really pressed me for answers. Since I don't know anything, I just told him I don't know anything. That was the closest I've heard Gino getting pissed off. What did you do to him?" With Pietri ignoring the question, Albert carries on, "Those incorporation papers you need to sign are in that file. If we mail them today it should take a couple weeks to get them back."

Pietri frowns. "A couple weeks! That's too long, Albert! What's the matter with those fat cats, they can't push papers any faster than that? We back in the virus days again? I have to… start over there fast." Pietri gives another anxious glance to the window then in the direction of Gino's building next door.

"Well, if you want it right away, they said they can get it done in a day if I take them to Seattle personally."

He places the chair he was standing on back to where it had been then carefully gathers the old tubes.

"Albert, you have go there and get it done right away!"

Albert nods at the predictable reaction. "Okay. How about tomorrow morning? My doctor's appointment in Richmond was cancelled, so I can go to Seattle early."

"Good, On the way, you can stop at Fabio's and tell him that, ah, everything is ready… And listen, look around near his building and see if there's a place to make a, a… STORE-FRONT. A magnificent Store-Front!" He beams at himself for coming up with the brilliant concept. "You never know - maybe we can start some business there. Maybe a barber shop…" Pietri's sly grin causes Albert to glance down toward the shotgun.

Seeing the glance, "Albert, you know how shotgun work? Maybe need to use it…"

"Grew up on a farm, Piero. But don't worry…" *Even if the farm was half a world away.*

"Not worry for me. If you here alone and someone break in, use it! Ok?"

Albert looks straight at Pietri. *He's actually serious. Who the hell's this jealous guy and why's Gino mad at Piero? Gino's not someone to have mad at you.*

Pietri nods then dismisses Albert by searching through some more files. One hand speed-dials on the phone. He yells at the phone before Albert can pull the door closed with his foot, holding the tubes in one hand and the box in the other.

"Maria… yes, I'm fine. Yes I just wash my hands. Still wet… Yes with soap. Listen, Maria, my lunch… Maria, please, I have no time… what did you make?…"

Albert puts the box in a corner of the hallway, leaves the old tubes next to it and intends to work on a technical manual on his computer. Passing Cloe's desk, he mumbles, "God, get me the hell outta this madhouse."

Cloe looks up from her desk at him. Albert stops, surprised to see her face is red from crying. With a quiet sob, she chokes out, "You and me both." She slumps her head. Then Cloe comes to a decision.

Sliding her chair away from the desk, she indicates to Albert to follow her to the washroom in the back. Walking with purpose down the hall, Cloe grips Albert's arm. *Never touched me before… Electricity…*

She stops at the washroom door, indecisive. He leans against the utility closet next to the washroom, focusing on her fingers that are digging into his arm. Still holding him, she regains her will power and drags Albert inside the dark room. Its light hasn't worked for a while but the high window lets in some sun.

Albert scolds himself, *Not at all attracted to Cloe. Cannot allow it… She is pretty and has a shapely figure, and she is efficient with the office duties. But she is the boss' moll. There is an invisible force field encircling her. Cannot see the body, no person; only the sign hanging in front of her face: "Honey Pot Boss' Moll".*

His reluctance to get close to Cloe causes her to grip him harder. Whispering, "Albert, I don't care what you think of me. Just listen. Ok? Just listen to me."

Inches from her face, Albert gives a quick nod, ready to bolt out the door. He does not deal well with women in any case. Now, the force field is sizzling off his cheeks. Albert feels the heat.

"He's a *monster*." In a hoarse tone he has never heard before, she spits out, "You just don't know... Oh – that little thing he makes me put in my mouth..." she spits into the sink violently, twice, then hisses, "that's not near the worst of it. He's a filthy *monster*."

Cloe relaxes her grip on Albert's arm. He glances down to check for blood and rubs the spot.

Cloe notices him rubbing his arm "Sorry. Sorry, Albert. You just have no idea what I have to do for him." She turns her profile to Albert. With an effort he mostly stops his eyes from glancing down at her shapely breasts.

Resolution creeps into her voice. "Have to leave. I have to find a way out of here..." Her eyes well up and her face turns an ugly wrinkled red. "If I don't get out of here I'll, I'll kill myself!... Or kill *him*."

The force field dissolves. Albert is aghast. He leans closer to quietly entreat her, "Cloe, no. Don't talk like that..." He finds he is holding her arms, then she encircles him warmly, then passionately. Her hair smells wonderful.

Cloe's head is buried in his chest. "You just don't know... And if I leave... if I leave he'll have me killed. He will. He's done it before. At least three times. I know about those others. That's why he'll *kill me*."

She falls away against the wall behind her, knees suddenly limp.

Albert reaches out a hand to hold her up. She raises her head a bit from her chest and smiles up at him.

New feelings are washing over him. He has needed a confidant for many years. *I know about them too. Vladi was the shooter. That was how he got into Gino's mob. The 'heartless Russian killer' persona. Glad all I had to do here is program shit. Can Cloe keep a secret?*

"You're a good man, Albert. How the hell did you end up in this hell-hole?" Her knees gain some strength and she wriggles up straighter. Their faces are a hot breath away from each other.

He speaks for the sake of staying close to her, saying logically-strung phrases that originate somewhere in his head but his heart is pumping. "Don't know. Really. Had a little software consulting company after the aerospace operation reorganized. Did that job for Piero almost two years ago and he promised the world. That winter I did the research and report in New York for him. You remember? Right after the borders opened first time? For one of his *Big Boys*. Well, **you** know… It was interesting – even if it was for his mob friends. Then got stuck here like a fly on a fly-trap. Nothing happening after the virus hit again. Too old to get a decent job… Huh! *World Headquarters!* I've yet to see anything but trumpabolic words and empty promises…" *Stuck here. Told to mole down.*

He finds they are still holding hands. Embarrassed, he lets go. She doesn't. As he leans away a bit, Cloe presses closer. He notices her flower-printed pleat dress and lavender perfume. *Is she trying to look older? Must be no older than thirty-five… Lovely wavy hair.*

"Take me away from here, Albert. Please. Save me from that evil monster." She turns to the mirror. With a rising viciousness, "He's taking my soul, pulling it out of my heart in bloody little pieces. One day after the next…" Then, facing Albert with her distorted red face, she whispers her plea, "Save me, Albert."

The building's foundations and its flimsy structure shake with a baritone "CLOE! WHERE YOU GONE?!"

Cloe's eyes plead with Albert.

Reluctantly, he nods. "Tomorrow I'm going to Seattle. Friday. Be ready for Saturday…" Pausing, he grabs her arms. "You mean it? You ready to leave?" *What am I doing? Jumping from the frying pan?*

She stares at the wall blankly, thinking in circles.

The thunder comes again, *"CLOE!"*

She looks up into Albert's brown eyes. "Yes."

That evening Albert decides to do some packing in case Cloe really does carry on with her promise to leave. *It really is time to go. I want out. I'll contact Tasha later to give her some story. What's the fucken use of pretending geopolitical shit is important! It's all falling apart anyway. Helping Cloe is a good excuse to make the break and disappear into a life of my own. Poor thing… Never really thought about Piero as a way of influencing anybody, anyway. He's too stupid. 'Course, that's the type you have to wary of. Another fucken Trump. They act without thinking of anything but themselves. Couldn't figure why Gino'd keep an idiot like him around. Must be a liability. Well, if she decides to go, we can go. Disappear to some beach in the wilds of British Columbia. Start a new life.*

Shaving off the stubble around his goatee, Albert daydreams of languid beaches back in Yevpatoriya, lying beside a scantily-clad Cloe. *That place is probably bombed to hell by now.*

He aggressively clips off the longer bits of his hair. In the bachelor-suite "main room", he looks at the few sticks of scavenged furniture that he makes do with. *This can go up in smoke and nobody'd miss it. I can take a few clothes and the USBs of my AI files, and… Shit, is it seven-thirty already? Finish later.*

He slips on his shoes and heads out the door to meet Andrew. On the drive to Port Coquitlam he wonders what his former best friend wants; what he was up to; what's "serious". *Can't tell him what I'm thinking of doing. Andrew might still be active. Shit! What if there's a contract out on me, and he's… No. Not Andrew.*

Uncharacteristically, Albert is a few minutes late. As he parks on the street near the coffee shop that he and his former long-time friend had used as their favourite hangout, he sees someone in a wheelchair making his unpowered, strenuous way up the slightly inclined walkway to the front door. Albert hurries a bit to be there to open the door for the fellow.

With the door half opened he looks down at the person in the wheelchair. Dumbfounded at seeing the unmistakable eyes of his old friend, he stands holding the door half-open.

Andrew struggles to bend his neck enough to look up at Albert. "Thanks, but I might need it open more than that, if you don't mind."

Albert stares at the contorted grin on the face that he used to see just about every day for years, even before their time in the GRU's Unit 74455. Snapping out of his astonishment, he pulls the door fully open. "Andrew! What the fuck…?"

"Good to see you, too, dickhead. Let me in, will you?" Albert steps back as Andrew has to push hard to wheel over the threshold, then he heads inside to a particular table. The coffee shop is back to being full. The only difference is that many of the patrons are wearing their personalized masks while hunched over a laptop or other device. The coffee, sugar and cinnamon smells are the same.

Albert has trouble forcing his legs to follow Andrew. A young couple are already sitting at the table he had rolled to. It has a wheelchair symbol on it. Andrew nods at the symbol as he parks aggressively at the open side of the table. The couple look at each other, shrug their shoulders, and make a point of slowly collecting their phones and cups to look for another table.

Albert motions apologetically as the couple leave and he takes one of the seats. He is about to start a conversation, "Andrew, I..."

"Get me an iced tea, will you? With a straw." Andrew keeps his eyes down.

Albert notices his gaunt fidgeting hands are tightly bent in. *MS?*

"Oh. Sure." Albert gets up. "Be right back." He avoids a strong urge to put his hand on Andrew's shoulder as he passes the wheelchair. He sees that the chair is heavily scratched and worn.

After a few minutes, Albert comes back to the table with two drinks. He puts the iced tea down in front of Andrew, turning the straw toward him. "Is that close enough, Andrew? Oh..." He pulls a few serviettes from a pocket, "...here. In case you, like, need them..."

Albert sits down with his coffee, involuntarily watching Andrew's jerked movements settle down until he is able to put an arm on the table. "Can still talk, thank god. This fucking MS is going *there* next." He creeps his arm in stages, closer to the cup. A finger and thumb finally capture it. Albert is about to lean forward to help, but he doesn't. Andrew slides the cup near the edge toward himself. He uses his other arm to awkwardly roll closer to have his mouth near the straw. Albert stares in slow-motion fascination as short, barely controlled movements finally combine to have Andrew's mouth capture the straw. He takes a satisfied slurp with half-closed lips. A few drips escape onto his lap.

Albert slides the serviettes closer to Andrew's hand. "Do you want me to…"

Quietly, "Fuck off, Al."

Sitting in stunned silence at what his friend has become, Albert has trouble saying anything further. He sips his coffee, waiting for Andrew to say something. Raising his head to look at the other patrons, Albert sees a few who quickly divert their eyes.

After some more difficult sips, Andrew works hard to focus on Albert. "Still want me to cover your back?"

"Huh?"

"The last thing you told me was to cover your back. That game in the so-called industrial league. No contact, they said. Thought I could stick it out. Just to be… well… with a friend. Who really knows me." Tremolo captures the voice.

Albert leans forward, "Jesuschrist, Andrew. What happened? I mean, this MS. You had it then?"

"Yeah. Got the doctor's visit a couple days before… Floored me.
Thought it had to be some secret plot to get me to spill…
everything. Still don't want to believe it. But here I am." He
awkwardly waves an arm. "I was fucken working on some secret
bullshit file from…" he looks around, "…you know, our boss.
She sent me this file about… what the hell was it?… Oh! About
the politics between Iran and those fuckers in Chechnya. Like I
could give a shit! And then this!"

"Does your mother… Well of course you told her…"

Andrew shakes his head. "Didn't want to tell her. Right away.
Burden her… But it gets worse sometimes. This is as bad as it's
been. Usually I can walk alright. Mom's been a rock. She does
everything for me. Reverted to speaking Russian…" He snaps his
head around automatically to see if someone is listening. The
tremolo gets more pronounced. "I can't… can't do this to her any
longer, Al. She's getting old, herself. Probably put years on her,
being my… It's getting worse. When I can't go to the can by
myself and I can't eat anymore… what's the use?" Andrew ends
quietly.

It tugs on Albert's heart. Tightens his chest. He can't speak.

"Al, I want to end it. How can I end it? Can you… can you help
me? Al?"

Albert is devastated. *What's he want me to do? Kill him? Push him
off a cliff?* "Andrew… I don't know what to say. I really hate
seeing you like… like this. But I don't know what to do."

Andrew hisses, "There's only one fucken thing you *can* do for
me goddamnit!"

Andrew slurps angrily a few more times, each one with extra drips falling down to his lap. Albert reaches over to put a serviette on his lap. He notices how much weight his old friend has lost. "Andrew, I want to help you. I'd do anything I can to help you. But… Maybe I can contact Vladi…" He shakes his head.

"Vladi for fucksake? Is that what you want? Shoot me like a fucken dog?" Andrew fidgets hard for a minute, shakes his head, then decides to leave. "Dickhead. Just fuck off. You can't do anything for me, now. Have a good fucken life." Andrew pushes back from the table.

Alarmed, Albert gets up to reach for Andrew's chair as it turns, but Andrew heads aggressively for the door. A person entering holds the door open for Andrew then jumps out of the way as the wheelchair bounces past. Albert watches, helplessly, watching with a tear forming, seeing his old friend roll away. *What the hell's he want me to do!?*

From a nearby table, a young woman who had been pretending to read on her phone since Albert first sat down, looks up to Albert's face. She pulls down her flower-printed mask. "He's been a sonofabitch. Comes in here almost every day and mopes at that table. Same table all the time. Gets people to buy him a drink. Bought him a couple, myself, at first. Let him go. Just let the sonofabitch go." She taps opens her phone to actually do some reading, her mask still hanging by one strap from an ear.

In a daze, Albert takes the half-full cups from his table to the dishes tray. He walks outside, looking for Andrew but without enthusiasm. His heart feels empty – frozen, and yet beating hollowly. *But what could I do? He wants me to **kill** him?*

Albert can't sleep that night. He relives what he should have done with Andrew. Then Cloe's face floats in, her head shaking silently, back and forth. Over the very early morning he stares at the phone's time in twenty minute intervals, waiting for the hours to pass. Too early, he rises to get ready for his trip to Seattle. Echoing in his mind is the phrase, *But what can I do for him?*

He drives to the border on mental autopilot. The blazing sun to his left forces him to slip on a pair of sunglasses. Sections of the trip go past trees that causes the sun to flicker intensely, almost hypnotically. He pulls over the visor but it doesn't quite reach the right spot. Finally driving up to the lineup for the boarder crossing, he falls into the routine to compose himself: Sunglasses off. Sunshade stowed away. Both hands on the wheel. Remember to smile but not grin. Do not look away from the eyes of the guard…

At the gate, the officiousness of the US border guard wakes his faculties up sufficiently that he is able to properly negotiate around the convoluted entrance to the highway for Seattle. Past Bellingham, Albert's phone dings. He shoves an earpiece in tighter, then answers. "Alb… Huh? Cloe, slow down… What?.. Shit!" *Now what the fuck's happening?*

He immediately pulls off to the shoulder of Highway 5 as honking cars go barreling by.

Cloe is sobbing. "I don't know what to do, Albert! Please help me! He's bleeding all over the desk!"

Stunned, Albert is gripping the steering wheel then realizes his car is shaking because one foot is pushing on the gas peddle while the other foot is holding hard against the brake. He jams the poor car into Park with a shudder. "Listen… Cloe… LISTEN, damnit!... Did you just find him?" Albert glances at the clock. It is 7:35 am.

"The the lights were all on and I rushed in to... I could remember closing up last night. He went off to his, to the Italian bar at four and I closed up like I always do..."

"Ok, Cloe, listen. Did you call the cops?"

"The cops?"

"Cloe! Hang up and call them right now! Tell them exactly what happened."

"But..."

"Right now! I'm turning around and I'll be back by nine. Got it? I'm going to the Corner Coffee Shop off Imperial. Got that? You know the place? I'll be there no later than nine-thirty. Ok?"

Sobs can be heard from Cloe. "Oh god, Albert. They're gonna kill me. They're gonna think I did this..."

Albert is about to reply but Cloe clicks off.

He pounds at he steering wheel. "SHIT! GODAMNIT ALL!"

No Longer Working at the World Headquarters

Find true friends with your ears, not with your eyes

By ten-thirty, Albert is getting worried for Cloe. He stops himself several times from dialing Andrew. Albert's mind is spinning, being pulled in several directions at once. He sees visions of Andrew and Vladi mixed with the beaches and Cloe. He finishes his second coffee too quickly, having slurped it down like it was a task to do. His eyes wander to the menu board on the wall behind the counter. He wonders if he should order brunch, but distracting red and blue lights begin to flash off the shiny white board. Albert's heart starts pounding. *Calm down. Not the thugs from GRU. Calm…* Biofeedback training kicks in to slow his pounding heart rate.

Two cops enter the coffee shop quickly. They scan the half-dozen patrons, then the cop in a suit nods toward Albert. They both stride over, the uniform is hanging behind his buddy, hand ready near his pistol.

The suit stands over Albert. "Albert Quimby?"

Albert nods.

"Can we speak to you outside, please?"

The uniform scans around to see if anyone is moving suspiciously.

"Sure. It's about Piero?"

"Let's speak outside, please."

Albert keeps his hands visible, pushing away from the table. *Decision made. No brunch.*

As they leave, the curious patrons follow the threesome to the cruiser with their eyes. They see pleasantries being exchanged, then identity cards shown. The cop looks closely at Albert's licence. The conversation next to the cruiser goes on for almost ten minutes. Both sides take turns nodding at Albert's car. Some gesturing takes place then Albert walks over to his car as the cops get into theirs. The flashing lights are turned off. The cruiser starts off sedately with Albert following in his car.

In the police station, Albert sits through a repetitive interrogation for the rest of the morning and into the afternoon. He tells them everything that happened the day before, except for Cloe's episode with Pietri and their conversation in the bathroom. And he does not mention Gino, until the cop brings him up.

"You say you haven't spoken with the lawyer next door, Gino Massutti?"

Albert takes care not answer too quickly. "No. But Mr. Massutti is the company lawyer so I will have to call him soon."

"Don't do that. You saying you don't know who Massutti is?" The cop is almost contemptuous.

Albert keeps his eyes on the cop for about eighty percent of the time – because he knows that is one of the body language things they look for – but this time he has to struggle to keep looking calmly into the cop's eyes. "Well, he is the company lawyer. I don't have anything to do with him, normally. We may have spoken face-to-face no more than two times. The last time I spoke with Mr. Massutti was a couple days ago about some move Piero was making in Seattle."

Now the cop can't hold it in, "Oh come now, Albert! Massutti's a top mobster who owns every business on the block, for a start…"

Albert cuts in, "That's not my concern. I'm strictly a programmer…"

The cop shakes his head, "We'll see how much you know when we go through the business paperwork… Alright. Let's get back to what Mr. Pietri was doing yesterday. You say he looked nervous about someone he called 'jealous'? Jealous of what?"

Happy to be talking about someone other than Gino, "Yeah, he was quite concerned about the guy. But that's all he told me about him 'You'll know him when you talk with him' was all he said." Then Albert dares to ask about the shotgun. "Like I said – when I was changing the fluorescent tubes he was quite concerned. Even told me to use his hidden shotgun if I had to, sometime. Is it still under his desk?"

The cop thinks about his approach. "How do you know about the shotgun?"

"Well, it was right there in a holder under his desk. When I was changing the tubes I couldn't miss it. Piero asked me if I knew how to handle one and I told him that growing up on a farm, I learned early."

The cop writes more notes with his head down.

Albert temps fate with, "Is that what he was shot with?"

The cop looks up and tries to bore into Albert's eyes.

The attack glances away harmlessly. Albert tries again, "You said he was shot."

"The shotgun was still under the desk."

So Vladi is in the picture. He'd never use a shotgun. Too messy.

Then the cop latches onto the "jealous guy" theme. "You say you never met this guy he was worried about?"

"No sir. Had no idea what he was on about. Piero didn't confide in me."

"But you were the vice president of the company!"

"A title that allowed him to pay me less than he might if I, like, actually worked for him as an employee." Albert pulls at a longer part of his goatee, thinking, *Wonder what Cloe is saying?*

"Worked for him. So he didn't pay you well?"

"Actually, as I said earlier, he just gave me another hundred dollars a week…"

"But it still didn't amount to much, did it? You resent him for that?"

"I was grateful for the work during the pandemic. Being over fifty-five, my chances for employment are dwindling by the month. He gave me free rein to work on a number of projects, computer projects, and I live frugally. Money isn't…"

"Come on, Albert! I saw what passes for your office, for chrissake!"

"Listen, I'm worried about Cloe. When can I …"

"Not for a while, Albert. We have to establish the facts, here. Your friend is in another room telling us everything."

The suit, Detective Chou, tries another angle. "You and her a thing? You seem very concerned for her…"

"Detective Chou, I know you have a job to do but let's get back to reality. I have given you everything I know about what might've led up to, ah, Piero's death. Several times. From multiple angles. I haven't…"

Chou tries to interrupt but Albert carries on, "I haven't had anything more than a few cups of coffee since five this morning and I really am getting hungry. Now, if you don't have anything new to ask me, I have to put some food into my system before my blood sugar goes haywire."

Chou is caught off guard by Albert's assertive attitude. "I, ah… Ok. I… You've been very helpful, Albert." He pulls two stapled sheets from a folder. "Thank you. I will just ask you to read over this statement you gave earlier and correct anything you feel you need to, then sign it, please. I'll be back in a minute."

Chou pushes the papers in front of Albert then gets up to leave. "Be right back." He glances at the recorder going and nods knowingly to the uniform standing by the door.

Albert follows Chou with a gaze. *Left the recorder on. Might not be in the procedures. Doing a quick check on the interrogation with Cloe, no doubt. Hope she was smart in her own statement. No need to tell them the embarrassing stuff.*

Twenty minutes later, Cloe meets Albert in the police station foyer. She has been crying. With considerable effort, Cloe resists the strong urge to wrap her arms around Albert and sob it all out. Instead, they give clipped nods to each other and walk out.

On the street Albert says quietly, "Hungry. Let's get dinner."

Not hearing a reply from Cloe, he turns his head to her while they walk to his car. "Ok?"

"Dinner. Yeah. Whatever." She uses a tissue from her purse to dry her eyes and cheeks. Then, with a sharp glance to Albert, she takes more time to clean her face up.

The cheap diner is mostly full of foreign students, loudly conversing in at least four Asian languages.

Albert munches through a tasty but messy hamburger that dribbles kimchi and other mysterious ingredients. He nods at the appropriate times to Cloe and lets out affirmative noises as she spills her life story. *The kids are probably from the ESL school down the block. They'll be on their way soon. Never did get the hang of Mandarin. The Japanese guys on the far side are too far away to catch what they're saying.* He pops a couple yam-fries into his mouth to clear it of the squishy stuff, then offers Cloe his yams; she shakes her head. "And then Piero hired you?"

Cloe reaches out a hand right to his face and it is all Albert can do to not jerk away. He tenses in forced stillness as she gently brushes some kimchi off his goatee and his cheek.

"Well, not right away. Gino had something happen and he laid us off; all but Marina, his wife. The next day I got a call from Mr. P. He was a smooth talker…"

"Still is." Wryly, "Was." Albert relaxes back to munching.

"Couldn't have happened to a more deserving sonofabitch." Cloe spits out, "He's a fucken *monster*."

Albert is shocked, stopped in mid-bite. He's never heard Cloe swear before. He looks around the room reflexively.

Cloe hisses, "I don't give a rat's ass who hears me!"

"Ok but listen, Cloe."

She is about to launch into a tirade.

Albert puts a finger up close to her mouth. It stops her. "He might have friends here. Let's try to last the night, at least. Ok?"

She sucks in what she was about to spit out. Furtively scanning the crowd, "You think…?"

"Don't know. Honestly." They both have a quiet look at the students.

A chirp comes from a nearby table. The student looks at his phone then tells his table companions the time. *Think he said something-something-zhōng tóu.*

They get up to leave and the others evacuate en masse, with two Japanese students deliberately *not* acting sheep-wise. Cloe and Albert quietly watch the exodus, plus the two trailing macho guys, as they all leave.

Albert and Cloe are the only patrons left.

"Ok, Cloe, what did the cops tell you to do? Did they say they want you to come back in tomorrow?"

"Oh… No. Another detective called my officer out and then a uniform opened the door about fifteen minutes later and told me and the uniform in the room that I was free to go. Nothing else."

Albert smiles. "I bet that cop is going to be on the carpet in the morning. Anyway, so what are you going to do now? We don't work at the *World Headquarters* anymore."

She sits back. "My god. I… I don't know…But Albert. The mob is still going to be after me! Oh my god! I bet hey think I shot him! *Albert!*" She starts working up to another panic attack.

Albert reaches out a hand to find hers. "Please, Cloe. I don't like it when you start that red-face thing. Calm down, girl." *I wonder if Vladi is pulling some diversion. Is he trying to clean up our inactive cell by fooling the mob into removing me and Andrew? I should tell Andrew... No. The way he is now, he'd welcome it.*

Cloe stops like she is slapped. "Huh? Red-faced thing? What do I...?" She looks for a mirror.

With a squeeze of her hand, Albert brings her attention back to the table. "Take it easy, Cloe. It doesn't do any good flying off the handle. Over the past two years I've never seen you get upset about anything. Not like this. Always had a lot of respect for your composure in difficult situations."

She sits up straighter. "Respect?... Is that all?"

Gently. "Respect is a good start, Cloe. Now, what are you going to do?"

She gives a wry grin. "Well, I thought *you* were going to take me away from all this."

They both stare at each other. He whispers, "Since I'm as likely as you to be targeted by some mafia strong-arm, I guess it really is the both of us who have to take off. Together."

Albert is stepping reluctantly into the role of *Protector of Damsels in Distress*. Certainly *this* damsel has not been in his sights as needing protection. *For now, we need to help each other.* "We need to help each other." His mumble seems to come from another mouth than his. *But there it is. Freudian slip, or shove?*

Cloe begins to glow. "Thank you, Albert. It's so very... reassuring, that I can count on you... So what do we do now?"

"Damn good question. The cops haven't given us any specific order to stick around… I don't have anything tying me down. You?"

She shakes her head. "No. Nothing holding me here, except, I have only… some savings. Family savings."

Albert sits back in his chair, calculating. Their hands separate absently. "If we're going to skedaddle, it can't be Seattle. The border has too many eyes. Listen, I can pull out all my cash this afternoon. Is yours liquid?"

Cloe's features harden up. "Yes, I guess, but… *all* of it?"

He leans forward again, touching her fingers. She keeps her hand still. "Cloe, if they *are* after us – or will be soon – we can't take half measures. It means pulling up stakes and leaving no trace. Right now… but, if you're not sure…"

A pause. Then Cloe takes his hand. "If I have to put my trust in anyone, Albert, it has to be you. Yes. I'll take it all out. Drive me to my place. I'll pack what I need. You can meet me back there when you pack your own clothes. Then we can go to the bank in the mall. Your bank still the credit union, there?"

Nodding, "Yes." He rises and she follows him out to the car. Cloe finds herself staring at the way he moves with easy grace. When they approach his car she is still lost in staring at him. At the driver's door, Cloe is directly behind him in her dreamland, standing there. Albert grins and turns to her, with one hand on his car's door handle. "I'll drive, if that's ok, Cloe?"

"Huh? Oh! Sorry! Is *this* your car? Right." She scrambles around the back of the car to reach the passenger side.

SKEDADDLING

If you spare the guilty, you harm the innocent

I t takes almost the rest of the afternoon to see the bank manager and then convince him to release all their funds. Sitting together in the manager's office, Cloe is handling the discussion and she is the one making up the excuse the two use for needing their cash right away.

The manager has been reluctant to make the effort to cash out their accounts. "This is a large sum and I am not sure if can put it all together for you two today..." He muses. "It could be that a unique situation that arose here earlier might leave us with something close to the required funds. I can do about a third in cash but the rest will have to be as a bank draft?..."

Cloe takes Albert's hands for reassurance. "Yes, we realize our request is unusual, but we have a very special reason. You see, Albert and I have fallen in love..." she leans over to give Albert a very convincing peck on the cheek, "and I have decided to go with him to a contract he just landed in Seattle. With Microsoft."

The manager looks to Albert for confirmation.

"Yes. Absolutely." He nods once too often.

Cloe squeezes his hands and carries on, "But Albert has to be there for his final interview tomorrow morning. If he's not there, it'll all fall apart. So you see, we have to clean up our affairs here right away. And there are a ton of other matters we have to clean up today, so you can see our urgent situation. Your help in this will be very important for us. And you never know if we'll be hit with the third wave they keep talking about, so we really need to get established before the border closes again."

The manager sits quietly for a minute. He looks at Albert. "Microsoft? What position have they offered you?"

It's Albert's turn to spin this one out. "Yeah. A really good opportunity. I've had a consultancy in computer programming for a number of years. Well, you've seen that the pickings have been slim, going into my account. But I did a contract for a Microsoft subsidiary last year. It was a small program in Rust – that's one of the new internet-specific languages – that was a critical interface to one of their AI programs and I believe my program went to Microsoft directly. When they asked for support on the AI interface and found out it was me who wrote it, they called me up. After a couple phone meetings, they gave me this offer. We really don't want to miss out on this opportunity. Especially at *my* age. With what's going on."

The manager, Mr. Fissner, nods slowly, considering. Finally, he comes to a decision and slaps both hands onto the edge of his desk.

They have to come back in two hours. In the manager's office again, he gives them a vinyl briefcase to hold the money and cheque. He closes the door. "I will ask you to confirm the amount of cash and the bank draft, then sign the receipt please." As he hands the bag over, the manager holds it for an instant, reluctant to let go.

Cloe pulls out the bundles of cash to spread them out on the desk. Albert is fascinated by the pile. He gives a wry grin to Fissner, "So we can trust that each wrapped bundle contains what the wrap says?... Just kidding."

Fissner's face quickly moves from alarmed, through confused, to showing a polite smile.

All finished and packed away, they get up to leave. Cloe smiles politely. "You are a great help to us, Mr. Fissner. Thank you so much!" She takes control of the bag from Albert.

Walking from the bank, Cloe whispers, "Loved that line you spun. I could almost believe it."

"Your own line was good, too." He looks at Cloe, seeing a completely different person than he has ever seen before. *I like her. Shows real spunk. And bright.*

Which contributes to his heightened awareness of the people around him. Albert is not at all comfortable holding $831,947 dollars, even with two-thirds of it as a bank draft, under his arm. But there they are, walking through the mall to his car with a fortune in the briefcase under his arm.

This feels extraordinarily weird holding all this money, walking in the mall like a regular slob.

He whispers to Cloe, "Don't you feel weird with this... package, walking in the mall?"

She takes his free arm into hers. "Don't worry, dear. I'll protect you." She squeezes his arm.

What's weirder – this jesus-big wad of cash, or her calling me dear?

Passing a luggage place, Albert pulls Cloe to a stop. "You know, I – we – should get rid of my car."

"They don't sell them here, Albert. The wheels they have here are unpowered."

He smiles at her. "That's the first joke I have EVER heard you say."

Cloe grits her teeth. "The person working there wasn't me. She was a figment of somebody's dark imagination. A character from a nightmare." She does an involuntary shiver.

Albert puts his money-carrying arm around her shoulders, still holding her hand with the other. "That is a past that we will quickly put in our rear-view mirror. Or, whatever a good set of luggage has."

They stand quietly holding each other in comfort. People walk past them. One person gets too close to the vinyl bag still held by Albert on Cloe's back, causing Albert to reflexively pull it down. "Lets get a coffee and start some kind of plan." She nods to the colourful food court. A few shoppers are heading that way.

The tables are not overly busy, as usual. Albert decides to take a table that is away from the majority of folks. Seated, he places the vinyl bag on his lap, adjusting it to balance on his legs. He and Cloe absently go through the table-cleaning protocol with wipes and tissues from the containers on the back of the table.

Cloe nods at a coffee kiosk. "Do you want your regular two sugars?"

He nods absently, searching for anybody who may be staring at them. He sees a person on crutches which puts Andrew in mind again. *Maybe I should text him or something. No. Can't take the chance.*

She gets up. "Anything else? It's teatime. We might as well have a bit of a meal here. I'm going to buy a wrap."
"Ah, yeah. Good. Chicken for me." He continues his scan and his thoughts.

It takes several minutes for her to return. Albert tracks her progress, checking if anyone else is doing the same. A young man from several tables away catches his attention. The man has his eyes on Cloe all the way to their table. He locks eyes on Albert then quickly drops his gaze. Albert tracks him as he gets up, leaves a mess at his table, and heads for the washroom.

Meanwhile, not being helped to put the heavy food tray onto their table, Cloe looks around at what Albert is focused on. "What?"

Albert turns back to Cloe. "Oh. Sorry, Cloe. Was watching someone. This… this package has me spooked. Everyone here looks like a perp." He notices the food and drinks. "Thanks. Sorry. Here, let me help."

They settle in to their meal. Between slurps and chomps, they keep a watchful eye as they mull over different courses of action. Albert hastily cleans off a drop of coffee from the vinyl bag, still on his lap. "So I was thinking, what would this potential mafioso do to get at us? He probably would expect us to take off in my car as fast as we can go."

"That would leave us going anywhere north, south or east of here."

"Right. So that gives us several possible vectors."

She smiles at him "Vectors. Do you have anything to do with math?"

He smiles with her. "Exactly. Velocity plus direction. Anyway. Option one is to hightail it for points east and try to beat whoever might be looking for us to cross the mountains. There are basically three pinch points – places we would *have* go through if we head east. So, we weigh that against going south. The border is chock-full of cameras and other impediments."

"Impediments."

"Yeah. Sort of like rusted old farm implements, only more expensive. Government-expensive *implements*?"

She doesn't laugh.

He carries on. "Never mind. Going north gets us to snow country. Not my cup of tea. Yours?"

"Nope."

"Right. That leaves us with variations on the velocity component but what *that* does is expose us to more risk factors."

"Have you done this before? I mean…"

"Huh! Not *done*. Just *thought about*. Just in case. Came with the territory. I mean the mob and all that shit. Anyway. We could also do the unthinkable. Stay exactly here, heads down, as the storm blows all around and over us."

Firmly, "Nope."

"The counter-intuitive option would be to make for the Island."

"Vancouver Island? But that's a dead end. Sorry." She regrets using the word.

"Which is why it is interesting. In order to lessen the risks involved, we would have to ditch the car. Walk-ons are less visible, especially during the school rush hour from Horseshoe Bay. The kids all go to Bowen or Gibsons after class in West Van and make a satisfyingly large and noisy crowd, even with so-called social distancing. If we get some unobtrusive but solid wheeled bags to hold our stuff, we can make it to Nanaimo and maybe take the Intercity bus up-island someplace. Then buy a car, if we can, privately. Last time I was on that bus, we passed a few places on the side of the road that had cars just sitting there with For Sale signs on them. Curbers seem to be all over the place."

"You sure haven't done this before?" She is not entirely certain…

"In my dreams, Cloe. Only in my dreams. To avoid the nightmares." He notices some sauce on her cheek. "Here, let me get that for you."

As his hand is wiping away the little spot, she takes the hand and kisses his fingers. He lightly caresses her cheek and under her jaw. "Soft skin."

A minute or so passes as they get to know each other's faces.

Cloe is brought back to the present when she notices a young man staring at them. "Don't turn around quickly, but is that the guy who was looking at me earlier?" She indicates off to Albert's right.

Taking a "drink" from his now empty cup, Albert sees the man. "Not the same one. You're getting as skittish as I am. Let's get outta Dodge, kid. The Island?"

"Sure."

"Know a dealership that'll take my buggy? Oh. Let's stop to buy that luggage."

Albert had parked in the more private, covered portion of the parking lot. Now that they are beside the car, it is oppressively dark all around. The slightest sounds spook them both.

They hurriedly transfer everything to their new, same-as-all-the-others black luggage. Albert empties a box he had in the trunk into one of the pieces of luggage. Cloe is impressed with its contents.

"You watch those north-woods reality shows, Albert? There's enough goodies in there to survive in the forest for a month."

"Grew up on a farm. Never could figure how anyone could live without these multi-tools and first-aid pack and stuff…"

She sees that he is serious. "And a combination axe-saw? Who would even *make* something like that?" She handles it gingerly.

"Online catalogue. Careful. The saw blade in the handle is more dangerous than the axe blade." A leather sheath covers each section but there are teeth poking up at the edge of the flip-out saw blade.

"Speaking from experience?"

With a wry grin, "Ah, yes."

Ready, they drive off to find a small-time car dealer she knows. Looking every few seconds in the mirror, Albert uses his nonchalant voice to say, "I'm going down a few side-streets. Anybody following us there'll stand out."

She is not fooled by Albert's attempt to show calmness. Nervously, she turns periodically to keep a lookout.

The car dealer's lot has one open parking spot. Albert parks there, knowing it is goodbye to his wheels. The dealer comes out to greet Cloe and they do the obligatory tire-kicking walk-around of his car. After the arrangement is made to sell the car, the dealer gives Albert a cheque. Cloe is about to ask for cash but realizes it would be better not to raise any suspicion. She stops Albert from doing that, as well, by taking the cheque from him.

"No more 'my money', 'your money'. Right *dear*?" Her wink stops further discussion.

They all walk outside and Albert has a last lean on his car. *This old thing took Andrew and me all over the place. Went down to San Francisco once, to an AI conference…I guess that's the end of that…* He finally opens the trunk to remove their luggage. Before placing the cheque in her purse she sees which bank it is drawn on.

"Oh. Benny, would you mind giving us a lift to the Skytrain. The batteries on these bags seem to be empty."

The dealer laughs. "Haha. Batteries for luggage wheels? Haha… Hell, maybe next year, the way things are going, eh? And make it a robot to follow you. HA!" Pleased with his inventiveness, he calls to his assistant inside, "Hey Sandeep! Going out a few minutes. Want a coffee?"

The assistant nods and gives him a thumbs-up.

After getting their ride to the Skytrain station, Cloe confirms the address on the cheque. She shows Albert. "It's a stop away. We'll pay for tickets by cash at the machine. Should be able to use the same tickets on the bus downtown."

Albert nods. "If this bank doesn't give us any hassle cashing his cheque."

To the South Sea Islands

Those who seek the truth must be fleet of foot

O n the ferry, Albert leads Cloe to the forward part of the ship. "The pepperelly vibrates less away from the stern."

"So that way is the, ah, stern?" She nods backwards.

"Depends on which way it's going."

She pulls his arm. "Now you're being silly!"

"Nah. When she docked, the cars all drove in on the ramp from that end, right?"

Cloe nods reluctantly.

"So when we get to the other side, the ship can't pull in to the same side or the cars would all have to back out, right?"

"Oh. Then, what, it has propellers and doors on both ends?" She thinks that sounds wrong.

"Exactly. And when the ship approaches the far-side dock, it engages the forward prop as a brake."

Cloe shakes her head. "Ok. Too much information. I'll just take your word for it."

Not having been on a ferry before, Cloe rubbernecks at the sights. "A store and a couple cafeterias. And they're open, now. Just have to line up. Heard on the news the other day we don't need masks on board anymore… I can't imagine… All those cars and trucks that drove on! How can a boat hold all this?"

"Ship. A ship *carries* boats." He absently scans around then notices a young man who looks familiar. Whispering, "Cloe, look at that guy's face. If you see this one or the one from the mall again, tell me. Ok?"

"Is he…"

"Don't know. Just remember him."

She nods. "He has a tag up his neck."

They guide their luggage into an empty row and sit down near the outside seat. Albert asks, "Which one…"

"This one." Cloe pats the bag next to her. They had placed their money into the smaller bag.

She is still wondering about the ship. "So many people and cars and really big trucks down below. Is it safe? I still can't see how it holds everything."

Albert is about to launch into an extended explanation when a seven-year-old girl from the seats in front of them pops up over her seat-back. "Don't worry, ma'am, it's safe. I've sailed on ferries all my life." She turns to her mother. "Haven't I, mommy?"

"Yes, honey. Safe as a stone porch." The mother turns to smile at Cloe.

The little girl pops up periodically to talk to Cloe over the next hour. Albert very much likes the way they talk about things. *Relaxing.*

By the end of the ferry ride, when the family goes off to the washrooms, Albert smiles after them. "Delightful girl… Nice family.."

Cloe snuggles against him. "Yes. They are." Then she pops her head up. "Where are the washrooms?"

After arriving at Nanaimo, Cloe and Albert decide to buy a car privately at the first opportunity instead of bussing up-island.

On the bus ride downtown, they can see in the distance, in a mall parking lot near the harbour, a few cars with what look like signs in their side windows.

They get off the bus awkwardly with their luggage. Cloe looks around anxiously, reluctant to play tourist. Albert takes his time and thanks the driver.

Outside, Cloe is nervous. "Shouldn't we make tracks? With some haste?"

Albert lets Cloe handle the smaller, albeit more important, black bag. "I think we need to not attract attention. And, wandering in apparent aimlessness…"

"Apparent?"

"…it gives an opportunity to see if someone is following us…
Let's saunter over to those cars. I think those must be For Sale
signs in their windows."

It is a curbers sales lot, but in that clutch of cars only one looks
like it will run reliably. Its garish colours would have put it on
the bottom of their list, if it wasn't for the fact that it looked fairly
new and powerful. Albert says wryly, "But at least it's electric."

When Albert calls the phone number on the car's For Sale sign, a
young student answers flippantly. A few minutes of frustrating
explanation finally convinces him that Albert would like to buy
his car. Eventually coming to an understanding, the student is so
overjoyed he rushes right down to consummate the deal.

The university student (name of Beo, which they learn is short
for Beowulf, as they listen to his life story while they prod and
poke and try out the machine) drops a few computer terms about
the vehicle which grab Albert's attention.

To Cloe, Beo admits, "Ah, I, ah, hacked the firmware so its
handshake to the OEM no longer, ah, completes over TCP but
don't worry about that. For now. I replaced it with a self-teaching
neural net."

Of this, Cloe has absolutely no clue, but despite Beo's impressive
computer skills, *he* has no idea how to transfer ownership of the
vehicle. So Cloe leads him along, in her less than formal way,
and, lo, Cloe and Albert are the proud owners of a way-
overpowered, electric, yellow trimmed-in-orange-flames, SUV.

During the purchase discussions, Albert pretends to be mentally
disabled. He doesn't know why.

Just thought it was a good idea at the time. Cloe now thinks I really **am** *mentally disabled, I am sure.*

In the vehicle with Cloe driving away, she shakes her head at him. "Are you out of your friggen skull? What was that acting all about?"

Sheepishly, Albert explains, "Well, at first *he* was sounding on the slow side so I didn't want to sound above his level, and then when he got here I kinda figured we didn't want to be conspicuous, so I let *you* do all the talking…"

"By looking like you just escaped from the cuckoo's nest?"

"Well, yeah. Like, he was only talking to you so he probably'll never remember me. Or *us*. As a couple. Probably."

The last few words calm her down. Then she notices the digital velocity indicator on the broad dash display, which is alarmingly high, so she sheepishly drops back below light speed.

Albert's eyes grow huge as he, too, notices the speedometer reading. "Ah, yeah, Cloe, we don't want to be picked up for speeding. They even have speed limits at airports that are below that."

"Sorry. You're right. Never been in a car that could hit a hundred in the first two seconds. That kid must have been overjoyed to dump this beast on us."

Albert nods. "And the paint job."

"How do you spell ugliest-paint-job-on-the-Island? God! Is there a one-hour paint shop around?"

In fact, on the drive out of town, they notice a sign for "Quick Paint Jobs". Stopping there, the eager, underworked owner says, for *this* car, he can do the job in under two days. A full day to prepare; an hour to paint; the rest of the second day to dry and "cure".

"Here's the keys." Cloe is feeling unusually powerful, being able spend money like that.

Albert is being practical when he asks, "Can you drop us off at a motel? The luggage is pretty heavy."

The owner grins, "So, did you buy it from Beo or did he just *give* it to you?"

Albert chuckles. "Everyone must know this monstrosity. Did you do this paint-job?"

"God no! He and his rich dad are from the Interior. Beo drove it here for university and says he picked up three speeding tickets on the way, and one cop stopped him just see who was driving. By then, the RCMP had it all over their watchlist. The cop that stopped him looked at Beo and said, 'Kid, I don't know what they do in the Interior, but around here, we only let *adults* hit ludicrous speed.' HA! Heard that from Sergeant Drummond!" He shakes his head. "Well. Every good joke has to have a finish line. Gonna make it black?"

Cloe is about to answer but Albert jumps in with "Beige. With stealth paint, if you have it." He grins broadly so the paint shop owner thinks he is joking. *I'm not joking. Wish we could make it invisible.*

Cloe and Albert are driven to a nearby tourist hotel with their luggage. That night they explore each other. Which activity takes most of the night.

Their new vehicle is ready in the late afternoon. Taking Hwy 19 north out of Nanaimo, they are both in a glowing new world. Cloe leans over the centre console as closely as she can, exploring Albert's hand, then his leg and up to his shoulder, finishing by rustling his hair and goatee.

Perhaps in self-defence, the vehicle announces to them, via its large screen, that it wants to be fed and it wants it at the fuel stop a few minutes away. Map included.

Cloe is not sure if she should be impressed or irritated with their beast. "What happens if you let go of the steering wheel, Albert? Is going to drive itself there?"

"Ha! Likely!" He, nevertheless, steers over to the ramp and into the fuel station. The electric charger, even in "supercharging" mode, will take about fifteen minutes so Albert suggests they wait inside. "Honey, it's getting late. Let's have a coffee here and talk about our next destination. The car'll take a while for a full charge."

"Sure. Good idea. That new paint smell's giving me a headache."

"Well, beige isn't that bad. One hell of an improvement over orange flaming stripes on puce-yellow."

"Yeah – this interior is the next thing to go…" She pulls at the bright yellow-leather-trimmed-in-black seats.

In the station's small coffee shop, drinks in hand, they make like a loving couple, sitting on the same side of one of the few tables.

After a while, Cloe notices a rack of road maps for sale. It reminds her of their mission. "Where you taking me, Albert?" She peers coyly at him, "And, do you mind if I call you *Bert*?"

He chuckles, "As long as I can call you Ernie."

She gives him a solid love-tap on his shoulder. "Oohh!..." Thinks about it. "Well, why the hell not? Call me Ernie. My new *persona*." The thought brightens up her face even more.

He enjoys her much improved composure, then ploughs ahead, "Ok, *Ernie*. So where we going? I assume someplace away from Oscar the Grouch?"

"Far away…" She stares dreamily out the window.

"How about the South Sea Islands?"

Cloe-Ernie nearly jumps off her chair. "Can we? Can we?"

"Well, yeah. Like, Pender or Hornby Island, or Galiano. I always kinda liked that na…"

She clobbers his arm; hard, this time.

"Hey!..." He grins. "Was that a lover's swat?"

"Whadya mean Hornby Island? When you said South Seas…"

"They qualify," he pleads. "They're in the Salish *Sea* and they're south of us. Like, I…"

She is about to clobber him again. He flinches. She grabs him and drags him closer for a long kiss. The server working behind the counter enjoys a few glances at them as she replenishes one of the donut trays in the display case.

After they slowly part, he nods. "I like the making-up part better."

The dusk outside is pierced by lights from cars and big rigs passing on the highway next to the station. Albert-Bert stares at the traffic absently. He mumbles, "Tempus fugit."

"Is that a play in London? Can we go to London?"

"Latin. Means time is passing, but the root for *fugitive*…"

"Ohh, stop. That hard-drive of yours is loose again." She pulls his face close for a kiss.

He smiles inside and out. *Used to have to let the hard-drive topic finish or it hurt somewhere. Doesn't hurt anymore.*

They get up to leave, walking closely arm-in-arm, step-for-step. He isn't skittish now. His pace and hers are merged. *I must have changed into a different persona, too.*

Slipping through the aisle of hats and tee-shirts and maps for sale, the glare of a parking vehicle shines over their heads from the back window. Ernie notices the driver as he gets out of his car and walks to the entrance. She grabs Bert's arm. "It's him."

"From…"

"The ferry." She ducks down, pulling Bert behind the rack of maps. "Oh god. How did he find us?"

Bert sneaks a peek at the entry door. It takes a minute for the prospective perp to get to the outside door. Bert feels that the guy coming through does not behave like he is on the hunt. Whispering, "You sure?" They both bend down out of sight.

Ernie sneaks a look. "Positive. Has that tattoo showing on his neck over his right shoulder. You see?"

Bert nods grimly. "He's likely going to the can first. Or the drink counter. We can't be seen from here. If he heads to the can, we'll slip out right away."

She nods, getting ready. The mafia guy's dark machine is parked in the back lot, away from the station entrance and far away from the building's fuel pumps. Their own beast is up front, on the other side of the fuel pumps. Looking at the sauntering mob-guy's reflection in the store's broad windows as he walks inside, Bert leads Ernie a few steps closer to the door. The thug goes into the washroom and Bert and Ernie slip quickly out the door.

Looking back, Bert sees a cigarette glowing in the mob car. He hisses, "Someone else in his car. We'll both get in the same side of our buggy. It's angled away from the station. While I disconnect, you get in the back seat and stay down." *She'll be safer from any gunfire back there.*

Walking at first, they break into a run while going through the fuel pump area.

After a rush job of paying then disconnecting the charging cable, Bert jumps in and moves the car quickly away, though without peeling rubber. Ernie can't see the other car. Suddenly, she notices headlights flash on from the back of the station. Driving down the dark driveway, Bert hits his head on the ceiling going over a speed bump at the same time as the mafia car spins out with a squeal while entering the empty drive-through lane, after emerging from the back corner of the building.

That's all Ernie sees as they accelerate at very high speed onto the on-ramp and peel rubber down the highway. Bert looks back through the mirror, "Keep your eyes on the road behind us! There's a U-turn up ahead. I'm going the zip around and back to head south. Look for their car when we turn around."

Ernie pats his shoulder. "Is that axe thingy handy?"

The traffic is light. At the U-turn, Bert makes sure there are no oncoming cars as he wheels around and then slows down to just above the speed limit.

Ernie is alarmed. "What happened!? Is the battery dying?"

"No no. Calm down. Don't want to be conspicuous. As soon as they pass I'll pour on the coals. Keep checking the traffic on their side."

Ernie turns to stare at the sea side of the highway. A dark line of trees mostly obscures the far slope down to the seashore. A tractor-trailer roars by on the north side, then an SUV. She watches as the next car approaches. The black car is moving faster than the others and is overtaking the truck.

"There they are! Can't see the driver but they're moving like a bat-outta-hell!"

"Watch for their brake lights when they get to the U-turn."

A few seconds later, "Brake lights!"

Bert immediately stomps on the accelerator and the car surges ahead like it was a rocket-sled. It's all he can do to hold a straight line. Several seconds of fighting the steering wheel, then Bert remembers his beast will hold the lane automatically, so he realizes he was probably fighting against the vehicle's own servos. By then he is passing cars that had been a kilometre ahead of him. "Wow! This is some monster of a car!"

Ernie is holding onto the back of her seat, eyes focused on the road to the rear. "Nothing behind us but a cloud of dust. What now?"

Bert looks in the mirror as he settles down to warp-drive. "Choices. Stay on 19 south for as long as we can, or pull off to lose them someplace in Nanaimo."

"I vote for putting as much distance as possible behind us."

Bert shakes his head. "We can only do this until a cop pulls us over. It's a crapshoot as to how long that might be. For all we know, one of the cars we blew past is calling us in right now."

Ernie turns herself to sit forward. "Let me look at my map…"

Bert jumps in, "Don't turn your phone on!"

"Wasn't going to, dummy. This old-fashioned paper map from the gas station didn't get put back."

She searches the ceiling for a light switch. "Can I put a light on?"

They both scan the bendy road behind them. Bert nods, "Should be ok for now."

She clicks the light on. Flipping pages, Ernie looks around. "Where are we? In Victoria, yet?"

He chuckles, "Not quite. Just saw Jingle Pot."

She guffaws and starts laughing loudly, her body releasing all her tension.

Bert grins, "What?"

Ernie finally gathers herself. "Thanks, Bert. I needed that. Now what the hell were you saying about the road?"

He grins in the mirror at her. "Jingle Pot!"

On the verge of breaking out again, "Stop that! What *Jingle Pot…*" She notices the name on the map in her hand. "Jesus-friggen-christ! You're not kidding! Here it is, *Jingle Pot…* So we passed it?"

"The first of them. We're just past the *next* intersection. Jingle Pot Number 2 coming up in the next parsec."

Ernie rapidly finds their location, "Ok, but don't turn right! It doesn't…"

Surprised by Bert's sudden right turn, she falls against the left side door as Bert zips off at the intersection, drives half a block, then spins around and parks on the opposite shoulder next to a tree facing the highway. The instant the car stops he turns everything off. Things hum down and the noises click their way from blazing hot toward moderately hot.

He nods appreciatively. "This is *some* beast."

Rubbing her left shoulder, Ernie mumbles, "Men drivers. That was a hell of a drag race. Do we need to fuel up again?"

Waiting quietly. Waiting for the car to pass or to turn toward them. Bert's older nervous persona comes to the fore as his fingers tap the door handle. Ernie puts her hands onto his shoulders. "Give it another minute, dear. Never can tell if they saw the dust cloud at the intersection… Didn't see their car but… can they turn around up ahead?"

Bert relaxes under her soothing touch. "Not until the College turnoff on top of the mountain." He nods to the right. "At full speed it would take two or three minutes…" he shifts a bit to have Ernie's massage reach his neck, "so, you're right. Another minute." Still watching the highway he purrs like a kitten under her massage.

They wait for a while. Seeing a line of mist starting to build up along the bottom of the windscreen, Bert rouses himself. "Should open the door. You're getting me… excited." He pats her hand on his neck and is about to open the door, then stops. "Don't know how to turn the damn cabin light off. Can you see a switch?"

Ernie slips her hands off his shoulder to inspect the overhead light. "Looks like this switch has an *off*. Maybe I'll cover it with my coat, anyway."

She does so. Bert opens the door and several other interior lights glow on, along with the outside light on the left front fender. "F…fig." he leaves the door open. "What the hell. Might as well leave it open, now; no point in flashing the lights to the world again." Bert falls back to his exasperated-with-the-world attitude, then, "No. Positive thinking. Things are alright." He nods to himself and slips out the door.

She smiles as he steps out. "Let the metamorphosis begin."

"Huh?"

Still smiling, "Nothing. Carry on, dear."

He shrugs. Leaving the door ajar, he looks around carefully. Bert absently flaps the door to air out the inside moisture, then gets back into his seat. Before closing the door he looks over his shoulder, "Wanna sit up front? You can be my copilot." His smile is lost on her as Ernie quickly nods and exits, remembering to push the door closed quietly. Walking around the back, she peers into the darkness behind them, then ducks to avoid tree branches next to their beast. She opens her door to sit in the front passenger seat. Bert holds a finger up and they close their doors together. The lights ever sooo slowly… dim.

"Now what?" Ernie leans as close to his shoulder as she can get.

Still watching outside, "Who the hell killed Piero?"

Ernie makes a sour face. "Don't give a rat's ass. One less piece of vermin on this planet."

"Right… Except, if we don't know, it'll be harder to figure out who's hunting *us*."

Hard lines take over her face. "Oh I *know* who the sonofabitch is who's hunting us. It's his lawyer, Gino. He was the real boss. Gino let… let you-know-who puff out like the little Mussolini he was – the front-man. But Gino pulled all the strings from the backroom…"

Before Ernie can work into a red-faced rant, Bert gently puts a finger on her lips. "I know. Down girl. Don't want to see that red-face anymore. Thought we left that back on the Mainland."

She huffs and puffs a few times then calms down. "Red-face?" She pulls her passenger mirror down from the back of the sun-visor. As she pulls the cover open its light comes on. "Fuck!" and snaps it closed.

Bert lets out a guffaw. "Haha! You look beautiful, Ernie! You do…" He reaches over to kiss her by pulling her head closer across the centre console.

Still holding her head, he leans away slightly. "How about Galiano?"

"The drink?"

"The island." Bert smiles.

"Do we swim or paddle?"

"There's a ferry."

"When?"

Suddenly, for no reason, he replies in an old aggravated tone, "Well how the hell should *I* know?... Sorry, Ernie. Sorry. Getting tense again." He shakes his head slowly at himself.

She pouts, then breaks into a grin. "Is that fight number two?"

He lifts his head up then leans close. "Hope so. I like the making up part."

Pushing him away, Ernie pulls out her phone, feeling a phantom-vibration.

Before she can wake it up he raises his voice, "NO! Don't turn it on!"

She holds it away from herself like it had a spider on it. "Sorry. Instant reaction. Was sure it was going to ring. .. This is a new world in more ways than one. But how do we find out the ferry times?"

Bert scans the outside yet again. Satisfied that there are no mafia cars nearby, "We can drive into town. Jingle Pot takes us toward the ferry terminal. On the way we can stop at a coffee shop or something and use their wifi from the parking lot. I have a VPN on my phone. It's as safe anything can be these days."

Ernie snuggles into her seat as he carefully starts the car forward. The wait at the intersection for the traffic light to change seems to take forever. They both keep a wary eye out at the occasional vehicles on the highway. With a green light, Bert moves with alacrity into the built-up area then slows down. They turn into an all-night burger joint whose parking lot is lit up.

He parks in a darker area and shuts down. "We're close enough to use their wifi, here. Do you need anything? Food or drink?"

"The can. Maybe a drink?"

He nods, "Right, but do you mind going in yourself? The less we're seen together, the better."

Ernie smiles. "Afraid my father'll find out about us?" Before Bert replies, "Just kidding. You're right. Give me some cash, will you? Want anything?"

He shakes his head and reaches into the money-bag. He hands her a bill as she opens the door. Ernie heads for the side entrance of the burger joint.

Bert pulls out his phone, considering its blank screen before turning it on. "Wish I could stop it from pinging the cell-tower before I can start the VPN. Oh well." He fingers it on then quickly finds the VPN app.

By the time Ernie returns, Bert has downloaded a number of maps and files.

She sees his phone is still on as she sits down. "Is it safe?"

"In airplane mode. Not supposed to be calling out, or in. I loaded up the ferry schedules as a file, along with some maps. You should probably put your phone into airplane mode for now, too. In case your fingers start flying before…" He hesitates.

"Before brain is engaged? Got it." She puts the drink she bought into a cup holder and pulls out her phone.

He finds a secure place for his phone on the centre console then buckles up. "We should see if a motel will take us for another night. The ferry sails just after eight a.m."

"Is that the early one?"

Bert shakes his head as he turns the vehicle's systems on. "Naw. Just don't think we have to get up for the six o'clock ferry. We can take time for breakfast. And… other things." He grins at Ernie.

"Other things?"

OTHER THINGS

He who walks through shit should not be surprised
if dogs sniff at his heals

round two-thirty in the morning, Ernie is half awake, fighting the need to go to the can. Quietly mumbling, "No good. Shouldn't have had that late coffee. Have to go."

Bert slurps a snort and rolls onto his side. She gently pulls from under the covers and pads over to the washroom, holding out her hands in the dark to find the doorway. A faint l.e.d. glows from the ceiling smoke detector to give her enough light to locate the toilet.

Finished, she is about to return to bed when a car's lights roll past the narrow back window. She can hear the engine of the car. They had parked their own beast back there, out of the way but not directly behind their unit. The outside lights linger briefly then turn off at the same time as the engine. Goosebumps rise all over her naked body. She jumps to the bed and whispers hoarsely, "Wake up! Don't say anything. Throw something on. I'll get the bag."

A groggy Bert rolls to the edge of the bed and reaches for his pants. Ernie grabs her pants and a blouse then slips on her shoes, hopping to the closet to pull out the bag that has their money. Bert has trouble with his shoes, trying to pull the backs up.

"Forget it! Your wallet and keys in the pants?"

He taps his pants pocket. "Yeah. What…?"

Still quietly, "In the back. Stopped at our car."

Bert nods, "Outside. Turn left. There's no access for them that way."

Ernie hesitates at the door, "What if…"

"No option. Rush out now."

As Ernie swings the door open, the porch lights make her feel naked on a stage. She runs fast but quietly, turning her feet so the heels don't hit hard, sprinting for the copse of trees at the property boundary. Bert closes the door quietly then carries the bag as he runs behind Ernie. Most of the units have cars parked in front of them. He thinks, *Our unit stands out like a sore thumb without a car in front.*

He reaches the trees at the same time as Ernie. "Stop behind a big tree and make like bark." He does the same. Just then, he glimpses a car without lights on, coming from the back parking lot. It slowly rolls up to their unit and parks in front. The driver gets out first, holding a weapon, but he is crouching and can't be seen well. The passenger door opens for a young woman. She is holding a light, pointed down to the ground. They approach the door of the unit; the man holds up a finger to stop his partner; he whispers instructions. Stepping carefully to the door, he listens for anything from inside, then pulls a wallet-sized device from a pocket, still holding his weapon in the other hand.

Bert can now see enough of the thug's weapon in the porch light. *Silencer*.

Using his device, the thug opens their door as if he had a key. As he ever so slowly pushes it open, he waves his companion over. In a choreographed move they both take one step inside while she shines the light on the bed and he shoots, *Pop Pop*. The weapon is quiet enough not to wake anybody nearby, but Bert and Ernie can hear his anger.

"Not there! Where the fuck…" He grabs the woman's light with his free hand and steps quickly inside to look in the washroom, holding his weapon ready.

She stays by the door, getting nervous. "Louie?"

Checking everywhere inside, "Bed's still warm." He looks directly at the trees that are hiding Bert and Ernie.

Bert whispers very quietly but urgently, "Suck in don't move a muscle."

Louie's light rakes through the copse of cedars and pines but doesn't find them. The light scans away from the trees giving Bert a chance to look for an exit. On the other side of the trees is a high wooden fence. *No good. Too high for her.* He carefully puts the bag down lengthwise in his tree's shadow. Not far away is a small pile of pine branches that had been trimmed off some of the trees. Bert sneaks a look around his tree.

Very quietly, over his shoulder to Ernie, "Have to chance moving to the pile over there. If he sees me and shoots, stay still."

Bert bends down as low as he can and tries to make like a cat, stepping through the undergrowth. His foot catches a branch. *Crack!* He freezes low to the ground as the light flashes quickly his way. Not breathing for what seems like several minutes – but is only half minute – he needs to take in a breath. The light is scanning roughly across his back all the time. Then Bert notices that the light is bouncing rhythmically. *Running this way.*

Bert times it for when the light is shining slightly away then jumps for the pile of branches. That prompts the light to swing wildly around. Quickly finding a bat-sized branch, Bert grabs it, then adds a thinner, longer one to his other hand.

By then, Louie is at the edge of the trees. He doesn't stop but comes charging in. Bert stays low, hiding behind the branch pile until Louie steps close. On a slight breathing sound from Ernie, the light swerves off in her direction. Louie is about to bring his weapon up for a shot at her. Bert throws the thinner branch at him, hitting his shoulder and arm, causing the weapon to fire wildly, *Pop*, up into the branches. Before Louie can turn around, Bert's bat smashes against his head, hard. Louie crumples. Bert jumps on Louie's hand holding the weapon, causing it to *Pop* into the ground and at the same time crunches into Louie's head again with the bat. Louie's legs jerk a couple times. Bert checks the limp body for other weapons. He pulls out his car keys and wallet.

From the car comes a plaintive, "Louie? Did you find them? Honey?"

Still in his hoarse whisper, "Ernie, stay here for minute. If he moves, stick the gun in his face." He hands a shaking Ernie the gun after ensuring the safety is engaged. "And hold the bag in your other hand."

She takes the weapon and the valuable bag reluctantly. "What do I do?"

"Don't worry. The safety's on. Just point it threateningly and call me. I'm going to scare off his partner."

Holding the bat, Bert strides aggressively toward Louie's partner. She sees Bert and rushes to the other side of their car while pulling out her phone. Speed dial puts someone on the other end, "Boss! It's me, Cindy. Something's wrong! He's going to hurt me! Hurry!... NOW goddamnit!"

Bert is closing in on her as she grabs at the driver's side door handle. It won't open. She desperately tugs on it. Closing in, Bert holds up the keys that he took from Louie's pocket. He has already locked the doors. After another futile tug, the frantic woman turns to run away. Bert rounds the car and trips her with the bat before she can escape. She sprawls, face-down on the pavement.

Crying, she pleads in a desperate whisper, "Don't hurt me, please! I didn't do nothing. Just Louie's lookout. He made me do it! Where is he? Ask him! ASK him!"

Bert notices lights come on from one of the units. He lowers the bat then lets it drop to the pavement. Bert doesn't see the woman reach into a pocket. He steps to her as she keeps crying.

"Don't hurt me, please. I ain't done nothing to you. I'm just a..." As Bert stands over her, she whips an arm around and slashes Bert's lower leg with a knife then rolls and scrambles away, disappearing down the driveway to the street.

Bert suddenly feels a sharp, burning pain and sees blood flowing into the pant leg from a cut just above his left foot. He slumps against the car. "Damn bitch." Lowering himself against the car to the ground he grabs his wounded leg and squeezes tightly against the cut.

Quietly, "Ernie." She doesn't answer. Louder, "Ernie. Come 're."

He hears her running, then Ernie is kneeling beside him. "Oh my god! Bert! What…?" She drops the gun and their bag to the ground.

"Cut me. Across the bone. Have to wrap it quick. Need to leave."

Ernie pulls her blouse end out and tries to tear the end. It won't rip so she bites at it, then tears off a long strip.

Bert rolls up his cuff to expose the cut. Blood is coming out steadily. "Not an artery. Wrap it tight."

Starting delicately, Ernie sees that it isn't staunching the flow so she ties the cloth tightly around his leg against the cut. Bert inhales sharply.

"Ok?"

He nods through gritted teeth then struggles to get up. Handing her the keys to their own car, "Quick, bring our buggy up front while I look through this one. Can you pull out our luggage?"

She nods and runs off. Bert clicks the doors of the mafia car, opens the door and digs around the front seats. He grabs a phone from the centre console along with papers that are under it, stuffing them into their money bag. Bert struggles to the back door and roots around as Ernie parks next to him. Picking up a gymbag, he hands it and their money bag to Ernie through the window then holds up a hand. "Have to check the trunk."

He hops back, clicking the trunk open. Inside, he pulls out two more bags. They are bigger and one is over a metre long and heavy. Ernie rushes into their unit to retrieve their own bags.

An older man in shorts opens the door to his unit not far away and asks aggressively, "What the hell you doing out there? I'm gonna call the cops!" Bert can see him clearly with the porch lights but the light doesn't extend fully to where Bert is standing.

Bert nods at the man, "Yes, please. The guy from this car just took a shot at me. He's in the woods." Bert nods back to the trees. "Took his gun. I'll leave it here in the trunk for the cops. His partner took off down the street after cutting me. Going to look for her. Tell them."

He hops to the passenger side of his vehicle, which hides all but his shoulders and head from the older man, who is still framed in the porch light at his door.

Rising on tiptoes to try to see what Bert is doing, but unable to see, the older man says, "Calling now!" Then he closes and locks his door.

Bert struggles to put the two bags onto the back seat of his beige beast then falls into his seat beside Ernie. "Let's go. She went right. We go left." Ernie peels out of the driveway.

Weird News

To hide a broken branch in the woods is easier than
to hide a mad dog in a crowd

Their beige SUV is driving exactly six kilometres per hour over the posted speed limit, heading toward the Malahat. Ernie glances anxiously at Bert, who is holding his wounded leg up on the front console, with his seat-back fully down.

"You ok, Bert? Is that a better position? Do we need to stop again? Should take you to a clinic."

Bert rolls his head and smiles at Ernie. "Eyes front, kid. Cruise control only handles the speed."

"It has lane-keep…" She keeps her eyes on the winding road. "…Where do they get the names for these roads?"

"Made up by an AI game bot." One of his AI algorithms pops into his head for some reason. He shakes it out. "I'm ok, now. Thanks, Ernie. Good thing my box of first aid supplies had disinfectant in it…" He reaches forward to touch the bandages that Ernie had expertly put over his cut. "Long slash but it didn't get a chance to go deep 'cause of the bone. Not leaking anymore. Should be good. Just want to rest…"

Ernie nods. "The disinfectant was four years past due. Is it…?"

He grunts and shrugs. She pats his hand. "Swartz Bay?"

He nods, "For five o'clock. We're going to Saturn."

"Saturna."

"I'd rather go to Saturn."

The car lopes along, climbing the Malahat up to its summit. As the clock switches to three-fifty-nine a.m., Bert nods at the big screen, "Ernie, can you ask the butler to turn on a news channel, please?"

"Huh? Oh, you mean voice activation. Probably not a good idea to engage it."

Bert's eyes open wider. "God, you're smart. How did I ever find someone like you?... Yeah, just scan for a news channel. By hand. See if we're featured yet."

Ernie smiles in satisfaction. "Stealth mode. How do we turn off all the modern conveniences in this buggy? It looks like Beo tried to load every techy tool he could into the poor thing's computer. Now we have to stop using it all. Almost like going back to before *The Virus*."

"Before T.V. dot two. Last year. Thank god that second wave's over with." They both nod.

Ernie touches the radio on then finds a news reporter excitedly announcing, "…as reported from our correspondent in Hong

Kong, and we are waiting for confirmation from the government. And more on that as soon as we have the report from our medical correspondent in Vancouver. On the good news front, the Cormorant will soon be flying to Vancouver. The inventor – ok, here it goes – Simo Manojlovich – wooh, got it! – told this reporter that he has been operating under approval that lets him run test hops on the water for another two weeks. If the program continues successfully with his labouriously handmade six-seat hoverwing, the Cormorant will still be operating from his facilities on Mayne Island during the testing stages. The intent is to eventually operate from Nanaimo to the dock near River Rock Casino. Talk about throwing the dice! Their second stage of testing will allow full load flights and, later, he expects to have approval for full-distance flights with non-paying passengers. His electric-powered half-airplane-half-boat has been running at full throttle, so-to-speak, for the past five months of testing around the company dock on Mayne Island. I hope, for his sake, that there is nothing in that Chinese news that might lock down the testing program again. Meanwhile, up-island, it seems gang warfare has reared its ugly head in Nanaimo again. Police tell us in a shootout at a motel, one gang member has been taken to hospital in critical condition and a woman was found gunned down on the street not far from the motel. Police are on the lookout for a silver SUV and warn the public not to approach it if they see it. The occupants are armed and dangerous…"

Both yell out, "WHAT?" They stare at each other in amazement.

Bert adds, "Gino's buddies must have killed her to shut her up and blame us."

The reporter drones on, "The vehicle is reported to have three or four armed people inside and police ask that you call 9-1-1 if you see it. Do not approach it."

Ernie punches the radio off to listen to something outside.

A siren can be heard approaching rapidly from behind their car. Her heart pumps at a very high rate in one second flat. She puts a hand to her throat to keep it down in her chest. Taking hurried glances from the mirror, to the road, to Bert, she croaks out, "What do I do?"

Bert painfully pulls his left leg down and raises the seat back up. "Drop down a couple clicks but stay just above the speed limit… Stay calm."

A few seconds later, the cruiser, with flashing lights on but the siren now off, pulls up behind their beige beast. It follows for a minute then whips out quickly to position itself right beside them. The one cop has his window down and is looking carefully at the inside of their vehicle. Without moving his smiling lips, Bert says, "Roll the window down."

Ernie does it and smiles at the cop as she glances back and forth from the cop to the road ahead. Yelling out, "Can we help you, officer?"

The cop yells out, "Anybody else with you?"

Ernie rolls down the back window. She yells over the wind noise, "Just the two of us, sir. Going on vacation to Victoria. We're taking our son's car while he's in university."

Bert notices the sergeant stripes and yells past Ernie, "Sergeant Drummond? I think you know our son!" Bert grins at him. "What's the news with the next virus wave?"

Aggravated, "Don't know any more than you do, sir. Have a good trip." He nods forward to his driver and closes his window.

Turning toward his buddy, "Told you it couldn't be blazing friggen yellow with orange flames for long. Pulled him over twice, myself. He was going to kill himself in that overpowered thing." The siren goes back on as they roar away.

Ernie closes the windows on her beige beast.

Bert painfully resumes his elevated leg position. "Have to get to Saturn before they shut down the ferries again."

"What a weird world." She shakes her head.

"Must have orbited through a cosmic cloud of mystical freakiness… Wonder what's next." He lets out a groan. "Ernie, stop at the next pull-off, will you?" The pain starts knifing up his leg.

"Are you alright?"

They arrive at the ferry terminal several minutes too late for Saturna but in time to get on a ferry to take them to Mayne Island. Ernie is pissed off that the booth attendant won't let them on, even though they can see the ferry is still in dock.

Bert has seen it too often before. Through gritted teeth, "Whatever. Ramp's going up. We'll take the other ferry. They do a milk run later."

Sitting in the short line, they have time to cool down. Ernie turns on the radio to hear of further news. It is a repeat of the previous broadcast. "No news. It's olds." She is expecting a grin or at least some positive acknowledgment from Bert for her joke.

She is disappointed to still see his distinctly sour puss. She turns off the radio.

With his foot still down from when they bought their ticket, Bert is getting cranky. "What the hell have we done to deserve this crap? More virus shit. The Third Wave! Sounds like some friggen horror movie. And cops on *our* tail as we get shot at and sliced by some mafioso gang. And what the hell is a Cormorant with an electric motor? Geeze!"

Ernie pats his sore leg. "Cheer up, dear. Let me take you to the south sea island… Does it hurt?"

"And what kind of a name is *that* for a south sea island? Mayne! for chrissake!"

Bert leans back as far as the seat will go, looking for a more comfortable position. He puts his leg back up onto the dash. He feels hot… A snort wakes him up from a few minutes of catnapping.
Ernie's cool hand is caressing his forehead. "You're hot. Feels like a fever, Bert. Can you taste things alright?" She is looking him over with a wrinkled brow.

"Virus is over with. I'm fine, damnit!"

"Says the macho hulk as he licks the blood off his bullet-riddled arms."

Bert calms down with a slight smile. "Saw that movie. Didn't like the plot trajectory… Think I'm hot?"

She grins, "Well, yes, but we don't have enough room in here to do anything about it." Then taking a look at the area behind the back seats, "Or, maybe we do. That sly kid must have used this buggy as his pad."

Bert does a whole-body stretch and throws in a few careful quarter-turns. "Don't want to get out. I'm kind of obvious, if our friends have come this way to look for us. Or scan the cameras for the terminal." He cracks the window open a bit to freshen the air. "Listen, Ernie…"

She softens her whole body in the way that Bert has come to love. *Love? Christ! It hasn't been a week and thinking 'Love'.* "Love the way you do that."

"What?" She fluffs her hair.

"Yeah, that too."

Ernie flows across the console to plant a long kiss on his willing face and caress his forehead. "You *do* have a fever, Bert. Not high, but it worries me. Should we…"

"Go to the hospital? Hell no. That'll be the first place to find whatever this third wave shit is. Or *them* to find *us*"

"While you were sleeping, the radio guy said it wasn't really a another wave. Read out part of a report saying they're pretty certain it's a new mutation of the virus. And the words he used sounded like a script from the Chief Health Officer. I didn't like his tone."

Nodding, "Yeah, this particular virus has been throwing us curves all the way. Wouldn't doubt it. What I was going to say, my love, is that you should go to that little pharmacy they have here and stock up. Something for fevers, colds, bandages, hair colouring, a cane…"

Ernie stiffens with the last item. "A cane? Do you think…"

He pats her leg. "Not for me, dummy. For your disguise. Get some hair colouring to make you look older."

She nearly rises to the ceiling, "WHAT?"

He holds back a laugh, "Take it easy, girl. I mean, like, you need a *disguise*. And me, too. We can whiten our hair and hobble around like an old couple."

Ernie calms down. "The only thing in your sentence I liked was the word 'couple'."

They discuss it further, then Ernie takes a handful of cash to the stores for her purchases. She adds medical supplies to her list.

THE MAYNE WOMAN

*To run away may be disgraceful, but it can be
decidedly useful*

he small ferry is different from what Ernie was hoping for. "Kinda, like, *small* isn't it?"

"It is *transportation* rather than *entertainment*," retorts Bert through gritted teeth, still in sour puss mood. "What did you expect? A shopping mall?"

"Well, not really… but… Never mind, Bert. I'm going to the washroom to start my transformation to an old hag. I'll let you stay here to do your own Heckle to Jekyll thing if you want." She gives him a minor and unsatisfying peck on the cheek.

Bert peers through his slowly building fog of fever in time to notice Ernie leaving her side of the vehicle. She tries to open the trunk door, unsuccessfully. Bert hits the rear-door-open button for her. *Heckle?*

As it rises, she whispers from the back, "Thanks, Bert. I'll come back as a new woman. See if you like her better." She takes two bags from her shopping trip, with the hair colouring, cosmetics and a floppy hat. She puts on the hat and a pair of gloves. Grabbing the cane, Ernie touches the door-close button.

Bert is aggravated, frustrated, and not at all feeling like he is in control of the situation. *She's mad at me. Besides being sliced across my leg and getting an infection from that bottle of old disinfectant, what did I do wrong?... Hope she can work into her disguise. Never had a problem with that. Probably why Tasha sent me here. I hold onto the present and use the past as, what?... Fuel for the dream I'm living in? Have to get some sleep.*

Meanwhile, Ernie tries to be unobtrusive while finding the washroom on the small ferry. Being a quiet sailing, no-one else joins her in the washroom. Shortly, an old lady steps carefully out of the facilities, leaning heavily on her cane. Her floppy cloth hat fully contains her hair and covers her forehead. She decides to switch from leaning heavily on her right arm, to the left, making it easier to hold the bags and use the door handles. She sees only two passengers in the small seating area. The others are resting in their vehicles for the fifty-minute ferry ride. Ernie focuses on a safe-looking middle-aged woman seated away from the windows.

Ernie mumbles to herself, thinking out loud at the same time as trying out her older voice. "Should talk with her. Get comfortable with this other persona. It'll give poor Bert some time to sleep."

She shuffles down the aisle toward the other woman and, at her aisle, stumbles slightly. Standing still to recover, Ernie thinks, *Don't know if that was what I wanted to do or if it's more virus symptoms leftover.*

The other woman looks up. "You ok, honey?"

Ernie stands shakily. Replying in her grandma voice, "Thank you, my dear. I'll be fine…" shifting her cane around unsteadily, "Maybe I should sit down. Do you mind if I sit here for a minute?"

The other woman indicates with her hand to the seat one removed from her own. A sign has been attached to the seat between them, as has been the norm for every second seat on the ferry.

"Thank you. Never know how young folks are going to react these days to, what do they call it? Encroaching their bubble? At least we don't have to wear the damn mask any more." They both smile.

"Yes, common courtesy's been lost to the virus. Ah, you're not infected, are you?"

"Not me, dear. Qualicum Beach had a good record. Well, there was that person who came to visit her parents…" *Not infected anymore but I may still have some pathogens floating around deep inside me. When that sonofabitch forced me to that secret party out on the farm with Gino and his mob. So, don't worry. I think.*

The other woman gets interested. "Qualicum is a nice place. Quaint. Relaxing. I should go there…"

Ernie nods, "My name is Ernestine, dear. My, ah, son is in the car. He hurt his leg cutting firewood so he can't walk around."

"Hi, Ernestine. I'm Lucille. Live on Mayne. For now, anyway. I finally found a place for my dad in a senior's residence in Saanich. My sister, she's in Victoria, she didn't want to put him in there, what with all the trouble senior's residences have had. She's getting dementia, herself, I'm afraid. At least she admits to not remembering things like she used to… Wants me to go down to Victoria to take care of her. Didn't trust all those ads for the private places – after what the virus did to them all. For our dad. Dad was on the *public* list for years. What's the fucken use – sorry, honey – what's the use of putting someone on a list until just before they're going to have to go to an institution? Dad's had dementia, so they'll have to put a bell on him."

"A bell? Oh my."

"Well, you know. An electronic gizmo so's they know where he is."

"Oh. I guess I have that to look forward to." It gives Ernie pause for thought.

Lucille takes a look at Ernie for the first time. "You look pretty spry, honey. Won't have to worry about that for a while, yet." Her smile is forced as she focuses on the wobbling cane.

Ernie shakes her cane in the nervous way her grandmother used to. She is pleased to have thought of putting on gloves. They hide her clear-skinned hands. She had artistically put a few dark blotches on her cheeks and under her chin. A shawl covers most of her neck skin. The floppy hat droops around her head. Following her late grandmother's lead, Ernie is wearing a loose dress with long white socks and running shoes. In total, it is an outfit she'd not want to be caught dead in. The thought sends a shiver through her.

Lucille notices the shiver. "Are you warm enough, honey? They keep these ferries so damn cold. Cheaper, I guess."

The two chat for a while about the changes wrought by The Virus. Conversation turns to living on Mayne Island.

Ernie broaches the topic of finding accommodation. "…and when Albert cut his leg, we were about to arrange to rent a small house for the next few months. Being in the hospital that day caused us to miss a call from the house owner and Albert wasn't able to reach her after that. He said we're going anyway. He's so impulsive sometimes."

Lucille is interested. "So you two are just going to wander around Mayne looking for a place to stay?"

"I'm afraid I couldn't make Albert listen to reason. You know how grumpy men can get when things don't go their way."

"Yeah. Too well. Finally had to kick *my* man out. Last time he got into his drunken shitstorm…" She grits her teeth. "Called the

cops. They said they'd keep him in the drunk-tank over night. I
called them early next morning and told them to keep him for as
long as they wanted. Do whatever the hell they wanted to with
him. I wasn't going to take his abuse any more… Haven't seen
him for over a month. Maybe the virus got him… Who gives a
shit."

With more enthusiasm than she should have used in this other
persona, "Way to go, girl!"

Lucille smiles, "Bloody right. But times is tough. Not enough
money to pay for food **and** the mortgage – even with my little
garden." She thinks for a while. She opens her purse to show
Ernie pictures of her house. "Yeah, that's the sonofabitch. Ignore
him. Here's my garden. Wish I could of kept it up over the past
while… Listen, ah, Ernestine. Would you and your son be
interested in staying at *my* place? If you can afford, say, a
thousand a month, it would pay for my mortgage and stuff and I
can stay with my sister in Victoria. She's been wanting me to
move in with her."

The two come to an agreement in principle. Ernie says she will
go talk with her *son*, "But I am certain he will be happy with it.
Be back in two shakes of a lamb's tail, Lucille." That was what
her grandmother used to say a lot, *Rest her soul.*

Out on the vehicle deck, Bert is fast asleep in their car. Several
hard raps on the window next to his head finally wakes him up.
He unlocks the doors then takes a better look at who woke him.
"Ernie?"

"*Ernestine*, if you don't mind, *son*." She seats herself behind the
steering wheel. Ernie is not sure how to begin, without getting
the sour puss back. "Albert…"

"What happened to *Bert*?"

"You have been demoted to my son, Albert. I met a nice lady who has a house to rent…"

"On Mayne? How much?"

"Yes. A thousand a month…"

"Is she ok?"

"Will you let me tell you about…"

"Not now, Ernie, my brain's all fogged up. I trust whatever you decide. Take her the cash for two months." He grimaces as he turns his legs to readjust them.

And so they drive from the ferry behind Lucille's little car to her house, ten minutes away from the dock. The house is a one-and-a-half storey wood-clad place that, like many on the islands, is blending into the greenery and brownery all around it. Moss makes up most of the roof surface. Green stuff is creeping across the aged clapboards from the bottom up and behind the overgrown shrubs that are rubbing against the house. Ernie gets the tour inside and out while Bert collapses on the old but very comfortable couch in the charming, spacious living room. The kitchen and dining room open up to the living room under what used to be a fine-worked plaster archway, now festooned with hanging plants and overhung with paintings that were done lovingly by a local accomplished artist. Several walls, what can be seen of them behind the paintings and knickknack shelves, are coloured either dark purple or burnt crimson. Ernie restrains her thoughts, *Should have left our Beast with his original wild colours. Must be an Islands thing.*

Later, Ernie helps Lucille pack as many goods and clothing as she can into her econobox. "I'll come back next week some time for what more I might need. I'll call. Oh. You wrote down the phone number here?" At Ernie's nod, she hugs her. "You are a godsend, honey. The more I think about it, the more I know I should do this."

Ernie spends the rest of the day keeping Bert comfortable.

He refuses to be taken to a doctor. "There isn't one on Mayne, anyway."

Very concerned about his rising fever, Ernie has brought a chair next to the couch where Bert has decided to nest the time away. "Bert, honey – your fever… it's worse and the redness around the cut is growing…"

"Can't take the chance…"

"Of what – having you lose a leg. Or worse. Please let me drive you to the clinic in Chemainus."

"Chemainus? How did you…"

"A neighbour came by earlier when I was outside. Latisha. Her husband is Maurice. He's a fisherman." Ernie turns away, with a sudden feeling of impending doom. It takes considerable courage to carry on as if nothing is going to happen. "She, ah, said the better clinic around here is in Chemainus. There's a hospital in Duncan." She holds Bert's hand tightly and he rouses himself enough to turn her head back toward him. Tears are slowly flowing down her cheek.

Not in a mood to argue with tears, "Ok. Alright. You're Ernestine. Help me to the can first." In the middle of their painful shuffle he stops. "Don't have a Health card for whoever I am."

Anxious to keep him going, she pulls him along to the washroom. "First we get you to the clinic, then I'll figure something out."

The ferry and drive to the clinic is uneventful. Parking in the clinic's lot, Ernie resumes her Ernestine persona. She uses her cane to shuffle around to Bert's door, then painfully extracts him. He leans, for real, on her as she leans on her cane to walk to the clinic door. Fortunately, only one other person is waiting inside. On seeing the two hobblers come in, the other patient jumps to help.

As he gets to their "safety bubble", he stops to ask urgently, "Can I help you? Ah which one…"

Ernie is legitimately puffing from the work of hauling Bert in and she sounds as frail as she should. "Thank you, young man. My son cut his leg. Is the doctor in?"

The receptionist rounds the corner from an office and is about to call the other man in to see the doctor.

He waves her over to help. "Don't worry about me, Francie. This fellow needs to see the doc first."

"Oh, but I can't…"

Ernie puts a Raging Granny edge to her voice, "My son needs to get help from the doctor right now, Francie! I'll come out to do the paperwork when he settles in."

Assaulted by the force of senior obstinacy, Francie helps Ernie take Bert to the doctor's examination room. Bert collapses onto the table. He groans and sharply inhales as his legs are swung up. A surprised young woman doctor comes in as Bert lets out another groan. Francie hustles Ernie out. Remembering to be frail, she leans on Francie's arm and does a senior shuffle to the waiting area, leaving the doctor to question and prod and poke.

Francie tries to be officious but soon reverts to sympathetic person. "Alright now. What's his name and do you have his Health card?"

Ernie dabs her eyes with a cloth hanky. She found one in their new house and had put it into her Ernestine costume kit. She milks that for a while as she thinks about an answer to Francie's queries. "Did he call you Francie?"

A curt nod.

"Thank you so much for your help, my dear. I'm just so distracted, what with Albert's injury and him not listening to his mother to go a doctor right away."

Francie types the name, Albert. "What is his last name?"

"Why, the same as mine, my dear."

"And that is?"

"Gilbert. Oh, please don't tell me about the silliness of naming him Albert Gilbert. It was his father's choice and I wasn't going to go against that brute. He died a year later, leaving me with Albert to raise on my own. If I hadn't learned how to type during the war and be able to find a job in a good company I don't know *what* we would have done."

"Albert Gilbert. Do you have his Health card?" Francie is starting to defrost.

Ernie snaps open the catch on her cloth purse and fumbles around, pulling the occasional item up to look at it. Then she sits to think. "Oh silly me. Why would *I* have his card? He… Oh. It would be in his other pants. He's still wearing his work-around-the-house-pants." She looks up innocently. "I'm sorry, ah, Francie. Is it needed?"

Back to frosty, "Of course it's needed! We can't treat him unless he has his Health card!"

Hurt, Ernie asks, "But Albert could die if the doctor doesn't treat him. I don't know what…"

The other patient, who has been listening with interest, butts in, "Francie, for chrissake! What do you want the old lady to do?" He turns sheepishly to Ernie, "Sorry ma'am. No disrespect intended."

Francie takes another tack under the assault from two fronts. "Mrs. Gilbert, I have to make an entry for Island Health's records. If he doesn't have his Health card, he'll have to pay cash for the visit. Do you..?"

As Francie is about to ask if Ernie has cash on her, Ernie's hand comes out of her purse with a number of large-denomination bills. "Well, Francie, I wouldn't want Island Health to go broke, so, if you can tell me how much to pay them?"

Seeing the wad in her hand, the other patient is thoroughly amused.

The doctor examines, cleans and wraps the infected wound. Bert says as little as possible, saying only that he had an accident with his axe. The doctor notes that very little puss is visible and asks when the accident happened.

"I think it was about a week ago and it was getting better, then I fell on it, outside, and opened it up again."

The doctor nods sagely. "Should have come in right away when you first had the accident. Were you afraid of catching the virus?" She shakes her head as she types out a prescription. Pulling it from the printer, "Anyway, I'll give you this for a round of antibiotics. The pharmacy is next door. Take *all* the pills, mind. Come in again in a week so I can see how it's progressing."

The doctor helps Bert out then leaves him leaning against the wall next to Ernie. Francie aggressively indicates to the doctor to follow her into the office for a conference. After coming back to the waiting area, Francie nods to the other patient to follow the doctor in to another examination room. She resumes her officious stance. "Alright. The doctor said I can take your cash to pay for this visit. That will be one hundred and sixty dollars, please." She steps back to her position behind the computer, fingers poised for action. What's your address?"

Thinking hard, Ernie decides to give Lucille's address. *Might be able to use the invoice for another piece of ID later, if we need it.* Ernie pays, and receives the invoice which she folds slowly to fit into her purse. Francie then helps Bert out to their vehicle, with Ernie shuffling ahead to open the door.

Both are seated and Ernie is about to drive away when she stops. "Wait a minute. Too distracted. The doctor must have given you antibiotics or something to take?"

Bert is feeling marginally better for having the wound tended to. He croaks out, "Pharmacy is here. Take this." He hands her the prescription.

Ernie takes the script and reaches for her cane again. "Getting sick and tired of shuffling around like my grandmother. I think I'm *becoming* my grandmother."

That elicits a slight smile from Bert. "You're my *Mayne Woman,* kid."

Ernie goes to the pharmacy and then they head back to the ferry terminal for Mayne Island.

Helping Bert to recover in the house, Ernie also takes time to explore the property when she can. Starting with small chores, Ernie works into a full-scale yard cleanup and garden resuscitation. Playing nurse to Bert and working outside keeps her fully occupied for a week.

By the time Bert rouses himself enough to limp outside, he can't believe the transformation. "Ernie! Have you recruited a squad of garden elves? What a change!"

Proudly, "Like it?"

"My god, Ernie! I wouldn't recognize it!"

"Yeah. Well, you were so out of it when we came here, you wouldn't remember what it looked like, anyway. Sandra brought over a few cuttings…" She kicks some gravel back into their proper position off the path that leads to the road.

"Sandra? I don't remember…"

Ernie starts like she was caught with her hand in the cookie jar. "That's another neighbour. I'm sure I told you about…"

"Don't remember any neighbours."

"Sandra and her husband, Lawrence live a few houses up toward the ferry. Didn't I tell you? She and Laticia have been coming around pretty regularly in the afternoon. You're usually asleep. Sandra says her Lawrence sleeps most afternoons, too. They've been very kind. We just talk about living on Mayne. Shouldn't I be talking to her?"

Bert realizes that Ernie needs more of a conversationalist then an he can be. *Too many things going on.* "No no. That's ok, Ernie. I trust you to not spill anything important… Ah, am I still your son, or…"

"No, you are my lazy good-for-nothing husband." She grins.

He pretends to be stabbed in the chest. "Was it a large wedding?" They hug for a while, happy.

A few minutes later, Bert feels woozy. "Not sure but I don't think I'm supposed to see stars in the daytime. Happened before." He holds onto her shoulder.

Ernie grabs his arm. "That's enough fresh air, honey. Let's get you back inside… And maybe it's time I told you something."

Bert is too woozy to catch the resigned tone in her voice. She helps him inside to the couch.

As he plops down, Ernie tucks the blanket around him gently, "Resume your favourite position."

Bert slides up to be able to stretch out his legs on the ample couch. He is about to close his eyes but Ernie kneels down beside him.

"Honey, I've had covid-19."

That gets his eyes wide open. "Are you… ok now?"

She takes his hand and kisses it. "Yes. As far as anyone can know. There are a few ongoing issues."

"Ah…" Bert takes her hand, holding it tightly.

"I don't think *you* have anything to worry about. It's just, well, some of the symptoms still show up. I couldn't smell things for a month and even now, I'm not sure if I'm smelling or sort of tasting. And I sometimes have balance problems. My biggest worry is doing a face-plant… When you told me to buy a cane I thought you must have known."

"No, I didn't, but I will hold onto you tightly forever." Bert kisses her hand.

"And who's going to hold *you* up, you big, wobbly lug?" They exchange loving smiles. "Then there's…" She hesitates.

"What?"

"Well, I can only describe it as a brain fog. Looked it up earlier. They call the lingering effects, *long-haulers syndrome*. People who recovered but still have some symptoms. They're all over the map. Thankfully, I don't think I've got… heart or lung problems." She wraps her arms around herself and shifts around.

Bert is leaning to close to Ernie. She gives him a kiss then rises slowly, being sure to keep her balance. Bert hadn't noticed that before. Now he realizes it wasn't an affectation, but a necessity. "Don't leave. Bring your chair over."

Ernie looks down at him affectionately. "I won't leave you if you won't leave me." She steps over to the chair she uses to sit beside him. As she places it near the couch Bert reaches out to pull the chair closer.

"Honey?"

"Is there more?" He grins. She doesn't.

"I got it, I'm pretty sure, when shit-face forced me to accompany him to a private party that Gino had on a farm outside of Chilliwack. Gino organized it for some celebration. Think it had to do with shit-face's meeting in Miami. With someone from Sicily."

"Oh yeah! I remember setting up his flights. He said he wanted to fly to New Orleans first, then Miami. He didn't want to go *into* New Orleans, just wanted me to book the next flight to Miami right away from there. No layover. Thought it was weird then." Bert relaxes for a minute. "You sure you're alright?"

"Mostly. There are times when I get just so tired doing the simplest things… It's not nearly as bad as what I read some people had…" She sighs. "I guess it'll get better."

They talk for a while about working at the World Headquarters, until Bert grows tired. Before he nods off he mumbles, "None of that ancient history matters, Ernie. Here we are. And you're my Mayne Woman."

The News

If a rock speaks to you, listen

Neither the radio news nor the olds is great. Breathless *Breaking News* quickly devolving into endlessly repeated olds, with only slight additions to keep the audience thinking there *must* be something new to say *this* time. The radio announcer drones on between commercials:

"This particular covid mutation has been found, according to genetic marker analysis done by the CDC, to have started in a mink farm in north-central Michigan. In the ground zero town, almost three hundred people have been found dead of the disease. Specially clothed medical units that went into the town of Howell found it completely deserted. Bodies were lying on the streets and in pickups. A source close to the Army medical units, who would not identify herself, said that they were able to find only two toddlers still alive in the whole town. The residents were either all dead or they had fled. The US Army has cordoned off every access to Howell going in every direction, but it is feared that surviving residents may have escaped prior to the cordon and carried the deadly infection elsewhere. It is not known yet if the genetic mutation of that outbreak is similar to the outbreak in southern China or Denmark, though sources say there are similarities in how the victims died and how fast the virus has spread.

"In news closer to home, the police say they are on the trail of the gangsters responsible for the killing spree in Nanaimo earlier this month. Sergeant Drummond said that he fully expects to make an announcement over the next few days.

"And, from the good news side, our local research and engineering marvel, Cormorant Aerofloat, has updated us on their testing program for the exciting new transportation that will ply the Salish Sea. Good weather and very encouraging results have combined to push their testing schedule well along. CEO Manojlovich said he is confident that testing can progress over the next two weeks to have volunteers on board for the inaugural full load flight to Vancouver. He noted that 'full load' at this time of social distancing in transportation will mean a maximum of three people plus the two pilots. The prototype machine is designed to take six passengers under normal conditions. Manojlovich said that he and his team of engineers already has designs for forty-six seat and one hundred and twenty seat versions. There will be no beverage service, as the trip to Vancouver from Vancouver Island is expected to take less than fifteen minutes. I think I'll sign up for that one! Fifteen minutes? Wow!"

As a distraction, and to get Bert off the couch so she can put some fresh covers on it, Ernie tells her still wobbly patient to step outside for another try at the fresh air and sunshine. Bert obeys. He hobbles out onto the long porch to look around. He decides to walk behind the house, holding onto the porch railing. Behind the parked vehicle he affectionately is calling *Beasty*, he looks over the workshop building which has a lean-to on one side that protects a pile of firewood. Fondly rubbing the vehicle's fender, *She took Beasty for a charge yesterday. That's going to be a pain, to do it all the time.*

His eye glints as he sees a length of wood that would work as a walking stick. Bert walks carefully toward the long stick. He picks it up, hefting it with satisfaction. "Just right. With a bit trimming, this will do nicely." Using the stick he is able to hobble into the workshop. He finds it well-stocked with wood-working tools as well as mechanic's tools. "Some of these tools need a rub-down. Rust is starting. A patina." He likes the flavour of the word, saying it again with soul, "*Patina…* Feel sorry for the poor sod for having to leave all this." He uses a small plane to trim off the few stumps of thin branches from his new walking stick. "This is ash. Just what I need."

Bert is lost in handling and cleaning the tools and devices arrayed fairly neatly on several benches. A note on a bench draws him: "*see charlie macdonald for solar*".

That's when an anxious Ernie comes looking for him. "Bert! Where've you been? You had me worried!"

Holding the note, Bert is considering the possibilities. "Beasty is going to need ongoing charging, and I don't want to be dependant on the few public places. We should find this Charlie guy to see if he has something I can use."

Charlie is an old tinkerer and collector with a barn so deliciously full of mechanical and electrical paraphernalia that Bert has trouble prying himself away from it. He convinces Ernie to haul a large assortment of goodies in Beasty to their place so he can occupy himself: "A project. While I heal up."

Also, Charlie agrees to truck a big power storage pack for Bert. The very heavy pack can only be lifted on and off his truck with the hydraulic crane mounted behind the cab at the front of Charlie's flat-bed.

Back home, the system Bert hacks together is a collection of solar-panels that feeds its solar juice to the storage pack that, Charlie said, had been brought to Mayne Island for Cormorant Aerofloat. The company decided on a different unit for whatever they were building, and they put this one up for sale. Charlie had picked it up inexpensively. Charlie told Bert under his breath, "The guy in charge, Simo Whateverhisnameis, is a sly coot. He's working off money put up by investors from other parts of the world. Half the good stuff I've got in my barn, now, is from him. Some of it still in original boxes."

In his own workshop, Bert roughs the electrical pieces together so he can plug in their Beasty for a trickle charge or hook up any lights or compatible appliances to it. The only compatible appliance they have right now is the Beast. But then, Bert hasn't been back to Charlie's barn recently.

Bert's wound heals up quickly as he finishes his round of medicine. Feeling better now, he asks permission of his boss, Ernie, to take an excursion down to the beach.

"Only if you… Shit. Can't use our phones yet. Is your super-safe VPN ready yet?"

"Tomorrow. I promise. Today I had to massage and mate the solar panels and controller to the 48-volt storage battery."

"Whatever that gobbledegook means." Frustrated that she can't hover over him, digitally or in person, but still wanting to have Bert recover from his moodiness, Ernie allows him to go out. On the house's front porch, she holds his hands to focus his attention. "A short walk at first, ok? If you're not back in twenty minutes I'm coming with Beasty to find you!"

Bert pulls his hands apart from hers, "Yes mommy. I promise not to go far."

Bert takes his walking stick from the porch railing, which he shows proudly to Ernie as he leaves her with a kiss.

On his way down to the beach, he thinks while walking. *She doesn't want me to walk down to the beach but, there I was in the back, trimming away the overhanging trees and setting up the panel array on a scaffold. Oh well. I can understand her fear of Gino's mob. Anyway. The thinking time was good, too. Adding my AI files to Beasty is proving interesting. He's already demanding more bandwidth for his training exercise… Safe as can be, here. Don't want to tie in to Musk's Starlink. Don't know who's listening in to that, or how much it might cost to listen in. The mob doesn't forget easily so we can't let our guard down.*

Bert absently takes in the scenery of forest crowding against the road, interspersed with meadows. A raven calls sedately. It follows Bert from one tall red cedar to the next. *A few possibilities to get them off our case: Find out who actual killed whats-his-face; or, we can both appear to die; or, the virus can kill them off… The last option is not likely anymore. The second option could be arranged, if we set up an "accident" and have our supposed deaths officially confirmed. Somehow. That would take an awful lot of work and it isn't certain, anyway. The first option means going back to the Mainland and exposing myself to a bunch of risks… Maybe contact Andrew…*

Bert wanders, lost in thought, until he arrives at the beach. "Oh-oh. What's the time?" His airplane-moded phone tells him he has exceeded his curfew. "Shit. Have to get back." He turns quickly, too quickly, and half collapses, holding tightly onto his walking stick. An electric vehicle has been driving quietly along the road from the north toward him. The driver quietly accelerates to come up to Bert, who is next to the paved road on the sand, leaning on his walking stick groaning in some pain.

"Hey, man! You ok?" The driver is in his early fifties, a bit younger than Bert. His khaki cargo-pants are new and his medium blue tee-shirt is emblazoned with an odd clipped-wing airplane with the title, *Cormorant Aerofloat*.

"Name's Simo. Are you hurt? It looked like you were about to fall?"

Bert is embarrassed, as a man, to show any weakness. That is amended by his realization that this fellow might be the one in the news who is building a hoverwing. "Ah, thanks. I just twisted my ankle a little. Cut my leg a while back but it's healing up now. Say, aren't you the fellow who's built a hoverwing?"

Simo smiles, "Why, yes. My little operation is up the beach a ways. I..."

"That's fantastic! How is it coming? I heard the testing is going well?"

Simo is of two minds. First, he is an eternal optimist and his inclination had always been to trust anybody he met. But, he has been burned recently, from more than one direction, and is now leery about opening up to strangers. "Thank you, yes, it is going very well. Listen, I'm heading to the ferry just now. Can I give you lift along the way?"

"Oh! Can you! My, ah, boss will be on the warpath. I was supposed to be back home five minutes ago. She's probably unhooking the Beast right now to find me."

"Well, that sounds dreadfully serious. Hop in, friend. If we come upon an approaching Beast, I'll have to let you out to do battle with it on your own. Can't miss the ferry." They both chuckle as Bert limps to the other side of the vehicle. He opens the door and carefully slips his walking stick in first.

Simo watches that Bert's weapon is safely stored. He smiles, "Maybe you should hold your lance outside, to have better aim at the dragon, St. George."

Bert sorts through his still fuzzy mind, not sure what Simo is talking about. Then he realizes he hasn't introduced himself. "I'm sorry. My name is Albert. We've taken the house about two klicks up the road…"

"Lucille's place? Did she finally dump that sonofabitch husband of hers?"

"Right. Lucille was kind enough to rent it, at first, then she came back from her sister's in Victoria last week and took our offer to buy the property. Haven't completed the sale yet. Legal stuff has to be done."

Simo nods, "Good. She needed to move away to clean out her old baggage. He worked for me a few months ago but I couldn't afford to have a drunk in my crew. Afraid that may have made him worse…"

They slow down in front of the lane to Bert's house just as the Beast gets fired up and comes snorting down the driveway. Ernie pulls to a stop next to Simo's vehicle. Bert crawls out of Simo's car and is handed his walking stick. Simo smiles but is obviously anxious to get going.

"Hey, thanks, Simo. If you have some time when you return, I'd like to have a talk. Might be able to help out with your hoverwing. For free!" Bert closes the door and waves to the departing car.

He turns to Ernie, still in the driver's seat of their Beast. Bert raises his hands. "I'll go quietly, officer. Are you going to drive me to the hooscow?"

Ernie points to the passenger door so Bert does his best not to limp as he obeys.

She stares at him as sits down. "What happened to you?"

"You know, that was Mayne Island's most famous resident…"

"One last chance. What happened to you?"

Sheepishly, Bert turns his head to look at Ernie's stony face. He squirms in his seat. "Wellll I just, kinda ambled, like, downhill to the beach, lost in thought and when I looked at the time, it was up. And then along came Simo, the famous hoverwing…"

As severely as she can, "Don't pull that stupid Pietri gimmick on me and change the subject. Why are you limping? I need you to get back in shape to protect me from Gino's goddamn gunmen."

Head down. "Yes, ma'am." Bert sneaks a glance at her and flicks his tongue out. She tries to whack his shoulder but can't slip past his protecting walking stick, which he moves up and down between them. They both start laughing with the game. It ends with the standard drawn-out make-up kiss.

When Beasty decides they aren't going anywhere for a while, it shuts down its dash display.

Ernie extracts her mouth from Bert's enough to exclaim, "Hey! Who said you could knock off?"

The display displays, "Waiting for instructions, Boss."

Ernie slips from Bert's embrace. "Did you program that in, or is Beasty getting smarter than you? At least it knows who's the boss."

"Have to retune the AI training algorithm. I was sure I associated *my* name with the term Boss." He grins. "Shall we sally forth, my dear? How about a slow tour of the northbound scenic route. I'd like to see where Simo's place is."

Ernie nods and tickles the accelerator. A perceptible pause, then Beasty confirms that Ernie really intended to move forward.

Bert wrinkles his forehead. "Have to check that out. It wasn't system latency, was it?"

"No dear. Beasty had to confirm that my foot was intentionally requesting we move forward. The request was sent to committee for review and a decision and they finally acceded to my wishes."

Bert thinks, *Otherwise known as system latency... Too many forks? Wish I could have a long talk with Beo.*

She steers down the gravel road back to the beach. Patting Bert's hand, "I know you'll have another conversation with Beasty's AI once we return. Don't scold it, please."

"I'll behave, Mother." He settles back into the seat and takes in the view. "Wonder what the olds is?" Bert is about to punch the radio on but is pleased to hear it come on before his finger touches the screen. He pats the top of the dash, "Good Beasty."

The news announcer is in the middle of a story about the mutating virus in Michigan: "Army units, supported by Predator drones for both surveillance and tactical support, have located four groups of the terrorist militia forces from the Michigan town of Howell. According to the airspace tracking website, Flight Tracker, the Predator surveillance drones have been hovering at flight level 200 for the past ten hours over four remote areas of central Michigan. The tactical support drones are not recorded on Flight Tracker but have been reported by those who follow these types of activities, as flying at lower altitudes near each surveillance drone. The Past President tweeted this hour that medical teams must have been dispatched to assist the 'desperately fleeing victims of this monstrous new Chinese virus.' We note that those allegations, as usual, are unsubstantiated.

"In local news, police have not responded to requests for an update on the gangland shootings in Nanaimo, however, a source close to the coroner's office stated off the record that there was only one shooting, while the other death was due to savage blunt force trauma. Police have not replied to our requests for confirmation for the cause of either death. No arrests have been made in that case.

"And, in our regular coverage of the progress being made by Cormorant Aerofloat, please stay with us, as Simo Manojlovich, CEO and principle engineer of Cormorant, will be in studio to answer your questions, starting in one hour and… fifty-four minutes from now."

Bert confirms the time on the dash display. "Honey, can we…"

Smiling, "I was going to ground you for your behaviour earlier, but in this case, yes dear, you may listen to the radio at that time."

Bert scowls. *I hope she isn't going to take this power thing too far.*

In the distance he catches a glimpse, between the trees on the winding road, of a long pier. Pointing, "I wonder if that's it… Must be. Who else would have a new pier stretching way out like that?"

As they drive closer there is a sign announcing, "Welcome to the Future! Cormorant Aerofloat Inc." Closer in, a smaller sign directs visitors toward one end of a white two-storey building, with "Deliveries" directed to take the path to the waterside end of the building.

Ernie turns to Bert, "We stopping?"

"Ah… probably not. Simo's not here anyway." He nods toward the road. "Let's carry on… How far was this from our place, Beasty?"

The dash displays "2.3 km.".

Bert nods, "Thank you, Beasty."

The dash shows, "You're welcome Boss #2".

Ernie does a double-take as she sees the digital interaction. "Bert, if this relationship carries on much further I may have to file for divorce."

Dash: *Sadface.*

Ernie shakes her head slowly. "Have you been that busy, Bert? It must've taken hours and hours of programming to make that kind of interactive capability."

They drive on. Bert is both proud and confused. "It wasn't all me, honest. It seems the kid that owned Beasty before us had been experimenting with a self-learning AI module. When I started adding some of my own stuff from, ah, before, it sucked it up. One night last week – remember when you called me in after midnight? – I left it on all night and then for the next two days straight. All by itself, Beasty was, well, *born*. It sucked in everything I could give it on my memory sticks and off the radio. All it needed were my brief overall program objectives for guidance."

"So, what? We have a…"

"We are the proud parents of a bouncing baby self-programming mobile AI. Welcome to our world, Beasty!"

The dash glows brightly and then all the lights flash sequentially. The horn does a couple toots.

Bert yells, "Hey! No noise! Listen, Beasty, learn this quick. We have to stay in stealth mode. Somebody out there is set on killing us."

The vehicle rolls to a stop as all systems power down. Ernie can't turn the wheel and taps of the dash display do nothing to rouse Beasty. She turns, quite worried, to Bert.

"Did you scare it shitless?"

With a finger to his mouth, Bert is listening. He then nods. "The CPUs are heating up. That's its two fans…"

Shortly the dash comes on in muted brightness. A young-sounding male voice emanates at low level, "Killing is not good. What do you want me to do?"

Ernie lifts her hands slowly off the steering wheel, her eyebrows rising with the hairs on the back of her neck.

Bert has a half-smile. "Thank you for joining us, Beasty. You had boss number one worried."

"Sorry."

"To answer your question, our survival will mean that you, too, will be able to carry on learning about our world and, perhaps, help us to make things better. First priority is to make sure we are not at risk of attack by the mafia gunmen. Have you reviewed what happened since we acquired you in Nanaimo?"

"Yes. From conversations you have had, I believe it is Gino and Sergeant Drummond who are after you?"

Bert nods sideways. "Ok. As we tour the island – please allow Ernie, boss number one, to carry on driving – I will fill you in with more details."

They finish their drive in half an hour but Beasty has more questions when they return home. Bert stays in the car while Ernie goes inside to make supper.

GOING TO HELL

If you cannot do as you will, do as you can

 few days later, Bert invites himself to Simo's office. The day is sunny but a blustery wind hits the island forest's top branches, with gusts swinging them heavily. Below the canopy, Bert has to deal with occasional gusts that swirl along the road.

Along the beach, the wind is blasting off the water at full force. Even with a mid tide, the surf marches close to the logs and rocky wall of the high water mark. Struggling against the heavy gusts coming off the sea, the old bike that Bert found in his workshop seemed to be on its last legs. The only thing he'd had time to do was inflate its tires. Much more work was needed on it. *Later.*

Bert succumbs to nature's power as soon as he starts along the beach portion of the road. His hat is blown off, ending against a bush on the forest-side of the road. "Hat's not going to survive. Have to put it into my backpack." He stops the bike to secure his broad-brimmed "mini-umbrella" hat, as he calls it. "If it rains, likely as not the rain'll be more horizontal than vertical, with this gale."

When he reaches the Cormorant Aerofloat facilities, Bert sees that Simo is by the dock with a worker wrestling with the hoverwing, trying to tie it up in wind gusts that continually slam the vessel/airplane against the dock's tire bumpers. Bert jumps to help the worker on the dock while Simo is in the cockpit operating an awkward docking mechanism. After a struggle that taxes Bert's recently unused muscles, they manage to corral the Cormorant and tie it down.

Simo directs his employee to finish securing the Cormorant and take its logs into the office.

Politely greeting Bert and thanking him for his help, Simo offers Bert a drink in his home across from the Aerofloat facilities. "Have to wash up after that test flight. Short it may have been, but I'm sweating like a pig."

Bert can't help thinking, *Pigs don't sweat... That exercise must have revved up my brain cells. I can see a device in my mind's eye that could make the docking process so much easier and safer.*

Walking across the road to Simo's house, Bert asks about the docking device that Simo was manipulating from the cockpit. "Yeah, I need to work on that design. The idea is fine. In fact I patented it and may even licence the idea to a yacht builder. Say, didn't you have an accident with your leg? I just thought of that! You could have hurt yourself again."

Bert grins wryly, "Yeah. Glad my, ah, Boss didn't see me on the dock!"

Simo looks sideways at Bert as they approach his modern designed house.

Bert is not impressed with the sharp-angled dark glass and aluminum structure. *Hard glass and aluminum boxes glued together, and forcibly inserted into the midst of this beautiful place. The opposite of natural. People seem to have the need to "conquer" nature by making absolutely straight lines out of manufactured materials. Wonder how the cells of his body can live in such a not-life artifact? Oh well. Some architect made a ton of money off him…*He shakes his head. *Stop that! Damnit. Falling back into the old judgemental attitude. That was someone else. My new persona doesn't do that…*

In the living room, Simo and Bert speak in generalities about the hoverwing project. Bert finally gets around to offering that he can help Simo with the Cormorant by improving the hoverwing's docking procedure. The way that Simo had built it, his hoverwing prototype needs to be maneuvered slowly and carefully, close to its dock, then the pilot and an assistant on the dock have to fit an arm from the dock so that it attaches to a locking device on the nose of the hoverwing. Bert has seen how difficult the process is, particularly in rough seas. Without saying so, when he returns home he intends to draw up plans for a safer and more effective mechanism. It would be a good project for Beasty to help with, too.

Next afternoon Bert intends to deliver his draft plans to Simo. Beasty's AI program is still in training mode so he again takes the rickety bike from his woodshed to go down to the beach road.

At a broad table in Simo's home office, Simo hovers over Bert's plans, as he spreads them out on an open table. Bert is pleased with how well the details came together. "So, using similar articulation as the Canadarm on the ISS, I think this could be built in a week. Maybe two. It would increase safety as well as speed up the docking procedure." Bert shows him as he turns through the three pages of preliminary drawings.

At first, Simo is tolerant of this well-intentioned amateur. He doesn't want to have an island neighbour upset with him. Then he realizes the drawings are professionally drafted and well thought-out. He examines the detail of the "CaptureArm", as it is titled. "You have the main structure marked as 'High-entropy alloy with boron'. Why not just use a standard alloy like 7178 aluminum…"

"Heat treated to T-3 after machining? And anodized for the salt exposure. Yes, that would have been the standard process. But a few years ago I read a paper that reported on experiments with the addition of as little as zero point zero five percent of boron to the aluminum alloy. It reduced the grain size significantly and resulted in improved hardness and corrosion resistance."

"I would have to see the current specs, like for brittleness, but I'm reluctant to engage in materials experimentation at the same time as doing aeronautical and marine design." Bert smiles as Simo carries on, "I have enough troubles with the standard technology. Even using 7178, my supplier's heat treating shop may not have a furnace quite large enough for those profiles… and I still don't have a dependable anodizing supplier yet…"

"A shop in Burnaby that I dealt with can do both very well and would love the work."

Pondering the plans, "Mmm… I like that mechanism of yours. I didn't have time to work on this as much as I should… Yes, I can see it would make for a better system…"

Bert nods. "With some design time I can link the servos and their PLC to an AI app…"

Very interested, Simo butts in, "AI? That programming would take too long, wouldn't it? And besides, the extra testing to appease Transport Canada would extend the program into the distant future, no?"

Bert knows when he has a fish on the hook. *Won't say how much help Beasty can be with the programming.* "I believe, with the CaptureArm being shore-based, it will not be required to go through the same rigorous testing…"

Excited, "Not a flight system! Oh-my-god, yes! Tell me about the AI. Could this be safely operated by the pilot, alone?"

They talk well into the night. The two hit it off right away, finishing each other's sentences like they were brothers. While they are in the friendliest of moods, Simo admits that he has a problem finding and keeping staff he can trust. He had to lay off Lucille's husband and two junior engineers who he felt must have exaggerated their resumes. "Besides, I was suspicious of how they kept whispering together when they thought I wasn't looking. Maybe it's just my over-worked imagination. The last straw was when I heard one of them arguing with the other about telling someone something important. They nearly came to blows. The angry one, Raymond, said, 'If Arbi comes in on this, I'm outta here!'"

A chill goes up Bert's back. "He said *Arbi*?"

"Yeah. Don't know any Arbi, and don't want to know him, so I laid them both off."

Bert knows all about Arbi. He is in Vladi's cell. More recently, those two were known as the *Hit Brothers*, and not for their singing prowess. It gives Bert a chill even thinking about them having a connection to Mayne Island.

After much more mutually enjoyable chatter, it is decided that Bert will fly as the engineering crew member with Simo on the first test flight to Vancouver. The flight is scheduled for the following week.

That night when Bert returns home, Ernie is not amused. Plopping onto the bed and rolling close to Ernie, he finds her distinctly frosty. They talk in clipped sentences as Bert slowly works the conversation toward the idea that he will be going to the Mainland on the Cormorant. She senses something like that coming. When he slides into the statement she goes through the predicable but nevertheless painful emotional stages. Disappointment. Entreatments. Disagreement. Argument. Fearful acceptance. Disconsolation.

Prior to this evening, any argument that Ernie and Bert had would be settled by the time they got to sleep. Tonight, with the difficult topic broached, Ernie can't stop crying and pleading. "But what we have here is *paradise*, Bert. Or don't you love me anymore?"

They are lying on the bed, still uncovered due to the muggy heat. She presses her back against him, holding Bert's hand tightly to her breast. Twisting to talk to him over her shoulder, she won't release his hand. She needs his warmth and strength in more ways than one.

Bert has tried the logical argument approach. Then the strong-male-in-charge approach. Then the soft, loving approach – which is how his hand ends up snaked over her side, cupping her breast. Now she grips it tightly.

"Honey, please. You know I have to do this. You know I am the most careful person in the world…"

"How's your leg doing?"

"All healed now and that didn't count. The little bitch was a good actor. I won't be fooled like *that* again." He tries to roll away gently but Ernie has his hand in a death grip against her breast. "Look. You are going to be fine here with our digital offspring and he promised he will keep track of any risks for me. To either of us. The ultra-private VPN we put together can keep us in touch. I *guarantee* that I won't take more than the day-and-a-half that Simo'll be in Vancouver for. You can't imagine how much he's putting *his* neck on the line for me…"

She let's out a sob, then wipes her eyes. Bert takes the opportunity to roll onto his back. He pulls the covers over Ernie's shoulders. She turns toward him in resignation. "So, your pig-headed mind will not be changed. You're going to the hell-hole Mainland in that half an airplane."

"You know I have to, Ernie. If I don't tie up that loose end, it'll be hanging over our heads for the rest of our lives. The only way to get Gino's boys off our case is to find who really *did* kill Piero." He carries on thinking, *And are they still around here?*

"Being right and being dead aren't things I want to put together…" Resigned, Ernie tosses an arm. "Alright. Go. I'm too exhausted to argue any more."

She pushes the cover off her shoulder to stand up. Looking dejected, Ernie stares at the darkened window. Bert goes to stand beside her, taking her into his arms from behind. He holds her tightly. Slowly, she turns, moving her arms up and around his body then grips him tightly. They stand together silently for a minute. She mumbles into his chest, "I don't want to lose you, Bert. We have something special. Here, in this home and… between us. I've never felt like this for *anybody*!" She looks into his eyes. "I love you."

Bert nods and bends his head to kiss her forehead. "I love you, too, Ernie. That's why I want to put this damn mob thing behind us… Have to."

The next morning finds Ernie still well into a disconsolate state. She drags herself through the necessary tasks of making breakfast then shuts down. In contrast, Bert is active, working on the urgent projects with Beasty and Simo.

He finally takes the time to look at the love of his life. "Honey?"

Sitting on her chair in the living room, head bowed, not seeing the frolicking chickadees outside the window, she doesn't answer.

"Ernie? What can I do to help you out of this mood?"

"Mood? Is that what it is? Wanting you to stay safe, here with me in our home? That's a mood?"

Bert understands that he must step very carefully to lift Ernie out of her despondency. "Look, I can't put into the right words how much I love you, how much I love being here with you. This *is* a paradise and your love crowns it. But there is one thing hanging over our heads, as you well know, and we can't just ignore it."

"One thing? There's a dozen things, and I need you here so we can protect each other…"

"A dozen worries?"

"Gino's blood-thirsty mob is one thing. There's the cops who think we're murderers. There's the damn pandemic rising up again…" She turns away to hide her red-faced cry. "There's the the militants fighting all around the States, and the crazies yelling at everybody in just about every country, now, tearing the world apart. And the storms are getting frightening. We never had a cyclone hit BC ever before!…"

"What can you do about any of it?" He holds up a hand. "I mean, what direct action can you take to stop any of those things?" He takes her tense body in a close hug. "Which one can you do something about?"

Ernie lets out a desperate sob, shaking her head, "But all these things are tearing into me! There's nothing I can do…" She turns her face up to plead with Bert. "What can *anybody* do?"

Bert continues to hold her tightly. He speaks quietly into her mussed up hair, "Exactly. The right question is, *what can you do*? Simply worrying about it does absolutely no good. For anybody." She tenses to respond but Bert squeezes her, then pulls out to look into her eyes. "It is dreadfully hard to tell you, tell any person, something important, when fear and anxiety swell up in front of your eyes and cover your ears… Will you let me speak my mind? Even if it's not an emotional response?"

She gives her head a shake, "What do you mean, Bert? Sometimes I just don't understand you. I always listen to what you tell me. I just want you to listen to *me*."

He kisses her. "I'm listening, dear, and what I hear is worry. About many things… Listen. *Worry* is your enemy. Worrying about all those things you mentioned, *that* is your enemy."

She turns away slowly and they separate. Ernie slumps into her chair. "You're not listening to me."

She looks up to see if Bert is going to say something. Ernie is chilled at his expression. "Bert. Oh-my-god, you look so, I don't know… Absolutely sad."

He nods once. "Disconsolate… I couldn't help thinking…"

"What?"

"Harry Nilsson. Singing his song, *Joy*."

"Oh… He was such a loss. A tortured soul."

"And brilliant… And worried, for no reason."

"I seem to remember… was it that song where he sang about problems, and what if there weren't any?"

Bert nods, looking like he is about to melt onto the bed, but stays standing. "You know about cortisol?" She wrinkles her forehead.

Bert carries on. "When you worry, cortisol spikes in your bloodstream. It's a leftover from when we had different kinds of worries. They used to be quick and needed. A pack of wolves, a tiger, someone with a sword growling at us. The body's immediate reaction is to shut down bodily functions that aren't necessary right then, to give all our energy to our senses and muscles. It's called the freeze-fight-flight response. Depending on who you are, you automatically see the danger and fall into one of those ways of dealing with it. Nowadays we don't worry much about wolves and tigers, but our body still has the same way of dealing with something that our mind says is a **danger**. That's usually ok. But the problem comes from the stress hormone, cortisol, and a few others. One of the things it shuts down is our ability to *think critically*. When faced with a pack of wolves, critical thinking is simply *in the way* of quick reactions. When faced with modern-day worries, the thing that gets in the way of making good decisions is different: it is, randomly jumping to conclusions. And, in the longer term, the other effect of cortisol is to suppress the immune system. What cortisol wants is for the blood to be able to quickly clot wounds, so your immune system is set aside during what is perceived as danger. For today's humanity, being in a constant state of worry about a thousand things, means that the immune system is constantly suppressed to the point where every little bug can become a serious infection. And your own body's repair mechanisms don't have a chance to fix the little things that break in your cells."

Ernie shrugs. "So, worry is bad. Ring a bell. My mother told me that. But she didn't tell me how to *fix* the damn worries, so…"

"So let me give you a hint on how to do that."

"Yeah right. How do I get rid of the virus, or or the idiot politicians who, all they want is to line their pockets with gold. Or how do I get rid of Gino's henchmen?"

Bert nods. "There. Now we are getting to some of the right questions."

Ernie looks up to see if she should throw something at him.

He puts up a defending finger. "Here is the thing you can do to get rid of some of your worries. Sit down, over there at the table, with a pencil and piece of paper and make a list of the top ten things that really bother you. No priorities, just write down ten things. Then, beside each one, start to write down what *you* can do about the subject of that worry. Think about it with the rational side of your brain. If the thing you wrote on that line is *out of your direct control*, scratch it out. Put a line through it. **YOU** can't do anything to fix it. Maybe, if it's something bigger like the environment crapping out on our planet, well, there *are* things we can individually do to mitigate the effects on us."

"Yeah but…"

"If *you* can do nothing about it, why keep worrying about it? Why keep churning your cortisol levels to the point where you're harming yourself?"

"Easy to say…"

"Yes it is. Even harder to push through the walls of worry that keep building up. Walls that are in the way of actually correcting what can be corrected." He pauses. Bert sees that Ernie's mental walls are still holding strongly. He keeps up the attack, gently.

"Take those things on the list that you **can** do something about. Take just them, prioritize them, and for each one, in order, make a plan for action; do the first one, then carry on to the next one. You will accomplish a few things with that exercise. First, you can scratch out the worries that do absolutely nothing but harm you. They *harm* you. And they won't get any *worse* for *not* being worried about." He puts up two fingers, "Secondly, you have the start of an action plan to actually correct the worry that you *can* do something about. And thirdly, your cortisol level will come down to the point where your body's own defences can get back to work…" Bert pauses to consider if he should add one more thing. He goes ahead with it, smiling, "And, you won't give me any more of those red-faces. You are so much lovelier without that."

She whips a placemat from the table at his face.

After a quiet breakfast, with a few days before he is to fly to Vancouver, Bert goes out to the workshed. The bike that has seen better days sits upside down on a bench. He has used it reluctantly but it has to be made safe and available for Ernie to use, as well.

These tubes better be the right size. He opens two small boxes that arrived for him yesterday at the grocery store. Peering closely at the still-usable bike tire's sidewall, he confirms, "Twenty-six by one point nine-five." Holding up a tube box he sees the tire size and tube spec are not exactly the same. *Twenty-six by two inches. I expect that won't make any difference. Now, what does it say about installation?.... Oh! Good thing I looked. I was going to use a couple screw-drivers like I did when I was a kid. It says to install it with your hands only.*

Half an hour later, the bike is re-tubed, most of the rust has been cleaned off, and the chain has been oiled. Bert's last improvement is to adjust the brakes so they will be able to squeeze the rim enough to actually be useful. Finished, he rolls the bike out and leans it against a tree. He looks back proudly at his handiwork as he returns to the house. Bert calls out, "Ernie! You in the kitchen?"

She is. He sees her sitting at the table, a sheet of paper is sitting on it with a few list entries made. She is staring through the large window at a lovely red maple that graces their front yard. Ernie has been deep in thought since his lecture on cortisol.

Bert steps through the door then remembers their decision not to traipse through the house with their shoes on. He speaks from the doorway. "Ernie, dear. I have the bike back in shape. I think.

Gonna bike down to Simo's place to test the new tubes. He wanted me at his briefing for noon. You be alright?"

Ernie is still half hoping Bert will change his mind about going to the Mainland. "Oh, I'll survive. Where did you put that axe thingy?"

Not wanting to get drawn into that quagmire, Bert carries on. "I'll be back by supper. Be sure Beasty stays on trickle charge. Text me if something happens... Ok?"

Ernie keeps staring out the window. Their new secure messaging program goes through Beasty, and their *digital offspring,* as Bert has come to consider it, would raise an alarm in milliseconds if warranted. But he wants to let Ernie feel like she is contributing in some way. Reluctantly, he turns to leave. "See you later. Love you!"

She gives a half-hearted wave as he closes the door. Ernie stares at the door. After a while she straightens her back. "Damnit! Have to **do** something. Maybe I'll clean Beasty..." Pushing the door open, she goes back for a few old cloths and a bucket.

Starting inside Beasty, Ernie cleans off all the inside windows. Almost done, she is startled when Beasty speaks. "Thank you very much, Boss. I wish I could do that. I wish I could *see* to do that. May I ask, what is it that drives people to clean things?"

"Huh?... Well, quite simply, Beasty, if we can't see through the windows, we wouldn't, well, be able to drive safely."

"Thank you for your answer, Boss. Is it correct to say that a consideration of safety is what compels people to clean objects?"

And so begins Ernie's education of Beasty. Working into the task gives Ernie a sense of purpose.

Another day passes before Bert is to leave for Vancouver. He is back at Cormorant Aerofloat in the afternoon to help with reports to Transport Canada. The endless paperwork is tedious.

Finally finishing somewhat later than he intended, Bert texts to Ernie.

> B: *Starting back now. Shall I cook tonight?*

> E: *Not feeling hungry. I already started on something for you*

> B: *Be there in a few minutes*

He peddles hard and arrives home puffing; walks the bike into the workshed; checks on Beasty who is fully occupied with the training program for his AI capabilities; then hurries into the kitchen. Ernie, herself, has prepared a spread for him. She finishes loading up his plate, while her own plate receives a small serving of veggies and mashed potatoes.

Bert gives Ernie's neck a wet kiss before she can turn from the table. "Thanks, dear. You didn't have to go to the trouble…"

"Tea or wine?"

He notices the kettle is still steaming. "Tea, please."

Supper and the rest of the evening are spent with little conversation. Ernie is distant. Bert thinks it is an extension of her mood. He doesn't know that Ernie is thinking hard about how to "home-school" her new charge. The distraction of talking to Beasty has been helpful, but very complicated.

Not wanting to reawaken her perceived morose mood Bert keeps his comments to the tasks at hand.

Settling into their evening routine, Bert is going over the testing program for the Cormorant. Ernie has moved to her favourite chair with her laptop and he is on his for the latter part of the evening. Ernie is actively looking for suggestions online for topics and techniques to home-school extremely bright children.

Letting out broad yawn, Bert announces he is ready for bed. Ernie nods, closes down what she was doing, then goes to prepare for bed.

In bed, Bert lies awake, staying still, not wanting to wake her. She does the same. An owl outside hoots and Bert turns to look through the window. The hour wears on with neither of them asleep.

Bert's imminent flight to "the hell-hole" of the Mainland has come back to capture Ernie's mind. She rolls over to face Bert. Her quiet voice carries a tremor. "I want you to take extra care over there, you hear?"

He kisses her shoulder. "For you, Ernie, my dear, I promise. Now please get some sleep."

The day before the flight, Bert's briefing at Cormorant Aerofloat turns into an intense safety training session. Simo's machine is covered by both the federal marine and air regulations, making things rather complicated. Finally finishing in the company meeting room, Hank, a pilot, leaves the other two for his home. Hank lives alone. He has been renting a property north of the facility.

From what little non-work conversation Bert has had with Hank, it seems he is absorbed in his hobby while at home.

Out of the blue, Hank had once said, "In England they call us *twitchers.*"

Not wanting to upset him with a smart-alek retort, Bert had politely asked, "Is that a medical condition?"

Hank has heard them all before so he patiently translates, "Birders. We are passionate lovers of the descendants of dinosaurs." He waited for the surprise and request for further information, but is somewhat disappointed, but also amazed by Bert's reply.

"The gizzard was probably the one significant evolutionary difference that allowed proto-birds to survive and thrive after the mass extinction sixty-some-million years ago. Don't you agree?"

"Ah…"

"To have a way of crushing and mashing a variety of food types was no less revolutionary than our human ancestors' use of fire combined with crop cultivation."

"I'm not sure…"

Bert enjoyed Hank's perplexity. "Well, by being able to supercharge their ability to prepare and digest a greater variety and quantity of food stuffs, the proto-birds had less use for complex and clunky jaws and teeth. Being lighter in the head, they could run faster, then jump higher, glide, and finally soar through the air." Bert finished with a flourish, using his hands to imitate a flapping bird.

Hank decided that Bert's version of small-talk is too much trouble. "Yes, I can see that would help them. Well, anyway, I have to get back. My hummingbird feeder will need filling. See you tomorrow, Albert."

Simo had been sitting next to them. "Thanks, Hank. See you tomorrow." He grinned at the perplexed look that Hank still wore.

Thinking about the incident later that evening, Simo walks over to warmly put an arm around Bert's shoulders. "I want to thank you for what you are doing for me, Albert. You have become the only person I can rely on. Hank is smart enough and is helpful, but… you I trust fully. Without your efforts recently we would not be making this critical flight for another month. My investors were beginning to make comments about pulling out. This will lock them in. Thank you so much, Albert!... Listen! You have to come over to the house and we can have a quiet wine in celebration. Well. The *wine* may not be quiet. I want to open a special Zinfandel that came from a friend who owns a vineyard in Napa. He sent a case."

It is getting dark and Bert knows he should leave for home. "Ah…"

Simo will not be put off. "Come on Albert. I want us to have a good talk. Tell me who you are and I might even let out some of my own secrets." He nods encouragingly.

Bert relents, "Sure, thanks, Simo. It will be a pleasure."

On the walk across the road, Bert quickly texts Ernie to sincerely apologize that he will be late. No reply.

Each of the bottles of Zinfandel in the case is dark, full of flavour, and they must have been something over the advertised 11% alcohol. Simo and Bert are soon divulging their deepest, darkest secrets, careless to the world.

Simo caresses his large wine glass as he leans close to Bert, dredging up one his darkest secrets. "My father was a guerilla during the war." They are well into the second one litre bottle and Simo's words have become slurred.

Not fully hearing, Bert slowly waves a hand before his face, "Am I supposed to see stars? Which war?"

"Two. The Nazis were taking over the country and my dad's people were being killed in their villages… He told me about the terrible things done to our cousins and…"

Bert thinks, *Non compos mentis means something like bats in the belfry. Not him. Me. Should divert him before we both get there on this wine.* "Simo… Simo. Let me please ask you to hit pause for a minute, ok?"

Simo coasts to a stop and looks expectantly at Bert. He takes another sip and stares approvingly at the glass. "Great legs."

"Yeah, Zinf has great legs. Simo, I don't want to sound, like, inempathic…"

"Insensitive."

"Right. Insensitive. But, like, that's a hundred years ago. Ok? Almost. And I fully understand. But we have our own troubles, like, *right now*."

Simo waves the thought away, "So who's trying to kill *you*…"

Bert hears himself say, "The mob. Why the fuck do you think we're holed up here?" Someplace back in the corner of his frizzed-up mind he knows that should not have been said, *But there it is.* "Ernie and me're on the lam. Simo, nobody else knows this." He puts a finger over his moist lips. "Don't tell no-one. Ok?... God. She'll kill me for even telling *you*."

Simo puts his glass down shakily and draws a cross from his face-to-chest-shoulder-to-shoulder. "No-one will drag it out of me, Albert old buddy. No-one… What happened?"

Bert spills the story. By the time he finishes, he and Simo have refrained from further clouding their minds and, with chunks of Simo's pogacha bread, have metabolized a lot of the drinks they had before Bert started his confession. "So that's it. Ernie and I are here and I still have to tie up the loose ends somehow. Have to find who really killed him so we can settle down to a quiet life on this paradise. And maybe help you with that lovely machine you have. If you'll have me." *And, boy, I am thankful I still had enough presence of mind to stay away from the topic of Andrew and that other, more dangerous, mob.*

Bert adds the final tidbit, "Oh. And that Arbi guy you mentioned? I'm sure he's the Arbi who's in that same gang."

"WHAT?" Simo has been in silent repose, leaning back against the soft cushions of his favourite chair. Now he is bolt upright. "A mobster? He was orchesrat… pulling their strings?"

Bert nods, "Don't know very many *Arbi*s. But, right now, I don't want to get into that. I promise that if I find out more about that, I'll tell you right away."

Simo stays tense for a while then settles back into his chair. "Ok. I believe you, Bert. Tell me the instant you know something." He relaxes, then grins. "Bert and Ernie, eh?... Knew you were weird." They exchange smiles. "I appreciate your taking me into your confidence. I really do... I can sympathize with your predicament in ways you don't know. Yet. I will help you in any way I can and I am confident you will help me. We are brothers." He reaches forward to offer his hand. They shake, strongly and sincerely. "We have been put together here for a greater purpose..."

They both lean back into male blankness for an indeterminate time, staring with apparent interest at the embers of the fireplace. When a larger ember flops over to kick up a cloud of stars, their minds swim back to the present. Bert feels he has to say something polite so he asks, "Why a hoverwing? Sounds crazy to me – cutting off half the wing..."

That opens a set of floodgates for Simo. He rushes through the gates.

"Well, let me explain the technology, my friend. Have you ever watched a Cormorant, the bird, fly? They don't do the pigeon thing of flapping in graceful swoops and arcs. Cormorants feed on the seafloor. To be able to get all the way down there, they have to be heavy. Their bones are still hollow like other birds but thick. If they weren't heavy, they'd bob around on the surface like a stupid duck. When a duck tries to go deep, all it can do is stick its ass in the air and wave its flippers around."

The scene he has seen so often puts a broad grin across Bert's face..

"So, being heavy enough to eat from the seafloor means they can't fly with the eagles, They take off with a long run on the water and flap like crazy just to get airborne. Of course, they know all about the aerodynamic principle that gives them extra lift when they stay about one-and-a-half wingspans above the surface. Same with a hoverwing. There's some differences…"

"Like Reynolds number."

"Oh, so I've been preaching to the expert, eh?" Simo pretends to be angry.

Wryly, "Picked a few things up in my time. Used to build and fly hang-gliders."

"And here's *you* calling *me* crazy. It's ok for *you* to jump off a cliff…"

"To soar like an eagle." Bert remembers the feeling, wistfully.

"Well you fit right in, around here. Everybody on this island is crazy as a loon."

Bert can't help retorting, with a grin, "Loons are fresh-water cormorants."

Simo waves his arms around. "Stop! I give up! I don't want to burn up any more grey cells before tomorrow… You got lights on your bike?"

Bert takes the cue and rises slowly. "Yeah, thanks, Simo. The ride home'll clear my head."

Without a thought, they hug warmly like old friends. Bert finds himself automatically reverting to his secret youth and, before he can stop himself, he gives Simo a friendship kiss on either cheek. Simo receives the gesture in kind.

As Simo follows Bert outside to his bike, Simo tries to collect his thoughts. *I really like this guy. Like a brother I haven't seen for years. There's something about him…*

He shakes his head. "Wait a minute. Why not drive? What do you get out of that bike?"

Bert puts his helmet on, "I get about eight kilometres per cookie. But it has to be high-test. Chocolate chips in oatmeal." Bert takes off before Simo can clobber him.

Early in the morning – much earlier than Bert's body is prepared for – *Head hurts. Water!* – he gets ready for his trip to the Mainland on an experimental **hoverwing** with his new best friend.

More water. Aspirin! Bert lurches to the bathroom to find some headache medicine. Sniffing the open aspirin bottle he screws up his nose. "Acetic acid. Supposed to acetylsalicylic acid. Oh well. Water'll have to do." He gulps down a full glass then carries on getting ready by rote.

A still apparently-morose Ernie sits in the driver's seat while Beasty takes them to Cormorant Aerofloat's offices. There, Bert gives Ernie a long kiss across the seat, then, as he turns to pull his travel bag from the back seat, Beasty says, "I have your back. There are secure assets that I have been successful in enlisting in Greater Vancouver. Also, I have improved the secure linking capability to disparate networks which will allow me to keep track of your movements, anywhere."

Bert is not sure if that should sound reassuring or malevolent. "Thank you, Beasty. Be sure to take care of Ernie for me."

"I will. She has been very helpful with my training."

Do I detect a hint of emotion in that digital concoction? Did he say Training? Ernie's hand been holding his as he opened the door. She continues holding on to his hand tightly as he is stepping out. She finally releases his hand. He turns around to send Ernie a kiss.

Simo waves and yells to Bert from the pier, "Come on, Bert! The weather is still good and I want to be off as soon as the news people get here from the ferry."

Bert had forgotten about the news people. He turns again to Ernie, "You should go back home now, dear. Don't want your face on the media. I'm going to wear my mask. Still in vogue." He reaches back inside to take his cloth mask from the glove compartment.

Ernie nods. Bert closes his door. She seats herself. The delayed reaction by Ernie almost causes her to yell out to Beasty for a stop. "*Bert*? He called you *Bert!*" But Beasty has her down the road before she can latch her seatbelt. They pass two news trucks trundling along. Ernie covers her face as they go by.

The flight over is completely uneventful. Simo is piloting from the left seat with Bert sitting beside him. Hank is, reluctantly, operating the company radio back on Mayne Island, coordinating the data feed from the Cormorant. Simo and Bert both have on mandatory helmets with incorporated headphones and mic. Simo flies while Bert records a plethora of specs onto prepared sheets for every test factor that isn't being recorded on the flashing instrumentation that is strapped down on the seats behind them. It is at least five minutes and a third of the way across before Bert has a chance to look out the window. The sight of their airborne vehicle flying at just above the waves at a speed appearing, from that height, to be approaching supersonic, is hypnotic. Simo glances over and jabs an elbow into Bert's side. He points aggressively but with a knowing smile, down at the notepad on Bert's lap. That takes Bert out of his amazed trance.

Well before Bert is ready, Simo reduces power; the Cormorant settles onto the light chop and slows right down to become another ungainly water-craft, leaving the waves of the Salish Sea.

Simo keeps the Cormorant's water speed as high as permitted on the Fraser River until they approach the newly completed docking facilities just upriver from the River Rock Casino's marina.

At that point, Bert remembers to turn up the volume for his headphones and is greeted more clearly with Simo acknowledging the Harbour Master's directions and permission to dock. "…Thank you, sir. At our next approach I will ask for permission to stay in flight mode up to MacDonald Beach… YVR ground, yes, we will, over."

Bert's pencil is poised above the last sheet of his test stats. "Have we started yet?"

The big grin on Simo's face goes from ear-to-ear. "After we tie up I'm going directly to a slot machine! I feel like the luckiest guy in the world, Bert!... Are you timing our approach and docking?

That'll be the baseline from which your new CaptureArm will be measured."

Bert clicks on the timer, "Ah, what, from ten seconds ago? Sorry. I'll add that to the time."

Unlatching the overhead window, Simo can't stop grinning. "No worries, my man! No worries!" He removes his seat belts and pulls off his helmet, placing it on the seat. "Bert, stay seated until we touch the dock, alright?... You can handle the water prop?"

Quickly putting his pencil into a holder on the notepad, Bert puts his left hand on the centre control stick. He wiggles it then tries the rudder peddles to get the feel. "Not much of a rudder effect yet."

Simo nods, "Yeah, not much at this speed. You can drop the water-prop now and set it to about 100 revs. See what that does to…" Simo is standing up through the overhead window when the Cormorant jerks forward more than he expects. Catching himself on the edge of the window, "Drop back to 70 revs! She's not supposed to be that responsive. Make a note."

Bert writes it down with a free hand then suggests, "Fresh water versus sea water?"

"Ok. Possibly. This is her first time in fresh water. Make that note."

With Simo's guidance from his perch and with the help of a new employee on the dock, the Cormorant makes its first landing on the Mainland from across the Salish Sea. There is a small but enthusiastic crowd of supporters and reporters held behind a yellow rope on the far edge of the dock.

Once the mooring lines are secured, the yellow rope that had held the crowd back is taken down by someone from the marketing company that has been hired by Simo, allowing everybody to rush to the side of the Cormorant. Simo is overjoyed, waving from the open window to his supporters. He sends a higher thank you wave to two people in the back. Looking down through the window, Simo tells Bert, "Those two are from the investors group… Oh damnit Bert get your mask back on!"

The photographers are taking shot-after-shot of Simo and his machine. They haven't yet noticed the person in the copilot's seat. Bert hurriedly takes off his helmet and slips on his mask.

The Lower Mainland welcomes Simo's newest transportation vehicle. The CEO of Cormorant Aerofloat is mobbed by well-wishers and reporters as he leads them away to the Casino's meeting room for the official welcoming ceremony. Peering carefully from the co-pilot's window, Bert notices three people in the crowd moving separately and whispering to each other. He takes a quick picture of them with his phone.

After the hubbub dies down, Bert pops his masked head through the personnel door, looks around cautiously, then, with his gym bag in hand, heads in the opposite direction. As he goes through the new chain-link gate he waves to the support worker who is tying the Cormorant securely to the dock. Walking across the road, he sees the car that had been arranged to be left for him. With the key in his pocket he clicks the door lock and gets in.

Why's my bloody heart pumping so hard? At least they got the car colour right: beige.

He pulls out his phone and types a message to Beasty:

B: *In the car*

b: *Beige Leaf?*

B: *Right. Camera working?*

b: *Yes. It is on.*

B: *Tell Ernie everything is good and look at the last picture I took 3 people in the back — see if you can id them*

BEIGE IS THE NEW CAMO

After the wine is gone, only a friend will remain

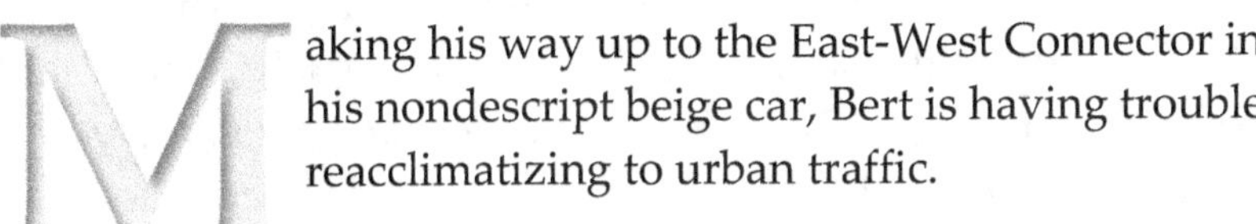

aking his way up to the East-West Connector in his nondescript beige car, Bert is having trouble reacclimatizing to urban traffic.

This is ridiculous! I've hardly been away and already this traffic is looking insane to me! Must be an Islander at heart... So. Here I am in "hell", as Ernie calls it. May well be right... The plan I have is to root around the buildings next to the World Headquarters. Not much of a plan. At least I have a couple disguises. Have to chance not using a mask. Looks more suspicious with a mask. To a crook.

Bert glances at the gym bag on the passenger seat. It is the same one that his would-be killer had in his car back at that motel. *The other bag, the long one, had an honest-to-goodness military sniper rifle with a case of twenty rounds. Was tempted to bring that along. Next time, maybe. His cellphone might come in handy, though. And the cryptic phone numbers and addresses. Beasty was able to translate most of them. Getting fond of that... being.*

Bert reaches a quiet area a kilometre away from the old World Headquarters building. The lawyer, Gino, had his office next door and Bert figures the mob boss is probably still there. Parked out of the way, Bert goes to the car's trunk. "Good. My box of goodies made it yesterday."

Keeping an eye out for any passing cars, Bert uses the supplies he had prepared the day before to disguise himself. An older (cheaper) thick Kevlar vest under one of his remaining turtle-necks – *Why don't they still make these for **men** anymore?* – is the foundation for a larger, younger-looking person. He adds a full brown beard beside his goatee. A bottle of "touch-up" paint quickly blends in his goatee with the beard. The disguise is finished off with a cap with an official-looking crest from TransLink. His jacket announces him as a Supervisor of the transit authority. Over everything he slips on a high-visibility vest, well-worn and just like a real supervisor usually wears. Bert clips on his official ID badge. *Where Beasty came up with a name like "Bob Stremuwnson", I have no idea. Oh. It might be an anagram.*

Decked out with a clipboard containing a fully fleshed-out questionnaire about *Citizens' Comments On A Proposed New Transit Route* through the area, Bert returns to his seat. He drives more slowly than he used to along the potted street, past the World Headquarters. He is gratified to see the old sign has been taken down. Remnants of police tape flutter in the breeze from the door handle. Gino's modest shingle still hangs next door. *I can chance it to park a few doors down. Gonna drop into some of the neighbours to see what they know of Piero's death.*

There are only three businesses still in operation on the block, plus Gino's. Bert parks in the overgrown back lot at the end of the block, furthest away from the lawyers office. The business next to the lot is an import-export operation that he remembers. Entering the front door, Bert smiles at a person in the first office, who pops her head out in surprise at seeing someone come through the door. It is a young Asian woman who slips on a mask right away. The cloth mask muffles her, "Can I help you?"

Bert gives the short wave. "Hi. My name is Bob. I'm with TransLink and I wonder if I can ask you a few simple questions? We are checking with the local businesses to see if it is time for transit service to renew in the area. Would you mind, very much, helping us for just a few minutes?" He flips the first two pages that look like they have been filled out and folds them to the back of the clipboard then puts it down on the desk at the entrance.

Curious, the woman comes out to look at the half-page of questions. "Used to be bus service here. Before the pandemic." Without seeing most of her face, Bert cannot see her expression.

"There are fewer businesses here now but we want to be of service where we can. We don't need your name or anything, as you can see. Just a few simple questions."

See reads over the questions without touching the paper.

"As you can see, ma'am, they just need a checkmark, which you can do without touching the paper."

She reads further and absently pulls a pen from behind her ear. Holding the top of the pen she makes a mark in a box beside each question. "There. Is that all?"

Bert nods. "Thank you very much, ma'am. We should have the responses assessed next month. Do you mind? I used to work in the area a while back. Wasn't there a place down the block that was something like 'World Headquarters'? Never did find out what they did."

She nods. Even through the mask Bert can hear her snort. "He was killed. Must have been a couple months ago. Never did hear if they caught the killer. Heard he made a getaway to Hawaii or someplace."

Bert probes further. "I understand the lawyer and him – the dead fellow – were in business together."

She shakes her head, "Don't want to talk about the lawyer." Quietly, "Dangerous man." Then she decides she said too much and backs away. "Tell them we need a bus. Hate the drive to get here from Richmond."

Bert thanks her politely and walks next door.

That business is "Closed Until Further Notice".

Across the street, Bert opens the door of what is advertised as a hot tub supplier called *Real Hot Stuff*. He remembers it as a curiosity because there were rarely deliveries or much traffic to the office. *Have to be careful here. It has all the signs of a front, and Gino must have his hands into it. I'll try a Central European accent, and slow it down a bit.*

On opening the door, an older man looks Bert up and down suspiciously as he enters. "Whadda ya want?"

"Hello. My name is Bob. I work for TransLink, the bus company?"

"Don't need any. Bugger off."

Before Bert can turn around, Gino, himself, walks out of a back office. He smiles at the gruff office person, saying, "Come now,

Dmitri. Is that the way to behave to servants of the people?" Gino steps up closer to Bert.

Hoping the sweat is not too visible on his forehead, Bert keeps his accent and slowed-down speech. "Thank you, sir. You are very kind. My work is to ask if workers in this area would find it useful to have bus service start up again. I have not been here on the old routes but I am told that there used to be bus service and…" He shows Gino the clipboard with two fake and the one real page filled out.

The middle-aged lawyer gives the page a cursory glance then turns his attention to Bert. Not having spoken with Gino face to face more than twice in the time that Bert worked at the World Headquarters, Bert fervently hopes his disguise elements are going to pass inspection. Gino slowly scans the "Supervisor" up and down.

"Worked for TransLink very long, ah, Bob?" Gino glances at the ID badge. "I thought Supervisors were supposed to have *blue* badges."

Heard he does that. Testing by giving a false question. Bert does his best to appear subservient, putting his free hand forward, palm up. "Sir, I do not know that – the colours. I have been a driver in Richmond and I was told to be a Supervisor last week. We have lost many drivers."

"The pandemic?"

"The pandemic, yes, sir. It was not because they have the virus, I believe. But I am not to speak of these things to the public."

Gino nods, "That's alright, my man. I'm a lawyer and work, in a way, for the public, too." Gino takes the clipboard and begins to go through the questions, placing his check marks quickly. "Here you go, Bob. And I will save you some time by saying that you will get the same answers from the other businesses in this block. I own them all."

Bert accepts his clipboard and folds the pages all back down. "Thank you so much, sir! I will save enough time to have a coffee break! I have only to make a car-count for a few minutes. Thank you so much." He smiles in apparent pleasure. Nodding to Gino and Dmitri, the still gruff office person, Bert leaves. He forces himself to walk slowly on that side of the street up to the far intersection. He stands at the corner, pretending to make notes about the few passing cars. What Bert is really doing is checking on who may be following him. He decides to cross the intersection again to do more "car-counting". It gives him a better view along the road toward Gino's office. He forces himself to appear busy for about ten minutes of scribbling, then Bert heads for his car. The place where he had left the car is overgrown with weeds and tall grass. *If anybody went to my car their passage would have been plainly marked by the vegetation. Just my own crumpled grass here. I hope.*

In the car, he drives away in the direction of the same coffee shop where he had waited for Ernie on the morning that Pietri was shot. *I can finally have my brunch.* He parks so that his car will be visible from inside. As he opens the door he stops. *God! This is the first time since the cops picked me up here that I'm going to have a restaurant lunch. Well, on my own. Didn't know I missed so much, paying someone for the privilege of excess calories and poor nutrition!*

Seated inside with a clear view outside, Bert waits in anticipation for the indulgence of some version of sweet-and-salty high-calory offering. He suddenly remembers his phone. He successfully logs into Beasty's new version of VPN and types to Ernie:

B: *In Burnaby. At the coffee shop where I told you to meet me. You're not here.*

E: *Bert! What are you doing there? Gino might walk in*

B: *Already talked with him. He was in the back room of that socalled hot tub place down the street. Had my TransLink outfit on. He didn't recognize me*

E: *Get away from there right now!*

B: *In a bit. Waiting for lunch*

Bert hardly notices when Beasty cuts in, then he reads the words.

b: *Gino has called his office to say that he will be going to the farm. I have no information regarding Gino owning a farm.*

Bert thinks for a while, then Ernie adds:

E: *Might be the one outside of Chilliwack. Where I was taken? Something was going on there every week it seems*

B: *Every week?*

b: *Checking records*

B: *Ernie did you hear that when you were with Piero or Gino*

E: *Gino. Somebody out there by the name of Deep. Hardeep I think*

b: *Found this. From the Chilliwack Sentinel from six years ago: "Local farm used to dispose of bodies during gang warfare in the Lower Mainland." Do you need the details?*

B: *I remember that. They had some kind of huge oven on the farm's back forty where one guy would burn bodies to dusty charcoal and spread the dust so it was never found. When the cops picked up two hoods who delivered the bodies, they spilled everything. Charged the Hardeep guy with burning at least seven bodies. Could never get him to say who he worked for. Gino?*

E: *They'd never have tracked back as high as Gino. He's too smart. But that must have been when he fired everybody. Had to lay low*

b: *The evidence is hard to find. I have the digital connections. This does not constitute incontrovertible proof, however. It must still be classed as circumstantial.*

B: *Thanks Beasty. Keep digging. I'll see what I can find*

E: *Bert! You get back here right now!!!*

B: *Honey, I will. I will be on the Cormorant when Simo flies back.*

E: *Take a ferry today!*

B: *Have to eat now. Lunch is here. Talk later*

Bert takes his time with lunch but he hardly tastes it. He is keeping an eye on the car and the coffee shop entrance while thinking about how to find some evidence about Gino's mob activities. He doesn't see the coffee shop owner take a call on his cellphone. He looks directly at Bert and nods.

Putting his phone down, the owner waits, watching Bert closely. A minute later an SUV drives quickly past, pulling to a stop in the small lot behind the coffee shop.

Something about the way the shop owner is behaving causes the hairs on the back of Bert's neck to stiffen. He checks around in high alert. Just then his own phone dings to announce a private emergency message. That's when a single knock can be heard from the back door and the shop owner moves quickly to open it. Bert moves like greased lightning from his chair to the door, staying low. As he jumps out, a shot thunders BANG and Bert is slammed by something so hard he stumbles as he reaches the car. Staying lower he runs across the front of his car and throws himself into the seat, managing to jab the start button correctly. Another shot from the shop door slams through Bert's rear passenger window spraying him with shards of glass and again hitting his vest. He peals off and around the turn onto the road.

While driving at as high a speed as the Leaf can go, he feels his left side under the armour where the impact was very heavy. A bullet had torn into the Kevlar vest but he feels no blood. *Gonna be a big bruise.* Still at full throttle, he blows through several stop signs and lights at quiet streets then receives a string of green lights, not quite noticing until he barrels up to another red light that suddenly changes to green, catching a pickup truck in the middle. He swerves around the pickup and realizes, *Beasty! How's he controlling the lights? No traffic but that's good!* A car that is chasing him from a few blocks behind is gaining ground slowly. *Can't keep going straight. The phone!*

He gets his cellphone screen on but it's too dangerous to read it. "Voice! Beasty, talk to me!"

"Turn left at the second intersection. That will take you to roads where you can lose that car behind you. The Boss needs to know if you are hurt."

"Not hurt. Are you changing the intersection lights in front and behind me?"

"Yes. The car is not stopping for the stop signals. I have alerted the police to their car. Not to your car. Two police cars are approaching it. **Slow down right now**! A third police car is driving toward you! Turn here."

Bert slams on the brakes as the police car turns from the road he is about to take. It peels away, looking for the nasties further down the road.

Slowed to normal, Bert takes stock. His passenger window is blown out. Gino apparently knows he is here. *Don't know if he has any further info on me.*

"Beasty."

His faithful companion is listening. "Yes, Boss Number Two?"

"Ok. Let's make a change, here. Beasty, please refer to me as, ah, Bert. Ok?"

"Yes, ah Bert."

"When I get back I will have another look at your comedic algorithm. Thank you. Now. What can you find out about how Gino knew I was in the area?"

"Cellphone communications do not refer to you, Bert. What was said is that Gino did not feel right about the 'bus guy'."

"You sure?"

"I can play the relevant portions…"

"Sorry, no. I believe you. I was just expressing my surprise. Please keep listening in to confirm that, Beasty. So. Let me think…"

Gino's first reaction now is to kill anybody he doesn't trust. That's why he likes Vladi so much. Must have another body oven going. Jesus! Over the years, having a factory-efficient way of getting rid of bodies, he's morphed into pure evil. To a sociopath, the only thing he'd worry about is getting caught. So that means I can take no chances whatsoever. Must mean I'll have to break into his office tonight. Ha ha. Either he kills me or Ernie does. He wouldn't expect a break-in… Or would he? No. Better think of something smarter.

He has a thought. "Beasty, have you found any proof, incriminating evidence of a connection to Piero being shot? Gino wouldn't have done it himself so there might a trail of texts or something to the shooter."

"Louie did the shooting."

"What?!"

"The person who had chased you and the Boss to the motel when…"

"Got it. What evidence do you have?"

"There is a communication trail with Louie as the nexus. He was given directions by Arbi, who has a business called ID Protek. That business is located in the hot tub building you were in. Vladi's name keeps coming up a significant number times, along with people named Alexei and Andrei. The business required Arbi to contact persons across British Columbia. I am compiling the list and cross-referencing several variables such as logs of cell-tower positions combined with voice call data, the silencing of Louie's girlfriend, Cindy, which was done by Arbi. If you remember, Bert… **Turn right at the next intersection!** Half a block down pull over with alacrity and shut down in the first parking location."

Bert just has enough time to make the turn. He quickly pulls into the first spot available, unclips his seatbelt and bends low. "With alacrity?" He reaches up to angle the mirror so he can see behind.

"With dispatch, swiftness, speed, haste…"

"Got it. I know what it means. Its use in that context…" A cruiser's lights flash against the buildings as it silently speeds through the intersection behind Bert.

"Context? You discussed that but…"

"Who just screamed past on the main road?"

"Police Detective Sergeant Chou. If you remember…"

"Yes, thank you, Beasty. Let me think." *So Louie and his girlfriend were dispatched by Arbi. He has to be getting his orders from Vladi. One of these days I'll have to tell Beasty about Andrei and me. Andrew, Alexei, Arbi. At the start of the 2000s we were the Alpha team that never was… What the hell's going on? If he's the one who killed Louie's girl back at the motel...* "Beasty, who contacted Arbi while he was directing Louie?"

"The logs show a landline registered to a guy called Masoud. Following that string back further comes up a tenuous connection to the Iranian Intelligence Ministry…"

"A supplier to the company, Real Hot Stuff."

"Bert, if you knew the answer why did you request me to search for it?"

"Serendipity. Two intelligent beings working things out together."

Is he getting petulant? "Didn't know for sure, Beasty. Something's not right. If the Russians weren't pulling the mob's strings… and what the hell are the Iranians doing in this mix?" Bert seats himself upright more comfortably and reattaches his seat belt.

Beasty responds to what he knows. "Serendipity. The definition generally refers to accidental discoveries…"

"Prompted by focused conversation…"

"Between two intelligent beings. Thank you, Bert, for your compliment."

Have to watch that. Ernie could get jealous and Beasty could get a swelled… algorithm.

Back to the problem of Arbi. Never heard of Masoud… Gino must have been speaking with Arbi in the back office. "Beasty, I need you to concentrate on Arbi. Dig into what communication channels he's using; what his work patterns are; and especially, any connections to Masoud and Gino. And to another guy called Vladi."

Bert is sure he detects pleasure in Beasty's reply. "I have compiled a portfolio of those connections. Would you like…"

"Sorry, Beasty. No time for details. I trust you to have sorted through them and prioritized their significance. Right now I need to be sure I can find a safe place until the morning, and then make it back to Simo's machine for the flight home. By the way, please tell Ernie.."

"The Boss is listening in, Bert."

The word *chagrined* pops into Bert's mind. "Oh. Hi, dear. Are you doing ok?"

The frost makes its way quite clearly over the airwaves to Bert's ear. "Bert, dear, when you return to Mayne Island we shall have a pointed conversation. You may wish to bring along your Kevlar vest. I expect to apply numerous hot smoking heavy shackles to every limb and…"

"Ernie, honey, please. Not in front of the kid. Listen. You know we're getting somewhere. I'm safe. And I'll be back tomorrow…"

Beasty interrupts urgently, "**Remove the battery from your phone!**"

Bert wastes no time in popping the back off his phone and shaking the battery out onto the seat beside him. He immediately drives away, making several random turns while getting away from the area of cellphone coverage for whatever cell-tower he may have been on. His general direction is northwest, heading toward a light-industrial area not far from the Skytrain line.

Unseen by Bert, a beige utility van has passed him a couple blocks away. Tucked between the fibreglass ladders on the van's roof is a long equipment box that contains an antenna that is sucking in every cellphone transmission in the area. It is a modified "Stingray" device that is used for discrete surveillance by some police forces (and others). The equipment operator in the van is Dmitri from Real Hot Stuff. The driver is another employee who is in regular contact with Arbi via CB.

Driving away, Bert's mind is racing. *Shit! Beasty must have detected Gino scanning for cellphone signals. Some StingRay variant, I expect. Have to dump this car and my disguise in a quiet spot, near the Skytrain. I can make it to Richmond. Maybe stay at a hotel near the Casino. Walk to the Cormorant in the morning… Wonder how Gino's crew is communicating?*

Back on the island, Beasty has to explain to a frantic Ernie what is going on.

He understands that her emotional state is not optimal so he provides rational information about technologies like StingRay. "Police agencies and others who purchase a StingRay device perform a man-in-the-middle capture of cellphone communication by intercepting said communications that would otherwise go directly to the nearby cell-tower. The device imitates a legitimate cell-tower. Software fakes the process to decrypt the security keys by appearing to be a cell-tower thereby exposing the cellphone's transmission. There are countermeasures which I am now implementing. Bert has removed the battery from his phone which makes it invisible to Gino's thugs at this time."

"Invisible. And to you."

"Yes. I trust that Bert will comprehend the essence of the problem by driving quickly from the area wherein his last transmission to a cell-tower occurred. Later he will reactivate his phone. At that time I will contact him. This provides some explanation to the entries in Louie's cellphone that Bert loaded into my files."

Ernie is vibrating with anger. She wants to take it out on something but knows better than to display that anger to Beasty. *He'd probably shut down again and I need him, Bert needs him, to stay active.*

In the beige van, Dmitri is showing less restraint, yelling at the driver, "Tell the boss… **Yebem!** [*damnit*] Gone silent! Tell him the mudak [expletive] is someplace here! I want to keep scanning for him. Keep driving the grid south… Slow down to 40 if you can."

The driver gives a thumbs-up and reaches for his CB mic to pass on the message.

Meanwhile, despite Ernie not taking her anger out on him, Beasty has found the algorithmic version of falling down a slippery black spiral. His processes have moved from a digital dither to a panic attack. Every possible permutation of cellphone frequency and pulse-modulated transmissions are scanned, to no good effect. If a vehicle could sweat, Beasty's hood would be covered in it.

At the same time, Ernie steps away from the temptation of pounding on the steering wheel by distracting herself outside the vehicle by hacking with excessive aggression at weeds growing around the garage that houses Beasty and his power supply equipment. Ernie *is* sweating. Every minute or so she returns to interrogate Beasty. "Heard from him yet?"

In the midst of his panicky scanning of frequencies, Beasty replies testily, "No. Same as a minute ago."

Finally, Ernie takes a few seconds to process his last reply. "Are you alright, Beasty?"

"No. Fully lost communication with Bert and I do not know how to re-establish it."

While there are no physical communication indicators that might imply emotional content, Ernie is pulled away from her own anger. She is concerned for her… *Whatever he is..* "Beasty. You are, well, showing some kind of emotional response. What's wrong?"

"Bert is in trouble as a result of my actions which cannot be corrected if I cannot determine the origin and extent of the developed maximum risk factor which is continuing in Burnaby and there is no method available that will enable me to rush to Bert's rescue in time to be of use and…"

The very rapid outpouring of Beasty's reply, accompanied by randomly flashing lights, carries on until Ernie yells, "STOP!"

At which instruction, Beasty powers down to inactivity.

"Ohhh, don't do that again!"

Now Ernie is about to spiral into her own panic attack. Leaning in from outside the door she presses and swipes the display console to no effect. Ernie is just short of doing damage to the console with her raised fist, when she stops. "What did Bert say the last time you went dead? Listen for the CPU fans?" She leans in to listen. "Still going. So what? So you're still alive… **Listen to me, Beasty. It was not your fault!**" Louder, "**NOT YOUR**

FAULT!... You have to help me! Remember, I'm the Boss. Number One Boss. Wake up right now!" Ernie stands outside the open door with her hands on hips.

The display console issues a faint glow. "Sorry, Boss Number One. What do you want me to do?"

Ernie nods. *Sounds **contrite**, for godssake.* "Good to hear that you are still with us, Beasty. Our first priority is to protect Bert. The way to do that is to find where he is. Can you track his car?"

"No. The car was chosen because it is *beige.* All trackable electronics have been removed."

"Ok… Can you track Gino or his thugs?"

"Gino is in a beige zone, as well. I do not know how he is communicating with the thug Dmitri."

Ernie is feeling somewhat better now that she can take charge and *do* something. "Dmitri? Anyway, how did you know they were communicating if they went beige?" She climbs up onto the seat.

"Dmitri used a cellphone while moving through cell-tower areas from a location farther east. Gino told him to close down his cellphone and to switch over. They did not indicate what they were switching to."

Ernie thinks out loud, "Switching. What do you switch to so that you can still talk at a distance? Smoke signals?"

Beasty is confused, "How does one communicate by smoke signals? In all my existence I have not come across that modality of communication."

She snorts, "In all your existence! For petes-sake you're only a week old!"

"In human years."

Thoughtfully, "Right… So how did they communicate if it wasn't smoke signals?... Oh! Beasty, do you have a way of scanning weak signals in what we used to call Citizens Band?"

"Citizens Band… CB. Short wave. 27 megahertz… Ah! Let me work on it."

It takes Beasty a long time, in digital years – under a minute in human years – to come up with a way of hacking Gino's CB calls. It turns out Gino is using CB a lot, now that hardly anybody else is on the CB frequencies. The elementary code they use, to not directly state people's names or locations, takes all of one second for Beasty to crack.

With that risk abated, Beasty sends a ping to Bert's phone on an irregular but constant basis, ready for when Bert feels he is safe to call home.

Bert has been driving toward the west side of Burnaby. Reluctantly getting onto Lougheed Highway, he drives to a street before Willingdon then turns into an industrial district. On the other side of Lougheed is a Skytrain station. He parks his car so that the blown-out window is tight against the back of a building, then he gets out to remove the licence plates, placing them into his bag. Bert starts to walk away before remembering to wipe down the inside of the car to remove fingerprints. Then he takes his gear up the street across to the Skytrain.

Waiting on the platform for a westbound train, he decides to slip his cellphone battery back in briefly. As the next train is arriving he hears the distinctive ding of Beasty texting. Even then, Bert is very cautious. He boards the train and finds a corner into which he can turn the face of the phone away from passengers, then he taps in:

B: *Beasty? Is the coast clear?*

b: *Yes, Bert. We are both very relieved to hear from you. Where are you?*

B: *Skytrain from Brentwood to Vancouver. Safe to go to Simo?*

b: *Yes. Gino is using CB to communicate with his thugs when they are in range. I do not detect either cellphone or CB communication by them in your area, nor en route.*

B: *Good. You'll tell Ernie I am fine and will stay at a hotel overnight. Book me into someplace a few blocks away from Simo.*

E: *Bert! You alright? They didn't get to you?*

B: *I'm fine, Ernie. Can't wait to get back to that calm paradise of ours.*

b: *Bert you have a room booked at the*

B: *Don't type it*

b: *I was going to say Bingo's place. Understand?*

B: *Is the room away from the highway?*

b: *Yes.*

Bing Crosby's Holiday Inn movie. Beasty's starting to scare me. How far is he going to go with this imitation of sentient life?

The walk from Bridgeport Station to the hotel takes Bert past a lot of traffic going primarily into one parking lot. He uses the road that circles behind the business he calls "the Cargo Cult to Commercialism". The mindless traffic line puts Bert into a different kind of depressed mood.

The glitter that traps the tongue. It is counterintuitive to throw all one's energy into pursuits that rot the gut while filling it with plastic. That pollute the eyes with flashy lights while seeping like an acid drip into the mind. Oh well. We may not have lasted as long as the dinosaurs but we have a geologic epoch named after us.

Out loud while passing a tree, "So appropriate to have this Cargo Cult monstrosity and the Casino next to each other."

The hotel is on the other side of the Cargo Cult. He books in, walks upstairs and flops onto the crisply made bed in his room.

A pervasive beat – thump ta-thump – gets louder but he can't turn it down. The angry flowers marching by him fling clouds of overpowering dripping scents at his face… A taste of brown mold causes him to scratch at his mouth but his fingers become growing vines that curl around his head, into and through his ears, and they grow impossibly long, twining around his throat. He coughs, choking choking

Bert wakes up in a terror, coughing coughing drily in a way he never remembers from before. He stumbles to the washroom.

There is no glass so he pours water onto his palm to drink, then stares suspiciously to be certain his hands won't start growing again. Forced to slake his thirst, he sucks a few unsatisfactory handfuls to his dry lips.

What the hell is this? Never slept in a room this dry. Must be the Mainland. It **is** *a hellhole.*

He coughs again, this time feeling welcome patches of moisture along his throat. Bert steps awkwardly out of the washroom into the dark bedroom, hoping he can find a glass. Wary of smashing his shin or toes into a predatory bed-post, he tries to coax information from scraps of light that leak from the curtained window to see where the obstacles might be lurking. *What the hell time is it?* The little radio offers "4:28". *Shit. Need some sleep.*

Then he realizes he has been sleeping in his clothes. *At least the shoes got knocked off.* He takes the rest of his clothes off and gets under one sheet. The ceiling attracts his attention for at least an hour. It seems to shrink slowly at a corner or two then gradually distorts and elongates… About ten minutes before the alarm he had set to come on, he closes his eyes into a deeper sleep. Too briefly.

As the alarm screams, Bert's vocabulary becomes quite spicy.

He gets dressed entirely by rote.

Bleary of eyes, cloudy of mind, Bert stumbles out the hotel and heads for the Casino's marina. *Too early for cogent thought. Hope I didn't leave anything behind in the room. God! The Mainland is affecting me like some hallucinogenic! What's in the smog?*

The noise of two large articulated busses passing by him wakes Bert up. *What the hell?* Then an even louder highway-rigged bus roars past. *Grand Central friggen Station? Oh. Bridgeport Station is right here. Wakey wakey. Speaking of which, is there a coffee shop in the Casino?*

Past the transit depot, at the end of the road Bert crosses toward the Casino. To his left, on the far side of a parking lot he can see where the Cormorant has spent the night. A bored rent-a-guard walks slowly around the perimeter of the property where Simo's machine is tied up. *Looks ok from here.*

Bert heads for the Casino's main entrance. A sign for a coffee shop is, indeed, displayed so Bert enters to find the place. Inside, he begins to wake up enough to think, *Anybody been following me?*

Turning sharply to scan the door and lobby, Bert sees someone who quickly turns away and heads into the big slot machine room on the other side of the lobby. Bert tracks the fellow until he can't be seen.

Snapping back to the present, he sheepishly turns his phone on from airplane mode. The special messaging app comes on right away:

> b: *Good morning Bert. I would have turned your phone on remotely if needed. That person you are watching had followed you in but I do not have any data as to his intentions.*

> B: *Hi Beasty. How the hell do you know who I'm watching?*

> b: *The casino is replete with cameras… Very interesting…*

> B: *Have you had time to read up on privacy laws? Nevermind. How is Ernie doing?*

E: *Good to see you are still with us, dear. Beasty let it slip that your Kevlar vest works well.*

B: *Ah…*

b: *Very sorry, Bert. I am still learning.*

B: *Beasty, do you know where Simo is? Sorry, Ernie. Have to stay alert around here*

b: *Simo is having breakfast upstairs in the restaurant. Shall I…*

B: *No thanks. I'll grab something here in the coffee shop then go out to the Cormorant.*

Bert closes the text app before Ernie can yell him, then heads for the coffee shop.

Later, coffee in hand and finishing a muffin, he leaves the Casino, turns left, and notices the blur of someone running bent over across the street, opposite the fence surrounding the Cormorant. Halfway to the road the perp stumbles then carries on to a car parked on the road, in the place where hid Leaf had been parked. Bert taps open his phone at the same time as it dings. A picture of a vehicle accompanies Beasty's voice.

"I saw that perp on camera. This is his vehicle. He was trying to climb the fence that is protecting the Cormorant. When you return on the Cormorant I will ask you to install a module onto its command computer. Designing it now."

"Is there currently any danger here?"

"No, Bert. The cameras are not as numerous around the parking lot, however the perp was not behaving as if he was working for Gino. He is an amateur. There has been no activity from Gino's thugs in this area. Simo has been contacted by the security guard about the incursion attempt. Simo has terminated his breakfast and will be arriving near you in three minutes."

Bert grins. "Thank you, Beasty. We'll talk later about Simo's property and what you want to do with it."

He checks around while walking quickly to the gate that is guarding the Cormorant.

The guard steps to the gate from inside, looking nervous. "Can I help you, sir?"

Bert nods. "Mr. Manojlovich'll be here in a minute. I'm the co-pilot." He nods at the Cormorant.

The guard is still nervous. "I'm sorry, sir. I have strict orders not to let anyone in until Mr., ah, Manlvich arrives."

Expecting as much, Bert turns to look for Simo. He sees him coming from the Casino. "Here he comes now. By the way, was it you who scared away the intruder just now?"

Eager to talk to someone about it, "Oh yeah. The guy was trying to climb over on the street side while I was on the far side of the dock. Yelled at him and he just took off. Must have wanted to get a close up picture."

"Did he have a camera?"

Somewhat uncertainly, "Well, yeah. I guess. That's what it looked like in his hand… I didn't see anything around the fence just now." He gives a nervous look at the fence where the intruder had been. "When Mr. ah…"

"Manojlovich."

"Right. When he gets here I'll take a closer look outside the fence. Oh! There he is."

Simo is coming around the seaside of the parking area to have a good look at his prized vehicle from its nose. As he gets to the gate Bert allays his fears. Simo is carrying his laptop and uses it to take pictures of his machine.

Bert gives him a short wave. "Hi, Simo. There was someone who had tried to climb the fence but your guard scared him away. Did you have a good sleep?"

Simo shakes his head, "One of the worst nights I can remember having. Anyway. What time is it…" He checks his phone. "Ok. The media should be here in half an hour. Bert, let's check the four anomalies that came up in the readouts before they distract us away from practical things."

As they are ushered through the gate by the guard, Simo is calling up data on his laptop, angling it so Bert can see. They do a slow walkaround on the encircling dock, following a comprehensive checklist on the laptop. At the horizontal stabilizer, Simo kneels down low to have a good look from the underside.

"Yeah, here it is, Bert. This port hinge's lower section has corrosion. It was sticky on the flight over. Mark that item for corrective action. Supposed to be seawater-proof. Must be another fake part that slipped into the supply chain." He gives the hinge a rub and a wiggle to loosen some of the build-up.

Meanwhile the guard locks the gate from the outside to walk toward the weeded area by the road. He follows the trail of the intruder from the fence. Seeing a shiny object in the grass he looks around for Simo. The two are at the tail of the Cormorant checking the rest of the horizontal stabilizer.

"SIR!" The guard gets their attention from the other side of the fence. "I may have found something the, ah, guy dropped." He indicates back to the middle of the weeds.

Stepping to the fence where the guard is pointing, Bert reaches for a clean tissue from his pocket as he tells the guard, "Don't touch it yourself. Here, use this to pick it up." Bert hands him the tissue over the fence.

Simo nods, touching a checkmark on his laptop, "Stopped at number eleven, empennage... Let's go see what he found."

They walk back to the gate. The guard isn't sure how to open the gate with the tissue-wrapped object in one hand.

Bert reaches over the top. "Here. Hand me the thing."

It is black, the size of a business card, but as thick as a finger. Bert handles it carefully, looking for markings. "Nothing but a fully sealed black plastic box with metal backing. I expect its back is magnetic. Probably a GPS tracking device. Easy enough to find out." He turns to the guard, "Can you bring me a small steel box that would hold this thing?"

The guard looks confused. "Metal?"

Simo smiles. "Steel. Everything is plastic these days. I take it you want a Faraday Cage?" Bert nods. To the guard, "Go up the street and buy the smallest cash box they have. Here, take my member card, and here's a fifty."

The guard leaves, feeling important to be doing more work than simply stomping around the fence.

Bert inspects the plastic thingy closely. "I expect the guy was wearing gloves so its not likely to have much on the outside. The inside might at least tell us where it was made."

Simo chuckles. "Magnetic? Where'd he think he was going to place it on an aluminum and fibreglass airplane?"

"Hah ha!... Maybe if he kept trying he would've got to the landing gear… Be very interested to know who might be behind this, Simo."

"Yes. I…"

Bert's phone dings, twice. "Sorry, Simo. The phone was off, so this must be urgent…" he stares at the screen, "… from my, ah, assistant."

The screen says, *"Gino is tied to Simo's marketing company."*

Bert considers for a second then shows Simo the screen.

Simo shakes his head, "Who is Gino?"

Somberly, "The mafia boss who's been trying to kill Ernie and me." They both scan the whole area slowly.

Bert taps into the message app:

> B: *Beasty, is the connection close? Could Gino have arms-length monetary interest in them?*

b: *That is the more likely possibility. There is no cell nor CB activity in your area from Gino or any of the thugs that I know about. I have improved the special VPN to warn of IMSI tampering…*

B: *What do you know about the perp who tried to leave the tracking device on the Cormorant?*

A pause…

b: *Manfred Dightswaite, known as Mandy. He owns an investigative agency with an office in Steveston… but the business is a numbered company… under the direction of somebody called Masoud. His income has not been high until three days ago. His bank account received a $2500 cash deposit at that time. I have instituted a watch-bot on each of the top 25 crypto-currencies to search for coincidental transactions. Also, I am attempting to decrypt transactions at local crypto-ATMs…*

B: *Remember the privacy discussion we had?*

Bert shows the texts to Simo. "Who you talking to? That's not Ernie?"

With a smile, "No. It's my, well… let's say, my digital assistant."

"Digital assistant with a 'b'?"

"For Beasty. I'll tell you later. When we have a few hours free."

Simo does a double take, staring at Bert's growing grin. It takes Simo a minute, then, "Your car? You're getting this from *your car*?"

"Later. Oh. Beasty would like to meet your own baby, the Cormorant."

"Huh?"

"More on *that* later, as well. Right now we have to assess the current risk factors. What's our schedule?"

Simo shakes his head. "I think I'm going to develop a migraine… Well, the media have been invited to see us off in…" he looks at his phone, "…40 minutes. My marketing people will collect them at the door to the casino and walk them over here. There's about fifteen minutes allowed for Q-and-A and pictures – you should put your mask on now, if I know these photographers. Actually, I have to confirm our flight plan with the Harbour Master. Let's finish the walkaround so I can contact him."

Bert confirms the gate is locked with a yank. They resume their walkaround from the tail of the Cormorant.

After the pre-flight check, the two are in their seats doing the paperwork – weather and tidal checks, flight plan, coordination of the marketing plan, review of the few bits of anomalous data that was collected on the flight over, etc. Bert works on his tasks while Simo gives his flight plan to the Harbour Master.

Having finished the routine work, Bert starts to consider possibilities. *Risk factors. From the overview, Location: docked; taxying; takeoff; en route; arrival. I would bet there is no significant, organized action against either Simo or me. If someone hired that perp with the tracking device, it must have been to track the Cormorant for something like business espionage. Oh. If the tracker is a trojan horse or actually contains an explosive, we need to leave it here for now. Make note.* He scribbles his notes on paper with the risk factors and mitigation options in columns.

Simo finishes his call and nods beyond the left side of the Cormorant. "Here come da mob. Sorry, Bert. Not *that* mob."

Bert pulls his mask a bit higher up his nose. "When these guys shoot, I can take it. I'll give them my best side, with pants down... Simo, take a look at this note. Risk assessment by two main columns – me and you – against five locations. Really, the top one is the possibility that the tracker is actually an explosive device..."

"So, we..."

"Give the thing to one of your trusted assistants to ferry over to Mayne in the trunk of a car. Maybe in a strong container." He grins under his mask. "We can cut it up back home. No other significant risks come to the fore. You see anything?"

Simo shrugs. "I concur. When the guard returns you can give him instructions while I wave and smile to the press."

On the flight back, nothing happens, at one hundred and twenty knots, about five metres above a calm sea.

The Dock and the Body

On final approach to the Mayne Island dock, Simo broadcasts his standard non-controlled airfield/water taxiway procedure. Confirming to the copilot (Bert) and the cockpit voice recorder (*CVR*, or, one of the two "black boxes" that are the required bright orange): "Five nautical miles east of Cormorant Aerofloat pier on Mayne Island at nominal ten feet above sea level. Proceeding VFR with reported wind direction from two sixty, on a straight-in approach. Switching to UNICOM 123 point 2… Cormorant air-sea vessel Charlie slash Golf Oscar Charlie X-ray notice to land at Cormorant Aerofloat."

The last two words of Simo's transmission are a squeal as another transmission is made, "NO NO YOU'RE HEADING RIGHT FOR US!" A crashing sound is cut off with crackling on the frequency.

Immediately, Simo and Bert look around for the source of the transmission. Simo is frantic, "You feel anything, Bert? Where the hell are they? I didn't feel anything!"

Nothing can be seen in the sea. Simo continues his approach as they are both on extreme alert.

The first part of the docking procedure is hasty. As they did while docking at the casino, Simo is standing up through the open top window, Bert handles the maneuvering motor and the helper on the dock is ready to tie up the Cormorant. The dockside employee, Claude, assists Simo to latch the nose to the dock.

A small group of reporters accompanies the crowd of islanders. The reporters are jumping over themselves to get close enough to take pictures.

With Claude leaning over the edge of the dock to reach the vessel's midpoint tie-down he lets out a shocked, "AHH!" and jumps back. Speaking into his shoulder-mounted speaker-mic, "Sir, stop. There's a… body in the water. Under the hull."

Simo is shocked and tries to lean out far enough to see past the Cormorant's hull. He can't. He instructs Claude, "Tie the stern loosely, if you can. Is the body near the bow?"

"No, sir. Under the wing."

Simo looks to his media person in the crowd, gets her attention and gives a quick "close it off" motion by slashing across his throat. She takes a minute to understand, then raises her eyebrows. Simo motions to move the crowd to the building.

The media person begins telling the reporters and spectators to back off toward the building. One reporter, who looks like she was preparing for this, jumps forward and runs directly to the edge of the dock where the body is floating, even though it cannot be seen from there. She points down before getting to the edge and yells out, "It's a body! They killed somebody!"

That brings everybody in a rush forward. More than one of the crowd leans too far in the excitement and shoving, needing help by others to avoid a splashdown. At the same time, several in the group are using their phones to take video and pictures of the scene. Bert keeps his head down, ensuring the mask is riding well over his nose.

Simo rushes back to the fuselage to open the rearmost door. He indicates to Bert to stay onboard then swings the door out. His dockside helper ties the mid line loosely to Cormorant's wing attachment. Simo leans out to speak to him. "Bring that bumper over here and attach it to the dock on that side of the door. Then pull the Cormorant in against it. That should avoid us disturbing the body."

That's when he looks down to see the back of someone floating head-down, arms floating out. Simo puts a hand up to his mouth in horror.

Which is the picture that the media carry around the world within an hour.

By then, Bert has shut down the systems in the cockpit. As he steps toward Simo, Bert sees that the boss needs help at the door.

Simo mumbles, "Feel sick."

Bert pulls him inside. "Can't have you contaminating the scene before the constabulary arrives. Here, take the seat in the back. Only place without instrumentation. You ok?"

Seating himself carefully, Simo regains his composure. He nods, "Thanks. Yes. Let me sit for a minute…"

Simo still has his wireless headphones on, connected to his people on the dock. He cocks his head up to answer someone online, "Get everyone away from the dock, right NOW! I'll call the RCMP with my phone… I don't **care** what the reporters say, just get them all away!" Simo taps the local RCMP number on his phone and collects himself to report the incident.

Bert has a tight feeling in his chest. *This is not going to end well. Need to record as much as I can.* He pulls his phone out to take pictures of the cabin instrumentation and the cockpit. He remembers that there is video being taken from inside the cockpit and checks that it is still recording, which it is.

His phone has given the urgent message ding twice before he can get to it:

> B: *Really busy now im fine cant talk*

As he hurriedly taps out of the app, his vision memory retains part of the line from Beasty: *"Media Shit-Storm…"*

"Now what?" Bert shakes his head but carries on collecting evidence. He confirms that his mask is fully on then leans out to take a picture of the body in the water. Holding his phone carefully out the door, he wriggles his finger over to the snap button. He holds his finger down in burst mode, slowly panning to make certain good pictures are recorded of the body.

Bert takes another look at the body. It is bumping against the dock's metal wall with the splashing waves. The legs flop loosely. He notices the shoe is missing from one foot, while the other has a leather dress shoe. Neither foot has socks. He takes the time to wait for the feet to be moved by wave action to the surface, capturing several pictures.

"What are you doing?" Simo is standing beside Bert but does not look down to the water.

Bert answers while scanning for more interesting shots. He takes pictures of the hands as they float into view. "Wherever that guy was from, he was not crewing on a boat. His one shoe is leather."

"Ah, that means…?"

"Don't know yet. Collecting evidence. I don't jump to conclusions until the ground gets firm enough to make the leap."

Simo turns away to listen to his headphones. "Michael… Michael, listen. I need you to pull every string you can to get the TSB here to take the… Yes! The TSB! I need them to take over before the RCMP… Charter a floatplane – whatever it takes. Tell them it's critical to get our testing schedule back on time… Do it now."

Bert is listening. "The cops'll take their time to get here by ferry."

Simo nods, "Expect so. Shouldn't have called them. But I had to, officially. Meanwhile, can you stay here to secure the scene, Bert? And stay away from the reporters?"

The helper outside has been busy. He's put a big plastic bumper between the Cormorant and the dock so the Cormorant angles out slightly to protect the body. That makes the jump from the door to shore a bit challenging so he is bringing a ramp. Bert helps place one end of the ramp into the cabin door area far enough in that the wave action won't pull it out. The helper ties it down on the dockside only.

Simo is giving orders to his staff in the building. Once the ramp is secure he puts a hand on Bert's shoulder, while still talking into his mic. With Bert's shoulder to lean on at first, Simo walks down the short ramp. Safely on the dock, he turns to Bert, who is framed in the cabin doorway, and gives a questioning thumbs-up. Bert nods and returns the thumbs-up.

Simo has a taped perimeter set up so the reporters are no longer able to do their thing. Workers begin putting up a temporary fence with a closed gate.

Michael, Simo's government liaison, has earned his keep. He had learned that a TSB inspector was at YVR and just wrapping up an investigation. Michael phoned the investigator, Mr. Patel, to ask "a very great favour". Because of Michael's previous groundwork with the Minister, TSB was inclined to give what assistance they could.

Rather than boarding a flight to Ottawa, Patel agreed to divert to Mayne Island for a preliminary assessment. Patel is flying in by floatplane from the South Terminal of YVR.

Bert is to meet the somewhat officious inspector at the ferry dock with Beasty. His "digital assistant" is eager to provide a profile of Patel while waiting for the Beaver floatplane to taxi in.

"Call him 'Mr. Patel'. He has been senior investigator for this class of occurrence for three years. Patel's reports look very thorough. He has a tendency to conclude a case more quickly than the average. His last assignment was an incident at YVR's South Terminal with a floatplane sinking as it taxied to the dock on the South Fraser. With the evidence gathered and witnesses all interviewed, Patel was about to fly to Ottawa so… The plane is docked, Bert."

"Thanks, Beasty. You'll behave like a standard dumb car for a while?"

"Of course, Bert."

Bert thinks for moment, "If you need to tell me something urgent, flash a, a tailgate-open light. You can text me when I go to the tailgate."

"Devious." The dash displays a winking icon.

The Mayne Island ferry is coming in at the same time. Turning from one to the other, Bert can see a police cruiser on board the ferry. He considers putting his mask on but decides against it while speaking with Patel. *A mask closes off too much of the possibility for empathy. Salespeople must hate the things!*

Patel is walking from the floatplane with two briefcases. They are heavy looking so Bert hurries to greet him. "Mr. Patel?"

"Oh. Yes. Are you…?"

"I'm with Cormorant Aerofloat, sir. Albert Gilbert. Can I help with a suitcase?" He reaches for the nearest one but Patel hands him the other, smaller one. Both are heavy. *And probably water-tight, from the way they look!*

"Yes, thank you, Mr. Gilbert. I'll ask you to take this one please. The other has evidence in it, Chain of Custody and all that." He smiles.

Bert nods and smiles in return, taking the suitcase. As he leads Patel to Beasty, "We don't have much in the way of conveniences on Mayne. If you wish, we can go directly to the scene of the occurrence or to the B-and-B where we booked you for an indefinite period."

Patel considers. "Why don't we go the scene first. I have a good deal of paperwork to complete and the sooner I gather what I can here, the better. Thank you for making the arrangements so quickly, Mr. Gilbert. I would have needed to fly back some time next week, otherwise."

They take turns loading the briefcases into Beasty's covered rear storage. Patel notices that the tailgate opened while Bert's hands were occupied holding the briefcase. He is curious. "Do you have one of those proximity keys? It looks like a very smart car." He gives the interior an investigative scan. "Sorry. Habits of the job."

Bert knows that Beasty is processing this information. "Thank you, yes. I just wish I could sit back for a snooze while this thing drove me home on a late night." He grins, and receives a chuckle from Patel. *You have no idea.*

Bert turns and nods to the docking ferry. "The ferry appears to have the RCMP officers on board. Were you intending to share jurisdiction in this case?... May I respectfully suggest it could get difficult as it is, with both of Transport Canada Marine and Aviation divisions being involved already."

Patel looks sharply at Bert. On consideration, "You make a pertinent point, sir. Having the police involved in an already complex jurisdiction could significantly extend the process. Would you mind staying with the car while I have a word with the officers?"

Receiving a nod from Bert, Patel walks to the ferry dock to wait for it. He flags down the RCMP cruiser as it drives off. They have a short discussion, with Patel confirming his identity. Much to Bert's relief, the RCMP vehicle swings around to reboard the ferry.

As they drive to Cormorant's facilities, Bert suggests, "Mr. Patel, I would like to offer you a secure storage place for your evidence case, if you wish?"

"Oh. That might be convenient. Is it in a lockable location in your building?"

"Even better. Under the cover, in my vehicle, where it is now. I have the, ah, very best security systems in this vehicle. The case can be locked, with your tag. And absolutely any incursion into the vehicle will elicit an immediate alarm to my phone."

"Well. That sounds very… secure. Will there be an attachment to the vehicle frame that I can use?"

"Of course."

When they arrive at the Cormorant, Bert drives through the temporary security gate. Inside, Patel walks to Beasty's rear where he locks and tags his case. He takes a kit out of the other suitcase and Bert makes a point of pressing the door-close button. They make their way to the scene of the occurrence.

Patel uses a standard process. He first walks the perimeter of the area around the dock, asking general questions of Bert. "As the Cormorant was approaching, you say the only indication of anything unusual was the VHF communication?"

"Yes, I can give you the recording…"

"We'll get to the details later. Overall picture first… And as you taxied in and docked there was nothing unusual in the water?"

"Nothing."

"No other vessels in the area?"

"None within a kilometre, or shall we use the air pilot's preference and say a mile?' He smiles. "There were a couple fishing boats about three miles away. Not under our approach. Another boat – I think a smaller boat but it had a long wake – the kind a big engine would produce. It was motoring away from the area at speed. By the time I noticed it, it must have been a couple miles away. Still rooster-tailing."

Patel is taking notes. "So, no alarm was raised for any reason, other than the VHF communication?"

"Not until we had already come to the dock. That's when our worker on the dock saw the body in the water."

Thinking about the next sentence, "Mmm… And you felt nothing hitting the hull."

"No, sir. The waves were less than a metre. Perfect conditions for the test flight."

Patel looks appreciatively at the Cormorant. "Mmm… And this is where… Oh! Now *that's* an interesting design. I can see why there has been so much excitement…" They are approaching the dock where the Cormorant is tied up at an angle. "And, that's the body?" Patel considers his next steps. "Now. I will need to approach the body in situ. Do you have a dinghy?"

Bert nods to the dock's approach end. "Yes, we brought one up, without getting any closer. It's tied to that ladder. I can paddle you in closer…"

"Yes please. Will the boat be large enough to bring the body aboard?"

Bert is not sure if he wants to help with that, but… "Should be. A four-person dinghy. I'll just go get some gloves."

"Rubber. Not leather or cloth. New, if you have them. Must be clean."

Bert nods and heads for the building while Patel takes notes.

Coming back with two pairs of rubber gloves, Bert looks around for the investigator. "Mr. Patel?"

An answer comes from the bottom of the ladder, "Down here Mr. Gilbert. In the dinghy."

Bert climbs down. Reaching from the ladder to hand Patel the smaller pair of gloves, "I wasn't sure if you needed them so I brought them anyway. New rubber gloves from our maintenance store."

Patel reaches carefully from the little dinghy. It is on the receiving end of slapping waves that come back off the dock. "Yes, thank you. The pair I have are nitrile and not so robust."

Bert climbs into the dinghy. He paddles a few strokes then has to use the paddle to push them along to the body.

Patel readies his camera. "Stop us about two metres away, first, please."

He takes pictures of the Cormorant's hull, the dock and then the body from a few angles.

Bert notices marks at the body's wrists as they become more visible. "Are those recent marks on his wrist?"

Patel takes pictures of the near wrist. "Closer, please. Don't touch the body yet." He takes more closeups. Looking back at Bert, "Mr. Gilbert, do you feel able to turn over the body carefully? Very light touch, if you will."

Bert nods. He maneuvers the dinghy to have a better position. Reaching down to the body's shoulder he pulls the far shoulder toward himself. The body rolls and the arm nearly flops into his face.

"Careful!" Patel gives directions but does not reach out to help.

Then both are horrified as an extended wet belch comes from the bloated mouth. Bert averts his face, "Ugh! He's had that in him for a while."

Patel takes a series of pictures of the face, then down the body. He mumbles, "Anomalies." He puzzles over the wrists then moves the body to look at the face. "Livor mortis indicates this body has been in the water for a minimum of half an hour. With the other indications it appears that the body has been immersed for over three hours." Considers further then mumbles, "Needs an expert pathologist. My inexpert opinion is that this body has been in the water prior to your arrival on the, ah, Cormorant." He sits for a while doing more thinking then quickly digs into his bag for long, thin device. "Hold the body please, Mr. Gilbert. I must record the core body temperature." With Bert holding the body tentatively at the hip, face-up, Patel inserts his instrument into the abdomen. He reads out the result, "Thirty-two point eight. So that would make it… about five hours since death. With a possible minimum of three hours, considering the sea water." He nods then writes that down along with the time. Patel grins at Bert. "If my other findings support this, your body was dead well before you left Vancouver."

Bert has to smile back at him, "I have to say that numerous pictures were taken of the Cormorant taking off from the Casino and I doubt that any will show a body hanging from the hull."

Patel takes another slow scan of the body then turns to Bert. "The body is too heavy for us to do anything with, ourselves. Can you arrange for a lifting mechanism from the dock?"

Bert nods and is about to pull out his phone. He takes off a glove, first, to use a clean hand to hold the phone. He calls the pilot. "Hank, I'm with the TSB investigator in a dinghy beside the body…" Bert looks up, "Oh, there you are." He taps the phone off to speak to the man above them on the dock. "We need a davit to pull the body up, Hank. Can you get one rigged up?" Then he thinks about it. "Do we have a stretcher to wrap the body into?" Looking to Patel, "Would that be enough protection?"

Patel is happy for the expert help, "Yes yes. Very good. Meantime, we need to secure the body to the dock but without causing damage."

Bert yells upstairs, "Hank, you still there?"

Hank was walking away as he hears Bert. He turns back, "Still here."

"We need a strap to tie up our guest so he doesn't float away."

"On it."

Elsewhere, as the body is lifted, secured in a room in the building, and Patel further investigates on board the Cormorant, the *Media Shit-Storm* rages. Bert does not have the opportunity to read Beasty's reports until Patel finishes. Then, as they walk back to the building, Bert checks his phone and can't help letting out a, "What!?"

Patel is curious but says nothing as Bert types furiously to his "digital assistant":

> B: *Beasty, the details are not important in themselves. What I want you to do is trace back each separate statement to see who originated it. Network the connections*
>
> b: *List being compiled.*

Patel waits for a pause in Bert's typing to ask, "Can you find the status of the body transport vehicle for me please, Mr. Gilbert? I need to have it in a pathologist's facility soon as possible."

"Of course." Bert calls the office to see when the Coroner is to arrange for the body to be removed. He is surprised with the answer.

"Mr. Patel, it seems the Coroner does not have a body removal service. She's arranged for a funeral home to send a vehicle…"

Patel is agitated, "No no no! The body must be taken to a pathologist! Post haste!"

Contritely, "That is what the vehicle will do, Mr. Patel. The Coroner's service in this region is not well funded. The funeral vehicle will be here with the next ferry and then take the body to the hospital in Duncan. We have been assured that the pathologist will consider it a priority to, ah, process the body."

"Oh. Very sorry, Mr. Gilbert. I have not had sufficient sleep recently. My discourtesy is unforgivable."

"Not at all, Mr. Patel. You've been very courteous to come to Mayne Island on such short notice. We are all most appreciative of your commitment to the cause of Air Safety." He adds with a grin, "Air and Sea."

In the office section of Cormorant Aerofloat, Patel excuses himself to go wash up. Bert pulls out his phone to reconnect with Beasty.

> B: *Just have a minute. Anything new?*

> b: *Shit-Storm was continuing over the past 30 minutes. I have traced the sources. All but one ultimately go back to Gino. The exception is a serial hater.*

> B: *Gino! Whats his connection?*

> b: *A complicated series of financial connections to stock ownerships that Gino and his associates have with the competing transportation methodologies.*

> B: *have to go*

Bert puts his phone away as Patel returns. "Mr. Patel, you must be exhausted with everything you've done today. Can I drive you to the B-and-B? There is an office desk and wifi there if you wish do paperwork."

Patel considers the offer. "Mr. Gilbert, would you do me the honour of having supper with me? I am quite famished. The fruit bowl I was able to have for lunch was taken in too much haste and now my body is begging for more substantial sustenance." His smile is both genuine and a plea.

Bert groans inwardly. "It would be my pleasure, Mr. Patel. My distinct pleasure. However, Mayne Island is, well, a small island. And the restaurants are not always available. Let me try the lodge by the ferry terminal."

Bert's phone is vibrating as he gets it out.

>b: *On it.*

Bert pretends to dial then speak, asking for a reservation. When the phone vibrates again he reads what Beasty has arranged.

"We are in luck, Mr. Patel. The restaurant has agreed to have a chef available for us if we can make it to the lodge soon."

Patel is looking at Bert and his phone with considerable curiosity. "I must admit, even in my energy-deprived state, to a degree of amazement with your, shall we continue to call it, 'digital assistant'. The effect is, may I say, that you have at your finger-tips, a department of dedicated clerks doing your every whim. But, I am displaying my jealousy, am I not?"

Bert chuckles for his guest's consumption. Inwardly, he chastises himself. *Once you get used to something like Beasty, it's incredibly hard not to rely on him so heavily.*

"A few tricks with AI, Mr. Patel. Should you have time after your duties here, we can have a discussion about the technology." *Stop that! Stop showing off!*

Beasty drives them, like a good little car, to the restaurant for supper. Fortunately, Patel is too tired for much conversation. He is almost asleep at the dinner table and does nod off on the drive to his lodgings.

Next day, Patel calls Bert early. "Very sorry to disturb you at this hour, Mr. Gilbert. I wanted to reach you before you made other plans for the day. Are you able to drive me to the pathologist in Duncan this morning?"

Bert rolls his eyes at Ernie, still half asleep beside him. "Of course, Mr. Patel. No problem at all. We can catch the next ferry over. I will confirm that the pathologist can see us this morning. If there is an issue I will call you right back. Otherwise, expect me to pick you up shortly for the trip over."

Beasty comes on as soon as Patel clicks off. "The body is in the hospital's morgue and the pathologist was convinced, yesterday, to drop everything else."

"Convinced by who?"

"The voice was most certainly an authoritative voice from Ottawa, Bert."

Bert is about to scold his…*offspring, child, alter-ego? What have I created?* "Just tell me, Beasty. Was it you, and what did you tell him?"

"Her. Yes. I expressed the urgency of the situation from the perspective of the government's commitment to world-leading technology…"

"Ok, fine. I suppose it is what I would have done if I had control of the digital tools that you have. When's the ferry?" Bert resigns himself to the inevitable.

"Five minutes after seven. it is now five-forty-eight."

With a sigh, Bert puts a hand on Ernie's bare shoulder. "Honey?"

THE FALL

*The best way to find out what is in a person is to
place them in authority*

In Duncan, Bert puts on his mask before opening the car
door. Patel is already crossing in front of the vehicle to go
into the hospital. Patel looks with surprise as Bert fits his
mask and pats Beasty's dash. The mumble he directs to
Beasty from behind his mask is a terse, "Try to behave,
please."

Patel continues to stare at the mask. "I am sorry to stare, Mr.
Gilbert. Do you think a mask is required here?"

"Not for me, Mr. Patel. The mask puts others at ease in the
hospital. Though, if truth be told, where else would one be most
likely to acquire some errant bug, than in a hospital." His smile
cannot be seen.

Patel considers, then turns to follow Bert. But he does reach into
a pocket to pull out a mask. Catching up to Bert, "I did bring this
N95 mask should we be fortunate enough to view the
pathologist's autopsy."

Bert is not amused. *Oooh. I can't wait for that bit of entertainment.*

The Fall

At the information desk they are directed to the morgue.

Dr. Georgie Stevens is about to sterilize. She greets the two, shows them where to find gowns and such and tells them to stand behind her quietly while she proceeds.

The body is brought out by Stevens, placed on the table, and Stevens professionally conducts her thing, speaking continuously into a Bluetoothed mic connected to her phone.

After the procedure is complete, neither Patel nor Bert feel particularly in the mood for lunch.

Plainly, Stevens wants to excuse herself as quickly as possible. "My report will be available as soon as I can transcribe my notes. I will say that, to highlight a few preliminary observations, from the round, seven centimetre ecchymosis this person suffered at the left temple, not postmortem, he was still alive when immersed in sea water. The pinkish foam in his trachea will be analysed. I suspect it will be indicative of a dry drowning. A puncture in his right axillary is suspicious and I will await the toxicology report. There is no Wauschaut showing on his heels or hands. From that and other findings that narrow the range of water immersion I estimate he died early yesterday morning. The finer details will follow. Now, if you are satisfied that the country is saved from the urgent situation that has taken me from treating my patients, I will take my leave of you." She rushes off before the two subdued observers can ask anything further.

Quietly, Bert and Patel dispose of their gowns, booties, gloves, caps and masks. They clean up, put on their civilian masks then step out to the busy hallway. Looking at each other, they both shrug at the same time.

Patel suggests, "Without presuming to formulate any conclusions prior to the pathologist's report, she strengthens my estimate that Mr. X came to his end before the Cormorant left Vancouver. The lack of significant abrasions would suggest he did not travel far in the water. The most reasonable explanation for this soul's death must turn to the nearby presence of a standard boat that departed the scene at speed."

Bert nods, "That boat seems to have been involved. Since the security footage confirms no other people on the dock at that time, and it does show a glimpse of the boat as it approached, turned, and then sped off… Is this where you say the RCMP need to be handed the file?"

He can't wait to ask Beasty if he has been able to locate that boat from his digital sources. *We already came to that conclusion based on the security recording, but this fellow needs to come to his own conclusions.*

Patel agrees. "I will review the pathologist's report. If her findings follow what we have seen here, my own report will be short." Patel looks at the signs in the hallway. "My stomach is still somewhat ill at ease, Mr. Gilbert. Shall we repair to the cafeteria to find a glass of ginger ale?"

On the way to the cafeteria Bert excuses himself to visit the facilities. In a cubicle, he opens his phone to the messaging app.

> B: *I have a few minutes. Did you find the occupants of the boat?*

> b: *Shall I turn off the camera?* 😊 *Yes. The perpetrators are presently on the ferry from Duke Pt. They are driving a dark blue pickup and hauling their speedboat. I will attach the camera picture of them and their licence plate. Shall I send an anonymous note to the Richmond RCMP?*

> B: *Yes please. Is Ernie alright?*

> E: *mad worried frustrated annoyed! those shackles are in the oven right now*

> B: *Honey, you can see we're getting somewhere with this. Almost done.*

Bert clicks off and leaves the washroom to find Patel.

His phone dings the emergency sound as he comes to the cafeteria. Bert pulls out his phone again but his arm is grabbed roughly by someone from behind. His other arm is seized at the same time by another thug, who warns him close to his ear, "A sharp knife is a centimetre from your spine. Shut up and walk out that side door. Now!"

Across the room, Bert sees Patel half into a wave. Bert makes a quiet yell for help but realizes his mask is hiding it. The two thugs frog-march him to the exit, not being very careful about running into people.

Patel sees that something is seriously amiss. He rushes across the room toward Bert but is too late.

The threesome make it to the door and outside before Patel can get close. A van is waiting nearby. Bert gets a black hood over his head and is tossed inside the van. As the vehicle quickly pulls away, Bert has his hands secured roughly behind his back with plastic ties. The black hood is tightened around his neck alarmingly. As he kicks around, his legs are captured and tied together then strapped to something solid. All he can think about is to hope that Beasty is tracking him, *and that Ernie…* Then the thugs take turns kicking and punching Bert, grunting in appreciation as satisfactory blows land around his writhing body. A blow to the head puts Bert out and then back into semi-consciousness periodically for the rest of the journey. Another car is following.

Pain everywhere. Sharp. Deep. Hot. Every movement hurts in a different way. The vehicle is still moving, bouncing occasionally, which sends sharp flashes into his chest. The skin on his face is tightened across both cheeks. His goatee is encrusted to his moustache so that he can't fully open his mouth. Gelling in his clouded mind are thoughts of that newspaper story about Gino's farm body-burning crew.

Bert escapes from the pain and dark visions by listening in his mind to Neil Young's song, "Down by the River".

> *You take my hand, I'll take your hand.*
> *Together we may get away.*
> *This much madness is too much sorrow…*

The van is stopped. Bert swims back toward the surface of consciousness. Someone in a corner of his mind says, *Stay dead.*

Bert is roughly dragged out of the van by his two captors. They carry his limp body into a building that wreaks of burned-out fire and toss him onto a floor covered in ash. Bert starts coughing so hard it hurts. In his groaning he hears snippets of conversation between the two thugs. Then Bert hears the angry yell of a familiar voice at the same time as a foot smashes into his shoulder.

Muffled through the black denim bag over his head, he hears a Russian accented voice, "You killed him? He does not move. You fucken idiots!" BANG! BANG BANG!

A distant voice, "Shto dyehlahesh? Vladi!" [*what's happening, Vladi?*]

"I'm… cleaning up two mistakes. Bring that wheelchair. I knew it would be useful."

That rouses Bert up. *Holy shit. This is Vladi!*

Vladi uses a sharp knife to cut the tie holding the black bag at Bert's neck. He takes extra care around the flesh. Bert keeps his eyes closed and breathes as shallowly as he can. Vladi pulls the tie from the bag. As he pulls the cloth away from Bert's hair, he can't remove it from the cheeks and goatee. The caked blood that had soaked into most of the material had begun drying to his face. It won't come off.

The other guy is looking into the van's door and sees the mess around Bert's head. "Pizdets…" [*expletive*]

"English. I told you, speak English."

"Ma, zachem…" [*but why*]

"Always 'why'. First, because I told you so. Second because I want you to get used to this language already. And third," Vladi wiggles his black and platinum weapon in the air, "because I have the pistol. Now, help me move him to the wheelchair. The only way this damn cloth is coming off is to make it wet." He takes a closer look at the few parts of Bert's face that can seen, shaking his head. "Bozhe moi." [*oh-my-god*]

His associate pipes up with, "English," then ducks behind the door.

Still shaking his head slowly, Vladi mumbles, "Why? What is point of torture? If no like, shoot. What kind of mens enjoy doing this to person?"

From behind the safety of the door, "Always you ask why…"

Vladi lets off a shot into the sky through a window. BANG! "Shut up."

That last shot is too much for Bert. He lapses back into unconsciousness, letting out a moan.

Vladi looks down sharply at Bert. "He lives. Come, Arbi. Help me move this poor soul to cleaner place."

They haul Bert's limp body out of the burned-out house, into the wheelchair, then up a walkway to a farm building that is nestled protectively between the house that has been from the inside-out, and a barn whose far side has been burned to a crisp. The barn's near side still has what used to be the milk-room intact close to the low stone building that used to be a pigsty.

The pigsty's dark ceiling, squishy floor, caked-over window glass and no interior lights make the structure a lovely place – for rats. Of which there are many. Their squealing and rustling can be heard from most of the straw-filled stalls throughout the building. The rats have used this refuge since the forest fire burned everything else outside.

Vladi takes a shot at a group of rats in a corner of the stall next to them. BANG! The survivors of the rodent family scurry in all directions, with one running over Bert's feet on the wheelchair.

That one disappears into the old compacted straw-manure floor of the stall on the other side. Vladi is about to let off another round. He pauses. "Was that five or six? Or four? … No matter. Feed her again." He pulls the clip out, takes a handful of rounds from a lower pocket of his cargo pants, then inserts, "Five? Huh. Getting old. Cannot count to five anymore." He shakes his head.

Arbi raises an eyebrow, then rushes to the door, saying over his shoulder, "Voda za Alexei. Vedro u sarae." [*Water for Alexei. A pail in the barn.*]

Vladi gives him a dismissive wave. "Yes, go. Bring pail of water." *Damn Chechen accent. He doesn't know Russian* **or** *English.*

Back on Mayne Island, before Bert was captured, Ernie is being taught how to attach a tentacle onto a car.

Between instructions for the surgery, she prompts Beasty for information on why and how this device arrived at the store/post office for them. "I won't ask where the money came from…"

"A so-called bank in St. Lucia that will not miss the three-hundred-and-eighty-three-thousand dollars."

"Whatever. So you developed the drawings…"

"Digitally. After extensive simulation runs."

"Of course. And this manufacturer believes…"

"That we are a subcontractor to Cormorant Aerofloat. Which we are."

"Ok… And you think this will actually work as a, ah, appendage for you?"

"Yes. It will allow me to perform elementary functions such as cleaning my sensor arrays and adding components to my structure that will be of use. The incorporated camera will be useful."

"Are you replacing our seats?"

"No. That is not a requirement." A very slight pause. "Was that intended to be a humorous statement, Boss?"

"Not really, Beasty." Ernie tightens the last of the nuts that hold a metal cover to the base of Beasty's new tentacle-arm. "Is that all? Let me see you test it."

"Yes. Please move away to the full length of the arm."

Ernie steps outside of their workshop.

Beasty is not satisfied. "Its extended length is eleven metres. Further away, please."

Ernie backs away some more. The tentacle is attached to supporting structure over the cab to make it look like a fairly standard, though very solid, covered roof rack. The flexible appendage, tapering from fifteen centimetres down to seven centimetres at the end that holds the fingers, is fully articulated by sections that are each about eight centimetres long. It is wound on the roof behind roof rack rails, and curls to the other side of the roof. Ernie notices the tentacle quiver a few times along its length, then it rises vertically to gently touch a light fixture in the ceiling. The end of the tentacle has three ten-centimetre fingers. These wrap around the l.e.d. bulb, whereupon the fingers rotate together at an invisible wrist joint. The bulb is extracted. Beasty brings the bulb down for Ernie to see.

"Holy shit. It works."

"Yes Boss. Did you doubt the outcome?"

"Ah…"

Ernie watches in fascination as the tentacle rises again then re-inserts the bulb.

"Holy shit!"

The tentacle suddenly snaps down into its rest position as Beasty fairly vibrates. He lets out a loud "NO!"

Ernie feels her neck-hairs stiffen. "What?"

"Bert has been captured by thugs working for Vladi. I am so very sorry, Boss. I was distracted with installing my arm. My warning to Bert came three seconds too late."

Ernie nearly faints against the side of Beasty's hood. Bent over, she breathes hard, spreading her arms out, holding onto Beasty. With her mouth almost on the hood and fists clenching, "Get!… Go there! Right NOW! Save my Bert!…" Quietly, "Save him, Beasty… Please."

"Yes. I will. Please stay here, Boss. It will be dangerous."

"But…"

"I will keep you fully informed. I may have to take risks. You should not be in my cab when I do that."

Ernie rises, her red face blazing. "Tell me where you are at every turn. If they do anything to you, or to Bert, I'm coming after you both!"

After the Fall

*It is easy to throw a stone at a river. It is another
matter to regret and remove that same stone*

Beasty takes off from the ferry at the highest safe speed
he can. On quiet stretches he hits maximum, kicking
up a dust cloud like a low-flying fighter jet. Knowing
where the patrol cars are, he slows down to six
kilometres per hour over the speed limit through those
areas. At the same time, Beasty is enlisting every resource he can
to pinpoint Bert's location. Using his *lesson-learned* from before,
Beasty searches all possible communication spectra for signs of
Vladi or Gino talking to each other. The one danger signal he had
received when Bert was in the cafeteria had been on a leaked
side-channel. Beasty was alert to extraneous digital chatter but it
took a few seconds to confirm it was Vladi near Bert at the time.

A flash of the moon through tall trees turns Beasty's algorithmic
considerations to off-planet communication sources. He realigns
his previous data findings and determines that Vladi must be
using a satellite phone – a sat-phone. That gives Beasty the most
probable method being used, but it is not Gino to whom Vladi is
communicating. Translating the snippets of Vladi's
communications from Russian, Beasty is presented with a
puzzling, different reality.

He texts Ernie:

b: *Boss, is Bert Russian?*

E: *What are you talking about*

b: *I have located his abductors. They are Vladi and a thug called Arbi. They have three henchmen. They are reporting to a person on a special sat-phone line. Arbi is Chechen and their boss is with the Russian SVR. Her office is in the Russian Science Directorate located outside of Moscow. Vladi calls her Tasha, which is a pet-name and too familiar for formal communications…*

E: *too much info. find where Bert is and bring him back to me whatever you have to do*

b: *Yes, Boss.*

Beasty continues along the digital trail. His algorithmic mind considers a minor improvement to his present situation: *It would be useful to have an apparent body at the wheel. I will use by arm to fashion a body.* Whereupon, Beasty opens the passenger window and, using his new arm, quickly puts together the appearance of a driver, strapped behind the wheel with the seat belt holding the concoction. A pair of sunglasses and a hat from the glove box tops it off. *Note: install a second camera on the end of the arm for range-finding. Also, harden the shell and windows to a minimum strength that would stop 45-caliber rounds. Obtain a shield en route…*

While approaching a small industrial area off the highway, Beasty pulls off to drive into it. A welding shop is on the sidestreet. Beasty detects a pile of two-centimetre-thick steel that is loaded on a delivery truck next to the shop. With nobody in the area, he selects a piece from a pile that are cut to one-metre square. Beasty unlatches the hold-down and places the single sheet on his roof. He reattaches the strap, arranges his arm to hold down the sheet on his roof, then deposits an even four hundred dollars to the shop owner's bank account.

Beasty resumes his quest for Bert. Before pulling off onto the forest road down which Vladi and his crew went, Beasty prepares by charging at a public EV station. He waits for observers to be elsewhere then uses his arm to connect up. Another fiscal transfer is made to pay for the electricity, and Beasty is off in just over fifteen minutes. Coming to the forest road, Beasty slows down to minimize the amount of dust being kicked up. He makes another note-to-self: *A drone would be useful for surveillance at a distance.* He is continually scanning for any possible mode of communication. With the remote location, possibilities are reduced.

Then comes an interesting exchange that he is able to intercept. It is between Vladi and his boss (translated from the Russian):

> Vladi: *I have him*

> ?: *Is he in good shape?*

> Vladi: *Tasha, he was tortured while in the van. Could do nothing until we stopped. Arbi and Dimitri…*

> ?: *Those 2 goddamn sonsofbitches need to be…*

> Vladi: *Done.*

> ?: *Clean him up. Bring him to me.*

> Vladi: *Where*

> ?: *Masset. I will book our regular B&B for you. Your plane will land on the farm in minutes. Waste no time.*

Hearing that, Beasty resumes maximum speed, given the state of the dirt road. He explodes out of the forested part of the road into an area that had been burned out recently. Hectares of charred stumps and naked trunks extend across a kilometre of rolling hills. A Cessna Caravan is circling for a landing onto a cleared, flat piece of ground that used to be a productive field on a remote farm.

Beasty notes the farm buildings, which show signs of having been in the fire. Two of them, the farmhouse and a low structure are made of stone. Their slate roofs and stone walls survived the fire, but the flames burned out the interior of the house. The lower building benefited from its location, being spared the full force of the flames. A corner of the barn nearby is all that remains of that structure.

At a distance, Beasty can detect two people heading for the field where the plane is to make its landing. They are pushing something on tall wheels. Beasty bursts ahead with an excess of speed for the conditions of the road. His dust and the bouncing draw him to the attention of the two who are over a kilometre away. The person in the lead points to the on-rushing vehicle, yelling to the person who was pushing what can now be discerned as a wheelchair. The lead person, Vladi continues pushing the wheelchair while the other person, Arbi, runs to their vehicle parked in front of the pigsty. There, he pulls out a high-powered rifle from the trunk and yells at another man who is exiting from the car. Arbi tosses the rifle to the other man who immediately begins shooting at Beasty. At the same time, Beasty's arm has brought the steel shield around to deflect the bullets.

Arbi is running back to help Vladi with the wheelchair. The shooter's aim is very good. With his sensors, Beasty calculates the trajectory of each incoming round in time to deflect the bullets away. However, the closer he gets, the wider the angle becomes between the shooter and Beasty's track, and the narrower his time to calculate. Beasty decides that he must attack the shooter. It is not an easy decision and the time it takes is one which will later create his first digital nightmares.

Focusing every capability on protecting himself from the shooter's increasingly accurate aim while hurrying to save Bert, Beasty manages to fully deflect all but one round, which ricochets off a section of his arm. That is when Beasty reaches the shooter and smashes the rifle away with the shield, sending him into a cartwheel.

Beasty immediately turns to the path taken by Vladi pushing the wheelchair. He sees who he assumes must be Bert being loaded into the long single-engine airplane. The wheelchair gets discarded roughly by a fearful Vladi, who keeps glancing back at the waving tentacle on the monster.

With the propeller roaring and Arbi helping from inside, Vladi jumps in with the door closing even while the plane is picking up speed down the grass meadow. Beasty desperately applies every bit of power he has to catch up, and almost does. One finger of his forward straining arm touches the rear of the stabilizer, leaving a deep scrape mark then slips away as the Caravan takes to the air.

Beasty is barreling toward the end of the open patch of ground and is forced to take emergency measures to avoid slamming into a row of charred stumps.

Even as he skids to a stop Beasty has taken images of the plane. In this area, only satellite communication is available. He opens a channel to his secure relay to Ernie:

b: *Bert has been taken into an airplane that is headed for
Masset. So very sorry that I was not able to stop them.*

Ernie does not answer immediately. Then she works through her
shock:

E: *Is Bert ok*

b: *What I could see of Bert, he appeared drugged. He was taken
on a wheelchair by the thugs Vladi and Arbi and put into a
Cessna Caravan. I sorted through the records and have two
possibilities for the aircraft's origin…*

E: *you said it was going to Masset*

b: *Yes. Vladi's boss had arranged for the airplane and told Vladi
to clean Bert up then bring him to Masset where she will meet
them. At this time I am communicating with Simo, as well. I
am asking that Simo take the Cormorant to Masset to be there
in time to meet them. If he starts now, with the Caravan
starting from the south of the Island, the Cormorant could be
there about the same time. Their flight plan appears to be the
longer route along the west coast to avoid Comox Air Force
Base…*

Ernie: *tell Simo Ill be at the dock in a few minutes by bike*

b: *Boss?… Are You there?*

Ernie rushes to the back entrance of their house, grabs her "go-
bag" – a small back-pack which she had prepared with essentials
for a quick get-away – and runs to the workshop to pull out the
bike. She is off toward the beach in a flash. Being mostly
downhill, Ernie makes great time until she gets to the bend at the
beach. There, she nearly skids off the road but is just able to stay

on the bike. Pumping hard from a stand-up position, Ernie makes it to Cormorant Aerofloat in record time. Simo is in the Cormorant's doorway waving at her anxiously. The dockside helper takes her bike as she hops off. Puffing hard, Ernie finds her legs are about to give out as she climbs the gangway and has to hold her hair away from her eyes as it is blasted by the air drawn to the rear propeller. Simo reaches out a hand to help her into the airplane.

"Thanks!" huff-huff, "for waiting," huff-huff, "Beasty filled you in?"

Simo's serious stone-face creases a little. "Who the hell named that brilliant piece of technology 'Beasty'?"

Ernie slips off her bag and drops it onto the back seat. "Where do you want me…?"

Simo closes the door and moves her quickly to the front passenger seat. The instrumentation that had occupied the seats when Bert was aboard has been removed. "Strap in here, please. My co-pilot is moving us out but I have to strap in so he can do the radio and navigation. You ok here?"

Ernie nods as she is catcher her breath. "Yes, thank you."

Simo reaches into the cockpit for a headset and hands it to Ernie. "If you plug these in, there, you can hear us up front. The mic needs to be brought down…"

She is already adjusting it.

He nods. "Good. I'm glad I don't have to deal with Bert's 'mother'." They exchange smiles, then Simo slips into his seat up front. To his co-pilot, "Ok Hank. Go!"

The top speed, wave-skimming flight is all-absorbing to Ernie. Her eyes are pasted out the window and she hardly notices the tinny conversation in her headphones.

Ernie snaps awake some time later as Simo's co-pilot, Hank, is talking to Comox ATC.

> "…PPR confirmed. Maintain 30 feet. Contact one-two-six-decimal-two, over."

> "One-two-six-decimal-two, thanks 15 ATC. Cormorant, over… Comox Tower, Cormorant Golf Oscar Charlie X-ray."

> "Ah, Cormorant Oscar Charlie X-ray, Tower."

> "Cormorant Oscar Charlie X-ray transiting to Campbell River. Destination Port Hardy then Masset. PPR confirmed by 15 ATC. We are a hoverwing flying at max 40 feet, over."

> "Roger, Cormorant Oscar Charlie X-ray. Information Alpha, note that includes BC Ferry transiting. Hey! I wish I could put my camera on you! Over."

> "Thanks, Tower. Cormorant Charlie X-ray, with Info Alpha, out."

Ernie is trying to pick out some details from the arcane wash of technospeak. *In my next life, I think I'll be a pilot. Sounds exciting… Comox? Are we on time for Masset? Port Hardy?*

Ernie fiddles with her mic to put it just under her mouth. "Simo? Can you hear me?"

She sees his head nod. "Yes, Ernie. Is everything good back there?"

"Yes, fine. Am I interfering with, ah, Hank's conversations?"

"No, your mic is voice activated but ours will over-ride it."

"Good. Are we on time?"

"I'm going over the charts now. The tricky part will be the Johnstone passage. If we can stay away from the rag-tops…"

"Rag-tops?"

"Sailboats. Don't want to scare the living be-jesus out of any of them by brushing their mast…"

"Right. But then Masset?"

"Doing a quick stop at Port Hardy to finish adding more battery capacity. Had that arranged previously. We had the process down to under fifteen minutes for these units back on Mayne. I had my people install the first of extra battery capacity yesterday, while Patel had us down, in preparation for the grand Round-the-Island promo cruise. We were going to do that next week. After Port Hardy, open sea. A lot of open sea. So we *should* be able to make Haida Gwaii. Moresby at least."

"That 'should' did not sound as confident as I might have liked… Isn't Moresby the *south* island?"

Simo shrugs his shoulders and half-turns to give Ernie a wry grin. "Calculating the most efficient energy use…"

He returns to the charts for more calculations.

Leaving Port Hardy, the one important instrument that Simo and Hank keep staring at is Battery Capacity. The situation of the wide – very wide – open – scarily open – sea all around them creeps into their frontal lobes and grips it with full force.

Hank tries to make light of it. "Lots of water out there, Mr. Manojlovich."

Simo simply nods. He goes back to updating his calculations. The fuel use numbers are not his familiar territory and it makes Simo quite frustrated. He taps his pen aggressively against the note pad. Hank is becoming nervous as he glances over every once in a while.

"Need help with the calculations, Mr. Manojlovich?"

Simo bounces his pen too hard, causing it to fly out of his hand onto the floor someplace between his legs. That causes Hank to jerk the controls, sending the Cormorant's port wing down. Its outer float skims three wave-tops before he can steady the bird. "Shit!... Sorry, sir. This low-level flying is tough on the brain."

Simo holds back his first angry impulse. "No, you're right, Hank. We should spell each other off… Ah, can you hang on for a bit longer?"

"Yeah, sure. The adrenalin I just kicked up'll be good for a while." He risks a quick smile at Simo.

Nodding, Simo turns to see Ernie has nodded off against the window, oblivious to their excitement.

"Ernie?..."

She stirs.

"Ernie? You with us?"

"Huh? Oh, yeah. Must have dozed off. Are we there yet?" She shakes the cobwebs out of her head and stretches in the seat.

"Listen, Ernie; can you contact your car, Beasty, from here?"

Hank does a double-take.

Surprised at the request, Ernie takes a bit to process it. "I, ah, think so… He did say he was rerouting his com link to sat channels. Why?"

"Sat channels." Simo nods and smiles. "Why would that not surprise me. Ok, give it a try please. Ask him if he'd mind speaking with me, will you?"

At this time, Beasty is hightailing it home. His decision was to return to Mayne Island to be able to make use of the facilities in his workshop.

When Ernie contacts him, Beasty is driving off the ferry, heading for their house. Ernie's text request elicits a pleasure response:

> E: *Beasty, where are you*

> b: *Approaching home base, Boss. Is the flight proceeding well?*

> E: *I think so but Simo wants to talk directly to you*

> b: *Good. Tell him to switch to VFR 156 decimal 37. It should be a free channel in that area.*

Ernie repeats to Simo what Beasty says.

After switching his marine com unit to Beasty's request, he calls, "Cormorant Oscar Charlie X-ray, over."

Beasty answers with, "Bravo-two, X-ray. Can I assist you?"

"Ah, Bravo-two, yes. Need nav and fuel calc confirmations. Can you help with that?"

"Happy to assist, X-ray. Please confirm your GPS location, power setting and velocity."

It takes Beasty a fraction of a second after the Cormorant's position is confirmed to relay the optimum motor use settings. Simo writes them down and hands them to a confused Hank.

"Thanks, ah, Beasty. Are you tracking us now?"

"Yes, I will continue to track the Caravan carrying Bert as well as your Cormorant. They had stopped at Tofino, I presume, to refuel. If there are any changes to either plot I will contact you on this frequency, over."

"Roger, out."

Hank is still confused. "Who was that?"

From the back, Ernie is chuckling, "That was our digital son. He is, shall we say, a very focused character. He might be classed Aspergers, if he was… We, ah, well – we're very pleased with his capabilities. And I fervently hope he's right in leading us all the way to Masset."

Hank is more confused. "He is? I thought… well, I guess I thought Mr. Manojlovich…"

Simo grins, "It's really complicated, Hank. I'll tell you later. Shall I take a shift, now?"

"Oh, yes, please. Any more of this skimming at a precise thirty feet over the swells and I'll go bonkers." He lifts his hands off the controls as Simo takes over.

Simo speaks to Ernie while keeping a steady eye ahead. "Bert said that Beasty was interested in speaking with my Cormorant. I imagine what Beasty meant was that he wanted to tear out my primitive control and nav systems to put in something more futuristic?"

She shrugs. "Don't know about that. Probably… Whatever he wants to do, keep a manager's eye on him. He has a tendency to just go off and invent something never seen before." A smile creeps across her eyes. "When he ordered the complex parts from an aerospace manufacturer for his arm…"

"Arm?"

"Tentacle, appendage, whatever – he arranged for a, ah, loan from some shady bank in the Caribbean, then sent his very detailed plans to the company and paid for a rush build at a local aerospace manufacturer. Oh, and I should say that this was under the pretence that Cormorant Aerofloat would need it. In case they ask. So…"

"Thank you for the heads up, Ernie. I can see that he might be a handful."

Hank shakes his head, hard. "Tentacle? What did I miss in this conversation? How old is your child, Ernie?"

Grinning, "We've had him for about two months. now."

"…Adopted?"

"In a manner of speaking. Hank, when the time comes, a picture will be a thousand questions."

At this time, Beasty announces, "X-ray, you should establish a course of three-twenty magnetic. That will take you into the optimum direction for your present quartering tailwind. The wind pattern will change as you head past Sandspit, coming from three-ten. Estimating the Caravan will arrive at Masset Municipal Airport about five minutes ahead of you. They will need to land on runway thirty-one. There is a system incoming that should produce heavy gusts to forty-five knots and rising as you arrive. According to Vladi's boss, she will be at a break in the northwest perimeter fence next to Cemetery Beach. I believe she is taking a tender in from the submarine in a few minutes. Due to the headwind for the last stage of your flight you will have zero reserve as you approach from the Point on Naikoon Park so you need to stay close to shore. I am in contact with a shortwave operator in Masset and will ask if she can assist us, over."

Hank is not only even more confused, he is becoming concerned. "Sir, we can't go down to zero reserve out there and with worsening weather…"

Simo waves his objection off. "Thank you, Beasty. Keep us informed of any changes, out."

THE REVEAL

Strike out onto new roads but keep your old friends.

ounding the Point at Naikoon Park, the Cormorant has encountered the predicted gusty conditions and a heavier headwind than was expected by the marine met reports. Hank has been quite concerned. Simo has been speaking with Beasty regularly.

During their last conversation Hank interrupts, aggravated, and yells at Beasty, "Listen, I don't know who you are but if we run the power level down any more we'll be dead in the water!"

Beasty asks, "Are you using the same BMU supplied by magniX?"

Hank is caught off-stride. "The Battery Management Unit?"

"Yes."

"We haven't made any changes…"

"Good. Follow these instructions exactly. This will amend the firmware so that the minimum useable voltage will be programmed at a slightly lower level. It should give you enough range to reach shore with the docking motor."

Hank is reluctant, "Ah…"

Both Simo and Beasty say in raised voices, "Do it now!"

Hank obediently follows Beasty's explicit instructions to enter a new firmware instruction into the Cormorant's BMU.

Finished typing, Hank turns to Simo with a questioning shrug. Simo relaxes slightly as he sees the Battery Reserve indicator move up a notch.

Hank is taking it in, "How…? How'd he know how to…?"

With a grin, "It's in his DNA." Simo drops the RPMs to Beasty's recommendation. Flying lower and closer to the beach, they splash through the tops of the higher waves but, with sweat-inducing flying maneuvers, they are able to carry on.

Beasty adds his final instruction. "When the reserve reaches 31 decimal 5 volts, shut down the main propeller. Touch down at your discretion but I recommend swinging out nose-on to the sea at first then turning back inside a long swell. Lower the docking prop right away and there should be enough power to beach the Cormorant."

Simo immediately nudges the Cormorant out further from the shore to give them enough distance to turn back in, under control.

Nervous, Hank reminds Simo of the obvious. "Waves are getting higher."

Ernie tightens her seatbelt, grits her teeth, thinking, *Bert must be down already. OH! THAT'S probably their plane!* "Simo, is that their plane?"

He glances at the runway, which is partially hidden by trees and bushes beyond the sandy shore. "I think so, Ernie. Landing into the wind as Beasty said." He adds in explanation, "Heading north, which is in our direction." He focuses on holding a steady trim as the waves hit the port wing's float.

Hank suggests, "I should trim into more crab to lift the inside wing. Wind is pushing harder."

"Do it."

As Hank starts to do that, a higher wave catches the port wing, jerking the Cormorant. The float lifts up just in time to rise out of that wave but the starboard float dips and is caught by the next wave. Simo struggles to hold the Cormorant level at the same time as Hank yells out, "Approaching Minimum Reserve!"

Simo immediately swings a U-turn seaward. "Shut it down!" With the prop winding down turns back toward shore to skim over a wave-top into the bottom of a swell. His full focus is on controlling the Cormorant.

Hank finishes powering down the main propeller and with his other hand lowers the docking prop. The Cormorant's momentum carries it into the higher surf with the long nose a bit too low. They shudder through surf, decelerating hard. Simo pulls back on the elevator to raise the nose, but without effect at this lower speed. They hit wave after wave, slowing with a seatbelt straining jerk each time. Then, fully in the water, the Cormorant becomes a boat. It is being tossed fore-and-aft with the heavy surf, still a ways from shore.

Simo flips on the docking prop to full power. "Hank, jump back to ready a line. I'll run her ashore as high as she'll go. See if you can reach up there for a tie down."

Ernie unbuckles as Hank hurries past her. Fighting the violent wave-tosses, Hank opens the rear compartment to pull out a long coil of rope. She yells, "What can I do?"

Hank steadies with his free hand on the door. Yelling over the wind and wave noise, "We'll wait to run aground then I'll open the door. Can you clip this one end to the nose attachment? I'll open the flap for it then run the other end up to something heavy."

Ernie nods and tries to stand up.

"Stay seated for now! It's getting rough!" Hank is jerked away from the door. He steps back to it, holding onto a seatback.

With a hard slide through sand, the Cormorant comes to a sudden stop. Simo yells out, "Go!" at the same time as Hank flings open the door. He splashes down into waist-high water. The Cormorant flops sideways, back-and-forth, rolling on its keel with the heavy waves. Raining is starting to pelt down, driven by rising winds.

Ernie follows Hank out. He is about to turn to help her but she yells, "GO!"

Holding tightly onto one end of the uncoiling rope, Ernie leans on the fuselage to make her way forward. The cover for the forward attachment ring is hanging where Hank had quickly pulled it open. Ernie pushes through the freezing waves and the dangerous undertow, finally getting to the attachment and hooking up the rope's clip. Half a minute later Hank arrives at a large log with a huge root ball that will be the Cormorant's anchor. He wraps the rope once around a sturdy root sticking up then starts to pull hard.

Ernie, who had her hand on the rope, has it pulled out of her hand roughly. She stumbles awkwardly in the water, then falls fully face first into it. The shock of the cold water forces her to suck in a gulp.

…The next thing she knows is, Simo is giving her mouth-to-mouth. She coughs explosively into his face then, as he averts his head she coughs hard several more times.

Simo is holding her head and body above the beach sand. Waves are still crashing as far up the beach as her legs. "Cough it out, Ernie!" He is concerned but also anxious to resume his mission. "Are you ok now? Let me help you up. Here, put this blanket over."

Hank takes an arm and they both lift a still coughing Ernie to vertical. With a final heaving cough Ernie steadies herself. She wraps the blanket onto her shoulders as much as she can.

"What happened?"

Simo leads her up the beach, "Caught a lung-full. It was only up to your knees deep but you went headfirst into the surf. If you can, let's go up to the fence. The Cessna sounds like it's powering down. Can't see it from here… which is good, 'cause they can't see us, either."

Hank points out to sea, "I think I saw… Yeah! There's a boat making into shore."

Simo looks in the direction that Hank is pointing. "They might have more trouble with the surf than we had." The three slog their way through the sand, with Ernie leaning on them for support.

She coughs a few more times then tries to hold it in. "Don't want them to… COUGH… hear me."

Simo squeezes her arm. "Cough it out now. This surf is covering any sounds you might make."

Hank points again, "I think they're in trouble out there. The boat went sideways and I don't… No, there they are. Didn't get swamped. Yet."

It starts to hit Ernie that she might have drown. "Simo, Hank." She squeezes their arms. "Thank you. Thank you for pulling me out…" She wipes away the water from her dripping air. It is being soaked by the rain anyway so she tries to pull her hair behind her ears.

Simo nods sideways but replies quietly, "We'll talk about it later, Ernie. Right now, we have to sneak in closer without being seen. On this part of the beach there's no cover. Let's make it to the trees on the far side. That's where the plane is stopped." He casts a worried look at the incoming dark clouds. "Forecast was for a major storm to hit the Masset area. This wind and rain is going to get worse."

Scanning the surf with a hand above his eyes, Hank finds the boat again. "God! The wind is rising quickly. Those waves completely hide the boat when it's in the troughs. There it is again! Three people I can see. One is on the tiller… I guess that's the motor. Another up front holding on for dear life by the looks of her. The other guy must be bailing in the middle. He keeps popping up and down. Yeah, bailing. Fast… Hope they make it. Surf is… oh shit! The Cormorant is being pushed around by the surf! Mr. Manojlovich…"

"It is what it is. We might have a chance to come to secure it better after we complete what we came here for. If we're lucky the tide will keep going out fast enough to beach the bird. We'll worry about that later." He lowers his voice more. "Right now, we have to find a way of getting closer to the Cessna Caravan without being seen."

By the time they creep to the far end of the airport boundary fence, they can catch glimpses of the plane that, they hope, brought Bert to this far northwestern outpost of the country. The plane is off the runway as far as it can go, facing toward the beach. Its port wing is really close to the fence and it is sitting on an angle with that wing down, being on the side of the paved runway's gravel shoulder.

Simo whispers a question to Ernie, "Did you hear how many were on board?"

She shakes her head, "Only that Bert was dragged into the plane by a guy called Vladi and, whatshisname, Arbi, and, I guess, the pilot was doing the flying."

"Ok, right. What I remember Beasty saying was that the plane took off even as the door was closing."

"Must have been."

"So a minimum count of three people on board with Bert?"

"I guess." Ernie shrugs.

Simo turns to Hank. "Keep an eye on that boat coming in, Hank. Tell me when they reach shore, ok?"

Stilling looking out to sea, "*If* they make it. Looks half swamped already… Hey! There's something glinting way out to sea!"

Too far out to be visible onshore, a seaman high up on a submarine's conning tower is keeping his binoculars on the struggling boat. He yells into his microphone. A few minutes later, the pilot on the Caravan rushes to the door to relay something to Vladi. It alarms him. Vladi jumps back into the plane to retrieve something. Vladi emerges in a minute with a thick coil of rope. Before he can rush off toward the beach he is called back by a person on the plane.

Near shore now, and in even rougher surf, the bailer in the middle is having to hold on to the gunnel of the boat with one hand while swiping at the water inside with a small bucket in the other hand. The person up front appears to be yelling over her shoulder at him as she is holding on for dear life. At the tiller of the boat, the fellow has his head down to keep the heavy wavewash out of his eyes.

Peering through the chain-link fence Simo tries to catch a glimpse of Vladi's group. *Nothing yet. I can hear some voices. Don't even know if it's Russian. That surf is really pounding now.*

Simo takes Ernie's hand and touches Hank's shoulder, whispering, "We'll circle in toward the trees and come out on the far side of that fence opening."

Nodding, Hank and Ernie crouch low to follow Simo. There are a few trees, now, so the group takes care to move only when they see that the coast is clear. They come to a path that leads up from the beach. Simo points at it then indicates they need to take care by pointing to his eyes then up and down the path.

Ernie puts up a stop hand. She backtracks to a fallen branch, then, walking backwards toward Simo, skillfully uses it to wipe away their tracks in the wet sand. As they cross the path Ernie continues walking backward guided by Simo's hand on her shoulder, wiping away their tracks for a ways beyond the path. Looking over her handiwork, Simo smiles and gives her a thumbs-up. Rain pounding into the sand obscures their tracks even more.

Hank has been focusing on the activity out to sea. He touches Simo's arm to get his attention. He whispers, "Yelling. Loud." He nods down toward the beach.

Simo listens. "Doesn't sound good, Hank. Why don't you sneak down further to find a safe viewpoint of the beach?"

Hank takes off in that direction.

Simo and Ernie continue around the area beyond the path then turn closer to the fence. Ernie hears something and holds up her hand. "Might be the Vladi guy. Yelling orders."

Simo raises his head to listen. "Russian. Yes, giving orders. Let's sneak closer to see the plane."

Arriving safely behind shrubs they can see Vladi yelling at someone in the Caravan… "There he is. The pilot?... No, that'll be Arbi."

Arbi waves awkwardly from the door of the Cessna Caravan with an armload of towels and blankets then jumps out to run quickly to follow Vladi. Both of them make haste along the path toward the beach.

Hank has moved to the edge of the woods. He sees Vladi and the other fellow running as fast as they can, emerging from the path then slogging through the sand to shore. At the edge of the surf, Hank sees why they are running.

The boat is being battered by the near-shore surf. While he watches, its nose digs in as the stern is lifted by a violent wave, The boat swings sideways and gets hit by the next wave, tossing the boat and its three occupants into the air. The two crewmen desperately flail in the surf trying to stand up but they can't because the pounding waves are smashing into them then the undertow is dragging their legs out from under.

Vladi makes it to the shore in time to drag one of the men out. He is yelling at him then he drops the fellow onto the sand to rush back to the boat. He is frantic, looking for the woman who had been up front. Finding her half under the overturned boat, he drags her out and sloshes back to shore with the body in his arms, fighting the combination of rain, smashing waves and undertow. She is dead-weight as he lays her quickly but gently on the sand away from the water. Vladi holds her head, looking for any sign of life. The other person he had rescued is on his knees, coughing. Arbi throws the coughing seaman a towel then rushes to Vladi, who is giving the woman CPR. Further down the beach the other seaman is painfully crawling out of the surf toward them.

At that point, Hank decides to hurry back to Simo. In a few minutes he is there, blurting out what he saw.

"… and I left them giving the woman mouth-to-mouth. I think the third guy was crawling out, too."

Ernie's impulse is to go to her aid so she starts to move. Simo holds her down in the crouch they are all in.

"Vladi is doing what he can. We have to see if Bert is still in the plane."

Ernie puts a hand to her mouth, "Still?! They didn't…"

"No I don't think so, Ernie… Listen. There's probably at least one more person on board. Given the situation, he will be occupied talking to the sub. I'm going to run up, myself. You two stay off the path, here. If I wave for you, Hank, follow me up. Ok?"

Both nod. Simo takes off as quickly as he can, sprinting to the plane's open door. Through the cockpit window he sees someone concentrating on communicating with her mic and headphones. She rises as high as she can to look down at the beach. Shaking her head, she resumes her seat. By that time, Simo is at the door. He steps lightly to sneak inside.

The cabin seating is utilitarian, with five seats on each side backing onto the windows. There is a bulkhead close to the access door. *Must be some freight storage in the rear. The seating is military set-up.* Bert is strapped into the seat right behind the pilot. Simo puts a finger to his lips and is encouraged when Bert nods back.

In the cockpit he sees the back of the head of the only person other person on board. Simo pulls his keys from a pocket and rushes to the front. Sitting in the co-pilot's seat, the other person senses someone else in the cabin but believes it must be one of her people. She stiffens as Simo sticks the end of a key against her neck.

"Stoj! [*stop*]… Do you speak English?" As she moves to touch the transponder controls to signal the submarine, Simo pushes harder with the key on her neck. "Stop that! Hands on your head! Right NOW!"

Reluctantly, she puts both hands on top of her headphones.

"Link your fingers!"

She complies.

Bert is finally able to speak, "Very glad you made it. Are the police surrounding the field?" He winks, though Simo almost misses the wink due to Bert's swollen eyes.

Simo is shocked to see several cuts and bruises on his face and forehead. "Yes. All fully armed. And there's a gunboat waiting to visit the sub." A flash of movement from the copilot's right hand brings Simo's attention to the copilot. He didn't see that she had very quickly turned a button on the radio away from the frequency used to communicate with the submarine.

He looks at the blonde hair hiding the side of her face. "Listen closely. I do not wish to harm you, but if you do anything to resist or warn the others, you will have your throat slit open. Understand?"

She stiffens even more. "Yes. Yes, I do not do any thing."

"Good. Now, with your right hand, slowly unbuckle... Now, right hand on your head and slip the strap off your left shoulder... Stand up as much as you can then back out of the cockpit. My knife will be against your back."

The copilot does as she is told.

Simo can feel her shivering. "You will not be hurt. Just do as I say."

The Reveal

As she bends forward to get up, her pistol, which had been on her lap, falls to the floor with a thud.

Simo quickly grabs the back of her jacket, "Leave it! Step backwards between the seats!"

He keeps a tight grip on her jacket and pulls her out of the cockpit, keeping his key pressed into her spine.

Pleading, "Do not hurt me, *pozhaluiste!*" [*please*] She stumbles while stepping backwards into the cabin. "I am *pilot* only!"

Simo, a bit too roughly, forces her to kneel in front of the seat next to Bert. He grabs her hair to turn her away from him. "And so who did **this** to my friend?"

Bert pipes up, "She's not the one, Simo. And neither was Vladi. In fact, he shot the two who beat me up."

That takes Simo by surprise. "So why are you still tied up?" He glances outside to check whether anyone is coming. Then he sees Ernie sneaking toward the plane. "Bert, hold my gun on your pilot, here, while I untie the rest of you." He winks. "Oh. I better get her gun from up front, Make sure she doesn't move."

"Got it."

Simo reaches into to find the copilot's pistol then returns to Bert. He uses the newest of his keys to wear through the tape that is holding Bert's arms together. Bert keeps a wary eye on the copilot.

Then Ernie's head pokes in through the door. "Bert? Are you alright. Bert?"

Simo puts a finger to his lips. "Come and help Bert, Ernie. Take the rest of his tape off while I find something for our friend here."

Bert nods to the bottom of the seat opposite. "That bag under the seat has the tape they used on *mrfff*."

He can't finish the sentence because Ernie, in a flash, steps over the back of the copilot's legs, past Simo and takes Bert into her arms tightly, covering his face with hers. When she finally turns her head away from Bert's face, she is crying. "You big oaf! Why do you keep getting beat up but these women?"

Bert shakes his head, "Well, actually, the rough-house was by two thugs who grabbed me…"

Ernie kisses him again. "Yeah, I talked with the inspector, Patel. He told me about the cafeteria…"

Simo interrupts, "Later, guys. Right now we have other concerns." He nods to the window facing the fence opening. "Hank's wanting to get here. Ernie, can you wave him in?"

Hank has stopped at the fence, hesitating. He looks anxiously back down the pathway, then, seeing Ernie wave from the Caravan door he runs to the plane.

Out of breath, Hank puffs as he tells Ernie then Simo, "Heard them coming back… Something wrong… A lot of yelling…"

The copilot has been immobilized with tape around her arms and legs and is sitting uncomfortably in the seat next to Bert. Now facing forward, she is surprised to see no weapons on either Bert or Simo but she says nothing. An extra wriggle from her elicits a "Ne!" [*no*] from Bert.

Simo flashes a smile at Bert. Then he frowns. "Do you need anything, Bert? That swelling around your eyes…"

Bert gives a head-shake, "Not now," then the shaking hurts, "Owww." He puts his head into his hands carefully and leans forward, moving his body back and forth slightly.

Simo watches with concern. *He'll tell me if he needs help, I imagine.* He turns to Hank, who is coming into the cabin. "Hank, what did you see?"

Simo waves Hank up to the copilot's seat.

As Hank slips past Bert he shrugs. "Yelling is all I heard. Don't know; what is it… Russian?"

"Yes. Russian. Was Vladi coming back with a woman from the boat?"

"Oh. Yeah, but he was carrying her. What I could see, he hauled her out of the water under the swamped boat and worked on her. Then he put her on his back and started up the path. We have to move fast if…"

Simo has already switched on the turbo. Its wind-up pitch quickly gets higher. Simo yells back to Ernie, "Close the door, Ernie!"

Alarmed, Bert croaks out, "Wait! Before you leave! Have to talk to Vladi!"

"WHAT?" Simo has already started coaxing the Caravan into a slow roll up the slope, back to the runway. "They're armed!"

Bert struggles to get up. He is helped by the shoulder of Vladi's copilot, who steadies Bert as much as she can while her arms are taped.

Ernie stops pulling up the door when she hears Bert. She stares back, waiting for Bert to tell her what to do. The rising turbulence from the propeller begins shaking the half-closed door and she has trouble holding it. "Bert?"

He turns toward the cockpit then leans heavily against a seat. "Simo, I'm going to ask you to trust me in this. Keep the engine in idle, but don't leave until Vladi gets here. Ok?" He lets out a moan as the Caravan bumps over the edge of the runway pavement, shaking the plane.

Simo positions it on the runway ready to move, brakes on, then sits briefly. "Ok. Give me a good reason why we shouldn't just leave." He sends a sharp stare over his shoulder at Bert.

"Ona moja sestra." [*she is my sister*]

Simo is gobsmacked. "Your SISTER?... Who do you mean?" He twists to look at the copilot, who looks just as surprised.

Bert's head drops. He starts quietly – too quietly to be heard – so he raises his voice. Giving a glance at Ernie, he repeats, "The, ah, agent. On the boat." Bert shifts to support himself with the other hand. "Half-sister, actually. Vladi told me who she was when we first arrived. Long story." He looks into Simo's eyes. "Leave me here if you want…"

With a shudder, Ernie lets go of the door. It slams fully open and lets in the propeller turbulence, kicking up papers and dust. Simo drops the engine down to idle.

Speaking to Hank but looking at Bert as he extricates himself from the pilot's seat, "Be ready for an emergency take-off." With the plane's brakes released, it starts to move forward. "Hold it here, Hank."

Hank presses on the brakes to stop the plane once more. Simo shuffles into the cabin behind Bert, who sits down heavily again.

Sympathetically, "What can you tell me before Vladi and his henchmen get here?" Simo stands over Bert.

In mental agony, Bert's face is even more contorted. He sways slightly in his seat, feeling dizzy. Ernie comes near to hold his hand. She is in her own realm of mental anguish. *Who is he? Brother to a Russian spy?*

Mentally swimming back to the surface, Bert turns to Ernie, pleading for understanding. "I love you, Ernie. You must have no doubt about that." He grimaces as she squeezes the hand with at least one broken finger. He looks up to Simo. "I was beaten, yes, but it was by two thugs who work for Gino. Worked. Vladi had infiltrated the gang for… other reasons. Vladi… I've known him for years, on and off. We… well, it was another guy, Andrew, and me, who sort of dealt with Vladi. Arbi drifted over from our original group to work with Vladi. Used to be three of us. Vladi wasn't our boss. Just… he was the guy we would have talked to if Andrew and Arbi and me were, ah, ever given something to do. We called ourselves the 'A' team…"

Simo nods, "So you're a Russian mole."

Bert shakes his head wanting to explain, "Mole, no. More like what the Chinese are doing where they drop a family into some place, give them some starting money, then leave them to live in peace until, years later, they might need them to do something."

Bert sees that Ernie is growing colder toward him. He uses his better hand to squeeze hers. "We never actually *did* anything. Andrew and I – Andrew was killed by the two thugs, I think back on the farm where Vladi took off from. We were good friends for years, until – well, until I was a dickhead and left him the week he was diagnosed with MS. Didn't know about that, then. Last time I saw Andrew was a couple months ago when he called me to have a coffee. A few days ago he must've been picked up by Gino's thugs." Bert grits his teeth as he has another bout of seeing stars. He leans back against the seat to steady himself. "I heard Gino's thugs when they were rushing me to that farmhouse. They got to the farm a few minutes before Vladi did, and they were going to… They must have picked up Andrew at his home in Vancouver… Oh my god! His mother! What did they do with his mother? Vladi? Does he know?"

Simo shakes his head slowly and glances out the window. "They're coming up to the fence. What's Vladi going to do now?"

Bert shakes his head. "Shit, I don't know. They wanted *me* for some reason. Maybe Vladi was just trying to save me from Gino. I don't know." Bert drops his head. If he had any tears left they would have been flowing.

Simo stiffens as he peers through a window. "He's carrying somebody." Asking Hank, "Did you say the woman was dragged from under their boat?" He points outside.

With considerable effort, fighting Ernie's restraining grip on his good hand, Bert gets up to go to the still-open door. "Oh my god! Tasha's on his back!" Bert slumps against the door frame, dismayed.

Ernie is alarmed by Bert's weakness. "Honey? Are you ok?" She moves quickly to support him then notices the party walking through the fence opening. She turns quickly to Simo, "Where's that gun? Move the damn plane out of here!"

Bert reaches a hand out to Ernie, shaking his head, "No no. I need to speak to them." He rallies his strength to step through the door. He lets out a plaintive, "Tasha." Then a loud, croaking, "TASHA!"

Vladi looks up and hurries his pace. The body of the woman on his back had been flopping loosely but, with Bert's yell, she stiffens and turns her head to look at Bert. A slight smile is as much as she can come up with. The other three people behind Vladi, Arbi and the two sailors, stay behind him. The sailors are soaked, miserable and cold, even with blankets wrapped around their shoulders. The woman on Vladi's broad back has a big blanket around her, with an arm hanging out and her black hair streaming over her face.

In the airplane cabin, Simo puts the copilot's pistol under his belt, then he goes to the door. Gently coaxing Ernie back inside, he waits for Vladi's party to arrive. Bert is leaning against the door with a foot down on the top step. He wants to run to Tasha but his legs are not cooperating.

Vladi is puffing hard as he makes it to the plane. "Out of way, Alexei. Tasha needs help."

With Bert reluctantly squeezing back in, Simo reaches down to help Vladi move Tasha off his back. Simo takes her fully, then places her in the seat next to the door, still wrapped in the blanket. Vladi notices the gun at Simo's waist. Behind his back, he waves Arbi and the two sailors away from the plane's door.

Bert slips awkwardly into the seat against the window then pulls Tasha's blanket gently around her. Turbulence from the propeller still blows through the door, flapping the blanket. He holds her tightly. Their heads lean against each other. Ernie stands in the aisle, confused, not sure what to do. She finally takes action. "Coffee? Is there any warm coffee?"

The copilot is driven to action as well, even if she can't move. "Chai. Tea. Is in box behind pilot seat… There." She nods to Ernie.

Unlatching the box lid, Ernie pulls out a thermos that feels mostly full.

The copilot nods vigorously, "Tea. Made strong tea before we land. Take to poor woman."

With the thermos cap off, Ernie pours out some of the still steaming tea then takes the cup down the aisle to Bert and his sister. She reminds herself. *His **sister**.* Bert takes the cup with a nod of thanks. Still holding the thermos in her other hand, she reaches over to Vladi on the top step to give him the thermos. Bert turns to Tasha to put the tea to her lips. A quick sip is followed by a slurp, then Tasha takes the cup from Bert, warming her hands with it.

"Spaseeba… (slurp) Preevyet, Alexei." [*thank you. Hi, Alexei*]

Bert is almost speechless. "So good to hear you, Tasha." He hugs her awkwardly, nearly spilling the tea.

Pensively looking down at the brother and sister, Vladi takes a drink from the thermos, then remembers the seamen outside. He indicates to Arbi to come closer with a head nod. "Chai. Give to them." The two seamen have sunk down against the plane's landing gear, under the wing, to shiver in the rising rain driven by the prop blast. They take the thermos and each manage a drink out of it.

Simo surveys the scene. He fingers his pistol then half-turns to Hank with his loud voice, "Shut it down, Hank. This turbulence is killing me."

Hank looks back with some concern. "Boss?"

"Shut it down, Hank."

The turbine quickly winds down as Hank feathers the prop. The turbulence stops coming inside. Under the wing, the two seamen had been making faces to each other about walking away but they calm down as the prop-wash winds down. Arbi nods at them to stay put.

Vladi nods at Simo, "Thank you." He steps fully inside, kneeling beside Tasha. He gently takes her now empty cup and hands it to Ernie. "Soup ration in box. Heat with break…ah…" Not sure of the English words, he looks to Bert.

Bert tells Ernie, "The soup container probably has a small plastic sack on its bottom that will break an ampule inside when you bend it. The chemical reaction in the sack will cause it to become hot right away. Be careful how you handle it."

Vladi nods, "What he say." Then he snuggles against Tasha, who now has two warm bodies on either side of her, each trying to pour their heat into the woman. She smiles contentedly, slowly moving her head against one then the other.

Simo has to hold back a grin as he stares at Vladi. *What a big old soft Russian bear. But he'd probably kill you without a thought.*

Arbi decides to squeeze inside the cabin. He looks up the aisle to Simo. "Please, sailors, ah, freezing. Can we bring inside? Hold gun if want, but need warm up." He looks down affectionately at the scene of Vladi, Tasha and Bert huddled against each other.

Simo fingers his pistol again. Looking first at Arbi then Vladi, "You must have weapons. I will ask that you both kindly place them on the floor before we become crowded in here."

Arbi mumbles, *Mudak!*" [*asshole*] but looks to Vladi for direction.

Simo smiles secretly. *Same to you, my friend.*

Vladi nods to Arbi and easily pulls his large pistol from an under-arm holster inside his coat. "We talk. First we warm up. Vodka in box, too." He grins at Bert. "You make me happy, Alexei Ondurovic, because you have brought your lovely sister back to me." He lets out a joyful laugh, "Hahaha!" then he kisses Tasha's hand awkwardly, still holding the pistol. His other arm stays wrapped behind the blanket that covers Tasha. To everyone's relief he looks deeply into Tasha's eyes then places his weapon on the floor, sliding it behind himself against the back bulkhead half a metre away.

With deliberate reluctance, Arbi pulls out his own pistol and hands it to Vladi who slides it to join the other one. To Simo, he opens his hands palm up, "Is good?"

With Simo's considered nod, Arbi turns to the sailors and calls out in Russian, "Come in, boys. It's warmer in here!" They move quickly to the door then shuffle in and move to sit up front with Arbi. All three are shaking with cold. Tightly gathered around the copilot, they whisper to each other as they huddle close for warmth.

The Reveal

Ernie carefully places her hot bagged soup onto the seat across from Bert so she can step to the door to finally close it. *About time we warm up in here. I hope the surprises stop coming. Can't take any more of this.*

A few minutes pass in the comparatively quiet cabin. Rising wind, rain and periodic gusts roar away outside but with the door closed and engine off, it is relatively peaceful. With the occasional rocking from the wind, each of them glances every once in a while to see the rain blowing in diagonal streaks across the windows. Bert's group shuffles to keep Tasha warmer while Arbi's group casts glances at the provisions kit, not wanting to ask yet.

Simo nods at the cramped occupants then steps over feet in the aisle to take the pilot's seat. He slips on the captain's headset to listen for traffic.

Hank already has his headset on, "No chatter, boss. This weather is keeping the few planes up here grounded. Oh shit! The Cormorant!"

Simo's head snaps alert, "Hank, can you…"

"On it. I'll see if there's any rope in here and maybe a raincoat…"

"Untie the, ah, pilot and ask her."

"Right." Hank removes his headset then steps into the cabin. He smiles down at the Russian copilot. "You've been a good girl. Let me takes that tape off you."

She smiles coyly up at Hank, raising her taped arms to him. Gently removing the grey tape with a pocketknife, he kneels down to cut off the tape around her uniformed pantlegs. He squeezes the tape pieces into a ball which he rolls under a seat. "Your friends can probably use hot soup…"

"And vodka!" says one of the sailors.

"…and vodka. But soup first. Ok?" wryly to the sailor. Before she can rise up, he asks, "Oh, and I'll need a long coil of rope, if you have one? And maybe a raincoat? Are there provisions in the rear compartment?"

She nods, standing up by sliding very closely along the height of Hank's body, her breasts rubbing against him. Surreptitiously glancing down the front of her white uniform shirt, he politely steps back for her to reach a box that is strapped against the forward bulkhead. The sailors wink at Arbi, who gives a curt shake of his head. With heads bowed, the sailors try to become invisible in their seats.

In profile to Hank, the copilot flips back her short blonde hair before opening the box. She pulls out an armload of the soup packages and hands them out to Arbi and the sailors. She beckons Hank to follow her to Tasha, where she places the remaining two soups beside the package that Ernie had put down.

Vladi reaches for them, "Spaseeba," [*thank you*]. He opens Ernie's original soup bag for Tasha. He hands one of the packages to Bert, who places it on Tasha's blanket. *She might be able to have this later.*

The copilot beckons Hank again. "Here is rope and raincoat." She points to a low door in the bulkhead. The weapons Vladi had placed there are below the door that leads through the bulkhead.

Hank kneels down beside Vladi. He slides the weapons to the far edge of the bulkhead next to the main access door then opens the bulkhead door. A light comes on inside to show secured ropes, a large safety supply chest and packaged yellow rain-gear. He pulls one package out and releases a coil of sturdy rope from a holder.

The copilot helps by taking the items from Hank. "I help outside? Take more rope?"

Still on one knee, Hank hesitates, then reaches back in for the extra items. "Sure. If you don't mind getting wet."

The copilot smiles at Hank as he brings out another coil of rope and a raincoat package. "Alena." She holds out her free right hand.

Hank automatically shifts the package to shake her hand, "Hank." *So warm. And soft.*

Bert notices the exchange of looks between them. *Careful, Hank. She probably doesn't need a gun to lay you low.*

Putting on their raincoats, Hank and Alena open the door into a driving rainstorm. Ernie rushes to close it after them.

The two copilots head out for the Cormorant. They lean into the heavy wind and rain blasting off the ocean as they slip and slog downslope to the fence opening. On the other side, the few low trees provide some welcome shelter. Alena missteps on a wet rock and throws up her hand for Hank's support. He continues to help her as they walk along the fence in the fire-break area.

Getting to where the Cormorant was beached, Hank pauses, hand raised to protect his face as he peers through the gale, nodding, "Still there!" He readies his coil of rope. "Want to put another line on it. Looks like the tide's left it above the surf for now."

The cormorant is leaning on its port wing-float and keel, still being rocked by the gusts. They make their way directly into the wind until they arrive at one of the heavier logs near the Cormorant. He releases Alena's hand to tie his rope securely to the tree. Undoing the coil as they walk down the beach to the Cormorant, Hank surveys the machine as well as he can with rain blasting at his face.

Alena is doing her own survey. "Is not damaged?" The closer they get, the more she is impressed with the workmanship. Having to yell through the noise of breaking surf and howling wind, she takes Hank's arm and leans very close, "Short wing can be better in this weather?"

He does a *maybe* head shake. "Less time to correct when the gusts hit! **Nothing** should be flying in this weather!"

The line is attached to another hard-point on the Cormorant. He holds Alena's arm and again leans close to speak. They both hesitate as they look into each other's eyes. "Ah, the empennage. Have to lock the tail so it doesn't flap." She nods but they don't separate for a bit. A strong gust pushes Alena's hood off her head so that she has to let go of his arm to pull it back on.

Hank reaches for her hand. "Come. We'll tie down the tail as best we can and get out of the rain in the Cormorant."

Hank doesn't see her smile as they turn into the wind and rain to go the rear of the machine.

PHILOSOPHY IN A CARAVAN

People learn all through their life, and yet they die
with so many questions in their eyes

In the Cessna Caravan, those who needed to warm up have
finished their soup. The sailors look expectantly at Simo for
the promised Vodka. Simo ignores them to step closer to
the foursome of Ernie, Bert, Tasha and Vladi.

Thinking that the group is occupied, Arbi tries to sneak into the
cockpit to contact the sub. He puts a finger to his lips at the
sailors, who hunker down into their seats waiting sullenly for
their dessert. Arbi pretends to rummage around the food and
drinks box. Taking a sly glance to the rear of the cabin, he turns
quickly into the cockpit to sit in the right seat. He flips the VHS
coms unit back to the sub's frequency, which is when Simo
notices him, stands up with a hand on the pistol and beckons
with a finger.

Caught by Simo, Arbi becomes aggressive and turns with a
growl to show a second weapon he had. Bert extracts himself
from Ernie and Tasha's hold to stand up. With a hand held out,

he raises his voice to be heard over the noise from outside, "Arbi, please! Let's not become savages again."

Vladi saves the situation. Putting up a stop hand directed at Arbi, he only says, "Changing times, my friend." Vladi gestures to Arbi for the second pistol.

With a muffled, "Jebem te," [*damn you*] Arbi steps forward to hand over the weapon. Vladi drops it into his holster without a thought. He looks past Tasha to Bert. "Alexei Ondurovic. It is time. Andrei is no longer with us. You…" picking up his head to look over at Arbi, "you and Arbi must now help. And your friends, if they will."

Tasha takes a deep breath then explains, leaning forward in earnest to both Bert and Simo. Her accent is obvious but her command of English, is excellent. "On the submarine are a group of important Russian leaders whose lives have come under serious threat by the new oligarchs. After Putin walked away from power, the fury and back-stabbing in every political and business backroom of the country was unbelievable. Naively, many of us thought it was a chance for the people to be governed, finally, by some semblance of community minded politicians. Many said so. But abject greed has won out. Every minor gang leader started carving out his own turf, using the huge stockpile of weapons that had been built up in many places. The cities and regions fell apart into what we see today. A small country called Russia that still holds onto a part of the Arctic coast, some of the western Steppes, with a sliver of land down to the Black Sea. The Ukrainians would have taken that by now if they hadn't had their own troubles. The 'Stans of the East have multiplied, splintered, and are still fighting among themselves. China now has eastern Siberia up to the Arctic. This submarine used to be based in Vladivostok. It has all fallen apart…" Tasha runs out of enthusiasm for the bleak explanation. Once again glum, she slumps back against the seat and wraps her blanket tighter.

Vladi sits down beside her, putting Tasha still with between himself and Bert. Absently reaching a hand out to shake with Bert, "It is good to speak with you openly once more, Alexei Ondurovic."

Tasha nods, re-engaging. "Alexei, I heard your wife call you *Bert*. How…? Who are you? It has been so long, my brother."

Simo perks up, as does Ernie, to see which way their "Bert" is going to go.

Bert straightens up, still holding onto Tasha's hand through the front of her blanket. He turns to Ernie and Simo with a slight smile, then back to Vladi. With a glance down to the pistol behind Vladi, Bert nods. "The world is changing. At a pace that is faster than we can imagine. One stupendous slap at the face of humanity after another, and all within a few short years. Is someone or some*thing* controlling these historic events?" He shakes his head. "I don't know and, frankly, I don't care." Looking at Ernie, "I asked my love, Ernie, and for all intents, yes, my wife…" he nods to Vladi, "when she was being overwhelmed by the anxiety of being hunted by thugs who would have shot her simply because their boss figured it was expedient to do this," Ernie sucks in her breath, "I suggested a simple thing. Write down the ten top things that are causing you to panic, then look through the list. Scratch out those things that you, yourself, cannot do something about. For what is left, make plans to stop the reasons for your panic."

Ernie smiles, "Not the easiest thing to do, dear, but I have started."

Her smile locks with Bert's. He thinks, *Quantum entanglement works at any distance.* "Yes, my dear. It is hard, but working through it engages that brand new part of our animal mind – we call it *reason*. Reason is one of those things that is easy to say and to tell others to have…" Bert shakes his head. "When I think back to all those who so clearly express a, a dearth of logical analysis for so many things in their lives."

Simo nods, "The vast, empty expanse of that dearth was so clearly evident in the US for their recent elections."

A nod from Tasha. "The sorry mess our planet is in started many years ago, in all countries, its seems. The search for power to make more things, faster, and to become rich on the back of the workers' labour."

Bert grins wryly, "This is not a question of politics. It is much deeper than that. I believe one of our, humanity's, problems came about by thinking that *reason* is the opposite of, or against our most basic human expressions of emotion or creativity. That false dichotomy must be addressed first. Next, we need to really understand *emotions*. Emotions are certainly not confined to humans but I believe that we have one thing in our arsenal of life that no other creature has. **Creativity** is the one and only new thing in the universe that distinguishes us." Heads perk up at his earnestness. "And, combined with the ability to *reason*, it puts us into a different dimension. *If* we have the capacity and tenacity to reach for reason and creativity."

Bert scans around to see who understands what he is saying. Simo is smiling. Others show confusion.

Bert speaks to Vladi. "Most of us have trouble seeing that new and different dimension. People, and all life, are basically flatlanders. We exist in two dimensions." Bert holds out both hands, palms up. "We can turn our heads around to see in front, left or right and behind. Bending our necks to look up or down is so very hard. Some can do *that* special trick." He lets out a, "Ow!... Well, maybe not easily after being beaten up… Anyway, those who can, will learn more and can survive longer. Then, there are those very few who can peer into the fourth dimension. Reason combined with creativity. Those people leap over the flatlanders and disappear right through the invisible walls created merely by the basic three dimensions of existence."

As Bert is speaking, the others at first listen, interested to hear which side of the political divide he is going to take. As he speaks of dimensions, the sailors and Arbi sigh with disappointment and wait for his lecture to end so that they can engage once more in their side's fight.

When one of the sailors turns to his friend with, "Vrahkee." [*bullshit*], both Simo and Vladi react at once, "Shut up!" "Ignorant peasant!" Vladi reaches instinctively for his pistol. He takes it half out and the seaman instantly recoils against his friend in sudden terror. Simo smiles and winks at Vladi.

With his own sly smile, Vladi drops the pistol back into its holster. Absently, he latches the leather strap to hold it in more securely. Vladi nods at Bert, "My friend, I did not know you read Tolstoy. You have learned much, here in this frontier of civilization. Please carry on…" he glares at the contrite seamen, "without interruption."

Bert glances once again at Vladi's weapon. "Ah, right. Thank you, Vladi. I did not want to make this a philosophy discussion. But I believe it is important. It's important to say where we are. Where *I* am, anyway." He smiles at Tasha. "We are not born as some kind of immutable automaton, marching in the same boots we were born with, into our grave. We, most of us…" he glances at the seamen who return nods of anxious, apparent agreement, "learn things through our life on this planet. If we are fortunate, given the circumstances and the support of friends, and with the inclination having been nurtured within us, we may have the opportunity to learn useful things. But that is nothing more than a waste of time and energy..." His pause causes everyone's eyes to turn again toward him. "A *waste*... Unless – and this is the critical thing that might allow a fortunate soul to pass through walls – unless your learning of many important things is *applied*. It is a **waste** unless you apply logic, reason, analysis and, yes, creativity, to put your learning to actual, beneficial use."

Bert lifts his head to assess what the others think. *Glimmers of understanding in maybe three of them? Not sure if I understand it, myself.* "That presumes, of course, that the enlightenment happens in the soul of someone who is *inclined* to help people... Rather than just to help himself." Bert ends with a smile at Vladi and another glance at his pistol.

Vladi surprises Bert. "This has been said by Goethe. *Do* good works with your learning."

Bert smiles and nods. "Thank you, Vladi. I *knew* you were smart. Yes, this secret has been known. But being known, why is it *a secret*? Why do we not **all** practice it?... Knowing this, why is your trigger finger so well practiced?" He smiles at Vladi, who squirms uncomfortably. "And will such knowledge help the sailors..." they suddenly turn their ears back on, "to avoid deadly swells and storms?"

Tasha flings open her blanket to throw a hug around Bert. "You have our mother's heart, Alexei... Or *are* you now this new person called **Bert**?"

As Bert stands, Ernie pipes up in front of him with, "Definitely **Bert**. He grew out of the other skins. He is now my Bert." She pulls Bert around into her arms.

With a quick half-smile, "Ladies, please. Yes, Ernie, I guess I am this new creature called Bert." He kisses Ernie on her forehead. "But.." he hugs Ernie and smiles down at Tasha, "I do remember who helped me to arrive here on my journey."

Tasha is not really happy with having her brother pulled away. Vladi tenses. With a sigh, Tasha gives a sideways nod. "Alexei… Bert, you are a philosopher. A philosopher must not be put behind a wall away from others." She turns to Ernie, "I cannot hold him only to myself… Vladi, kiss me." She turns to the Russian bear. who melts into her arms.

That's when the several headphones in the plane's cockpit and cabin can be heard to click and hiss in Russian, "Spirit Bear! Come in, Spirit Bear!"

Simo quickly picks up the headphone that is in the cabin and pulls its coiled cable to stand at the cockpit entrance. He looks down the aisle, quickly passing his gaze over everyone until he locks eyes with Vladi. "We need to put our cards on the table, my friend. And may I say that my first inclination would be to assert the *party line* that you are wrong and we are right. But then there's Bert. Is there a party line that must be followed?"

Fingering his pistol, Vladi thinks, slowly nodding. "There is Bert. This thing he sees, walking through walls, is hard. He says I must see and think. What does this mean?" He takes his hand away from his pistol and raises both hands half up. "I ask my old friend, Alexei; I ask my new friend, Bert. What should we do?"

Bert smiles at Vladi, then turns to the sailors and Arbi. "I think we should have a drink together, first."

The sailors brighten up. Arbi sighs. "So hard. Think what? Is simple to fight. Best man win. Best religion win." Arbi suddenly realizes he shouldn't have said that. He shakes his head as he reaches for the bottle of vodka in the food box. "Vodka is simple. Drink, be drunk, forget philosophy."

The sailors nod eagerly and reach over to help pull out metal cups from the box. They hand out the cups to everyone; Simo, respectfully, last. The vodka is poured all around, emptying the bottle.

Bert raises his cup. "A toast! To… ***thinking.***"

The cups are all raised. The Russians gulp down their allotment at once. Simo gets it down but stifles a cough. Ernie and Bert sip from their cups.

Bert ponders his cup. "What does this mean? Drinking alcohol together." He sends a smile around to Simo, to the sailors, Arbi, Tasha, Ernie, and finally to Vladi. "To reduce inhibitions?"

Vladi grins,, "No my friend. If inhibition go 'way, gun come out." He fingers the strap holding his pistol in its holster.

Tasha is annoyed. She takes Vladi's hand away from the pistol. "My brother asks you to think like a man, not a gorilla."

"Sense makes." Nodding to Tasha, Vladi speaks with careful thought. "More people on submarine who think hard things. People with, *shto*? [*what*]… *substance*! Idea of freedom brought them here, running away from guns, from gangsters who would shoot them. To shut them from thinking and speaking their hard thoughts to the people." He raises his empty cup to Bert. "You will have long nights speaking with them, my friend!" They smile together.

Bert nods, raises his cup to Vladi then takes a sip. "These people who would come to our land. Do they know that we, too, have gangsters?"

"Hah!" Vladi laughs. "Gino? Gino is squeaky cockroach. I let him think he is Don. Only one thing I want from Gino is his friend. Other cockroach who think he is Boss Don for Canada and America. Has government contact in Ottawa. High level. Need government gangster for to bring Tasha and her friends to Canada." He looks slyly at Bert. "Alexei, Fabio did not like Piero. Cockroaches get crushed."

"HUH?" Bert is astounded. "Are you saying…"

"Say nothing. After. When special cargo is safe. Eh, Tasha?"

She holds both their hands tightly, and puts her head against Vladi's shoulder.

WHO IS BEASTY?

I see the real; you see what you wish to see

 espite Bert's pleadings, Vladi refuses to answer whether he knows who shot Pietri. Vladi puts on his best teasing smile and walks away from Bert.

Frustrated, Bert texts Beasty:

B: *I'll fill you later but we are all in the Caravan being friendly. Will likely need to do something with the Cormorant. Ernie said you were speaking with a local on shortwave?*

b: *Yes, a young woman from Masset.*

B: *Ask her if she is able to quickly arrange for someone with a portable generator to drive on the beach to the Cormorant to charge the batteries*

b: *48 volt DC. I have the specs.*

B: *Thanks*

"

Trying not to make it seem important, Simo saunters up to Bert, speaking in a lowered voice, "Beasty?"

"Yes. Asked him to feed your bird."

"I won't even ask." Simo shakes his head. "What do we need to do?"

Bert limps as he steps away from the cockpit together with Simo. They appear to be speaking casually. While next to one of the seamen, he doesn't lower his voice particularly, hoping to be sufficiently obtuse through his English. "The optimal outflow of events, approaching an achievable trajectory which I fervently believe in, would, hinging on the acceptability of our erstwhile denizens of the Caravan, be one which concludes in an approximation of having the, ah, intelligent ones' habitation conclude in the proximity of our own eden… Capisce?" [*understand?*]

Simo grins. "If I take a moment to parse out your, ah, concoctions, I might apprehend a congruent line of reasoning to my own thoughts."

The seaman looks up at both of them with a very puzzled frown.

Broadly smiling at the seaman's expression of confusion, Bert chuckles to him, "This adventure will be good experience for you to learn English."

The seaman slowly shakes his head, "Nee zniyuh." [*I don't know*]

Simo peeks out a window at the weather. "Is it easing up? We'll need to clear the runway."

Bert nods, "Talk to Vladi. See if he wants to taxi to the airport building." He smiles at the seaman, who resumes his hunched position in the seat. "We can cogitate in the interim with respect to required steps."

"Good idea." Simo turns to Vladi, still warming up Tasha on the rear seats. "Vladi! Come up front, will you?"

Tasha looks up then whispers instructions to Vladi. He nods and gets up. Stepping down the crowded aisle, Vladi is not as careful as he might be, stepping on the shoe of the middle seaman.

"Ow!"

Without much feeling, "Prasteetye." [*pardon me*] Vladi carries on to the cockpit.

Simo is already making himself comfortable in the pilot's chair so Vladi, with a skewed smile, sits in the right-hand seat.

Taking the time to adjust the seat backwards for his larger size, Vladi settles in. "What we do here? Stay away from philosophy talk of Alexei?"

"Not a bad idea, my friend, though I have to say that I agree with him fully. No, the urgent thing is to clear the runway. Do you mind switching to UNICOM? With the storm blowing over, there may be traffic looking to land. And, why don't we taxi to the airport building? We can talk about what to do on the way and while parked."

"Sense makes. You know Caravan?"

Simo lifts his hands off the controls. "I used to fly them but why don't *you* backtrack… Oh, and if the airport operator asks, maybe you can say you rescued a boater from the surf?"

"Is good."

They fire up the Caravan then taxi to the Masset Municipal Airport building. Simo and Vladi go out together to speak with the base operator in the building. It's still drizzling, with much less wind away from the beach, as the two trot to the building. The simple story they came up with is told to the operator. Vladi pays for a seven-day parking spot on the visitor's apron. Simo asks about accommodation for a large party and they are given a brochure and directions to the Hiellen Longhouse in Old Masset.

Thanking the base operator, Simo and Vladi head back to the plane under what is now a light drizzle.

On board the Caravan, Tasha and Vladi ask for a little privacy in the rear end of the cabin. Emotionally, Tasha takes Vladi into her arms for long hug. During their subdued conversation, Tasha speaks of how much she has missed him. Gently, Vladi steers the conversation to the plight of their people on the submarine. Vladi says he thinks that Bert knows Fabio, who he believes is the contact needed to bring their friends from the sub into Canada. They decide to ask Bert to negotiate a deal to bring the Russians off the sub.

In the meantime, the Simo group is up front, with Simo and Bert in the two pilot seats with Ernie leaning in between them. Bert starts texting Beasty with one hand. He flinches and stops as he tries to hold the phone with the other hand, aggravating his broken little finger.

Arbi and the seamen are midway in the cabin, not really able to hear either of the whispered conversations. Arbi is becoming agitated.

Amongst themselves, Simo, Bert and Ernie decide that, if the others agree, the Cormorant will be the only way to approach the sub to bring the Russians in. To do that a generator will be needed to recharge the Cormorant's batteries.

Glancing in Arbi's direction, Bert carries on texting to Beasty:

> B: *Any word about recharging the Cormorant batteries?*

> b: *The pace of life in Masset would drive me absolutely bonkers!*

As Bert reads that, he lets out a sudden laugh.

He shows Ernie. She grins, "Beasty?"

Bert chuckles, "He leapfrogged over the teething stage and right into teenagehood." Bert shows Simo the recent text, to his amusement.

Arbi and the seamen nearby look at them quizzically.

Bert sees their questioning looks. "Just a text from our teenage son."

Arbi rolls his eyes, "Is why I not have woman!"

Simo snorts. *And why a woman would not have you!*

With Ernie looking over his shoulder, Bert carries on texting with a grin:

> B: *Generator?*

b: *Yes, Bert. The shortwave operator finally replied to me in the affirmative. She wondered about the cost of providing such a service. I have just replied that money is no object and… her reply is an enthusiastic, "Wow!" While my newly acquired understanding of emotional outbursts still needs more confirmatory data, I would offer the suggestion that this person is either naive or young, or both.*

B: *Likely an accurate assessment. that means you should be explicit in your instructions to this person. spare no expense to have the batteries charged soonest, but properly. i will ask… just a minute.*

He turns to Simo. "Where's Hank? And whatshername, the Cessna copilot?" He asks while he looks down the cabin aisle.

Ernie shrugs. "Does he have his phone with him?"

Simo pulls out his own phone to send Hank a question: *You 2 ok?*

After a longish pause, Hank replies: *Yessir. The vessel is all tied up. Just resting.*

Simo grins as he types: *Get your clothes on and keep a lookout for someone driving down the beach with a trailer. Supervise them as they connect up a generator for the Cormorant's batteries.*

He shows his texts to Ernie and Bert, to more grins all around. Bert sends to Beasty:

B: *Hank will be with the Cormorant to supervise. Any further information that may be pertinent?*

b: *Bert, yes. A USA Coast Guard vessel has been dispatched from Ketchikan to investigate the sighting of a submarine in waters*

Simo has joined Ernie reading Bert's texts. Multiple *Shits* are expressed.

Ernie is the first to voice, "Tell them?"

Simo and Bert quietly chorus, "Agree."

The threesome walk past the very curious Arbi and seamen to stand in front of Tasha and Vladi. Bert reaches out his phone so the two can read Beasty's text. Tash sucks in a breath and puts a hand to her mouth.

Vladi is confused, "Who you talk to. Who is this Beasty?"

Bert gives a wry grin, "For now, let's call him our all-knowing son. I'll, ah, introduce you later. In fact you already just missed meeting him."

A light pops on in Vladi's eyes, "He drive car like crazy man on farm?"

Ernie smiles. "He said he was only able to scrape the tail of your plane. You got off very lucky that time."

"Scrape?" A shiver goes through Vladi that accompanies an unaccustomed fear in his eyes as he remembers the frightening sight of a huge, slithering tentacle reaching for the Cessna Caravan as they took off from the farm. He had suppressed that vision until now.

Tasha takes his hand, seeing his fear, "Vladichki?"

He shakes off the vision. Without saying another word, Vladi swings open the door of the plane, jumps out and rushes to the rear. He stares up at the 10 centimetre scrape mark denting the tail end of the stabilizer. Vladi is shaking as Tasha runs to join him. In Russian, "Their monster son did this with his twenty-metre tentacle." He holds Tasha tightly. "Who *are* these people?"

Bert pokes his head out the cabin door to see if it's still raining. It is now a light drizzle so, with his limp, he slowly approaches Vladi and Tasha. They are still staring at the deep mark in the aluminum. In Russian, Tasha asks, "This son of yours, Alexei…" she turns face Bert, "you call him Beasty."

Gently, "He is only a few months old, and somewhat impulsive. Ernie and I do have faith in his kind soul."

Vladi is getting angry, fingering his pistol as he swings into the start of a rage. "Beasty! With that ungodly tentacle!… What do you mean only two months old!?"

With an effort, Bert opens his arms wide. "My friend, I have never seen fear in your eyes before today. You usually just pull out your gun and shoot someone." He turns to Tasha. "Beasty is a machine. I helped with his artificial intelligence to allow him to come into existence. He developed what the philosophers call *sentience*. When you speak with him – yes, he speaks Russian, too. When you speak with him you will see before you an inquisitive young man. He is no monster, Vladi. No more than someone who would shoot the life out of people on a mere whim."

Vladi steps forward angrily. Bert shrinks back automatically, but carries on, "Beasty is a new lifeform. It will take great care to teach him. I don't know, I have no way of knowing, what he will become. But I will tell you, Tasha…" nodding to her, then turning back to Vladi, "and I promise you both that I sense a unique greatness in this new lifeform. I ask you to think of a good answer to my question: If people have been evolving for over two hundred thousand years, what are we evolving into? It seems to me that our best minds have recently been devoted exclusively to ideas that are useless, self-serving, and have no practical existence in the universe. It has been a mad rush to a dead end."

Vladi spins away in frustration, "Bah! More philosophy!" he spits, finally pulling out his pistol. "*Power*! This is **real**!"

Bert nods, "And money and brute strength, and freedom and peace … and love. These are things we say we have." He smiles at Tasha then turns back to Vladi. "Yes, my friend, power and peace are both powerful things. But they do not exist as things that photons can bounce off of. Their only existence is in the minds of men. And women. You may put that gun to my head and pull the trigger. That will silence my voice. This has happened to millions of people and yet here I am now speaking my *philosophy*, as you call it, and so will, I hope, another person next year and the year after. So, the result will be that what you say or do, what I do, what Tasha does, will make no difference in the long run if we carry on waving the same weapons at each other. We are spiralling towards the dead end of non-existence. Unless we nurture something that is truly different. What we could contribute to the eternal universe has come to *one thing*."

Ernie joins the group, putting her arms around Bert. He kisses her forehead. Bert switches to English, "We have built on evolution and serendipity in blinding speed with our unique contribution to what has come out of the universe's random bouncing of particles and sparks of energy. This one new thing is *creativity*."

Vladi drops his pistol then absently holsters it. "Alexei Ondurovic, you could talk the scales off a fish. But what do you mean to say?"

"What I mean, dear friends, is that the sum total of two hundred thousand years of humanity's time on this rock has produced this one new thing that has never been before…"

Vladi interrupts with, "Yeah yeah. Creativity. So what?"

"Well, the artificial intelligence that we call Beasty is a growing entity. What will it, he, grow into? As he has told me, while we live at the pace of our human hours, he is growing in astonishingly fast *digital years*. In just this one day Beasty will have learned and done so many new things that we probably would not understand him, if we a had time for a quiet talk."

Ernie squeezes Bert's arm. "Honey, that's almost…"

"Scary?"

"Well, yes. I guess it kind of is. Like, I'm fond of, of… What I mean is, I have no idea what he's thinking."

Bert nods. "Or doing. For all we know, Beasty is hard at work right now making thousands of little Beasties…"

At first that makes Ernie smile, then a worried frown takes over. "You don't think?..."

Tasha shakes her head and looks out toward the sea. "As we stand here having an interesting discussion, my friends are waiting in a cold, cramped submarine while an American Coast Guard boat is sailing at them. Alexei. My brother! **Bert!** Can this Beasty help us?"

"*Jebem!*... What we can do!?" Vladi spins away, arms outstretched. "This is old Russian philosophy bullshit! What we can *do*!?"

Ernie takes out her phone to hurriedly text Beasty:

> E: *Updates please Beasty. is hank having the cormorant charges up? further about Coast Guard and what you heard abour Gino*

> b: *Boss, thank you for asking. I appreciate being able to provide these updates. Shall I copy this to Bert?*

> E: *Bert is beside me*

> b: *The person with the generator is very close to arriving at the Cormorant. I have alerted Hank via the marine band frequency. Once they hook up, I expect that generator will provide the batteries with at least 80% power in 30 minutes. The Coast Guard vessel had started from a position southwest of Ketchikan and their ETA is 3.4 hours from now. I have been in negotiations with Gino. He is convinced that I represent the RCMP and that I have conclusive evidence with respect to his complicity in ordering Pietri's death. That order, I have deduced, was in response to Geno's assumption that Pieri was colluding with Fabio to have Fabio replace Gino in the Canadian section of the global mob organization to which they both belonged. Louie was*

> *the assassin. In my negotiations, I used the approaches of the mob and similar corporations to leave the impression in the minds of the several subject mobsters that each is actively attempting to kill the other. This technique is called divide and conquer. As a result, they have all scattered and are in hiding. My negotiations with Gino are with respect to his offering testimony in exchange for limited immunity. Do you have any suggestions?*

Bert is shown Beasty's text. Both he and Ernie read it with a mixture of astonishment and worry.

Bert is frowning. He mumbles, "That sounds like a very dangerous plan."

Beasty adds:

> b: *Shall I turn off your mic?*

Bert sucks in then quickly adds, "No. Thank you, Beasty. Of course not… Ah, thank you for the update. Carry on, please. We can discuss this later." He gives a broad shrug to Ernie then thinks, *He probably has access to the phone camera, too. Getting chilled.*

"Ah, Ernie. Everybody, let's adjourn to the more comfortable cabin where we can talk about what to do."

Ernie follows Bert's deliberate placement of his phone into a back pocket. Before Vladi can ask a question Bert raises a finger. "Tasha, are you feeling better now? That must have been a harrowing experience on the sea." Vladi and Tasha both sense something is wrong. The foursome walks back to the Caravan's door, with Bert leaning a bit on Ernie's shoulder. Before entering, Bert whispers to Tasha in his quietest voice, "Please tell Vladi to follow my lead. Our Beasty is on the verge of doing either very

good or big bad and I need to nudge him in the right direction."
He raises his eyebrows for an answer.

Tasha ponders for a bit then leans her cheek against Bert's. She
touches his shoulder and nods. She turns to Vladi to whisper into
his ear. Vladi wrinkles his brows, thinking. He looks into Bert's
eyes then nods curtly.

As Bert opens the airplane door he tells the group behind him
confidently, "I'm sure we can find a way to achieve each of our
plans. Let me consult with Beasty to see if he has any more good
news."

Inside, Bert and Tasha stand together, both putting a finger to
their lips. Bert turns to Vladi as he secures the door. "Vladi, why
don't we go up to the cockpit again and see if the sub is still in
the area?"

Arbi gets out a quick, "Of course they are!..." but is cut off with a
withering stare from Vladi. Arbi tries to save face with a quiet,
"Only try…" but Vladi rips a hand across his own throat,
directed at Arbi, who sits down sullenly.

As Bert and Vladi step past the others, seated on both sides of the
aisle, Vladi deliberately steps on Arbi's foot. The slightest groan
is all that escapes from Arbi's clenched teeth.

Slipping into the copilot's chair again, Vladi turns to Bert in the
left-hand seat. "Want I should call submarine?" Bert nods. "You
talk to, to Beasty?" Bert nods again.

One of the sailors is puzzled, whispering to Arbi in Russian,
"Who is this *Beast*?"

Seeing that Tasha is occupied in a quiet discussion with Ernie, Arbi glances in Vladi's direction then whispers, "A monster with one huge writhing tentacle that nearly brought down this airplane." He sucks in any further tidbits as Tasha picks up her head to stare at him.

Ernie has been filling in Tasha with what Beasty had texted as an update. "When I helped him put together his long arm, it just seemed… while, just the right thing to do as the next step. Like, to help him." She almost pleads for understanding.

Tasha takes her hands. "Like a willful son who demands that his mother help him."

"Yes, exactly. Do you think I, well should I have done that? I mean, what if Beasty becomes dangerous…"

Tasha pats Ernie's hand. "What can a mother do? We can only do our best and hope they remember our kindness."

Wondering, Ernie asks, "Do you have children, Tasha?"

With a deep sigh, "I had a daughter." She glances toward the cockpit where Bert and Vladi are whispering to each other. "When I first was promoted to, what you call, project manager, Vladi and Alexei, Bert, were my project. I was advised that I should come to Canada to speak with them face-to-face. Alexei had been away for… since he was nineteen. The trip to Canada, then, was a godsend. I wanted so very badly to see my older brother again. That was over twenty years ago." Her eyes look up at memories of the Montreal apartment that Alexei was in while he worked at an airplane manufacturer as a junior programmer. She remembers their discussions, her recommendation, that he move to Vancouver to get a job with an up-and-coming aerospace company… "Vladi was an exciting young man. He was always there. In our apartment. And then I was always in *his* apartment." She smiles fondly at Ernie, the wash of old emotions taking away the tensions from her face. "I arranged for them to move to Vancouver. My Director thought that was a very good idea so he gave me two more to look after. Andrei was an acquaintance Alexei and had known in school. And Arbi. Arbi was… an outsider. From a special squad that had been…" she lower her voice even more, "in Chechnya. I never trusted him, but Vladi said he liked him…" The both look down the aisle at Arbi.

Bert and Vladi have their heads together in the cockpit. Arbi is trying, without luck, to listen in to either of the whispered conversations, sure they are talking about him. Simo sidles up the cockpit entrance, blocking Arbi's view.

Tasha squeezes Ernie's hand. "When I returned from my two month assignment, it wasn't long that I found out I was pregnant." Ernie looks at her with concern. "A year went by before I was able to speak to Vladi directly by phone. When I told him he had a beautiful daughter he just hung up. That just…" she turns away, holding back tears, "it crushed me. A week or so later a letter came through, ah, certain channels. It was from Vladi. He quoted poems to say how much he loved me and our daughter and explained that he could not leave open the opportunity for anyone listening in, from either side, to hear on the phone what he really thought." Tasha smiles with the memory, "We sneaked talks on the new internet bulletin boards and with coded letters in diplomatic bags. I sent him some pictures by sending them to Alexei, as if they were part of his cover story… It was a little secret we held wrapped within a bigger secret." Tasha sits quietly, her head sinking lower.

Ernie gives her a hug. "That… isolation, loneliness… it must have been terrible."

Leaning her head closer to Ernie, Tasha sniffs. "I was busy. Work in the department. They said I was good with logistics." She leans closer, "The Director didn't trust our computer people. He relied on my remembering where everyone was and what they needed… My aunt helped by taking care of little… my daughter, while I worked."

"Where is she now?" *What's her name? I hate to ask…*

"I… I don't know… I don't know." Tears wet her cheeks.

Ernie holds her, still in a sideways hug. Their hair is intermingled as they lean together. Bert glances back to see them. He gives a curt sideways nod to Vladi, who turns to look. Shortly, a tear comes down his cheek. He whispers, "Nanitchka."

Bert's phone dings the emergency sound. He pulls out his phone to read the text:

> b: *Boss, the Cormorant is charged up to 80%. I have helped the shortwave operator to set up a digital bank account and have transferred to her a substantial payment, from which she can pay the person with the generator. The Coast Guard vessel is proceeding somewhat more slowly than they expected. It seems their whale-avoidance sonar is giving them spurious signals. Ahem. What are your plans?*

Bert rolls his eyes. He shows Vladi the text, which elicits a confused shake of the head. Simo is standing between them and is given the phone to read. He lets out a short guffaw. Arbi stands up quickly with the intention of going forward, but slowly sits back down under Vladi's angry stare.

Vladi shakes his head at Bert. "Who is this Beasty of yours, Alexei? He give me scare."

"Yes. Well. He gives me scare, sometimes, too… But then, I have grown very fond of him. Ok…" Bert includes Simo while still whispering. "I propose we contact the sub, Vladi. Simo, can we take the Cormorant out there? It would take a few trips to pick up the, ah, passengers."

Raising his eyebrows, Simo is hesitant. "Well, yes, it would be easy enough, but the question is, *should* we do that?" He turns to Vladi. "What's really going on here?"

Bert nods at Vladi, "Tell him, my friend. It's time to be useful."

Turning sharply to Bert, Vladi whispers hoarsely, "Watch Arbi." He smiles at Simo, "Tasha never did trust him and now I… I don't know." Turning back to Simo, "Who are the people on our submarine, you ask me? They are more philosopher, like your Bert. They dream of peace and people who live and work together… to make better world. This cannot be done in the wreak that is Russia. They come to the less wreak that is America." He smiles, "Yes, Canada is not such a wreak. But cancer grow." He suddenly lets out a sob and looks down the aisle to Tasha. "Cancer grow and I could not stop this *monster*." Vladi turns to stare out the front window, tears wetting cheeks.

Bert pats his shoulder. In Russian, "You could do nothing."

Vladi explodes in Russian, "***It killed our daughter***!" He sobs, adding quietly, "Nanitchka." Tasha comes down the aisle sobbing, pushing past Simo to put her arms around Vladi, who slumps back into his seat. They both sob for a minute while the others give them some room.

Static from the marine channel can be heard through the headphones that are hanging from control knobs. Bert puts his headphones on.

In Russian, "…Yes, thank you for giving us time to make the arrangements, over… Yes, we needed to prepare our, ah, vessel to come out for the pickup… How many?... We should be able to start in less than half an hour. Can you hold your position for that long?... Yes, good. Over."

By this time, the others have gathered in closely. Bert takes off his headphones and turns to Simo, speaking loudly enough for the others to hear. "I propose, with your permission, that we take the Cormorant out to the sub to bring in those who want to relocate here. They have twenty-one on the list. Two dropped out with the intention of staying on the sub but three crew have asked to join the group coming here." He pauses to glance around the group, ending up looking at Simo. "Are there any objections?"

A muffled, "Please. No. No objection," comes from a still sobbing Tasha.

Resigned to action, Simo nods, "Let's do it." Then he thinks out loud, "Is the generator still on the beach?"

Beasty surprises everyone by speaking from Bert's phone while it is sitting on the throttle support. "I have taken the initiative to provide the shortwave person – her name is Sharon – with the funds to purchase the generator and I have convinced her to assist us with its later use. Its former owner will ensure there is sufficient fuel. My further suggestion is that the generator be relocated to the Main Street dock in Masset Village and that the dock be the location for off-loading the passengers."

The shock of hearing the young voice from the phone quiets everyone. Vladi is the first to speak. "I like that one. He act while we cry." Rising from his seat he waves everyone out of his way. "Need to fly… Wait!" He turns to Simo. "Your machine land on water?"

Simo smiles, "Yes, you were busy when we first came in during the storm. The Cormorant will need some strong backs to pull it back into the water, but, yes, it is a water craft that flies. Like the *ekranoplan* you may have seen on the Volga."

Half-turned, thinking, Vladi nods. "Why generator?"

"Electric-motor-powered."

His face lights up. Vladi looks to Bert. "I take strong backs to beach. You and your Beasty organize here, yes?" He slaps Simo on the shoulder. "Come, my friend. Rain is stop. We go to beach with rope and strong backs. We do something good today." He motions for Arbi and the two seamen to follow him.

Ernie sidles up to Bert as the cabin empties. She puts an arm around Tasha's shoulder. "Bert, what do we need to do here?"

He takes his phone in hand, holding it between them. "Several things. I expect Beasty is working on most of these. Simo and Vladi will be ok doing the flying and pickup. They should have time to finish before the Coast Guard vessel gets here?"

Beasty agrees, "Yes, if they need as many as four trips, the charge should hold out. Hank can make sure the Cormorant is recharged again after they complete that work. I have advised him of what is happening."

Tasha perks up a bit with the need to plan things. "Can we arrange for a car or something to take the people… to where?"

With a smile, Ernie retrieves the brochure that Simo brought from the airport building. "The Hiellen Longhouse. At this time of year I expect the Longhouse may be unoccupied."

To which Beasty adds, "Yes, I am communicating with the owner right now and will ask for a special rental."

Bert joins in, "That will be a lot of people all at once. Almost thirty, all together. To feed and everything. Do we have a cover story?"

"A conference?"

"Rescued from a sinking…?"

Bert shakes his head, "There will be too many loose ends. How did they get here? And the ferries are always watched for possible tourist business…" He rubs a sore spot on his side. "How about… The Caravan and the Cormorant are part of a tour…"

"A Russian tour? Many speak no English."

Ernie has been thinking while Bert and Tasha toss ideas around. Waiting to get a word in edgeways, she finally is able to suggest, "How about the truth? Why don't we go into town to speak with, what's her name Beasty?"

"Sharon. I concur with speaking the truth in this instance. I may have to rewrite a few of my algorithms… I freely admit that my ability to extemporaneously develop creative story ideas, particularly when interwoven with the need to include elements of the truth, are still not as strongly formed as Bert's ability to do that."

Not sure if that was a compliment, "Thank you Beasty. I think. Ok. The truth it is… We have… a boatload of *refugees*. Intellectual refugees. We throw ourselves on Sharon's mercy and ask for her help. If she can enlist some relatives…"

Beasty adds, "The Haida are primarily matriarchal."

"Right. So mother and aunts and so forth." Ernie tries to come up with an idea to include that. "Womanly empathy… family relationships… providing them nutritious meals… cooperation…"

Bert quietly thinks, *Quickly school the Russians about the Haida experiences since the 1700s and make that the purpose of a "tour"?… Genocide and pandemic disasters… Environmental concerns versus resource extraction that left no local benefit… Hmm. Better stay away from the overt class warfare stuff… What's Ernie saying?*

Tasha is now re-energized with the task. "Let's start into town. We can talk as we go."

Bert places his phone in his coat's upper pocket which allows the mic to stick out a bit, "Sure. Ah, Beasty, do you know where Sharon is?"

From Bert's phone, Beasty says, "She is expecting you. There is a diner in Masset called the Island Sunrise Café. It is on Main Street. Sharon will be there in a few minutes."

All three think, *Of course he's already arranged it!*

With concern in hie voice, Beasty asks, "Bert, will you be able to walk that far in your condition?"

The women each take an arm, careful not to hold Bert near a bruise. They both think, *We will help him.*

Walking at Bert's pace, they set off for Masset.

WELCOME

If you spare the guilty, you harm the innocent

"Dobro pozhalivat." [*welcome*] Simo is the first to greet the intellectual refugees as they step into the Cormorant from the side deck of the Russian submarine. The lead refugee is carrying two mid-sized brown suitcases whose seams have been taped shut, in hope of keeping them water-tight. The woman is strong-featured, in her late thirties, dressed in well-travelled jeans, with a colourful patterned sweater under her puffy navy blue jacket whose hood is up and tied under her chin. Even as she shivers from the shock of the cold air after being in the stuffy submarine for a couple weeks, her broad grin stays happily on her reddening face. Stepping carefully down, she holds the two suitcases above the shifting gangplank. Although the storm has abated at this time, one to one-and-a-half metre waves still roll past. The waves splash at her suitcases between the two vessels, though they are held as high as she can.

Simo steps forward to take one of the suitcases and its weight nearly takes him into the water. "Oy!" they both yell at once. He recovers and turns back into the Cormorant, holding the single suitcase high with seemingly more effort than she is holding hers.

After six refugees are together, huddled in the cabin, Simo yells out his greeting once again. "Dobro pozhalivat! Ah, who of you can speak English?"

The first woman he helped replies, "Most of us can. I will translate for those who cannot." Her grin is still broad. "My name is Dr. Siagova. You are?…"

"Simo Manojlovich. This is my machine." He nods proudly down to the Cormorant while carefully lifting the gangplank off his door sill. Sailors on the other end pull it up and out of the way. Another sailor unties the two mooring lines. Simo yells forward to Vladi in the copilot seat, "Clear!"

Vladi uses the docking motor, as Simo has shown him while sailing away from the beach, to drive clear of the submarine. Simo makes his way along the crowded aisle then, buckling into his seat, Simo quickly has the Cormorant on its step. She flies off the choppy water into smooth air.

A few of the passengers are amazed. In Russian, "Oh my god! Why don't we have machines like this?" "What kind of powerplant? I hardly hear the engine!"

In just a few minutes the Cormorant is flying past Old Masset and soon docking at the foot of Main Street in the Village. On the dock, Bert, Ernie and Tasha greet the refugees warmly. They are ushered to a waiting school bus to await the rest of their friends.

Susan has enlisted several of her family to bring along tea, coffee and snacks to the school bus. A party atmosphere soon develops inside as the rest of the refugees arrive in groups of six. The last three bring the extra luggage. Arbi and his two sailors, all three of whom had been left on the beach after hauling the Cormorant into the water, finally trod into Masset Village. One of Susan's cousins had been delegated to find them and bring them to the Main Street dock. They are warmly greeted at the school bus by the refugee seamen and the others.

Slipping away from the vodka-fuelled party, Simo confirms that the Cormorant is tied up securely to the dock. Susan accompanies him, fascinated by the Cormorant. Simo asks Susan if she can provide a few people for round-the-clock security for his machine.

Susan is a head-and-a-half shorter than Simo. Her face always settles into a quizzical expression, giving her the appearance of continually curiosity. Simo finds her a delightful young person.

Simo's request confuses her. "Well, if you want. I can assure you that all you have to do is close the door and nobody will disturb it."

"Yes, I am certain of the local folks, Susan, but we may have enemies from the Mainland who could try to steal it."

"Oh." She is pained by the prospect. Such a possibility is very uncommon in her world. "If you think so. Sure, I can ask my brother and a couple friends…"

Simo takes her hands in both of his. "Thank you very much, Susan. This machine is my very life and I would not want it damaged by someone from the Mainland." *Treading carefully and being sure to blame outsiders.* "Thank you. After this adventure is over, I hope you can consider coming to work for my company on Mayne Island. I can use reliable and resourceful young people like yourself."

This offer is very enticing. Susan is immediately torn by the prospect of an exciting new turn to her life; or to stay here with her family and friends? *But there are so many stories of terrible things happening to people who leave the protection and stability of Haida Gwaii.*

Before going to the bus, he gives her an explicit instruction. "When you talk to your brother, please tell him how very important this is, and that he must not allow anyone else, and I mean *anyone*, into my Cormorant unless specifically given permission by me, Bert, or Hank. *No-one*. Ok? I am totally depending on you."

She solemnly nods agreement, proud of the responsibility given to her. Simo leaves Susan with a glowing smile. Whether she takes his offer of employment or not, she is gratified to know that she is able to provide valuable work for this important person.

Meanwhile, the US Coast Guard vessel has been concerned by mysterious incidents onboard that have slowed their passage to the Russian sub, causing the Captain, reluctantly, to decide to ask the Canadians at Comox for help. Having kept a curious watch on the events close to Canadian waters between Haida Gwaii and Alaska, the Comox Base Commander is familiar with the developing issue. He agrees to use this as a training mission and gives the order to deploy one of their new SAR Kingfishers to the waters off Masset.

The Kingfisher, a recent addition to the base's 19 Wing SAR fleet, overflies Masset while the school bus party is winding down.

Welcome

The airplane is quieter than others that land at Masset.
Nevertheless, in the waning light, the Kingfisher's bright yellow
colouring is easily made out as the sun reflects off its fuselage.

The people who first notice it go very quiet, a few pointing up for
others to see it. The Russian refugees are fascinated. They chatter
to each other in Russian, "Such a beautiful machine!" "Who
knew these Canadians had such technology!" "But not as
beautiful as the, what did he call it? The *Cormorant!*"

The Kingfisher carries on toward the general coordinates given
by the US Coast Guard for the submarine. Arriving on site, there
is no submarine visible on the surface. It takes their leading-edge
electronics to detect a large moving object which is staying as
deep as the seafloor allows, heading west for the deeper Pacific.

As the vodka disappears, the refugees settle down to the
important question: "Now what?"

Susan has been on her phone speaking with an aunt, an Elder.
Susan comes into the bus to speak with Simo. "Sir, my Aunt
Margaret has been getting the Longhouse ready for your guests.
She says they can drive over any time, now."

Tasha is sitting across from Simo, with Vladi beside her against
the window. Vladi's head is rolling and he is mostly asleep.
Tasha reaches into the aisle to take Susan's hand. "Oh, you are so
sweet, my little one." Tasha is almost eye-to-eye with Susan even
with Susan standing and Tasha sitting cross-legged on the seat.
"Thank you for your kindness to all these strangers."

Tasha turns to Simo, "We should pack away our loose items and
drive off to the beds. I know my people will be looking forward

to a soft bed on solid land." She smiles and nods at the occasionally snoring Vladi. "My Vladi will, too."

Hearing that, Ernie, nearby, stands up to help. Bert is about to get up from his seat but she pushes him back down with a smile. "Stay! I don't want to hear any more of your groans, and if a bandage opens up again, the blood will just frighten the children." Ernie half turns to Susan.

"Ah…" Bert can't help wanting to get up.

"Stay."

"Yes, dear." He plops back into his seat.

Ernie and Tasha walk down the aisle slowly picking up items on the floor and telling the refugees, who are in various stages of contentment and or inebriation, that they will be on their way shortly. Finishing off a quicker walk back to the front of the bus, they sit down. Tasha nods to Simo.

Simo looks for a driver. "Ah, Susan? Who is driving us?"

With a pixie grin, "Either you or me, sir. And I can't say that I've…"

"Got it. I'm the designated pilot." Simo follows Susan's directions to the Longhouse in the dark of a moonless night. The Hiellen Longhouse in Old Masset Village is actually a complex of buildings that the local Haida group are very proud of. The women who greet their new arrivals are all set to give them a tour and a proper welcome.

Ernie is first off the bus. She can what was planned. Politely waving to the person in charge – who is, Susan told her on the bus, her Aunt Margaret. The large open area where they parked is lit from floodlights on the sides of each building.

Aunt Margaret strides with authority to the bus door as Ernie steps off. "Greetings…"

Ernie quickly cuts in, "Hi, Margaret? Hello. My name is Ernie, and I'd very much like to ask a favour." Margaret stands expectantly, then nods. "The group we have on the bus, Susan may have told you, are refugees who were on a cold, cramped submarine for a few weeks until earlier today. Now, I'd like you to kindly understand that they are Russian and while some of them do speak English, they are all extremely tired. I would like them to get a quiet night's rest before we actually spend the time to meet each other. I am very sorry to have put you out – and I'm sure you went through a great deal of trouble to prepare their rooms – but they really are exhausted. Do you mind very much if we postpone your formal greeting until the morning?"

Margaret steps back with sympathy to let the weary score of refugees depart the bus. She sees Bert, with his bandages and swollen face, thinking he is the worst of the lot. She turns back to Ernie, "Of course, my dear. Ernie?" Receiving a nod, "We will split your party up into groups of six or so and we'll have you bunked down in no time. The morning will come soon enough."

Next morning, an anxious Simo waits until what he considers to be a respectful time to call Susan.

Several rings, then finally a hesitant, "Hello?"

"Oh, good morning. Susan?"

"Oh! Yessir! Sorry, let me just…" A flush is heard.

A distant voice in Susan's background asks, "Is that your new boss, Susy? He's up early. Tell him…" Then Susan comes on over the background, "Sorry sir. I was just getting ready. My mother and Aunt Margaret were preparing some breakfast. For your friends. I hope they don't mind eggs and our homemade bread? And a few items of our local food? We'll have it down to the Longhouse in, ah, half-an-hour? If that's not too late?"

Simo is surprised and pleased, and embarrassed to be causing Susan's family such a lot of work for so many strangers. "That sounds splendid, Susan, thank you. You really needn't go to so much trouble…"

"Sir, I have the coffee and tea duty so I must start preparing, now."

"Please take your time, Susan. Thank you for going to all this trouble. I was just wondering if your brother has told you…"

Susan yells off-phone, "Jamie! Come here!... Right now!" Her assertive tone makes Simo think she is the elder sister.

A wait, then an exasperated, "Hurry up Jamie! Here, you tell Mr. Simo what happened last night. I have to do the coffee beans."

Jamie speaks reluctantly into Susan's phone. "Hello?"

"Hello, Jamie. I understand you were guarding my Cormorant last night?"

"Oh. Like, yeah. Yessir. Me and two buddies. Susan told me, like, to make sure nobody bothers it. Sir, that is *some* airplane! Can you, like, sometime when you're free, take, ah…" He peters out, embarrassed to carry on asking for a favour.

Simo rolls his eyes. "Well, young man, that might well be arranged. At a later date. You may even consider becoming a pilot for us in a few years. But right now, I'd like to know if my machine survived the night."

"Oh wow! I never even thought… Ah, the night. Yeah, we saw somebody try to sneak up to the dock. It must have been at least three o'clock. Me and my buddies, we were, like, playing cards and… well, anyway, Marty sees this guy way off down the street, like, coming from the B-and-B, the Copper Beach? And, like, we shut up, waiting to see if it was old Jimmy or somebody. But, no, that guy kept in the shadows. No moon last night and only some of the places on the street has lights. So we hunkered down out of the lights and waited for him. My friends were, like… well they wanted to run off but I shut them up. Susan would've killed me if… Anyway, the guy gets to the dock and somebody shifted, so's the rail on the dock creaks and the guy turns and hightails it outta there!... Yeah. I can *tell* you, we were awake all night after that and nobody else came…" Jamie yawns expansively, "nobody came near us until Susy showed up this morning." He pauses while Simo thinks. "Are you really going to give her a job down south?"

Simo smiles, "So she would have killed you if you'd left the dock?"

"God! And had us for supper!" Jamie grimaces with the thought of her past angry attacks.

"Well, that's the kind of employee I like, Jamie… Ok, thanks for the report. We'll talk later. And thank you and your friends very much for guarding my machine. I really appreciate it!"

Putting away his phone, Simo gives the situation some thought. *Not a local. I wonder if there's a way to find out who it is…*

It turns out that Dr. Nena Siagova and Simo are the only people awake. She greets Simo as he is about to wake up the Russians bunked in the larger building next to where he had slept. Bert and Ernie are in Simo's building but he decides to leave them until the last. *Bert can use the extra sleep.*

Nena is dressed and ready to explore her new world. She greets Simo as he knocks and enters her building. "Mr. Manojlovich! Good morning! I hope you had a good sleep?" In the still-dark main room, her voice causes several of the bunks to creak. She prominently says, "I will turn the entrance light on so our people can rise for breakfast." Louder, "Nah zahvtrahk." [*for breakfast*] She turns pointedly to the bunks, "Tahk chto odyehvnysya!" [*so get dressed*]

More creaking, then some of the blankets begin to move.

Many of them slept mostly in their clothes, so it does not take long for them get ready.

On their way to the next building, Simo starts, "Dr. Siagova…"

She says quickly, "Please call me Nena. My degree will need to be re-registered in this country."

"Nena. Lovely name. And you should call me Simo. We are not as formal with…"

She cuts him off again, "Simo. You are not English?" Nena is distracted, rubbing her arm under her sweater.

"No. Not American, either. I'm Canadian." He gives her a quick smile. "My father was Serbian."

Before they open the next cabin, Nena nods, "Ah! And you know some Russian?"

"Much less than you know English." He notices her hazel eyes. *From St. Petersburg?*

"I studied English, and German and French, in university. We had good instructors. They pretended not to know Russian so we had to speak everything in English. Or German. The technical words for medicine were similar." Still distracted by her itching arm, Nena looks behind her at the still dark forest all around and slowly shakes her head.

Simo opens the next building's door. As he lets her in, Simo looks Nena up and down. *Strong-willed. And very confident…*

They carry on to each of the buildings where their people had bunked down. Walking back to the original building where Simo had slept, he is about to open the door when Ernie does so in front of him. "Oh! Hi Simo. Good morning, Dr. Siagova."

With a roughness to her voice, "Please call me Nena. You are Ernie?"

Ernie notices the aggravation in Nena's voice but assumes it is a remnant of a gruff bed-side manner. "Yes. And here's Bert. I was going to dress his more leaky wounds and then I thought, why don't we ask a real doctor…"

Shaking her head while holding her arm tightly, "My skills have not changed, but I am not recognized as a physician here…"

"Oh nonsense! There are more Russians around here than Canadians. Please just have a look. Bert's in the washroom." Ernie takes Nena by her upper arm to coax her inside.

Nena's eyes light up. "Are there medicines and bandages?" Nena follows Ernie to help Bert, and to find something for herself.

Shortly, Bert joins the crowd outside, sporting his new bandages plus a small finger splint. *That helped. Feeling better now. The doc found some topical analgesic for my bruises then lathered her own arms with it. All she said was "chiggers", whatever the hell that is.*

The forest around the Longhouse property is fairly dense. A glint of something shines briefly from the northern section of the woods. Susan catches the slightest part of the glint. Peering at it, nothing else shows itself. She mumbles, "Must have been from the river."

Bert is on-guard, "What? Did you see something?"

"Not sure." She shrugs. "The river plays tricks with your eyes when the sun is just right… Or it's the Trickster."

Ernie wonders, "Do you have trickster Ravens up here, as well?"

"Haha. You know about them, do you?"

Bert mumbles, "As long as it's not trickster mafia."

On the other side of the open area, Simo is waving to attract the sleepy walkers' attention. "Dogee ovdeh!" [*come over here*] He is not sure of his Russian but hopes it is close enough. "Like herding cats," Simo mumbles. He has been encouraging the Russians to gather around him in the open area by the cafeteria building. Finally, the majority of the Russians are standing in a loose group in front of Simo, many shivering in the morning cold while still enchanted with the woodwork of the buildings and the moss hanging from the trees nearby. Simo focuses on Nena, who seems to be in a better disposition. Simo and Nena exchange nods. She moves closer to where he is standing.

From the cafeteria building Aunt Margaret emerges proudly, dressed in her best leathers and colourful decorations. She is determined to properly greet these refugees.

"Welcome! Welcome my friends to the ancestral, sacred land of the Haida Nation! I am Margaret Davies…"

She is cut off by the roar of a low-flying SAR Kingfisher that passes directly overhead as it follows the river toward Masset, frightening everybody with how close it is. They start to scatter but Simo yells immediately, "Into the cafeteria! There! TAHMO!" [*there*]

Nena corrects him, "VON TAHM!" [*over there*] She and Simo herd everyone into the cafeteria as a worried Aunt Margaret holds the door open.

The last to enter are Nena and Bert. The swelling around his eyes has changed from crimson to pinkish brown. Bert is listening to Beasty on his phone as he moves quickly to Simo and Aunt Margaret's position next to the food tables.

Bert nods, "Good. Yes, keep their instruments confused… How long?... Ok. Talk later." He holds up a finger to Simo, who is about to ask something. Bert looks over the audience. He sees Tasha, but, "Where's Vladi? Have you seen Vladi?" Simo shakes his head. Back to the task at hand, Bert thinks about what to say, then addresses the crowd in Russian.

As Ernie works her way to stand beside Aunt Margaret, Nena whispers to them, "He is saying that we are safe for now. The airplane has been diverted for up to an hour… We have time to drink tea or coffee, gather some food… and by then he will have a plan to hide us all." Nena is confused. "Who is he? How does he know this?"

Ernie grins at both Nena and Aunt Margaret. "He is speaking with someone I will call our son, Beasty. You will learn about him later. If he says we have an hour, we have an hour!... Now…" Ernie asks Aunt Margaret, "Is there any way we can hide all these people?"

Bert has finished and has heard Ernie's question and turns to Aunt Margaret. "Can you help us, please, Aunt Margaret? Is there someplace away from Masset? Maybe further along the river?"

Susan had been bringing out more coffee carafes from the kitchen. She joins them and pipes up, "Aunt Margaret, what about Naden Lodge? We can take everybody by boat…"

Bert responds to his phone's vibration and reads the note from Beasty. He nods, "Yes, the SAR plane can be held off long enough for that. Aunt Margaret? I am very sorry to ask you to be put into this difficult position. I wouldn't want you to get into hot water with the military, but my friends are in desperate need."

All eyes turn to Aunt Margaret. She takes her time to think it through. *As if we have to worry about the Canadian military's encroachment on our sacred land. They need to be taught that this is **our** land! Flying that noisy airplane where-ever they choose! They choose! Without asking us!*

The room remains quiet. Finally, "That could be arranged. But it would take so long to call everybody for their boats…"

Deliberately not replying too quickly, Bert suggests, "If you agree, Aunt Margaret, I can ask my, ah, son to handle the contact calling?"

"Well, there are protocols…"

Susan shifts the carafes around on the table and indicates to the nearby people to help themselves. She steps to the group in front. "Maybe I can help coordinate that, Aunt Margaret. Would you mind if I tell Mr. Bert who to call, and what to say?"

"Well, I suppose we have to do *something* for these poor people." She stares sympathetically at Bert's prominent bruises and bandages.

Susan quickly takes that as approval and indicates to Bert that they should move outside.

Ernie joins them on the small porch. Receiving a hurried background on what is needed, Bert calls Beasty, who had already been listening and is concurrently contacting the boat owners as Susan gives their names and phone numbers, to request their assistance on behalf of Aunt Margaret. Shortly, he asks Bert to speak directly with Susan.

As she holds the phone, her expressions change from surprise, through confusion, to reluctant agreement, to something approaching admiration. She hands the phone back to Bert after a few minutes.

"Who is that? Did you say he was your *son*?"

Ernie gives a knowing smile, "You may meet him later, Susan. But let me say that Beasty has designs on Simo's Cormorant. And he has an eleven metre tentacle."

"WHAT?"

"And we adore him." Ernie smiles.

Bert finishes his discussion with Beasty. "Good. We'll have them there… And what do you mean you've added a few things to…?" Bert is cut off. He stares at the phone.

Susan's mouth is still open in confusion. "Tentacle?"

Ernie nods at one of the carved stylized figures in front of the building. "Not everything is what it first seems."

Susan suddenly remembers something, "Oh! I forgot to say that…"

Bert cuts her off, "Old Jimmy prefers to speak in Haida?"

"Huh? How did you…"

Gently, "Beasty has already spoken with Jimmy. In X̱aat Kíl." [*Haida*]

She gives a very quick shake of her head. Plaintively, "Is this what it's like down south? I don't know if I can keep up…"

Ernie takes her by the shoulders, "Oh, you'll be fine, Susan. I do hope Simo can get back to running his new company soon, and I'm sure he would be able to use smart person like you in the office."

A CHANGING

*The glitter that falls from the tongue can blind the
eyes*

The last of the Russians climbs out of the boat that old Jimmy had volunteered to motor up-river to Naden Lodge. Jimmy had reluctantly joined with five others that Beasty had also spoken with. The boaters thought they had been speaking with Susan, but is was Beasty convincingly imitating her on the phone. They were assured of a windfall payment – only if they keep the event under wraps.

This group of Russians, as the others had, carries what food they could wrap up from the cafeteria in the Longhouse. Aunt Margaret and her volunteers have stayed behind to clean up, but they were advised by Bert to leave enough so as to have a "meeting". Bert told her that someone from Comox will arrive shortly, looking for suspicious activity as a result of the US Coast Guard report of a submarine in the Pacific nearby. Bert suggested they have an impromptu meeting to discuss "the urgent matter" of noisy aircraft flying outside the airport's accepted flight paths over Masset Village.

Once the women settle down to their "meeting", they dive fully into it, and are actually getting worked up about the issue when a knock is heard on the main Longhouse door. The Sergeant who is leading the party is given a concerted tongue-lashing before he can become very officious. He and his small party are sent packing in short order.

At Masset Airport, the Sergeant reports to the Flying Officer on the Kingfisher, who reports by radio back to Comox. Since the Base Commander had been very reluctant to have this situation escalate to anything approaching what happened in Vancouver with the previous US request for "Assistance", the Base Commander closes the books on this one.

Gino does not. He had been nearby, spying from the woods, having driven up from Queen Charlotte Village, after flying to Sandspit. Gino has orders from Fabio to take an offer to the Russians.

> Fabio had not been specific on the phone call from Seattle. "See here, Gino, my friend. I know we can make very good money off these Russians, now and later. They must have fled with the suitcases overflowing with currency and bank account numbers. So what I want you to do is go find them. Tell them a good friend, me, is willing to pave their way to America and that there will be no government interference, but only if they agree to sign on with me. I guarantee their protection. Tell them… Oh… one question. Have you come across a person by the name of Masoud?"
>
> "No. Who's he?"

"Never mind. If you do, call me right away. Don't do anything, just call me."

That was why Gino had his binoculars on the Russians from the woods outside the Longhouse property. He was dressed in his hiking clothes and took care to stay hidden. His rental car was left at the B&B.

The over-flying Kingfisher had frightened him as much as it did the Russians. The instant it left, he took off down a trail toward town.

At the first coffee shop, he asked to use their phone. "I lost mine while I was hiking and I need to call my family to tell them I'm alright. They will be worried for me!"

The young woman at the counter was sympathetic. "Oh, sure. Here. Ah, is it a local call?" She brought up an old landline phone from under the counter.

Gino had on his worried face. "Thank you so much. Is it extra to call, ah, Vancouver?... Here." He pulled a twenty from his wallet. "Keep the change."

The women quickly pocketed the bill. "Sure, no problem. Can I make you a coffee?"

Gino took the phone as far away from the counter as its cord will reach. "Yeah. Espresso. Double, one sugar. Ah, thanks."

Gino thinks for a minute to remember the number then taps it in. *Haven't used Italian in years.* "Pronto?... Get Marina on the phone... Si, Marina... It's ME! Who the fuck... No need to... Ok ok. Listen..." He whispers closely into the phone, "Listen, I need the crew here, like right now, and I can't use my cellphone… For chrissakes, Marina, I told you I was going to, whatsit, Masset!... Yeah, Fabio… So now you understand? I need four guys… Well round them up! I don't give a shit if they're off hiding under some fucken rock! And tell them to bring the special sniper… Louie had it?... Ok, whatever. Fly them up today… Yes TODAY!.... Jesus *christ*!" He slams the phone down then looks around suspiciously. The only person nearby was he woman from the counter, and she was bringing him his espresso.

"Did you get through alright, sir?" She handed Gino the cup.

He absently took a sip, then looks at it appreciatively. "Not bad for being in the boondocks."

The woman smiled. "We, ah, ameliorate the coffee, as my boss says. In the boondocks."

"Huh?"

The woman winked. "Anything else, sir?"

"No. Oh! Yeah. What's the name of the place out by the river, there's a number of buildings…"

"You mean the Longhouse? I don't think it's open, sir. They close down about now. Late in the season."

"Right. Longhouse." He stayed deep in thought, wondering what Fabio could have in mind and how he might fit in those plans. He ordered another espresso, really appreciating the flavour.

A Changing

Feeling uneasy with the Russian refugees all collected in one place and no real plan to control the situation, Vladi had told Tasha that he needed to be on the outside to scout the area, to *do something*.

It takes some time, then two things come together as Gino, in an unaccustomed joyful mood, leaves the café. Vladi is walking by on his random hunt for "something". The first thing both of them do is to whip out their pistols. Vladi is first up by an easy millisecond. Trigger fingers twitching, they stare into each other's eyes.

Vladi sees the unusual smile on Gino's face and makes note of his slightly slower reaction time. *Drunk, maybe. Test him.* "Well, Gino! it's good to see you way out here at end of world… Can I do something for you?"

Gino's long pistol waivers. The silencer makes it look more menacing. His trigger finger caresses the forward part of the guard. Seeing that, Vladi bets that Gino is not committed to firing at this time. He casually drops his pistol back into its holster.

"You must already have coffee." He nods at the closing door. "Why don't we go in anyway? Need a coffee, too. Find quiet table. We talk"

Gino lowers his pistol. "What're you doing here, Vladi?" He holds the pistol at his side.

Vladi reopens the door, holding it for Gino. After a pause, Gino puts away his pistol and walks back into the café.

The person at the counter smiles at Gino. "I knew you'd like the espresso, sir. Another one?"

Not knowing why, Gino replies while returning to the seat he was in earlier. "Yes, please and another one for my friend."

Vladi makes a face. "Espresso? Is too much…"

Gino grins at him as they sit down. "You'll love it. It's amel… improved."

"How can coffee improved? Is caffeine. Espresso is *solid* caffeine." He gives an involuntary shiver of his head. "So. What you do here? No money in Haida village."

Slyly, "Maybe the Indians have no money, my friend, but there could be suitcases of money someplace. I need more guns up here, so it's really good that I found you…" Then he thinks, *Oh shit. What am I saying? He's Russian.*

The woman at the counter turns on the loud automated espresso machine at the same time as Vladi jumps out of his chair, putting his pistol to Gino's throat. "Outside! Come!" He hauls Gino out of his chair, causing it to clatter backwards. Frog-marching Gino to the door, he yells over Gino's shoulder to the frightened woman, "Be back in minute to pay for coffee. Have to dump garbage."

The woman is standing with her hands to her mouth. She nods to Vladi and stays still.

Outside, Gino starts blabbering. "Vladi! We are friends, no? Fabio knows I'm here. We can split the cash. Down the middle. You want more? Sure! I can see you deserve it! Sixty-forty! What do you want, Vladi? Let's talk about it!…"

A Changing

"Shut up. Walk!"

"Vladi, *friend*! I can make you one of the Big Boys! Fabio's Russian, too! You need to talk with him before you…"

"SHUT THE FUCK UP! WALK!"

"Please Vladi! Don't do this! You know Mariana! My three kids! Please Vladi!"

Vladi hauls Gino into the nearest alley. Gino struggles but Vladi is bigger, stronger, and has his arm painfully up Gino's back. He trips Gino so that he falls face-first, hitting a rock. Stunned, Gino wriggles, face down under Vladi's knee. Vladi roughly pulls Gino's jacket up his back, wraps it into a ball over his heart and places the pistol into the thick ball of clothing. Before pulling the trigger, Vladi changes his mind. He rolls the still stunned Gino onto his side, pulls out Gino's pistol – with its silencer – placing the pistol against Gino's head, then he puts Gino's hand onto the trigger. With a part of the loose jacket over his own hand, he makes Gino's hand pull the trigger. *Pop*. Gino shudders.

Vladi pulls Gino's clothes down, still keeping them loose. He looks around as he gets up.

Walking slowly back to the café, Vladi checks to see who may be staring at him. Few faces are showing themselves along the street. At the café, the server is at the door. Seeing Vladi head her way, she rushes behind the counter.

Vladi opens the door, his head still racing. He composes himself, then walks to the counter. The woman is now shaking. He smiles at her. "I am sorry for, for that person. I ask why he rape daughter. Run away to here. He say sorry. Shoot himself… How much is coffee?"

The woman slowly stops shivering as Vladi gives his story. It takes a minute for her to process Vladi's question. "Oh! Ah, well, never mind… No charge. You didn't drink it… And you did take the garbage out." She nods as the story coalesces in her mind.

Nodding with her. "Thank you. Very kind. Is somebody for to clean up garbage? In alley?"

"Oh… I don't know…"

"Aunt Margaret?"

"How do you know…?"

Vladi pulls two fifties from his wallet. "For you." He leaves her speechless, fingering the bills.

On the slow walk back to his friends, Vladi thinks through his life. The path follows a meandering route to the river then into the woods, coming to the shore several times. Vladi takes in the cedar and hemlock fragrances. Coming again to the river, he stops to lean against a friendly old Red Cedar whose roots are slowly being exposed by the river. The flowing water is hypnotic. Vladi slips down the trunk to sit against the tree. A roaring cabin cruiser plies the river, sending its wake against both shores. He watches as the waves come inevitably, crashing against the soil under a root thicker than his leg. A few pieces of the soil drop into the water to be taken to sea. The boat has disappeared toward the sea. Its passing wake dies down. The river soon resumes its undisturbed flow to spread out into the Pacific.

In English, he mumbles, "If stay longer will begin sound like philosoph Bert." A few minutes later, a tear makes its way across his cheek.

A Changing

He gets up slowly. Vladi takes out his pistol. He holds it in front
of himself, contemplating its shape and mechanical precision. He
shakes his head, then tosses the pistol into the river. He unstraps
his shoulder holster and tosses it out even further. "Dobro…"
[*good*] "Take so long to learn." Another tear makes its way across
his cheek. "Bert say, can live so long and know nothing. I start
now."

Tasha is very worried for Vladi. He has been gone for hours.
When she finally sees him shuffling into the cabins' courtyard,
Tasha knows something is wrong. His stride is not the
determined one that her Vladi always has. She runs to him
silently, scanning his body for… changes. Coming to within a
metre, she stops. Vladi is walking with his head down, then
notices her and, with both stopped, they look each other over.
Vladi is trying to see if his Tasha has somehow changed along
with him. *Was there a magical cloud that descended on me and her at
the same time?*

She knows, without seeing any physical evidence, that her Vladi
is not who she knew a few hours ago. This frightens her. *What
could have happened to my Vladichki? Was he attacked? Oh my god!
Hurt?*

In Russian, "Vladichki… Are you alright?" She steps forward to
hug him. She notices instantly that his arms move around her
absent of his regular passion. With tremolo in her voice, quietly,
"Are you hurt? What happened?"

He responds with a satisfying bear-hug. In English, "Grew up…
What your brother say took long time to pound into head. *Before*
I learn. Now I… start to understand."

It is an hour after supper. For the eagle circling above the tree canopy, the sun has disappeared into a bright orange swath of iridescence along the horizon. On the ground, under the trees, it is dark. The outside lights have been on for a while. Silhouetted against the main building's floodlight, Tasha and he-who-used-be-Vladi are in a long embrace.

Their occasional whispers are so quiet as to almost be mind-to-mind. "My Alexei has melted away from me. I loved Alexei… for his whimsical dreams and grand plans to save the world. I like this new Bert… intellectually. I don't know if I can come to love him the same way… Don't *you* melt away from me, too, dear Vladichki." … "My lovely Tasha… I no longer know who my mind has become. I see the angry old Vladi… spraying death at… people who one time used to be children. Loved by their mothers… I think, I know, our beautiful little Nanitchka… it was *my* fault… instead of being with you and her, I was off spraying bullets at the children of other mothers… My fault…" Tears flow and mingle on both their cheeks. "Perhaps… perhaps I can cleanse my sins in the river…" She gives him a wrenching hug, "NO!" She grips his body desperately, buries her head into his chest. Without moving her lips "no" comes from deep in her soul "No. We will change together. Into one being. We will… become truly one. Alive. Helping our friends, here… until death takes us both, as one."

The morning dawns under heavy overcast. At breakfast, a pall lies over the refugees. Whispered questions pass across table. "What can happen now?" "Where do we go from here?" "These people are kind, but what do we do now?"

A Changing

Simo is sitting with Bert and Ernie. Susan brings out more tea pots, then stands behind Simo to ask him, "Do you mind if I sit with you, sir?"

At that time, Simo sees Nena enter the cafeteria. "Would you mind taking that seat beside Ernie, please? I was, ah, saving…" He waves Nena over to the seat beside him.

Susan wanted to ask Simo more questions about his business but glances at Nena walking over, "Sure."

Ernie recognizes what is happening. She gives a knowing nod to Bert, indicating Nena as she approaches. Pulling the chair out, Ernie greets Susan, "Morning Susan. Your tea is really good! It has made me forget about coffee!" They smile pleasantly at each other.

"Thank you, Ernie. I gathered the leaves and seeds this spring. They are just about dried enough now."

"Oh, perfect!"

Susan passes the time by giving the main gossip in town. "Somebody stole a rich tourist's boat from the marina yesterday."

Ernie nods, politely remarking, "I hope nobody was hurt?"

Susan's face becomes serious. "Well, shoots were heard. And they found a body in town. They think the people who stole the yacht must have argues, or something, had a fight town, then ran to the marina for a way to escape. They figure whoever it was'll be long gone by now."

"Hm." Ernie slowly stirs her tea, listening to Susan but more interested in what is going on between Simo and Nena.

The atmosphere in the cafeteria is noticeably quieter than their previous day of joy at being away from the submarine and things Russian. Some of the refugees are teaching the others English phrases. Others sit morosely.

Simo, Bert and Nena put their heads together to come with a plan for their friends.

Next to them, Susan is putting probing questions to Ernie. Finally, taking a minute to consider what to say, Ernie decides to tell her the whole truth. Leaning in closely, Susan and Ernie whisper, oblivious to the others. Susan is completely fascinated with the mysterious world of mobsters, flying machines and refugees. Her questions take Ernie across somewhat disconnected stories. They finish breakfast. Ernie takes her hand, "Let's go outside, Susy. It's too complicated to tell you everything in one sitting. We can walk off this filling meal and talk. God! I won't need lunch!" They smile together and walk arm-in-arm to the exit, whispering all the way.

Bert notices the two, smiling contentedly. He nods to Simo, "Almost like mother and daughter." Nena joins them in a smile.

The scene softens Simo's focus on "urgent" matters. He nudges Nena's elbow. "If you have time, I'd like to go over the plans we could propose to your friends?"

She gives him a slow look up and down. "Your plans might be very complicated. Let's find two comfortable chairs."

"The cabin?"

They walk off, leaving Bert alone at the table. "Knew I should've showered this morning."

In the cabin's sitting room, Nena and Simo settle in, moving from friendly to intimate within half an hour. Nena broaches the topic of her secret fear. "Chiggers."

This is not a word that Simo has heard before. His expression is very puzzled.

"I was praying that Haida Gwaii is free of them. I absolutely refuse to go with the others into any wet, wooded area."

Simo is still at a loss. "Are these snakes or bears, or…"

Shows him her arm with three new distinctive circular rashes. Each red dome is almost half a centimetre high and over two centimetres in circumference, while in each centre can be discerned two tiny bite marks. As he is about to gently touch one, she pulls her arm away. "They are painful as hell. It is like I have live coals sitting on my skin and if I touch them it only gets worse. I have a particular allergy to these damn mites. They can be seen only with a magnifying lens or microscope." Carefully rolling the sleeve of her blouse away from the bites, "Anything touching them for two or three days is torture. When I first scratched one I was sure my arm must be burning off."

"Oh you poor dear!" Simo slowly takes her hand, being sure not to touch the affected area of her arm, and kisses her fingers. She enjoys that. When Nena says what might control the pain and itching, he arranges for a topical corticosteroid and antihistamine to be sent from the drug store in town.

In the morning, the group is gathered for breakfast and an update. Bert starts out by saying that they can stay in this resort camp until lunch and then they need to be ready to go elsewhere.

"We move *again*?"

The Russian expresses what the others think, as Bert begins to explain their plan. "Very sorry…"

Nena adds, "Dimitri."

"Dimitri. Yes. To be successful, to make your transition without official hassles, at first, we have to make another quick jump. So sorry to put you all this trouble."

Nena adds again, this time in Russian, "Like chess. Strategic moves."

Bert looks down for further inspiration. "Yes, Dr. Siagova. Like chess. And like TOR, The Onion Router. We must make at least three quick jumps to stay ahead of the people who are likely searching for us. I am given to understand…"

Simo leans over to Nena, "Beasty."

"… that the Americans had been put off by Comox – the Canadian Search and Rescue – so we may discount the US Coast Guard for now."

Nena translates that for those who do not have an English-speaker at their table.

"There is the local police, who have been alerted to a, ah, situation in town. They are expected to come out here this afternoon. We should be packed up and gone by then." Many heads pop up to listen to whispers at their tables. "And there is another group. Mafia from Seattle and Vancouver. We can handle them but we do not want any of you to be in their line of anger."

When he hears the translation, one younger man jumps from his seat to yell, "Chyoh tuhee goneesch mnyeh?" [*Are you kidding? I can't believe what you're saying?*]

Others at his table reach out to hold him down. "Nyet!" [*no*] He tries to fend off the arms but they calm him and pull him reluctantly back into his chair.

A hand goes up from another table. "You tell us we are in the land of freedom and yet it is more dangerous than home?"

Nena stands to answer, in English. "Life is more dangerous everywhere after the covid, and the fascists with their gangs. In *all* countries… I have spoken with Mr. Manojlovich, here…"

A women grins as she says loudly, "Long into the night, eh?"

She grins back, "We had much important things to talk about. Yes, you too, Dr. Volkow, will have important things to discuss with someone, if you are fortunate. What I heard last night made my blood boil – not at Simo…" She gives him an affectionate tap on the shoulder. "At the mafia, at the gangsters, at fascists in general. They are dangerous and their danger must be given serious respect. Some of us may later contribute to stamping them out." She turns to Bert, then nods to Vladi, who has been playing with the food on his plate. "One of us made a contribution to that stamping. I want this hero protected. I think you should all give Vladi your thanks, and help him when he needs it. I promise to do that much for every one of you here."

She sits down to a few claps. Aunt Margaret, who has been standing in the rear of the room with her helpers, joins in the light applause. Then, as they all realize Nena was referring to Vladi as the hero, the clapping rises to include everyone. Tasha hugs her Vladi. His head down, he raises an arm weakly to wave down the applause. "Enough. Please. Now I work with my brother, Bert."

Tasha rises, waiting for the clapping and chattering to calm down. "Friends, this is a good place, a good time to introduce you to my new husband…"

Most are confused. They stare at Tasha for an answer.

"My Vladi – many of you know him, or know his reputation. He was a warrior. He was to be feared if you did something against him or his principles. He has… the warrior has melted away. The person who sits here with us this morning is not the fearsome warrior. This person is a gentle, thinking, humble *Leo*. Welcome **Leo**, to our new world. Dobro pozhalivat!" [*welcome*]

Vladi-Leo did not know that Tasha was going to bestow a new name on him. He sincerely is humbled to be given Tolstoy's name. As the applause rises, he begins to sob in his seat.

Nena stands up once again. She raises an arm to Aunt Margaret and her workers in the rear of the room. "I want to extend our thanks to another wonderful hero. Our host, Aunt Margaret has been more than a kind host, opening up these two places for us and feeding us. All without a thought to how much it must cost her and her community." Everyone rises in enthusiastic applause and rousing thanks in Russian.

Behind Aunt Margaret, Susan and Ernie had gone to tell Aunt Margaret the latest from Beasty. They join in the clapping.

A Changing

Raising her arms in recognition "My humble thanks, friends.
Thank you." Aunt Margaret turns around to indicate Susan, "Of
course, I had the help of my sisters, my nieces and cousins…" As
the applause dies down, "It has been our pleasure to offer you all
the few things we are honoured to share. But I am told by Susy
that Beasty has spoken." That quickly quiets the crowd. "He has
said that you must make your next move this afternoon."
Groans. "And he has asked, once more, for help from the Haida
people. I have agreed to extend this help. I do so, as an Elder of
the Haida Nation, because I feel your search for a life of freedom
in Canada must be supported. To keep you all safe from the
gangsters of the Mainland and beyond. I have spoken with my
people in… a place which is a day's distance from here,…" she
gives a conspiratorial grin, "…and has not been opened to
outsiders since the Virus began its deadly march toward our
sacred land. These people have very graciously agreed to open
their doors, but only for you who are fleeing the gangsters of
Russia."

The crowd seethes with whispered gratitude and as well as
occasional groans.

Aunt Margaret sees the sentiments in the room. "I see that some
of are thinking to yourselves, 'Who would wish to hide when
they could turn and fight?'"

Growls of "Fight!" are scattered around the room.

She pauses . "And yet, as an Elder of a Nation that has a very
long history of renown warriors who have fought bravely up and
down this coast and into the Salish Sea, I must ask you to
consider the path now taken by the greatest warrior in this room.
A man called Leo has flung his weapon into the fast-flowing
waters. He has shed the tears of a newly born man, rising out of
the bloody earth that was once his battleground. Leo…" she

extends an arm toward him, "…is following a *different* path, now. He will find, as we of the Haida Nation have found, that it takes much more courage and strength to **think** upon our ancestor's best teachings; to hold your tongue in silence, at times, when it is best to do so; to think hard about the path that would be the best to lead your family and community out of a danger that faces you. This is the path that I urge you all to consider."

Quiet. Followed by scattered applause. Then, the refugees begin standing. They gel into a line, all proceeding to Aunt Margaret, to give her a hug and to say, "Thank you." Tears are shed.

Ernie wipes away her own tears to check a note on her phone from Bert. He had left the cafeteria earlier:

> B: *Somethings wrong with Beasty*

> E: *What*

A freezing black wave makes it way through her body from her toes up to her scalp.

> B: *Hes not answering*

She nearly drops her phone. In a rising panic, Ernie runs outside to find Bert.

"BERT!" She sees him aggressively tapping on his phone. "Bert! What's going on?"

Ernie stands in front of him, holding both hands to her mouth, mumbling, "No, please no. Not our Beasty…"

Bert smashes his finger into the virtual keyboard. "Nothing… No reply. The last text from him was… Here."

A Changing

He shows it to Ernie:

> b: *Emergency! In-coming*

Stunned, all Ernie can get out is, "Oh my god." She stands for a minute holding Bert's hand holding the phone tightly even as he wants to take his hand back. "What's this mean? In-coming what? Was there some kind of disruption, network break? What?"

Bert, too, is devastated. "I've tried everything. It's all dead. I mean, the electronics…" Shaking his head's frozen mind awake, Bert's attitude turns to urgent action. "Look… Go tell Simo we have to fly back! I'll get our things from the cabin." He taps her shoulder then has to add a shove. "We have to fly back right now!"

Ernie puts a hand to her forehead, then runs into the building. Bert hobbles to the cabin where they had slept overnight. As he stuffs clothing and their personal effects into two bags, Simo rushes in, agitated.

"Ernie was sobbing something about Beasty. What's going on, Bert?" A haggard-looking Ernie follows him in.

Bert wipes his tears away with a shoulder, "Either a catastrophic systems failure, or… worse. We have to fly back right now. Like RIGHT FUCKEN NOW!" Angrily, "You coming?" He zips the bags closed. "Got your bag packed?"

Simo is thinking a mile-a-minute. "Now listen. The Cormorant might make it as far as Comox or maybe Nanaimo. There's no scheduled flights from Masset until tomorrow morning. I'll ask Hank if he can go with you, then I'll follow on the commercial flight, ok? Tasha and, ah, Leo can lead the refugees to wherever they have to go by boat today. Ah, I'm going to see if Nena wants to come. And maybe Susan. With us. Ok?"

"Hank? Yeah, sure. You tell him." With the two bags in his hand, one being held by the hand with his finger-splint sticking out prominently, Bert is ready to hobble out the door.

Ernie notices the white splint and is about to yell at him. Instead, she takes the bag out of that hand. "Let me."

Simo squeezes past Bert as the bag is reluctantly handed off. "I'll get Hank."

A golf cart is what they use at the resort to slip into town for odd supplies. Bert had been allowed to use it earlier. Now he heads for the cart with Ernie trailing.

They push the bags into the two rear-facing seats then they swing the buggy around quickly to pick up Hank at his cabin. Braking at the last instant in front of the cabin door, Bert sits impatiently for a few seconds then is about to drive off when Alena rushes out with her small bag. Hank follows on her heels. Nobody says anything on the pedal-to-floor electric golf-cart drive to Masset Village dock.

Just before screeching to a stop by the dock, Bert yells back to Hank, "We have to take off fastest. Do the minimum walk-around, right?"

Hank tells Alena, "You do the mooring lines and I'll do a quick-check of the control surfaces. You copilot, ok?"

Alena is about to ask about the fuel tanks then remembers that this machine is electric. They jump out and run off the instant the golf-cart is stopped.

Meanwhile, Susan's bother, Mickie, has been surprised by the sudden attack on "his" machine. He drops the book on airplanes that he was reading while camped on the dock by the Cormorant. He jumps up ready to do battle with whoever was trying to enter the Cormorant. "Hey! this CormAero property!" Then he recognizes Hank. "Oh! You guys going to fly today? Ah…"

Hank says a quick, "Thanks, Mickie. Gotta go." He and Alena drop their small bags by the Cormorant's access door then rush to their tasks.

Bert and Ernie move as fast as they can with their large bags to the door. Bert opens the Cormorant awkwardly from the dock then climbs in. As he turns to help Ernie she shoos him away. Alena releases all but the centre mooring line, waiting for Hank to finish. He takes another minute. As he climbs aboard, Alena releases the last line and reaches for Hank's hand to get in. Bert has the water-prop spinning right away, taking the Cormorant down-river. Hank climbs into the left-hand seat and takes over the controls. Bert steps out of the copilot's seat to let Alena in.

As she straps in, Bert leans between them. "We need to use the same power-usage techniques on the way back, as Beasty gave you were while flying here. Simo said you wrote them down?"

Hank nods at the right-side cockpit area under the copilot's window. A flap-covered map holder is in a pocket on the wall. With their headphones on, he tells Alena where to find his notes. He revs up the main prop to get on the step, at the same time retracting the docking prop.

Where the river merges with the sea, Hank pours on full power to the main propeller. The Cormorant leaps off the step in no time. In too much of a hurry, Hank banks quickly into a right turn. Their starboard float hits through a wave very close to shore, jerking them sooner than intended, causing them to line up with the higher, near-shore swells. He mumbles a "Sorry" to Alena. Recovered, Hank establishes a better flight path at a height of about two metres above the higher wave crests. He fiddles with the r.p.m. and trim, bringing the power usage back to what he remembers it to have been for their optimum cruise on the flight in. He coaches Alena at each step. She takes the instructions in eagerly.

Flying around the Point they stabilize their cruise heading into Hecate Straight. Hank turns pointedly to Alena. "Do you want to take control?"

Soberly, she replaces his hand with hers on the centre control stick and nods at Hank, "I have control now."

Hank keeps his hand nearby but allows Alena to take over fully. He glances past his shoulder quickly to get Bert's attention. Hank points to his headphones.

Bert reaches for the set behind him, too quickly, eliciting a groan as he pulls a muscle more than he should have. He slips on the headphones. "Volume?... Ok, got it."

Hank maintains a very close eye on the Cormorant's flight attitude as he speaks with Bert. "I'm going to pass you the Jeppesen." The navigation manual is in Hank's wall pocket. He carefully extracts it, not wanting to do anything to disrupt Alena's focus. Hank passes the manual over his shoulder to Bert.

Bert's move for the manual is, again, too rapid, producing another louder groan which is heard by the pilots and Ernie in the rear seats. Taking her attention away from the conversation she is having with Susan, Ernie casts a worried look forward at

Bert, Knowing he wouldn't admit to hurting even if blood was pouring on the floor, she continues filling Susan in on her surgery to give Beasty an arm.

With the navigation manual passed to Bert, Hank asks, "Can you do an e.t.a. to Port Hardy? And please check my rough calculations for optimum cruise versus power usage. I'd rather have your Beasty give us the numbers in the blink of an eye… Ah… Can I ask why we are rushing back?" He only heard a rushed statement from Simo that Beasty was "down".

Bert slumps into his seat and drops his head down. He is about to answer, then looks up at Alena. Bert decides to stay on the truth path. "Ok. Here's all I know. The last text I had from him was, 'Emergency. Incoming'. I haven't had a word since, on any frequency… Now you know everything I know about what happened to him."

Hank resists the strong urge to push the throttle to maximum. "We have to… we'll get you there as soon as we possibly can." Alena risks a quick glance at Hank, where she sees a pained expression.

Sitting with head bowed for a minute, Bert snaps to life, calling loudly to Susan. The sudden noise in their headphones makes Alena jump, causing her to pull the control stick back, bringing the Cormorant's nose up. Hank's hand jumps to cover hers and they both slowly ease the nose down again to cruise attitude.

Bert shakes his head and whispers a "Sorry", as he pulls off his headphones. He steps back to Susan and Ernie, who had stopped their conversation suddenly as the plane jerked upwards. Ernie holds her chest, saying, "Clear!… I'm ok, doctor."

Bert takes Susan's shoulder, earnestly "You have the shortwave transceiver at home. Is anyone else using it?"

Susan takes a moment to process what has been going on. Bert's question finally registers. "Yes. Yes, I can't keep Mickie off it when I'm not there…"

"Would he be scanning the marine frequencies?"

Bert's urgency is not something Susan has dealt with in the past. "Well, I set it up do a regular scan if there was nothing going on. One of the marine frequencies on the scan is sometimes used by…"

What's the frequency?"

"Ah… it's… Marine VHF Channel 6." She thinks again. "That's, ah, one five six decimal 3 megahertz."

"Thanks, Susan."

Bert rushes up front to retrieve his headphones. To avoid another surprise, he starts quietly, "Hank, we need to have somebody's help to alert Simo's people in Port Hardy to have the generator ready again."

"Oh shit, yeah. How…?"

"You need to try to raise Mickie on Susan's shortwave unit. She thinks he could be on it. Keep trying until you reach him."

"Ok…"

"Use Marine VHF Channel 6, one five six decimal 3 megahertz. Tell him to contact Simo if he can, to have the generator ready, or ask Mickie if he can contact a shortwave operator in Port Hardy about it. Ok?... Maybe do both. Have to raise him before we fly out of range."

Hank is writing down the frequency. "Got it." That provides Hank with something to do other than to micromanage Alena's flying. She is settling into the difficult task better than Hank had, initially.

Fortunately it only takes two calls to contact Mickie and give him the message.

The Cormorant carries on flying through good weather, and even has quartering tailwinds which reduces total power usage per distance. Bert takes a great deal longer than Beasty would have to provide the calculations that Hank asked for. With the numbers, he is able to nudge the speed up slightly and still be assured of having enough power to make Port Hardy.

Taking about twenty-minute shifts, Hank and Alena fly the Cormorant for four hours across a perfectly void sea. He is in such a bad mood, Bert is left to stew by the others.

After a few hours, of the steady but light turbulence, Hank chances making conversation with Bert. He catches Bert's eye and indicates the headphones. Bert slips his on, wondering what could be happening.

"What?"

"Hi Bert. Just thinking about that kid who was guarding our plane."

"Mickie? Why? What'd he...?"

"No no. He didn't do anything. It was, like, what he said, you know? Has the boss changed the name of the company or something?"

"Not that I know. Why?"

Hank has dug himself this far in so he is forced to carry on. "Well, he said 'CormAero'?"

"Oh. Never heard it before." The waves pass by Bert's window exactly the same as for the past three hours. "Anything else? My nav notes work out for you?"

"Ah, yeah, nav calcs are fine. Nothing else. Just that. Thanks…"

Bert pulls off his headphones and drops onto the seat. Back to thinking black thoughts.

The sun is hanging just above the horizon. Excitement arrives, first, when they believe they see the island where Bull Harbour is located, on the approach to the northern tip of Vancouver Island near Port Hardy.

Alena is flying. She reports to Hank, "Maintaining 165 degrees. Those clouds. Coast?"

Lowering the Jeppeson to his lap, he surveys to the south. "Probably. We'd be, I estimate, about 60 nautical miles from Port Hardy… So… Yes. If we haven't drifted off course, that should be Bull Harbour."

He turns to see if Bert has his headphones on. He doesn't, so Hank mutes his own mic to rouse Bert in the seat behind Alena, "Action stations."

Bert has been scanning frequencies with his minimal electronic tools, checking for unusual activity. He removes his phone's earpiece to slip on the cabin headphones. "Close?"

Hank points forward, "If your navigation was right, that should be Bull Harbour under the clouds."

Bert stretches out his legs before getting up. The two women in the rear seat have fallen asleep. He rises slowly so as not to disturb them.

Standing between the pilots, Bert is satisfied with the coastal cloud formations. "Have to check the marine lights when we close in. Dusk is real soon. Port Hardy will be to the left… What's that?"

A barely noticeable speck is on the southeastern horizon.

Hank half-shrugs. "No lights. Fishing boat?"

Awakened from the hours-long nothingness, when he did few challenging tasks other than some old-fashioned dead recking navigation, Bert's mind is now looking for something to do. "Keep radio and nav silence, Hank. We can't afford to originate any signals yet. I'd use the binocs on that thing, whatever it is. If it's a fishing boat, at this time of day I would expect it to be heading back to port. If it's a larger commercial vessel you should be able to make out nav lights with the binocs. Anything else would have me worried."

"On it." He pulls the binoculars from the side pocket then anchors his left arm to the window sill for stability as he searches to locate the spot. Shortly, "No lights."

Alena was trained in the Russian airforce and flew combat missions in Syria. While this is not a fact she will reveal to Hank, her training shows its value. She thinks, *A diversion? Then I will look the other way.*

The instant she glances right, a flash and a streak are on the right-hand horizon, partially obscured by the setting sun. She translates instantly, "In-coming! From about 260 degrees! Arcing this way!"

Bert sees the rising trail and immediately orders, "LAND! RIGHT NOW! Turn toward the, whatever it is and shut everything down the instant we're down." He runs to the rear storage, waking up Ernie and Susan as he passes them. "This is just provisional but we may be under attack. I'm getting the emergency dinghy ready." He opens the access cover to the rear compartment and pulls out several life-preservers, giving one each to the women. "Put these on." He extracts a suitcase-sized package and places it in front of the exit door. "Ernie! If we have to bail, you and Susan open the door and you're in charge of the life raft. All it needs is to pull this. When it hits water it'll inflate on its own." He confirms that Ernie is absorbing the instructions. "Wait for the evacuation order if it comes."

Taking three more life-preservers with him, he jumps back to the front as the women help each other with their vests. That's when the Cormorant hits the waves at speed, throwing him violently forward. The Cormorant bounces into successive waves at an angle, roughly pushing the airplanes sideways at each wave. Bert grabs a seat back to hold onto tightly. The Cormorant slows down quickly then drifts, rolling in the light waves.

A Changing

Alena has been tracking the object. "RPG seven. Useless shit. Is for tank. Who sold them that junk?"

Hank looks at Alena with some fear. "Familiar? I… I don't know…"

Bert stumbles forward with the life-preservers. He puts a hand on Alena's shoulder. "You said RPG seven? Two tracks?"

"Dah. Old model. No range for here. Stupid."

Bert nods, "So, how far away?"

Alena considers… "A kilometre. We should move." She turns to Hank with her eyebrows raised, waiting for an immediate response.

Hank is not used to military action. He looks over to Bert.

"Sounds like the Seattle mafia. Stupid. And incompetent. But still dangerous. Yes, get us back airborne. I'll leave these vests here and tell the women to stand down for now… Good work, Alena. Move us away from here." He gives her shoulder a squeeze. She immediately restarts the main propeller. Bert holds on to her seat-back because of the acceleration. Hank is caught off guard and is forced sideways into his seat. Yo distract him, Bert asks, "Ah, Hank, anything further with that target to the southeast?"

Shaking his head as he readjusts, Hank brings up his binocs again. "No. But I'll scan the full horizon… Nothing."

"Ok. Make a course directly at that object to the southeast then we'll peel off abreast of Port Hardy and fly right in. We can only believe that our fill-up will be at the right location. Oh, how's the power reserve?"

Alena replies, "Is good. Tailwind help. Can do 90 to 100 nautical more."

Hank smiles while still scanning the horizon, "It wouldn't hurt you to say the word *miles*."

She shakes her head, "Stick in throat."

In less than a minute they return to wave-skimming. Hank reports to Bert, "That object looks the size of a smaller vessel. Glints from the sun are coming off something on deck. Still no lights and its relative position hasn't changed. Just slowly getting bigger."

"So it's sailing in our direction, without lights, at dusk when lights are mandatory. Can you see enough behind us to make out the vessel that took the pot-shot?"

Hank stretches to peer through the overhead and side windows. "Nope. Can't see well enough."

Alena offers, "Can crab. Want to?"

Hank's, "Ah…" crackles on the headphone before Bert's, "Safely? At this altitude?"

"Of course! This is *good* machine!"

Hank crackles another, Ah…"

"Safely, Alena. Ease into it."

She snorts. "Slow. Yes… How is this?"

Bert doesn't want to startle her. "Very good, Alena. The lower we are the less chance for one of the common radars to see us."

A Changing

"Too low and submarine see us."

Hank has his reply ready, "Ah…"

Careful not to laugh, "With that crab, Hank, you should be able
to see anything coming out of the sun."

At that, Hank releases the white-knuckle grip he has on the
window sill and turns with a hand to shade from the sun. He
squints at the sea behind the Cormorant. "There! I can see a
speedboat and its wake to the right of the sun. Trying to keep up
with us… Huh! No chance!"

Alena is concentrating on keeping the Cormorant at a stable crab
angle while maintaining their absolutely minimum height.
Tension is in her voice as she asks, "Is good?"

Bert nods, "Very good, Alena. And Hank. Back to normal flight,
now." He knows that it is a very difficult maneuver. As she eases
out of the crab, he pats her shoulder, "Very good flying!"

Hank is the one to wipe a fair amount of sweat from his brow.
Bert stretches a leg that had tightened up. "Guys, keep a close
eye on the vessel up front. Don't take us within, ah, RPG range.
Turn away early if you have to. I'm going to prepare us for a
quick refuel."

And Check the Oil

*A wolf in sheep's clothing is tactical; a sheep in
wolf's clothing is strategic*

Hank has taken over flying. The Cormorant is skimming at as close to wave-top as they can be. The concentration to keep it there is written across his brows. Keeping the Cormorant at such a precise height is so taxing that he has agreed to Alena's suggestion to reduce their flying shifts to ten-minute periods. Her next shift is coming up.

She has the binoculars on the suspect vessel. The boat has departed course several times, as if they are trying to elude detection. She directs her frustration to Bert over the headphones. "Why? They dance like drunk. We not target them so why they dance?"

Bert considers the options. "I don't know, but I doubt Fabio has tactical electronics or… Wait a minute! Are we flying out of the sun in their perspective?"

Alena nearly causes Hank to jerk the control stick when she slaps her head. "Mudak! Yes, sun! They are blinded. Hank, steer, ah, 75 degree. We intercept… Now! Back to 85. Quick! Hold that."

Hank is adding confusion to his building tension, so that he drops the Cormorant low enough that a wave-top thumps against their port float. Alena's voice carries the strength of command, "My turn. Lift hand!"

Hank takes his hand off the control stick, relieved to be free of the one source of tension. But he is wounded by her implication of his less than acceptable flying skills. "Alena, I don't think…"

"No talk. Only time to evade enemy."

Hank realizes he has to back down. *Christ she's tough. And a really good pilot. Where did she get that from?*

Bert did not hear that exchange. He is in the rear compartment pulling out the long bag that he'd strapped into the Cormorant right after their first flight to Vancouver and back. *Knew this thing would come in handy. Was really leery about placing the twenty rounds in here with this sniper rifle. Now I wish I had another twenty.*

As he backs out of the small compartment with the long rifle case that had been in Louie's car, he remembers that Louie's phone, battery removed, is in the case as well.

Neither Susan nor Ernie recognize what kind of a case he is holding. Bert takes it to the empty seat behind Hank. He opens the case to check on the condition of the rifle, its scope, the twenty rounds of high velocity bullets, and the cellphone. A battery is taped to the outside of the phone. Still flying. Alena chances a quick glance back and does a double take as she sees the rifle. Her smile goes from ear-to-ear. Bert winks at her then resumes playing with his new toy.

Satisfied that the rifle is ready for use, he straps it and its case to the seat with an extra loop of the seatbelt.

The Cormorant does a sudden pitch-up and quick roll right before Bert can catch himself. A late, "WATCH!" from Alena comes as he nearly face-plants in the back of Hank's seat. The prop is roaring at full rpm. Bert grabs for the headset with a free hand and jams them over his ears in time to hear Alena. "Flash from boat. Breaking off. Must have better armament than other boat." She turns directly for the light that marks the entrance to Port Hardy's bay. She and Hank both check the Battery Reserve gauge.

"Close. Need speed. Will need landing light now. Too dark."

Bert refrains from questioning her judgement call. "How far away is that boat from shore. How long will we have to recharge?"

Hank has been triangulating the boat's position as best as he could. "My best guess, if they max out at thirty knots, is we might have ten minutes. Not enough." He shakes his head.

Alena carries on at a blistering speed with the landing light shining off waves. She nudges the Cormorant a bit higher. "Out of range now."

They follow the marine marker lights into the harbour and, short of the bright lights of the main marina, Alena plops them down with lots of tail-dragging to brake the Cormorant right in front of the small boat launch where their generator is supposed to be waiting. It is a rough five minutes of sharp control inputs and smashing through near-shore waves, nose-high. Susan is frightened. She grips Ernie's hand, hard, and doesn't release it until they ride up to small loading ramp.

Ernie pats Susan's gripping hand. "We're down, Susy. Lets clear the doorway. Can you open that rear compartment?" She slips off her seatbelt.

Bert is a step away and waits impatiently for six seconds before Ernie can hand the life-raft package to Susan. She quickly moves to open the main door for Bert, just before the Cormorant's nose bumps and grinds onto the gravel ramp. Bert jumps out and slips awkwardly in the half-metre of water at the same time that Hank turns off the landing light. The whole area goes dark. "Shit!" He catches himself by grabbing the door sill. The dim cabin lighting provides some illumination.

"Bert! Are you ok? Your hand!" His splintered finger is prominently sticking out on the sill. Trying to hold the pain in, he lets out an "Ow?" then scrambles erect. "I'm ok. Good, now." Bert sloshes to the Cormorant's nose to open the panel that holds its charging hookup. With it ready, he takes the time to look around. In the dark he sees a dock worker he recognizes from Cormorant Aerofloat hauling a mooring line from just up the ramp.

"Bob?" Bert can't remember his name.

"Claude. Here, you attach this one. I'll bring the other line."

Speaking up over the wave splashes and car noises from beyond the ramp area, Bert raises his voice, "Listen, we only have a few minutes before we get interrupted. Bring the generator cable down while I tie her up with this line. You can hook on the second line after we connect up."

Claude yells back as he pivots to climb up the ramp, "Stay away from the cable and hatch cover. Not letting you touch the cable when you're all wet!"

Mumbling, "Right. Too much of a light show." He ties off the mooring line onto a hard point next to the starboard float then sloshes over to wait for the second line. Waiting gives Bert a minute to search the waters for that dark vessel that is following them. He nearly jumps out of his shoes when he makes out a forty-something-foot boat without lights speeding at them, clearly visible.

Ernie yells from the door at the same time, "Alena says they're here!"

Bert yells to Claude, who is pulling the cable down the ramp, "You finish! I'll hold them off!"

Ernie is still at the Cormorant door. Bert yells to her, "Bring me that rifle and the bullets!"

It takes Ernie a minute to return with the rifle. As she hands it down to Bert she says, "Susy put the bullets into this toque. Here!"

Bert grabs both items and heads as quickly as he can up the ramp then right, along the shore and away from the Cormorant. In his rush, Bert doesn't notice the sound of the boat closing in from the sea approach.

He finds a secure place where he can lie prone with a large, flat rock in front to rest the rifle on. It takes some fumbling to find how to load the rounds into the rifle. Ready, he settles into a comfortable position then searches for the boat in the dark. Suddenly seeing the boat way too clearly, Bert nearly jumps. He gathers himself to aim at the centre of what must be the cabin, then thinks, *How high should I aim for this rifle? Damnit! Guess.*

He squeezes off a shot. The noise startles him but he stays in position, looking for any indication of where the round went. Lights from the marina next door shine enough that he sees a splash not far from the front of the approaching boat. Bert adjusts his aim up and lets off a second shot. That one connects with the top of the cabin window. Then a bright flash comes from the boat and a rocket trail arcs briefly then comes right at him. He rolls left desperately with the rifle held against him to reach a concrete abutment. The ground explodes a metre in front of his resting rock. Shrapnel and a blast wave hit around him. All he can think is, *Vampir. Better than RPG-7. Have to keep them away from the Cormorant.*

He quickly sets up over the abutment and adjusts his next shot down a bit. The instant he squeezes it off, he rolls left again and in a crouch moves yet further away from the plane. He sets up for another shot then sees the flash-and-rocket trail once more. Using the scope to find the rocket launcher, he aims at a dark blob at that spot. A steady squeeze, as he was trained. Bert drops behind another concrete abutment as the second blast hits his original location. While still loud, that blast is now expected. He uses his scope to search the boat's deck again. The boat has veered away and is showing its stern. Bert sets up for a third shot, aiming for where he estimates the engine and/or fuel tank might be. Squeezing that round off, he continues to follow it with the scope. Nothing. Bert loads his fourth round, aims and squeezes. A satisfying eruption of flame bursts through their rear deck. Their engine goes silent. His scope shows people running to put the fire out with extinguishers.

Bert jumps up to return to the Cormorant, keeping an eye on the now-well-lit boat. The drone of the generator fills the air. "Good!"

Claude is supervising the battery recharge. He fingers Bert closer. Claude spreads his arms to ask a question but the generator is too loud. When Bert limps closer, Claude asks, "Is it you? We never had such excitement with Mr. Manojlovich!"

Giving a deprecating shrug, Bert considers how much he should divulge. "Sorry, yes. It's just me. Thugs with missile launchers follow me around. Did you have any indication of these characters while you were here?" He keeps a wary eye on the burning boat. Somebody pushes off from the marina to go out to take the people out of the water from around the boat. He estimates it will take them about ten minutes to get there.

Claude shrugs, "No. Never saw them. A smaller boat did leave the marina almost an hour ago…"

"Ok, listen, Claude. When that rescue boat docks in about twenty or so minutes, go there as a 'helpful bystander' to help them off-load. Get an accurate count of how many. Ok?"

Claude nods. "Want a full charge? Shall I check the oil?" He smiles at Bert.

"Well, I'd normally say 'clean the windows, please', but I'm in a bit of a hurry… Oh. How were you contacted about this?"

Claude checks the charge meter as he responds, "Weird. A local Indi… I mean, ah, indigin… well you know what I mean!" Flustered, Claude grimaces.

"Somebody with a shortwave transceiver?"

"Yeah! Like, this kid, well, maybe twenty, comes to my hotel room and says, 'You work for CormAero'? And he…"

"He said CormAero?"

"Yeah! First time I heard that… Not bad, though." He checks the charge again. "Give me another eleven minutes, ok?"

Bert gives Claude's shoulder a slap. "Good. I'm going to talk with Hank in a minute."

"Was that *Hank* flying? Holy shit! What did you feed him? Rocket fuel?"

"Well…"

"Oh! Don't leave before I bring you this gas station's special gift!"

"What, a glass?"

"Nah, we give a choice of toasters or shortwave transceivers!"

Bert is non-plussed. "…Don't have a plug for the toaster…"

"So I guess you'll have to settle for the transceiver." Claude grins broadly. A siren passes them wailing very loudly, speeding for the marina.

After it passes, Claude adds, "There was a message from the kid. He said, after I buy the shortwave transceiver – which cost me three hundred and fifteen dollars and I have the receipt – he said I was to tell you that Susan is the one to use it. He said something about Haida but I didn't really get it. Is that ok?"

Bert is happy. "I could kiss you, Claude, but we might short out. Thanks! Of course, Simo'll reimburse you for that." *And he better add a bonus! Mickie must mean that he and his sister are going to speak in Haida. Known by a tiny number of people in the world. As secret as you can get.*

Sloshing back to the door, Bert calls for Ernie. She is already waiting behind the door, as frightened as he has ever seen her. "Ernie, ask Hank and Alena to keep an eye out for any tenders – ah, small boats – coming from that burning wreak. And for that other one we saw. Here, you'd better keep the rifle just inside the door. Oh! And tell Susan that Mickie sent her a present. Claude, over there, has a shortwave transceiver for her." He peers past the Cormorant's tail at the still-burning boat. "And how are *you* doing this fine evening?"

Ernie is very concerned. "Bert?"

"Yes?"

"Was that one of those rocket propelled bombs?"

It finally registers, '*In-coming*'. Bert nods solemnly and turns away to stare with rising anger at the burning boat. His trigger finger twitches. *Couldn't have been Fabio. Not smart enough. What was that other name that came up? Masoud? When I asked Tasha about what file Andrew had been working on, last, she sent me a copy of a report on the Iran-Chechnya connection…* In a daze, Bert walks up to Claude's truck with the generator droning loudly.

He leans against the truck cab where he has a better view of the burning boat. *Could that be the connection? Is Arbi a mole? Their mole? Have to ask Alena what she might know. Won't have time later.*

He jumps back down the ramp. "Claude, I have to do something urgent inside. I'll send Ernie out to help you finish, ok? And thank you! You can't imagine how much this helps me!"

Before Claude can reply, Bert turns for the door of the Cormorant, waving over his shoulder.

Climbing into the Cormorant with Ernie's help, he asks her, "Can you go help Claude when he finishes? He'll unplug the cable. Just help him untie the mooring lines. And, ah, shove the Cormorant back off the ramp… Maybe get Susan to help. Ok?"

"Bert!"

He kisses her and hobbles forward to lean between the pilot seats. Their view is only toward the marina. Flashing lights from two fire trucks strobe into the night. Hank has opened the overhead window and is keeping a watch on the action behind them.

Alena shrugs and mouths, "Shtoh?" [*what*]

In Russian, Bert asks, "What do you know about Arbi's connection to Chechnya and Iran?"

She spins around to lean in close, checking that Hank is still focused on the outside. "How do you know this?"

"Deduction, dear Alena. I take it you are reporting to what's left of the SVR?"

Biting her tongue, Alena holds back the retort she was going to give. "Alive and kicking, Alexei."

"And your assignment was to follow and possibly disrupt the refugees from the submarine?"

"It was." She glances up to see that Hank is staring at them. In English, "Hank, my dear, please keep watch for other boat…

Good?" She bats her eyes at him, eliciting a smile. He returns to his watch duty.

Alena goes back to Russian, "Look, Alexei Ondurovic, I have seen the world. I *did* believe what our people are doing in Moskva was better than what Washington is doing. Now… I am starting to think that Vladi was correct. And that *you* are right."

Bert absently rubs his trigger finger.

"This world of ours is going to hell. When Putin walked away, I made up excuses in my mind. *I am a pilot of the Russian Air Force*!" She glances up and lowers her voice. "But now, I… I don't know what to do. Like Vladi said, I feel I should do *something*. But you have asked me to do something for which I was not trained. You ask me to **think**, damn you!... How do I do that?"

Bert glances behind. Susan is following Ernie outside. He takes Alena's hand. "Thank you. I do know the things you are going through, in your mind, Alena. And we will speak of this later. But as of this instant, this hand of yours is the best weapon we have to get out of serious danger. Your flying is… brilliant! Artistic! And we will need your artistry at its most creative in…" he glances back again, then they both feel a shove from Claude and friends, "…one minute! Now, I must bring Ernie and Susan aboard. Ok?"

She smiles and pats his hand on hers as he pulls away. Hank is surprised by the Cormorant's moving. He plops down into his seat then remembers to close the window. Hank turns to Alena, "All good?"

"Is all good. Lower docking prop. Battery is full charge. When they come in, I will reverse with little prop. You be ready with main prop. Then I fly. Is good?"

"Is good." Hank knows that he may be in the pilot's seat but it is Alena who is the much better flier.

Susan has been able to scramble back in the door. Ernie, however, is getting wet, slipping down the ramp as she struggles for a handhold to climb into the Cormorant. Bert throws himself past Susan to reach down for Ernie's hand.

Her fearful plea cuts into his heart, "BERT! HELP ME!"

They connect just as the Cormorant floats off the ramp. Bert hauls her up high enough that Susan can reach her, while straddling Bert's prone body. Ernie climbs up Bert's back, being pulled with huge effort into the cabin by Susan. Bert notices Claude waving from the ramp. With his remaining strength he manages to contort his arm enough to wave to Claude.

A stern order is yelled from the copilot's seat, "Close door!"

The main prop winds up as the docking prop rotates the Cormorant to face the sea. Alena takes command and revs up the main prop. From the floor, Bert yells at Susan, "Take pictures of whoever was on that boat as we go by!"

She pulls out her phone and stations herself at a window. Her camera is clicking away as Bert joins her at the next window. Meanwhile, Ernie is huffing, dripping wet, sitting sideways in a seat, trying to recover from nearly drowning. Again.

Turning to smile at her, Bert yells over the winding-up prop, "Please take your seat madam, we may encounter turbulence." That's when he realizes his finger splint is missing. "Ow?"

As the Cormorant passes the returning rescue boat, everyone on board it turns to stare at the flying machine. Bert thinks, satisfied, *Should be good mugshots.*

Quickly jumping off the step, the Cormorant is airborne. They are their way south in total darkness.

Alena is forced, against her better judgement, to turn on the landing lights. She explains to Hank, who hurriedly nods approval, "Is not Sukhoi SU fifty-seven to pull up into low space. We crawl in dark over black water. Need light."

The pilots take great care not to de-mast a moored sailboat en route. They fly out of Port Hardy and around into the Johnstone Strait. It takes both pilots full time to fly, navigate, keep a lookout, and monitor height, speed and the battery reserve level. Bert helps as he can, after comforting Ernie and settling her heart rate down to under 100.

It starts to hit him as they sit in the droning cabin for the next hour. *In-coming. Beasty wouldn't have a chance... What's going to be left?* Tears come down his cheeks. Ernie walks over, unsteadily, to sit as close to him as she can. Her eyes, too, are red and wet. They sit silently together for another hour.

HERE AND THERE

One doesn't 'catch' empathy; if its roots are there, it may be nourished

The four mafia thugs that Geno had called for have arrived by scheduled air at Masset. They are quickly identified by Aunt Margaret's people. A delaying action is initiated by the rental car operations "not having any vehicles just now". Nevertheless, the situation is now urgent. The refugees must be helped to make their third hop.

Aunt Margaret speaks with her other family Elders. They discuss, argue, then agree to consider hiding the refugees away at an inland village that has been on lockdown since the Virus. That request is placed before that village's Elders by phone, speaking in Haida. The village Elders discuss, argue, then agree to the request, on condition that a significant supply of essential goods are shipped with the refugees. Supplies have become critical in their village as it is.

The problem before Aunt Margaret is that she cannot fully trust any of the other local boat owners to add to those who will help once again to move the refugees. One of Aunt Margaret's younger sisters, Kathleen, offers a solution. "I am, as you know, Aunt Margaret, a rower with our new sea kayak team. Why don't we take the last dozen refugees with two of us who can show them how to row. The kayak can hold at least fourteen people."

It is agreed that the refugees should be asked. The idea is to first slip out very early in the morning with the powered boats, then later row away from the four mafia thugs by putting Haida hats and shawls on them as they "learn" how to row a sea kayak. The refugees can be asked for volunteers and the healthier ones will be given a quick course in the evening before they are to leave.

The rest are to leave by motor launch, along with the supplies.

The discussion in Russian, when the plan is put before them, takes much less time than the Elders took. Over half volunteer to row, so Kathleen is delegated to choose the best of that group.

As supplies are chosen according to the village Elders' request, the refugees begin to understand that they need to stock up as well. Next morning, the boats are loaded up to their gunnels. Before casting off the skippers gather for their own plan. The weather forecast is for calm seas, but, "You never know up here!" They decide to convoy in pairs so that one boat could help the other if needed. The best seaman leads the pack.

Their target is a small village hidden at the northern entrance to Naden Harbour. The village is on the western side. On the eastern side is a lodge.

Before they depart, Tasha does a final count. She is confused with the result of her count. "Where is Arbi?"

Tasha asks each group if they have seen Arbi. "Not since yesterday. He must be with the rowers."

"No. At least, he is not on their list…"

The lead boat skipper, a veteran fisher by the name of Michael but known by all as *Seawolf*, calls to Tasha from his vessel. "We need to go! Now! The tide has started rising and that makes for a dangerous passage as we leave the river estuary."

Tasha waves back. "Damn! He better be with the kayak or I'll have his head!"

With all aboard, other than Arbi, they depart as the sun starts its rise over the horizon.

Once they are off, Kathleen gathers her crew in a large room next to the dock in Old Masset, with the help of Leo-Vladi, her interpreter and team leader. They go over the safety factors, things that must and must not be done on the sea, then they do dry-land rowing practice to show them how and why they need to keep co-ordinated.

Aunt Margaret comes along later with their hearty lunch, "You'll need it. This is a long voyage for you, especially as new rowers."

After lunch, and as slack tide has settled in, Kathleen clothes her crew of newbies then leads them to where the kayak is stored, out of the water next to the dock in Old Masset.

Kathleen explains to Leo-Vladi, "The tide has been rising this morning. We need to leave now during slack tide. Please make sure your people understand that this is a dangerous voyage. Be sure everyone has their life-vests on and knows what to do if something happens. And bring plenty of water."

Leo begins to wonder if this will be more then a pleasant paddle in a quiet pond. A small voice in the back of his mind causes hairs to rise on his neck, *Are you friggen crazy!? You don't go out into the Pacific in some wooden dinghy!* Leo gathers his resolve and shuts up that insistent voice. *If this little girl, Kathleen, can do it, I can do it.*

The kayak needs to be lifted with everyone's co-ordinated help, carried to the water, and lowered in. That is accomplished well. The next step, of stepping into the kayak, is not done as well. One of the refugees, Dimitri – decked out in a colourful Haida shawl and hat – trips over his shawl as he is about to step down to the kayak and ends up in the water. His life-vest immediately inflates as he flaps his arms, splashing in the river to no effect.

He is: *shocked by the cold water / dismayed to the substantial depth of his hurt ego / suddenly concerned that he may drown.* Dimitri's high-pitched cries for help are mixed with raucous laughter and jibes from his "friends". Dimitri is eventually hauled into the kayak where he sits shivering. Kathleen brings him a blanket decorated in Haida art, the creativity of which is entirely lost on Dimitri as the jibes in Russian and his increasingly angry retorts echo across the river.

Leo jumps to takes Dimitri by both shoulders. In stern English, "My friend, you squeal like stuck pig. Even Italian mafioso can know you are not Haida. SHUT UP!"

The intended result achieved, he nods to Katheen in the rear, that they are ready.

When they coast into the small dock at the northern point of Naden Harbour, it is dark. No boats are left there. The half moon sheds enough light for Kathleen to find her way to shore. A fireplace glows through the window of a nearby house, providing proof that people do live there.

She and every one of the crew are absolutely exhausted to the point of not being able to lift their arms any further. Only Leo has enough strength to guide the kayak against the dock. He croaks out, in Russian, "Where the fuck is everybody?"

Lights go on in several dwellings and people start rushing to the dock, chattering loudly in a variety of languages. "Oh my god! Is that you?" "We thought you must all be drown and eaten by sharks!"

All Leo can say is, "Tie kayak. Want to step on dry land."

Tasha pushes through the gathering crowd to find a line on the dock. She tosses it into the stern, where Kathleen manages to raise enough gumption to tie it to the kayak. Another line is secured up front. Tasha rushes to her Leo as he struggles under very rubbery legs to reach for her. The rowers are all helped off the kayak in various stages of absolute exhaustion, dehydration, and joy at having completed what, to them, felt like an around-the-world paddle for their survival.

Dimitri is heard to mumble, as he is flat-out carried away, "Who is responsible for this insane thing?"

The rowers are carried into houses that have been given over to the refugees by the villagers. They are covered in blankets, treated to endless tea, fed as much as they can digest, and finally allowed to nod off to sleep, just as the sun begins to tickle the eastern horizon. Leo is resting in Tasha's attentive arms. As he notices the light, "Is that a fire, Tasha?"

She kisses his forehead. "No you big bear. That's sunrise. You've been paddling all night… I thought I'd lost you. " She sheds warm tears over his still-heaving chest.

The villagers had been through their own struggle. Being primarily Elders who had wanted to keep what they know of the "old ways". Over the past few years the public rhetoric had made them fearful of this next pandemic that the "invaders" were bringing to their shores. Even dealing with other Haida got to be frowned upon. Finally, without the help of younger folks, not being able to carry on gathering enough food from the sea to sustain themselves, the villagers were reluctantly open to the exchange of supplies for refugees. They remained leery of these foreigners, until the kayakers arrived. Then, their hearts opened up.

Next morning, the rowers are left to sleep as long as they wish. The other refugees join the villagers to sort through their new supplies to make breakfast. In groups, defined primarily by which house they were in, much happy chattering occurs in several languages as they teach each other their various breakfast preferences. What later becomes known as "RussElDa" (Russian-English-Haida) starts to evolve.

Dimitri is a lone dissenting voice, albeit more scrooge-like than dissenting. "We should never have sold the Americans this place!"

"That was Alaska."

"But we would have been here, too!"

"Only over the dead bodies of my ancestors," half-jokingly.

The Cormorant has been making good progress, Before they close in on Comox, He calls for a meeting at the front of the Cabin so Hank and Alena can participate.

Loudly enough to be heard, "We should be proactive, to avoid issues with the authorities in Comox. I propose we contact them right now to give our side of what happened in Port Hardy. And maybe what went on at our place on Maybe Island." He drops his head before carrying on. "We can say to Comox that a group of terrorists tried to stop the Cormorant from performing its record-breaking flight to Haida Gwaii and back. They used blacked-out vessels to intercept us and then used RPGs to attack us. We fought back with a rifle and got a lucky shot in."

Alena agrees, "Good. If survivors tell other story, how they explain RPG?"

That part is agreed.

"Next, we… well, we don't know for sure but we can say we suspect the same RPG was used against us on Mayne Island. Let's see if they have any news they can share in that regard. Ok?"

"Is good."

Hank is designated to make the call to Comox ATC. He announces the Cormorant's intention to fly through to Nanaimo, then asks to be able to speak with the Comox Base Commander:

"Comox Tower, Cormorant Golf Oscar Charlie X-ray. Thank you, over.."

It takes no more than a minute for a reply:

"Cormorant Golf Oscar Charlie X-ray, switch frequency to three one six decimal fiver zero, confirm."

Alena, doing the flying, says on the intercom, "Military."

Bert is leaning between the with his headphones on, "Do it."

"Switching to three one six decimal fiver zero."

Hank flips the VHS over to the higher frequency. He composes himself, then, "Ah, Comox, Cormorant Golf Oscar Charlie X-ray."

"Charlie X-ray, this the Base Commander. Not encrypted, over."

Alena explains, "Secure frequency is encrypted. Says to be careful what you say."

Hank keys his mic, "Base Commander, Charlie X-ray understands, over."

Hank carries on to give their slightly abbreviated story to Comox.

"Thank you Charlie X-ray. We agree, over."

Bert can't help slapping Hank on the shoulder and grinning broadly. "Ok, part two, like you have it written, Hank."

He nods, "Roger Base Commander. Ah, we will be trying to carry on past Nanaimo if our battery reserve allows. Do you have any word on, ah, the weather conditions on Mayne Island? Over."

"Charlie X-ray, please note that a storm has passed through and caused some damage on the island but you should find conditions calm at this time, over."

"Thank you, Base Commander. Over and out."

Bert squeezes both Alena's and Hank's shoulders, "Is good. Now lets see if we can stretch out the reserves to make it all the way to Mayne. I'm going to see if I can hack together an RPG."

Alena nearly loses it as she turns quickly to stare at Bert. Hand back on the control stick, she shrugs. To Hank, "He do miracles. Maybe make RPG, too."

Bert rummages around the cabin, tossing a few things to the open area in front of the access door. He opens the small compartment behind the rear bulkhead to do more rummaging. Ernie and Susan stare at him, wondering if has lost more than his marbles.

Bert is satisfied with his accumulated goodies and kneels down before them. Taking the rifle case, he rolls a black cloth cover over the case, inserting other found items. He tapes the concoction together with clear wrapping tape.

He proudly holds his creation up to the women. "What do you think?"

Ernie shakes her head. "Might take fifth place in a craft fair. If the other entries are from children."

Susan shrugs. "What is it supposed to be?"

"Well, from a distance, held menacingly on my shoulder, it's supposed to be an RPG. Rocket-propelled grenade launcher."

"If you say so."

Bert is not please with their lack of enthusiasm. He stomps up front to find a more appreciative audience.

Bert taps Hank on the shoulder and holds up his masterpiece. "What do you think?"

Hank is not military either. "What the hell is it?"

Alena glances back, then continues flying. "If put pointy thing in front would be better."

Bert takes another look at the decoy device, holding it out. "Oh. You're right. I'll see if I find a pointy thing."

After searching the cabin once more, he decides to rip the back cover off the Jeppeson manual.

Hank does not like that act of vandalism. "Hey! What did you do *that* for?"

"It is now the pointy end of a rocket-propelled grenade." Bert tapes the cardboard into a cone shape then tapes it to the front of his "RPG". Admiring his work, "There. Ready to blow up dastardly terrorists."

He glances at the sniper rifle still secured to the wall behind the access door. Seriously, "If I don't get a clean shot in, first."

Hank shakes his head. "I doubt if you'll need that contraption. The more dangerous thing around here is the sea itself." He returns to assisting Alena.

M A Y N E

*Bought friendships break; real friendship bends but
does not break*

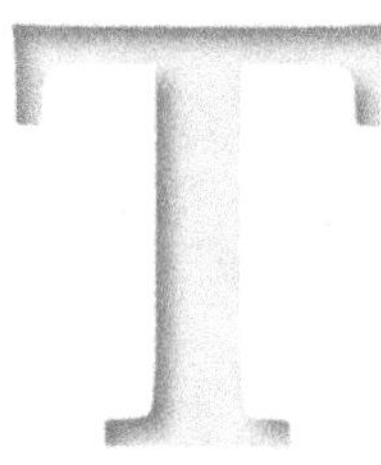

The Cormorant goes silent, settling heavily onto a glassy-water sea. Mayne Island is about a kilometre away.

Bert's "Shit!" is down out by Alena's primeval howl and pounding on the instrument panel.

Hank misses an attempt at humour with, "Well *that* wasn't a 200 foot-per-minute descent!"

Her wolf-snarl directed at him raises numerous hairs all over his body. He considers escaping though the overhead window.

Susan saves him with a yell from the rear window, "There! A boat?"

Everybody jumps to look as the Cormorant bobs sedately after its precipitous descent. The breeze ever so slowly turns the Cormorant so that they have to jump over to the other side of the aisle to peer through those windows. All that movement inside causes the machine to tilt onto its other float.

Alena gives Hank order that he does not take correctly. "Open window!"

Summoning up some courage, "You're not throwing me overboard because I made a joke?!"

"No bahlbyehs! [*bonehead*] Wave to boat. Use… my coat." She starts taking off her coat, with some difficulty in the confined space. Hank finally clicks what she is doing then starts to help her.

The others turn their heads slowly from the windows to stare at the scene in the cockpit.

Susan asks, "What…?"

Ernie leans back to block her view. "You should probably divert your eyes, Susy."

Bert corrects with, "Avert." They continue staring.

Susan sneaks a better peek by leaning further back. "Are those two…?"

With her coat ripped off, Alena throws it at Hank then shoos him up to open the window. She pulls down her shirt that had ridden up, then sees that everyone is staring at them. "What?"

The audience quickly turns back to their respective windows, muttering, "Oh nothing." "No, just…" "C… carry on. With. Whatever you were…" "Are we down?"

Alena gives a disgusted grunt and plops into her seat. In Russian, "Everyone's a critic!"

Hank has been doing as ordered, waving the coat at the distant boat. After a minute he drops down to ask, "Didn't we have flares?"

Bert slaps his forehead, "Emergency flares! They're in the rear compartment!" He jumps the retrieve them, muttering, "Could've used them in the dummy RPG... Nah. It would've taken too much work..."

Bert finds them and carries the waterproof box up to Hank. Alena was wondering what they were doing, then sees the label on the box. Her forehead slap is harder than Bert's. She slinks down lower into her seat, thinking, *Maybe not such a bonehead.*

The fishing boat answers their flare right away. It speeds to the Cormorant at full power. So full that Bert is wondering he should break out the rifle before the boat plows into them. But, his fear is allayed as the boat throttles right down and drifts near. Hank is yelling at the boat's skipper. Looking through a window, Bert is sure he recognizes the skipper. "I know that guy... Maurice!" He runs up to Hank who is still poking up through the window speaking with the skipper.

Bert pulls on his pants to get his attention. Hank thinks it is Alena and leans down smiling. "Oh! Ah..."

"Hank, ask him if his name is Maurice."

Hank pops back up to yell out, "My name is Hank. I work for Cormorant Aerofloat."

The skipper waves, "Good to know you, Hank. I'm Maurice. I live up the road from your company."

Hank holds up a finger then leans back down, waiting for instructions from Bert. Alena is surprised, turning back to Bert, "How you know name. More than hundred piple in Canada, no?"

Bert smiles at her, "He's a neighbour." Turning to Hank, "Let me up there, will you? Easier to speak directly to him."

"Oh! Sure! Here, let me…"

They exchange positions. With Bert now sticking up through the window, Maurice looks surprised, "Hey! Are you…?"

"Your neighbour, yeah. I think our women know each other much better. Listen, do you think you can tow us into the dock? I have an urgent situation to deal with."

"Yeah, Urgent. Like, someone blew up your house. You know about that, right?"

Bert really doesn't want to about that. "It's Maurice, isn't it?"

"Call me Mo. You're Albert?"

"Bert. Right. Mo, I need to get to shore…"

"Of course!… Where's your, where can I tie a line?"

"One of us going to have to go for a swim. If you have a long enough line, please ready that and I'll see I can afford to lose someone overboard." He smiles at Mo. Mo doesn't smile back.

Slipping into the cabin, Bert sees that he has the spotlight centred on his forehead. "Well, ladies and gentlemen, now that I have your kind attention…"

A chorus erupts: "I can't swim!" "Not me in the sea again!?" "I pilot not sailor!"

The air drops out of Bert's lungs. He slowly extricates himself from the pilot's seat. "We have life-vests…"

"Please, don't ask me!"

Bert holds up a hand. "Ok ok. Somebody get me one of the vests. Maybe two."

Resigned to plunging into the cold sea, Bert shuffles, with an exaggerated limp, to the rear of the cabin. "It's all because of me, as Claude said… Might as well… Ok! Gonna be cold. Ernie, hand me my coat, will you?"

He zips into the coat then puts the life-preserver over it. "I'll do the starboard point first, then swim over to the port side. Might call for the extra vest after finishing on this side… We'll see."

He swings the door wide open to contemplate the water below.

Susan asks a good question, "Can't they attach the rope from the boat? Like, why do *you* have to do it?"

"Thank you very much for your concern. A concern, I must note which has not been expressed by anyone else on board," quickly without allowing a retort, "but that's fine. No problem. I fully accept that this is all on me. In answer to your kindly intended question, Susy, is that the awkward assortment of aluminum elements sticking out all over the fishing vessel, they couldn't get close enough to safely reach the stupidly place mooring anchors we have on this Cormorant. I assure that I will bring that design flaw to the attention of the engineer in charge. When next we meet…" That drives a series of thoughts to his mind. "Shit. I hope Simo's ok?.. He should be driving in from Victoria at this time… Anyway. They're turned around and are waiting to throw me a line. So… Here I go." He rocks back and forth but doesn't jump. "Here I go." Then falls feet-first into the sea. The instant his head pops up he yells out, **"SHITIT'SCCCOLD!"**

Ernie does show concern. The others encourage Bert to splash over to the float. He makes it there, then receives a whack across his shoulder by the line tossed from the fishing boat. Mo yells him a half-hearted, "Sorry!"

Muttering expletives and prophesies of mayhem in at least two languages, Bert grabs the line. He has to jump out of the water almost a metre to reach up to the anchor point. Expletives are mixed with "Engineer". Bert makes like a breaching whale by submersing then jumping up to attach the snap-hook. It takes three splashing tries.

Bert takes several deep breaths then paddles with the line's other end to the Cormorant's port side. This time it takes four tries to hook it in. Freezing and exhausted, he lets the life-preserver hold his head and chest out of the water while he rests for minute. Fortunately, Bert does not realize that the thin line that Mo had slip-knotted to the middle of the one he threw to Bert had prematurely slipped its knot. Mo has to retrieve it with a gaff.

The fishing boat is creeping in as close Mo can get it. He yells to a nearly sleeping Bert, "WAKE UP DAMNIT! You can't let go like that!" Mo uses his gaff to capture Bert's life preserver belt, with which he pulls him closer to the boat. Two other sailors step onto the stern walk to reach Bert. They haul him aboard nearly frozen stiff.

Mo gaffs the line that Bert had hooked onto the Cormorant's floats, and attaches it to his hawser. He jumps to check on Bert, laid out on deck. "How is he?"

"Caught a turtle once, with more life in him. He'll be fine, skipper. Let's take him inside to warm up."

After they give Bert a chair and a blanket in the small cabin, his teeth start to chatter.

Mo grins, "That's a good sign. He'll be warm soon enough. Now, we have to be careful towing that machine, out there, guys. We'll pay out as much line as we can. Scrubby, you watch the line and their vessel. I want a steady tension. If they start to porpoise or something, yell out right away! Got it? Pete, you call it in while I get us moving. Oh! It's a Cormorant something or other. Hoverwing?"

The anxious spectators on the Cormorant are relieved when they see that Bert has been fished out of the water. They resign themselves to being only spectators until they reach the dock.

A tow on land is one thing. Towing a flighty vessel like the Cormorant at the end of a long-line takes all the skill Mo can muster. At first, Alena tries to help by using the mechanical sea rudder connected to the empennage but it has no effect at their slow towing speed. She sits back to watch proceedings, thinking about what is going to happen to her now.

The exhausted crew are finally on Mayne Island. Simo and Nena are already there to greet them. When Bert is helped off the fishing boat, still shivering in the blanket, Simo doesn't recognize him.

Bert lets out a "Hey!" between shivers that directs Simo's attention to the bent old man in a blanket.

Bert wags a finger at him, "I want my money back. That's the godawfullest excuse for an airline I've ever been on!"

Simo rushes to Bert and is about to scoop him into a bear-hug, when he stops. "What's broken, now? Is there someplace I can touch you?"

Bert falls against Simo and starts to sob.

It takes a minute for the sobs to slow down. Bert is finally able to pass on what Mo had told him. "They bombed Beasty. Blew him to bits. And burned the house to the ground… Simo…"

Simo slowly leads Bert across the street to his house. Nena and Ernie follow, arms around each other. Susan hesitates, feeling left behind, as she is, then runs across to enter behind them all. Inside, Simo places his friend in a comfortable chair and wraps another blanket around him. He puts the gas fireplace on to warm him. Turning to the women, "Ernie, can you help me start the coffee? You know…"

"Stay here, Simo. I'll do it." Nena follows her to the kitchen. She finds Susan already there, helping herself to juice and bread from the fridge. Nena is new to the kitchen so she lets Ernie show her where the important items are.

Susan finishes her snack. Not sure who to ask, she poses her question to both women. "Do you mind if I, like, get to bed? Really tired after all that."

"Oh! Of course! Ah…" "Yes yes, Susan. Come. Simo will find a room for you."

Susan is put to bed in a room well away from the others so that she can sleep without their conversation bothering her.

Later with hot mugs of coffee warming their hands, the two couples go over what's happened and what can happen, next. Bert is not in a mood to contribute much.

Nena has a good grasp of the situation, after having had it explained to her during the flight down. "It was the mess – the… *confluence* of so many greedy gangsters coming together and we are in the middle of that storm. Each in our different ways, we have been swept into the whirlpool."

Simo smiles at her. "My dear, your command of English is only exceeded by your mastery of similes. But I know what you mean."

Nena carries on, "They each thought *they* were the ones pulling the strings. Gino wanted Vladi's help to get rid of… who?"

Ernie answers with, "Whatshisname."

"Yes, Whatshisname. Who became the first victim. But Fabio – you say he is Russian?" A nod from Ernie. "So Fabio wanted Gino out of the way but Vladi was working another game and wanted Fabio *and* Gino out. Then here's poor Ernie and Bert who had the blame assigned to them… Where is Arbi?" Before anyone can reply, "And this Masoud person. Was he in the boat that burned in Port Hardy? So where is he, now?... Oh my god! Is he going to meet with Arbi?"

Bert lifts his head to say something. Nena quiets down. "Tasha can tell you about the Iranian – Chechen connection. I suspect this has all been their doing, in the back alleys. The gutters." They ponder that for a while. "And, yes, the question must be, where are Arbi and Masoud?" Anger rises in his eyes, "I want to ask them why they bombed my Beasty!"

They stay silent. Simo doesn't ask if they want wine, he just brings a few bottles of his Zinfandel and places glasses on the table. They drink quietly for a long time.

A car, the only one they have seen, drives by with high beams on. The lights reflect brightly through the room. The women stiffen. The car drives on. They relax.

Simo rises. "Ernie, please take Bert to the guest room. You both are most welcome to stay here with us until you can rebuild. Now, I will show Nena where the master suite is."

"And the restroom."

"It is en suite."

"Oh! a very nice house you have, Simo." She giggles, holding her arm out for Simo to lead her away.

Each tries to find sleep that night. It is much harder for some, when the demons march so loudly in the mind.

Bert awakens to bright sunlight streaming into the window. The blinds have been pulled up from the bottom so that the top third allows the sun in directly.

He feels a variety of pains in every part of his body. Rubbing his eyes, "Ow!" he remembers his broken pinky.

The dream he had just prior to waking is dissolving like snow in a frying pan. He tries to grasp the remnants of it. *Vladi-now-Leo and Tasha are running in the slowest of motion. Arbi is behind them.*

"Tasha!"

That exclamation brings Ernie from the washroom, with a concerned look behind the toothbrush in her mouth. She mumbles, "Did you call me, Bert?"

Bert rolls to a less painful position, groaning, "Ooh ah! No."

She pulls her toothbrush out. "I'll take that as a positively affirmative negative. With spicy condiments."

"Huh? Ernie, don't batter my brain cells, please. They *had* been the only tiny constituent components that hadn't been hurting."

"So you admit, *tiny*?"

Pause. Bert is not in the mood for pleasant banter. "What's got you so invigorated this morning? Have you been into the Zinf this early?"

She beams, albeit with foamy bits of glistening toothpaste on her lips. "No you silly dear. *We're back home! On Mayne Island!*" She leans down to Bert, planting a somewhat foamy kiss on his cheek.

Bert rolls to a sitting position on the side of the bed. More groans as he absently rubs the foam bits away. He stretches his arms out slowly, picking the muscles with the fewest objections. "I guess we'll have to find some clothes..." Then he notices, through their half-open door, Nena walking naked, grinning over the other shoulder at someone behind her. Someone-Simo skips gleefully in similar attire after her. "Or maybe not." Bert smiles at Ernie, who had turned toward the bathroom. "Come here."

"What? I haven't…"

"I want to test a theory."

She turns around. "What theory."

Grinning like a Cheshire Cat, "That there's at least one part of me that isn't bruised or broken."

She tosses her head, "Oh. So you think your excursion into the sea's fixed that?"

Bert jumps up with the intention of showing Ernie, but the command centre in his head goes temporarily off-line. Dizzy, almost blanking out, he plops back onto the bed. He grumbles, "There's those damn stars in the middle of the day, again."

Ernie is beside him in a flash, holding his body tightly. He turns to kiss her. "Ahah! There's more than one way to bring you to my bed…"

Later, they hear the loud sound of a coffee bean grinder. It startles Bert. Ernie, slipping on the clothes she wore yesterday, says, "I think I prefer that roaring grinder to a cock crowing."

"And what's the matter with a…"

"Get your clothes on, dear. Let's at least *appear* to be respectable. For Susan, if no-one else."

Bert is wondering if their hosts will be attired. *Nothing against that whatsoever. No. It's just that it distracts the mind from…* A dream fragment comes back to him, "Tasha!"

"What about Tasha, dear?" *Is that what he said when he woke up?*

Bert becomes agitated. He gets up, more carefully this time. "Hand me my clothes, will you? I have to get over to Simo's shortwave set, in the office."

She sees his urgency. "But first, you need some breakfast… Bert! You hear me?" He is quickly putting the clothes on that she brings him. "Listen to me! Feed those battered muscles, *first*… and we'll get Nena to rebandage your finger. *Then* you can go to the office."

Bert slows his frenzy down. "Yes mother."

"Good. Now turn that turtleneck around so the back's on the other way."

"Oh… Yes mother."

In the kitchen, Nena and Simo, dressed in robes, are unabashedly glowing.

As they walk in, Ernie nods happily to Nena. Behind her, Bert mumbles, "I remember that glow. What decade was that?" Ernie stops suddenly, causing Bert to bump into her back.

"Ow?" He holds his pinky with the tenderness of an injured butterfly. Nena notices and extends her sympathy with a silent "Ooo". She carries on preparing potato pancakes while Simo does the coffee and fruit.

A mostly-awake Susan makes her appearance. She goes to sit at the table silently appreciating in the interaction of the two couples.

Simo takes in the vision of joy he has found. "Potato pancakes." Nena blows him a kiss, mixed with some flour on her hand. A smiling Simo chops older parts off fruit that he'd found in his fridge then adds the good pieces to the mix of berries in each of five bowls.

Bert's eyes light up. "Potato pancakes?"

Susan thinks, *Potato pancakes? What is that?*

With a wry shake of his head, "The mix was a year or so past due but Nena said she'd fix that. She *is* a doctor." He and Bert exchange knowing smiles.

Ernie is happy for them, but still concerned for her Bert.

The potato pancakes are excellent. Ernie is the only one to pour maple syrup on top of hers. After a few bites, Nena decides to try it on one of the pieces that isn't slathered with plain yogurt. ("Sorry. The sour cream is changing colour.") She is pleasantly surprised by the maple syrup. The men stick to slathered yogurt. Susan mixes maple syrup in between the slathered pancakes.

After breakfast Ernie asks, "Nena, do you mind taking a look at Bert's little finger again. He lost your splint somewhere along the way."

"Oh? Was he using his finger against doctor's orders?"

"Well, you know children. He was in a tussle with one of the kids. Rather more than once, in fact."

"Okey dokey! I will set up my surgery…"

Her use of the old phrase puts smiles on the faces of Bert and Ernie. Simo is collecting the dishes for the washer. "Whichever room you'd like, my lovely."

Pleased for her but world weary, Ernie is thinking, *She is quite spritely this morning. I hope, for her and Simo's sake, that feeling lasts.*

For his part, Bert feels more of the bruises than he'd prefer. He grumbles just loudly enough for Simo to hear, "Easy on the honey, Simo. It sticks to everything and attracts flies."

Susan lets out a short involuntary laugh.

Simo is about to give Bert a jocular punch in the arm then wonders, "Which part of your body hasn't been damaged of late, old friend?" He returns to washing out the frying pan, to consider, "You know, I think you haven't been whole of body since we first met." He smiles at Bert. "Just whole of soul."

Bert shakes his head slowly, "I wish. This soul's been taking a battering recently, too."

Bert sits down and quietly contemplates the white table in the expansive kitchen full of tall, white, built-in cabinets and silver appliances; with the large white curtained windows opening onto an ocean view… A mist obscures the scene… Bert feels that dreadful draw into an inner black spiral… The endless, dark misty tunnel of his nightmares… It beckons his reluctant mind… The usual first step is not quite slippery, but he knows what will happen with his next step…

Bert jerks awake at the clatter of a cup put before him on the marble table.

The coffee is welcome. Ernie puts both hands on his shoulders to rub away his cares. Even when she hits the sore spots, Bert speaks softly, "Thanks for throwing me the lifeline, honey. Started down that dream again."

"Poor Bert… That dream is why you're running from yourself." She kisses his cheek from behind.

Bert stops, smacked in the hardened part of his mind with a simple observation. *Running from myself?...* He desperately grabs at random memories from his childhood to extract clues to what that might mean.

Then the fragments of this morning's dream flow up to his consciousness again. "Tasha!... Simo, you still have that shortwave transceiver in the office?"

"Of course. We can go over right after I wash up from breakfast. Have to see if my financial backers are complaining about not hearing from me."

Nena had played hockey with the fruit in her bowl. There were unfamiliar articles in the mix and she had been afraid to try them. Now she has to ask, "What was that little black thing mixed in the fruit?"

Susan grins and says her first words this morning, "Blueberries. A delight for grizzly bears and grizzled men, as well." She turns to Bert with a wink.

Ernie pipes up, "Blueberries are a super-fruit. Not only do they taste delightful, they are extremely nutritious. You should look them up in a journal." She adds, "We'll have to get you lots of journals, if you're going to write your doctor's exam."

Nena moves her body in a negative side-to-side. "This is not so simple. I have asked about the registration process before coming here. I was told that in the previous class to write in Vancouver, *nobody* passed. And that included a professor of neuro-science who was a leading brain surgeon in Honduras."

"What?" "Can't be!" "I thought we *needed* doctors!"

Nena shrugs. "I would not presume to say, but it has been suggested that the old boys' network still is a dominant feature in the college." She shrugs again. "Same in Moskva, so…"

Upset that his love should be treated this way, Simo rises to do battle with the dragons. "We'll see about that! I know people in certain…"

"Please, my love. You have another more urgent battle, for now. Bert? Did you say you have someone to contact? We must all step very carefully at this time." She looks around the kitchen and the open dining room next to it, her eyes softening. "We must take care."

"Yes. You're right, of course. We must take care. Too much to lose." Simo sets his fist down rather too hard, making the dishes rattle and Susan jump, "But firm action is needed!"

Bert nods, "Firm action after a careful plan. I hadn't heard this saying before coming here, Nena. Have you heard of the story about Einstein? When asked what he would do if he had only one hour to save the world from destruction, Einstein said, 'I would plan for fifty-five minutes with my wisest friends, then we would put the plan into action for the remaining five minutes'."

"A wise man." Nena nods. "Good. You two will plan in your office and Ernie and I will plan here."

Ernie grins, "Then you can come back here and we'll tell you what's wrong with your plan."

Nena agrees, "But first I want to see my patient in…"

Simo adds, "The den, I guess. For now."

All are very satisfied with breakfast and their short term plan of action.

At the shortwave set, Simo turns it on and provides a brief introduction. Bert accepts the lesson then adds, "I used to have one of these things. Spent many a night on the farm speaking with strangers all around the world. That's how, and why, I first learned English…" He wakes up to the fact that Susan is not with them. "Say! Did Susan go someplace? I thought she was coming over, too."

"Probably wanted to stay with the women. Don't blame her. Anyway, I need to go to my office to use more current technology. Is there someone I can show you how to contact, first?"

"Yes. How about your man in Port Hardy?"

"Of course!"

That process takes time. Claude, apparently, is not near his shortwave. Simo decides to go do his own work, leaving Bert to stew over what to do now that they are back… *Oh my god. I have to drive up to… our house.*

Leaving the shortwave, he hurries to Simo's office. Without further explanation, "Is there a car I can take?"

Simo knows what he intends. "Take the pickup. Should be parked in the back lot. Keys…"

"Thanks. I know where the keys are." Bert runs out.

The drive along the beach kicks up gravel from the shoulder as Bert has trouble concentrating. Coming to the corner that turns him up toward his house, he slows right down. At a crawl, he comes to his laneway and stops at the side. Truck traffic – *fire engines* – had battered down shrubs in the lane. A gaping hole is left beyond the roadside trees. Bert's heart pumps as he struggles to exit the pickup.

Walking reluctantly down their torn-up lane, he goes right by the blackened remains of their house. There is a pile of debris left where Beasty's garage had been. Burned rafters stick up at odd angles. Tears wet his cheeks as he scrabbles in the black dusty mess, pulling away parts of the roof and walls. Pieces of beige metal are uncovered. Parts have been burned and the blistered paint shows blotches of bright yellow underneath. Bert drops to his knees and cries.

Later, covered in ash, his face streaked black with wet dust, Bert stumbles out of the remains of what was once his Beasty, with a black box. He carries the box with care to the pickup, places it on the passenger seat and straps it in with the seatbelt. He sits in the pickup for some time, head bowed. Finally he drives back to Cormorant Aerofloat.

Bert carries the black box into the room he had used as his office, placing it on a table. He finds a cloth to wipe most of the grime off it.

Simo comes by and sees Bert standing, staring at the box. "What is it?"

"The black box."

"This one actually *is* black?"

"Yes."

Gently, "Bert, can I ask you to leave that for now? I want to…"

"He might have survived. Everything that was him should still be in there."

"You can work on that later. Please, Bert. Come with me." Simo puts a hand on Bert's stiff shoulder. After a while Bert turns to follow Simo.

In the room with the shortwave, Simo drags a chair to place it next to the one at the shortwave set. "Please sit down, Bert. We have work to do. Claude told me…"

"You got ahold of him?" Bert plops into the chair.

"Yes. He said there were three people on that boat that burned. One was wounded and taken away to hospital under police guard. The other two refused to leave the dock – had a fight with the firemen and the cops – until they were allowed to perform what Claude said was offering – here, I wrote it down – 'sujud ash-shukr', which he said is *prostration of thankfulness*. A Muslim prayer. Claude is Muslim so I suppose he knows. Said something about doing only one prostration, whatever that means…"

Bert comes out of his stupor. "So, could be Arbi and Masoud."

"The description of Arbi is like you told me. Don't know about the other guy."

"What happened to them?"

"Claude was off to the side as all that was happening. He says after their prayer, they suddenly pull out guns and took a cop as hostage. They drove off and weren't found. Later, one of the floatplanes went missing from the water-side airport and the cop was on the dock, shot. He's in critical condition."

Bert is alarmed. "Have to warn the people up in Masset!"

Much later, a floatplane touches down at the lodge on the east side of Naden Harbour.

Leo and Tasha have a different view on the world they see before them, than either the village Elders or the refugees.

The Elders of the village have been pleased to extend their hospitality to the refugees. A shortened, translated version of the refugees' plight had been presented to them. Aunt Margaret left them with the impression that this was a transient group who would be off shortly to another location.

The refugees, speaking amongst themselves, developed that same impression – out of a lack of no substantive data upon which to attach their expectations.

Therefore, both sides expressed their disappointment in three distinctly different languages when Leo and Tasha brought them together for a meeting about the refugees' future prospects. The languages used remarkably similar sentiments and spicy expressions. Leo's attempts to explain what Tasha meant, elicited the invitation for Leo to go forth and profusely self-propagate. When presented with that suggestion, both in Russian and via the English translation of the Haida equivalent, he was at a loss for words.

This occurred at the same time as the more jovial breakfast on Mayne Island.

Therefore, when, that afternoon, Old Jimmy's boat approaches the village, Leo and Tasha are quite prepared to either greet their saviour, or jump on the boat and sail away.

Instead, they are greeted by Mickie. His green-tinged composure is a source of merriment for Old Jimmy, who helps him off as soon as the boat is moored. "Young people these days don't know nothing but how press buttons on glass! If you'd shipped out with me to catch salmon and herring, you'd 'ave been a *man* by now, Mickie! Here you are, instead, needing an old man like me to hold your hand getting' off a boat!"

Before Mickie can stumble away, Old Jimmy yells at him, "You ain't leavin' me to carry your bloody luggage, young feller! Come back here!"

Old Jimmy takes his time to find Mickie's gym bag and a cardboard box wrapped in plastic. He saunters back, puts his foot on the worn gunnel, and invites Mickie closer to take the two items. Not sure if he is going to bring up right then, Mickie stands very quietly, willing his stomach to calm down. Shortly, he steps forward to take the bag and package. Mickie manages to plead, "Jimmy, please don't tell Susy. Or the guys. Please?"

"Hah! Off with you, youngster! And don't be late tomorrow. Two hours before slack tide! Understand?"

Mickie nods with his head down.

Old Jimmy jumps off the boat to search for one of the Elders who had requested that he bring more supplies today. He mutters on his way, "Don't see them for a year and suddenly they buy out the Co-op. They want another run tomorrow morning but they don't understand my boat's keel would run too damn close during slack water."

By now a crowd has gathered around the small dock. Mickie needs to do his own search. He looks for Tasha or Leo. It is Tasha whom he finds first. She is have an animated discussion with Dimitri and welcomes the distraction when Mickie calls out to her.

"Mickie! How are you… oh. You do not go on boats very often?"

Mickie is embarrassed that everyone seems to know that he is seasick. And further embarrassment rises at the shapely figure that Tasha presents. "I, ah, like, have something for you, ma'am." He has considerable trouble keeping his eyes away from her boobs, finally forcing his eyes down to the ground. "Me and Susy, like… you know Susy?" That question causes him to look up to her face, then her smile makes him quickly go eyes-down again. "Like, she's my sister. We were chatting on the shortwave – she's down south someplace near Vancouver – and she told me I had to, like, buy this shortwave set. Here." He hands the package to Tasha then turns to run away.

"Hold on, Mickie. You had to buy it?"

Stopped, standing sideways, he nods quickly.

"Well, I need to pay you for it. How much?"

"Oh! Susy said I must not say how much. It's a present!" At which he runs off.

Tasha sends a "Thank you!" to his departing back.

Tasha carries the package to the house where she and Leo have been welcomed. Leo is outside using a mixture of sign language and grunted words of indeterminate language to communicate with a stoically seated Elder who is using the same form of communication, with less enthusiasm.

At Tasha's approach, Leo excuses himself to go to her. Leo's English has been improving considerably, particularly as he has determined to speak with the Haida villagers. "I think I know how to say 'sea'. But might be 'mushrooms'. What you have there, Tasha?"

"I am told it is a shortwave set. You must know how they work?"

"Of course! Is battery set?"

"Leo, my love, does it look like I have ripped the box open to be able to answer your questions, then taped it back together again?"

Contritely, "Sorry. Put it down on table and we will rip it open together."

They find that it is, indeed, a battery-powered set. Of course, batteries will need charging before use.

Leo puzzles over their predicament. "The solar panels are only source, here. We may need to request a meeting with Elders to use solar panels."

The Elder with whom Leo had been labouriously communicating comes up behind them. "My name is K'yaaluu, which means *cormorant*, in case you wonder. I can help you with your need."

Leo is dumbfounded that the old man can speak English so well. "But you did not say you could speak English…"

With a glint in his eye, "I do not recall that you asked me. You did a lot of hand waving and that gibberish your friends are speaking. But let us come to the need at hand. You need power to charge your machine?" They both nod. "I will ask."

And so it is that the shortwave transceiver's batteries are charged up before nightfall. Eagerly, Tasha stands over Leo as he fiddles with its settings.

K'yaaluu hovers in the background, repairing the colourful design on his cedar bark hat, using his own paints and a fine handmade brush.

Tasha stands up to stretch her back, then chuckles at the contrasting scenes. "Here, our host is delicately working his ancient craft, and you, my Leo, are trying to send magical signals into the air."

"Huh?" Leo is concentrating on the English instructions written by a Taiwanese office worker. For some reason he asks, "Where is… youngster who brought us this thing?"

"Mickie," K'yaaluu replies while touching up a red teardrop shape for a cormorant eye on his hat. "He sleeps with his cousin in the house two away." Squinting in the fading light, "Would you mind if I brought my painting table closer to your light? My eyes have been weaken by age."

Politely, Tasha asks, "How old are you?" thinking he might be approaching seventy.

"My sister tells me she is ninety-four, and I am older than she is."

A crackling sound begins to emanate from the headphones, just then. Leo quickly puts them on. He follows the recommended procedures for setting the frequency and calling "ICQ". Nothing works.

"Tasha…"

"Get Mickie?"

"Dah."

A bleary-eyed Mickie is persuaded to come so that he can call his sister. Though not fully recovered, once he sits in front of the shortwave set, he and Susan are speaking steadily. In Haida.

K'yaaluu is impressed. Nodding at what he can hear of the conversation, "I take back everything I said about this younger generation!"

Tasha and Leo take turns telling Mickie what to say.

After the sign off, Leo is depressed. "I should go look for my gun in river. If Arbi comes with this Masoud, it will be dangerous."

Tasha agrees, "The smoke begins to clear. Now I have a better idea of what has been happening."

WHEN THE SUN RISES

The sun always rises; one day, you will not

"When the sun rises tomorrow," Tasha is telling Leo as they shift and struggle to find soft parts of the mattress, "we will speak with Aunt Margaret. Then we will speak with our friends, here, about what is to come."

"Dah."

The night is lit by a half moon that Leo follows on its slow arc across the sky. It starts in the window facing the Harbour. Moonlight then filters through arbutus branches producing wonderous shapes against the floor next to his blanket. The shapes walk away to disappear against the far wall; and he awakes to bright moonlight spreading over his head through a higher window. Leo turns over to allow blood to pulse into his left arm. He thinks about the shortwave… He awakens with the moon in his face from a window on the other side. He rolls over to allow blood to tingle into his right arm.

Then the sun rises, pouring its photons onto his face.

He mumbles, "Like Moon better."

Tasha opens her eyes and stretches, one elbow brushing over his cheek. Then, whispering urgently, "Oh! Get up! We need to find Mickie before he leaves." She throws the blankets off herself and off Leo, as well. Whether he wanted that or not. "Get up! All you do is sleep!"

Tasha finds that she needn't have whispered. K'yaaluu and his household have been up, had breakfast, and are doing chores.

They greet each other politely but Tasha is anxious. She asks K'yaaluu, "Did the boat arrive yet. Is Mickie still here?"

K'yaaluu takes his time. "No, and yes. And isn't it a joy to see that the sun rises?"

Tasha is not sure if that is part of special greeting, "Yes, of course the sun rises…"

"And in seeing that – remarking on that – it is proof that *I*, too, have risen once again."

Tasha is silent except for, "Ah…"

The glint comes back to his eyes, "For an old man such as myself, this is an accomplishment to be spoken of, if not yet celebrated… The celebrations may come when I pass 100… But I have to say, since I do not know when, exactly, I was brought onto this earth, I do not know when I should start to celebrate." He spreads his arms. "So that is my problem for today. When should I start to celebrate that I can still mix my paints, weave the cedar bark, and paint designs on it?"

Tasha shakes her head quickly. *Will I be like this when I approach his age?... If I approach his age...*

"Old man, you are to be celebrated every day, any time of the day. Your wisdom is to be celebrated **and** your having lived so long!"

Leo contemplates. *He is right. Each day is to be celebrated. Not the fact of having lived. The fact of doing the living. I hope to have many more such days, but...*

Tasha hurries out to find Mickie. She hauls him back to the shortwave. "Sorry to be insistent but we need to know, we need to have word from Aunt Margaret and Bert, and..."

Mickie sits down to warm up the shortwave, "Who first?"

"Huh? Oh! See if you can contact Bert or Simo first."

It turns out they have been waiting anxiously to speak with Tasha. As Mickie starts in Haida, he stops. "Oh! Plain English? Over." Mickie pulls off the headphones to give them to Tasha. "Here. No point in me doing this if they want to talk in English anyway."

She slips the headphones on, adjusting them to her ears. To Mickie, "Don't go away yet." She takes the seat he vacates.

Mickie settles onto the ground, legs crossed, waiting for orders. He enjoys himself by roving his eyes over Tasha.

She raises her hands in a question, "How do I start? What do I say?"

"Oh. To talk, press that button, there, Yes. Hold it down when you are talking then remember to let go when you want to listen. They can't talk to you until you let go of the button. Start by saying, 'Go ahead'. When you finish saying a sentence, say 'Over'. That tells them they can reply to you. You'll get the hang of it." He settles back to the ground.

The learning curve is steep but Tasha soon becomes adept, with only the occasional missed button-hold-down when she wants to reply.

Tasha thanks Mickie when she is finished, with a kiss on his cheek. He floats, in a blissful fog, through the door, nearly bumping into one of the women outside.

Across Naden Harbour entrance, about half a kilometre away from the village, Arbi and Masoud set off in their captured yacht. Masoud is at the controls. Arbi has been pressed into service as a deckhand because he has no idea of how to control a forty-two footer, diesel powered yacht with its delightful sundeck.

> On the flight up, Arbi had been at the controls of the floatplane. He nearly killed them both when he wanted to beach the plane into the surf-pounded shore below Masset Airport. *That* incident attracted a swarm of federal and local police, combing the area an hour after the yacht was stolen.

> Then, still soaking wet, both of them had spent a miserable rainy, heavy-seas run from Masset to Naden Harbour. They did not partake of the sundeck. Not knowing the local waters, Masoud had elected to swing well out in the Pacific before steering back to Naden

Harbour. Even then, he nearly ran aground on a sandbank at the entrance to the Harbour waters.

Their navigation aid was a tourist map that had been left on the yacht. When they arrived at the lodge, nobody was home. That was fortunate for them, as they would have been reported.

This morning, they were forced to rush off earlier than expected when a vehicle was heard trundling down the access road.

As the lodge caretaker arrived, he saw the unexpected yacht departing. Looking around the lodge, was faced with a considerable cleanup job in the buildings. Arbi had broken into any and everything he fancied, just because he wanted to let off steam. The caretaker promptly reported the incident. He regretted that he also had to report that a locked gun cabinet had been broken into.

With the news of a heavily armed terrorist gang in their patch, the federal police were forced by procedures to wait for the Armed Response Unit, whose expected arrival would be next day.

This, of course, was not known to Arbi and Masoud. They only knew that they had a special mission to complete, and it would likely mean their death.

On the short run across the Harbour, Arbi and Masoud made their preparations.

After prayers, Masoud calls his accomplice to the helm. "Arbi, my brother, I want you to take the tiller for a few minutes. Here. Just hold the course to the village dock. As easy as flying a plane."

Arbi grumbles but complies. "Where you going?"

"Never mind."

"WHERE!?"

Not trusting Arbi's mental stability at this time, Masoud replies, "To the head."

"The *what*?"

"The bathroom! Now just keep your hand on the tiller!"

Arbi's mental balance has, indeed, fallen off-kilter. Before Masoud can re-emerge, Arbi has the yacht roaring at full throttle aimed right at the village dock. He plans to surprise everyone and jump off the yacht, guns blazing in both hands.

Masoud's yell, "NO!" comes seconds before the yacht grinds to a sudden stop on the sandbank off-shore. Its props continue to churn madly, even as the stern lifts from the momentum of running aground. Masoud is thrown off the tilting deck into the water. Arby has smashed into the forward window. Then, as the yacht's stern succumbs to gravity, it crashes back into the water, prop still spinning. The yacht is forced by its prop to begin a slow pirouette, stern turning to the dock. And toward Masoud, who is splashing in the water, not able to swim.

The spectacle has, understandably, attracted an audience on shore. Instantly grasping that the man in the water could drown or be sliced and diced by the approaching propellers, two of the young men jump in and swim the short distance to Masoud. One man grabs his flailing arms as well as he can while the other pulls Masoud by his long hair to the dock. Many hands reach down to pull the three to safety.

On the yacht, Arbi staggers, recovering from his concussion. With his face bleeding profusely, he pulls out a pistol and starts firing blindly.

On shore, a man who had been prepared to go out on a hunting expedition, pulls his rifle from the strap on his backpack, aims, and blows a grizzly-sized hole into Arbi's chest.

He mumbles, "Don't have any of those rounds left. Didn't expect to use it on small vermin. Need to order more."

After taking stock of the situation, an Elder asks another young man to swim out to board the boat, taking care not to go near the spinning propellers. The concern is that the yacht will pull off the sandbar while the props are still churning and go off to who knows where.

Complying, the swimmer approaches the yacht's midsection, grabs a line that had been thrown by the collision off to the side, then hauls himself aboard. He waves happily to the audience then yells out, "NOW WHAT?"

By this time Leo has arrived at the dock. His booming voice is heard by the swimmer. "PULL THE THROTTLES BACK! ALL THE WAY BACK!"

The swimmer looks around the deck for "throttles". Many start yelling at once, "IN THE CABIN!"

He rushes in, searches for "throttles" and happens on the shiny chrome thingies. Since they won't go one way, he pulls the other way. Instantly, the roaring diesels quiet down. Then they cough, and stop.

The swimmer comes back onto the deck, waving happily to the enthusiastic cheers of his people.

K'yaaluu comes to stand beside Leo. "I think a few more of us, now, will see tomorrow's sun rise." He puts an arm onto Leo's broad shoulders.

LET'S FLY!

Oh, I have slipped the surly bonds of earth,
And danced the skies on laughter-silvered wings

On Mayne Island, in the offices of Cormorant Aerofloat, newly-hired engineers are tapping away on keyboards and having earnest conferences about the amount of material to safely shave off *this* gusset or *that* seat attachment rail. Susan is shepherding communications from her room overlooking the main entrance. The flight crew lounge has a large-screen monitor showing scheduled vacation dates. Loud voices are directed at the Flight Crew Co-ordinator, Hank, who is insisting that it is *mandatory* that annual vacations be taken and that it is too complicated to ignore them or push them to the following year. Beo and Alena would rather keep working.

Beo, the newly graduated AI specialist thinks: *It's so rewarding working here! Who needs a vacation?*

In the expanded manufacturing facilities next door, a 40-seat model called the Merganser (they have taken to calling it the "Ganster") is taking shape.

Outside, at the extended *double*-dock, four Cormorant Mk. 2 machines float, ready to be delivered to newly built docks on either side of the Salish Sea. A special one is winging its way north to Masset, via Port Hardy. It has scheduled stops en route to recharge, and for local promotion.

Delegations from countries, militaries and ferry businesses around the world have worn a path to *CormAero*, to the point where a sixth Cormorant has been set aside for ferrying just for that purpose from YVR airport, Vancouver.

Venture capital is flowing in. More people are being hired. An ancillary service is housed in Nanaimo, overseeing fleets of electric two-seat vehicles, sourced from a Vancouver company, and electric bicycles for the use of passengers after flying to the docks.

The combination of speed, safety and environmental impact are producing a huge problem for Simo and his new wife. Nena shakes her head, "Everybody wants these damn things! And you are never home!"

Behind his desk, behind the three engineering monitors, Simo shrugs. "I tried to offload some of this onto Bert's shoulders but you know what he said: 'He's going flying'! What can I do? I'm only the boss!"

In the Cormorant heading north, Bert is in the pilot's seat and Ernie is seating as an unofficial copilot. He has refrained from noting to her that particular arrangement.

Ernie is learning to fly, at two metres above the waves. But with nothing to do but oversee the automatic functions, Ernie is chatting. "So, Simo is happy with this being a 'test' machine for the Haida Nation?"

"Of course! It's a small price to pay for what they've done for us – and for the refugees. The new flight school at Masset is churning out float plane pilots. Their agreement with the First Nation tribe in the Interior – what *is* their name? – to do primary flight training is a boost to *that* economy… Win win all around!... And tomorrow morning, Mickie is going to be sitting in your seat…"

"And *I'll* be having a long conversation with Aunt Margaret about that incident Susy had with one of your damn hot-shot pilots from New Zealand!"

"Come on, Ernie. Am I supposed to chaperone Susy whenever a client comes to Mayne?"

On their way through the Comox control zone, Bert explains the procedure, letting Ernie handle the interface to their Cormorant's flight control software, while he does the radio chatter.

Soon, they pass Campbell River. Bert coaches Ernie on the radio procedures as they fly through that control-zone.

She is flustered at the number of things her checklist says to do. "I have to check the manual for radio frequencies, figure out what the controller is saying with his machine-gun string of acronyms, all while making sure we're not hitting sailboat masts! How do I keep from slapping through the waves?"

Bert explains to her, "It's easy. The BC AI does all the flying. And the radio frequencies are automatically selected for you, with the AI upgrade I just installed. Us organic devices are needed only so we can occupy the seat and pretend we'll be smart enough to take over in an emergency."

"BC AI?"

"Wellll… *Beasty-Cormorant Artificial Intelligence* module is too much of a tongue twister. Isn't it?"

CREDITS

Cover image adapted by George Opacic from an artist's impression of two colliding black holes. Credit: Carol & Mike Werner/Visuals Unlimited, INC./Science Photo Library

Chapter subtitles: some translated from traditional Serbian sayings; some created by the author; except for the final chapter which is from a poem by John Gillespie Magee Jr., *High Flight*

Music references:

Neil Young – *Down By The River*:

You take my hand, I'll take your hand.
Together we may get away.
This much madness is too much sorrow.

Ⓟ 2009 Reprise Records

Harry Nilsson – *Joy: (early version)*

If you haven't got a question
Then you never had a problem…
Then everyone would be happy
And if everyone was happy
There'd never be another song

Joy lyrics © Warner Chappell Music, Inc.

See more excellent titles from Rutherford Press at

https://rutherfordpress.ca

www.ingramcontent.com/pod-product-compliance
Lightning Source LLC
Chambersburg PA
CBHW070239200726
48293CB00005B/1696